IN LATE 1936, eighteen-year-old Isidro Elejalde leaves his Basque village in Northern Spain, spurred to join the fight to preserve his country's democracy from the insurrectionists by the rousing words of a political essayist. Months earlier, Spanish generals launched a military coup to overthrow Spain's newly elected left-wing government. They assumed the population would welcome the coup, but throughout the country people like Isidro remained loyal to the ideals of democracy, and the Spanish Civil War began in bloody earnest.

In Bilbao, Mariana raises her two young children while, with her writing, she decries the fascist-backed coup attempt and their German and Italian allies, imploring the world to support democracy. As the Nationalist forces assault the country, Mariana and Isidro's lives intersect fleetingly, yet in meaningful and lasting ways.

Through a chorus of voices—a female soldier in an all-male battalion, a reluctant conscript recently emigrated from Cuba, a young girl whose parents have abandoned her in order to fight against the fascists, among others—we follow Isidro and Mariana as they struggle to maintain their humanity in a country determined to tear itself apart.

Julian Zabalbeascoa is a fierce and assured new talent, and *What We Tried to Bury Grows Here* is a remarkable feat of research and imagination, as well as a transcendent literary accomplishment.

Praise for
What We Tried to Bury Grows Here

"*What We Tried to Bury Grows Here* is a startling book, beautiful and horrific, that navigates the complexities of the Basque Country during the Spanish Civil War, in which fascism and communism, regionalism and nationalism, and faith and skepticism do battle across a brilliantly evoked, suffering landscape."

—PHIL KLAY, NATIONAL BOOK AWARD WINNER, AUTHOR OF *MISSIONARIES*

"Julian Zabalbeascoa is the real deal, a major talent, and the story he's telling here is both riveting and terrifying."

—RICHARD RUSSO, PULITZER PRIZE WINNER, AUTHOR OF *SOMEBODY'S FOOL*

"Debut novelist Zabalbeascoa's decision to tell his story through a plethora of individual narrators perfectly captures the messiness of a civil war... [*What We Tried To Bury Grows Here*] builds to an emotionally compelling climax."

—*KIRKUS REVIEWS*

"One of the strongest and most evocative novels of 2024. Zabalbeascoa's debut uses multiperspective narration to excellent effect as we are pitched across Spain during the Spanish Civil War. Essentially a series of soul-stirring short stories stitched together to give one a glimpse at the horrors of modern war. If Paul Lynch's *Prophet Song* is a document of a future battle with the far right and this a harrowing account of past struggles the only conclusion to be made is that the fight against fascism will never be over. For me, though, it is this novel's use of quiet moments and fragmented domesticity that brings everything home. Can't recommend this novel enough, a modern classic."

—DOUGLAS RIGGS, BANK SQUARE BOOKS (MYSTIC, CT)

WHAT WE TRIED TO BURY GROWS HERE

a novel by
JULIAN ZABALBEASCOA

Two Dollar Radio
Books too loud to Ignore

Two Dollar Radio
Books too loud to Ignore

WHO WE ARE TWO DOLLAR RADIO is a family-run outfit dedicated to reaffirming the cultural and artistic spirit of the publishing industry. We aim to do this by presenting bold works of literary merit, each book, individually and collectively, providing a sonic progression that we believe to be too loud to ignore.

TwoDollarRadio.com

Proudly based in
Ohio
TURTLE ISLAND

 @TwoDollarRadio

 @TwoDollarRadio

 /TwoDollarRadio

Printed in Canada

Love the
PLANET?
So do we.

Printed on Rolland Enviro.
This paper contains 100% post-consumer fiber, is manufactured using renewable energy - Biogas and processed chlorine free.

 100%   **PCF**   BIO GAS® ENERGY   PERMANENT

SOME RECOMMENDED LOCATIONS FOR READING:
Pretty much anywhere because books are portable and the perfect technology!

 COVER PHOTO⟶ Courtesy of the Robert D. Farber University Archives & Special Collections Department, Brandeis University.
COVER DESIGN⟶ Eric Obenauf **AUTHOR PHOTOGRAPH**⟶ Katie Sticca

Two Dollar Radio would like to acknowledge that the land where we live and work is the contemporary territory of multiple Indigenous Nations.

For Katie and Nico

Spanish Civil War
Timeline of Events

1936

FEBRUARY 16 — Spaniards go to the polls in the third general election of Spain's Second Republic, which had formed in 1931. In the run up to the election, leaders from both the political right and left invoke the threat of a civil war should their side lose. The Popular Front, a coalition of left-wing political parties, wins with 47.2% of the vote. Violent confrontations occur throughout Spain, resulting in the deaths of sixteen people.

FEBRUARY 22 — General Francisco Franco meets with Generals Emilio Mola, Juan Yagüe, and José Sanjurjo in Madrid, where they plot a military coup.

MAY 20 — The government closes Catholic schools, citing the threat of potential arsonist attacks. One hundred and seventy churches have been burned across Spain. Anti-clerical violence will soon intensify, with the murder of nearly 7,000 priests, nuns, and monks in the months to come.

JULY 12 — In Madrid, Falangists murder José del Castillo, a socialist who was a lieutenant in the Republic's Assault Guard. The next day, in retaliation for Castillo's murder, Assault Guards and leftist militiamen arrest and execute José Calvo Sotelo, a leading monarchist. The political right seizes upon the assassination to initiate their planned coup.

JULY 17 — The coup begins with a military revolt in Spanish Morocco. Nine days later, Adolf Hitler offers military support to the Nationalist cause. Mussolini soon follows.

AUGUST 1 — Concerned the conflict in Spain will pull Europe into another war, Great Britain and France propose the Non-Intervention Agreement, which bars the world's major powers from participating in the Spanish Civil War. Ultimately, 27 European countries support the initiative, in addition to the United States. Despite signing the agreement, Germany and Italy lend resources to the Nationalists, while Russia sells arms to those defending the Republic.

OCTOBER 1 — The Second Republic grants autonomy to the Basque Country for their support in the war. The Basque Country is considered the most Catholic of all regions in Spain. Franco sees the Basques siding with the government as a grand betrayal.

1937

MARCH 31 — General Mola begins the Nationalist's campaign against the Basque Country, declaring on the radio, "If your submission is not immediate, I will raze Vizcaya to the ground, beginning with the industries of war. I have ample means to do so."

APRIL 26 — Meant to occur a week earlier as a birthday present to Hitler, German and Italian planes attack the Basque village of Gernika in what will become the first carpet bombing of its kind in history.

JUNE 11 — Basque forces retreat to Bilbao to defend it as their last stand against the Nationalists' assault. Eight days later, Bilbao falls to the Nationalists.

AUGUST 24 — In the seaside town of Santoña, the Basque Army surrenders to Italians. Franco nullifies the terms of the agreement and demands that Italians hand over the 22,000 Basques who are immediately imprisoned. More than 500 will be sentenced to death.

DECEMBER 15 — The Battle of Teruel begins. It will be one of the bloodiest actions during the Spanish Civil War, waged in an area of Spain which will endure its worst winter in decades.

1938

APRIL 15 — Nationalists conquer Vinaroz, cutting the Republican zone in half.

JULY 5 — Hoping to persuade Germany and Italy to withdraw their troops, the Non-Intervention Committee pressures Prime Minister Negrín to remove the International Brigades from Spain.

JULY 24 — **NOVEMBER 16** — The Battle of the Ebro, the longest-lasting and most decisive battle of the war, ends with the Republic's defeat.

1939

JANUARY 26 — Barcelona falls to the Nationalists, leaving only Madrid and Valencia in the hands of the Republic.

FEBRUARY 27 — Britain and France recognize Franco's Nationalist government.

MARCH 15 — Germany invades northern Czechoslovakia.

MARCH 28 — Nationalists conquer Madrid and, two days later, Valencia.

APRIL 1 — Franco declares victory. The United States recognizes his government.

SEPTEMBER 1 — Germany invades Poland. World War II begins.

...all the world's mistakes and its hopes were concentrated in that war, like a lens concentrates the sun's rays, causing fire, and Spain was lit by all the world's hopes and its mistakes, and the same fire's splitting the world today.

—Leonardo Sciascia, "Today Spain, Tomorrow the World"

I am a part of all that I have met

—Alfred Tennyson, "Ulysses"

WHAT WE TRIED TO BURY GROWS HERE

ONWARDS!

A new Spain is being born, the old dying. We are the midwives, the gravediggers. The world welcomes the infant screaming. Who among us would allow another to quit us of our last breath?

This, readers, will not be easy.

As with any war, an enemy is positioned against us. We know them well. Monarchists, nationalists, the military, the church, the wealthy: fascists. Those who possessed power for so long its loss now is a galvanizing trauma.

Democracy didn't serve them, just as they suspected it wouldn't. By force, then, they'll drag us to the past. To a time when women's voices weren't heard, before the church and military lost their position in the political sphere of our lives, before the working class could challenge their exploiters, before all the supposed problems our new freedoms have caused. To a Spain so rooted in fear that individual liberty is its greatest threat.

But we are also fighting against apathy—our neighbors' and the world's democracies'.

Do the politicians in Paris and London truly believe that Hitler and Mussolini's planes are crowding our skies to bring order? Is this so-called order why, at this very moment, insurrectionists are executing thousands of political opponents in Seville. I am fortunate to have known peace in my life. It bears no likeness to what has become of Spain these past weeks.

And are we in the Basque Country any better? So long a part of and apart from Spain, it takes little effort to reassure ourselves that the civil bloodletting in Madrid and Barcelona and Granada will break like a wave against the mountains closing us off from the rest of the country.

To impose their desires upon the rest of Europe, Hitler and Mussolini need the iron embedded in our mountains.

First we will know, then the world: what has begun in Spain is determined to spread.

But it is not too late. The future remains ours to create.

A truth to rouse, a responsibility weighted like a burden.

Allow me now to address several of my critics: search my previous writings. Leading to February's general election, not one saber did I rattle, not one bugle did I make sing. Policy, the merits and failings of communism, socialism, anarchism, republicanism, even the benefits and costs of regional autonomy—this is how I bored my readers then. However, after the fascists' coup attempt, what choice remains but war?

I want peace, to raise my children in the new and just world we were on the cusp of bringing forward. I am before my altar every morning that half this country will come to their senses. Until they do, we must fight them with the weapons they've loaded against us.

Our brothers and sisters in Madrid are only partly right—Madrid *shall* be the tomb of fascism. Sure, of course. But we will also bury them in Bilbao. If we must, in Barcelona and Malaga, we shall make corpses of their men. In Valencia and Toledo, Córdoba and León, A Coruña and Burgos, we will plant their rotting dead.

The free and the oppressed of the world are watching. It's on us to show them the way. Onwards!

—ERLEA
AUGUST 7, 1936

Two and a half years of war—now it's my turn to die.

The captain barks an order that sends the other prisoners shuffling backwards to the pit's edge. I don't move but study the soldier in front of me, this man who will be my executioner. Unlike his fellow soldiers, he cradles his rifle awkwardly and winces at the crackling reports of distant fighting. Might he hesitate? A few seconds is all I'd need to escape.

When we emptied from the lorry's back, I noted the dark forest of poplars and pines in the near distance. Prisoners and soldiers crowded me then. Not now. Now those trees are just off to my right and nobody is in my way. Beyond the thin trunks, the world calls to me.

I startle at a hand on my shoulder. "Isidro," Soto says and motions for me to step back with him and the eight others. All but one or two are from Andalucía. I'm the only prisoner from the Basque Country. "It's over," he says.

"The trees," I whisper.

Soto doesn't acknowledge this. He's blinking against the chill in the night and the wind moving the pines, the stars through them. When he's alongside the rest of our men, he draws in a deep breath and composes himself. "Courage," he says to the eight at our left.

My heels hang over the lip of the pit. Impossible, I think, that I'll soon be down there, yet I make fists to control the tremors. Despite my efforts, they move through me, draining heat from blood. I've never been so cold. One of the prisoners down the line hiccups, the sobs beginning. Another hisses at him, "Don't give that to them."

I hear our breaths quickening. It can't be too late, I want to insist but flinch for the captain yelling at his soldiers to load their weapons. It's accompanied by the click-clacking of bolts feeding bullets into chambers. I know what comes next. The command to raise rifles and take aim, the command to fire, the quicksilver flare from muzzles flooding the world with noise and light.

But my executioner, he's yet to loop his finger over the trigger. I look away from him, slowly, so that he might follow my eyes to the silhouettes of poplars and pines, the puddles I'll need to avoid. Is he seeing what I'm seeing? Beyond it all is a darkness that could swallow me if I reach it, and in it a certain kind of hope.

"Rifles up," the captain shouts, then tells them to aim for our hearts.

1

THE FASCISTS CONQUERED neighboring Irun then San Sebastián but inexplicably halted their advance at our doorstep in Bizkaia. The war continued elsewhere—Madrid, Galicia, Málaga—ignoring the rest of us, and as the months passed I began to hope it might always remain an abstraction, resolved without my involvement. On a chilly night, though, along our province's exposed southern rim, our lorry's thin shivering headlights swept over two bodies gracelessly arranged at the side of the road, and I understood the nightmare had finally arrived.

I stayed in the lorry's bed, making space, while our lieutenant scratched his chin, weaving around the bodies, and said, "I see how it all happened. I see it." Then, "She was last. They forced her to watch."

Isidro and Gabriel struggled to lift her to me. All her weight pooled in the middle, folding her. Her face was tipped back and dark with blood, the white kerchief bounding her hair black from it. Easy to imagine a shadowy man, his boot toe. Harder to picture was his face as he kicked—his anger, his certainty. It terrified me. I was incapable of understanding it let alone possessing it. "Venga, Félix," Isidro said through his teeth, encouraging me.

Blood dripped onto the gravel from her chewed back. I saw my hand go out to correct her head, relieve it of its weight. I stopped short. I had a chance to save myself—perhaps. It was selfish, I knew, but if I touched her, I'd be accepting an invitation to cross a threshold.

Isidro repositioned his slick hands. "Félix," he hissed, "bend down." I wanted to tell Isidro he was an impostor, that we didn't belong here, but maybe it was just me.

"They're still warm," Gabriel said, looking behind him. "Whoever did this is close."

I shook my head and retreated to the lorry's far corner.

"No me jodas," Gabriel said. Isidro ignored him and pushed as much of the body as he could into the lorry bed, then climbed up to drag in the rest of her. I felt guilty but turned from them as they went for the man. "We're trying to rid the world of a plague," Gabriel said, jutting his thumb at me, "and Félix here wants to keep his hands clean." The lieutenant was too distracted by the indentation in the grass to notice, his eyes narrowing in meditative consideration, watching, it seemed, the killings as they occurred. "Those bastards took their time with her," he said to no one.

After Isidro pulled the man in, he covered the two with a tarp, gently, as though putting them to bed. I thought I might be sick. Gabriel laughed at whatever expression I must have been making. A bitter and venomous laugh. "What did you think this would be like. It wasn't for the marching you enlisted, since you're shit at that, too." I hoped Isidro would defend me in some way, but he set his eyes on the tarp, and the sound of our lieutenant starting the lorry—the engine turning over was a cannon report—muffled whatever Gabriel said next. I only heard the cruelty in his voice. Since meeting him two weeks ago I told myself that every fascist was as much a bastard as him, that were it not for geography, were he not Basque, he'd have been right alongside them, part of the rabid masses rushing into the streets when the rebel generals wrestled control of Morocco and those first planes and ships full of insurrectionists crossed the strait. His approach to life was that his misfortunes were the fault of everybody else, and now there was this war—thank god—to hold them accountable. He just happened to be born among those defending the government.

The truck bounced in and out of the ruts in the road, and I drew my feet close, away from the rippling tarp. Behind us, moonlight tinted the dust cloud blue. I kept my vision there while Gabriel glared at me. "Coward," he shouted and gave a quick half-kick to the tarp—fingers showed from under it. I didn't respond. Cold air whispered off a nearby lake as a beech forest emerged to our left. The trees were monstrous hands—the naked branches long and malformed, grasping at something in the sky—and I became aware of a widening space between Isidro and me.

He had convinced me to enlist with him toward the end of July, when we took my family's sheep to pasture. The war was a few weeks old then. It hadn't marked its course north yet. Aside from Isidro, everyone I knew believed it never would. I don't think I'd heard anybody else call it a civil war.

While the sheep grazed and Isidro quoted every recent article by Erlea, the clouds' gray and torn undersides brushed silently against the mountaintops until late in the afternoon when they spilled into the valley. We tightened the flock to take them home, Isidro continuing on about the war, unfolding pages torn from pamphlets, reading from one then another of Erlea's writings. It was a made-up name. No one knew who she was. Despite this, she'd become, for many, the political consciousness of the Basque Country. "'We deserve the chance to make as much a mess of the country as the kings before us.' That's it in one sentence, no? Spain belongs to its people. We should be the one mapping its course, right?" He didn't pause long enough for me to answer. "And listen to this one. 'In Granada, fascists have executed so many that the cemetery's caretaker has gone mad and had to be committed. This, you see, is what they want for us. Since the very beginning. Since before their coup attempt.'" He was building to his proposition.

"Enough," I said. "Even the rams aren't as single-minded."

So out it came: "Sooner rather than later we'll be worm food. Last I checked, there's no coming back from that. But right now, we're alive and young and able to fight for something good, just as there's a fight for the soul of this land." Weeks earlier, Isidro's middle brother had completed seminary and joined the priesthood in San Sebastián, a decision their father, a devout believer and strict disciplinarian, celebrated. He'd lost a laborer but was now guaranteed his heavenly seat among the choir and a reunion with his wife, despite his every sin. You didn't think it possible, but he became an even more intolerable son of a bitch. His wife had died from pleurisy when Isidro was not yet two. In sixteen years, he hadn't managed to fool another woman. Isidro possessed no memories of his mother but took from her early death the galvanizing knowledge that this life will soon be pinched from you, tomorrow if not today. He was the most restless boy in the village.

Xabier and Isidro had been close, the two closest brothers I knew. I envied them that. Xabier entering seminary surprised us all. He was abandoning Isidro to their father and older brother, both of whom aspired to no greater ideal than the beasts in the field. Isidro searched the ranks of village boys for his brother's surrogate. How it exhausted us. From the start, Isidro, the youngest of his family, approached the world as though he'd received orders to improve it. After Xabier joined the priesthood, we knew it was only a matter of time before Isidro enlisted. For as long as it mattered, boys who didn't inherit the family house and didn't want to emigrate to the New World had two options before them: priest or soldier. The brothers were playing out an old story with all the intensity of people convinced they were the first to take the stage.

"The fight's in Spain." I widened to the right to bring in more of the sheep, wondering how many of our friends he'd already tried to convince. Likely several, possibly many. Nonetheless, though I was certain I'd tell him no, I was excited he was asking me.

"What happens there affects us as well. We can't wait for others to save it, or us for that matter."

I watched his figure merge with the fog, partly believing he willed this fight to occur—it would be his grand energy versus the worst of us. I decided I'd have nothing to do with it.

One of the ewes I circled must have thought itself joyfully alone in the world. Its head was down as it nibbled on dry brush. At my sudden appearance, it startled, pinching out a string of pebbles, and dashed into the fog. As signs went, I wasn't pleased with what I'd been given.

The lieutenant banging on the outside of his door returned me to the present. He pointed to the village we approached, a few lights dotting it, the moon low and full. "We'll find them there," he shouted. I'd never been this far south. Spain was somewhere in the darkness, across an invisible and sacred border that we Basques believed in but which, for the Spanish, was no more remarkable from the ground on either side of it.

The houses' facades were stone and mortar, each hauntingly white like the snow-capped mountains in the distance. They'd recently been scrubbed or painted, as if the villagers were anticipating some-body of importance. Our lieutenant stopped in front of one whose window let some light through. He knocked on the door, and shortly an older man stood in the doorway, occupying as much of it as he could. We watched from the lorry bed while the two talked, our lieutenant jovial, his voice light, a salesman's charm. He repeatedly hitched his thumb at the lorry as though it held marvels. The old man was leery but eventually allowed our lieutenant to guide him to us, where the smile fell from our lieutenant's face, and he ordered the man to peer into the lorry's bed at the tarp between us, its raised contours, the oily red fingerprints smeared on it, the muddy shoes it didn't cover. Gabriel began lifting the tarp until our lieutenant wagged a finger.

The old man rocked on his heels and sighed. We were the tide returning a horror. His village was now trapped in it, this back and forth, one group of bodies for another. He appeared to be weighing his sense of duty against an obligation to keep safe whoever was in the house. This close to Nationalist-held territory, allegiances weren't so clearly defined. Neither was the balance of power. Tomorrow you never knew who would throw you against the wall for the actions of today.

Our lieutenant asked, *so then*, and the old man said and the old man said the carnicero did it—the butcher. We'd find him at the village's tavern.

It was just a short walk. Our lieutenant leaned into the lorry for the keys, retrieved his rifle, and checked the chamber. The silence overwhelmed me. I sensed it could drag me across the border. I jumped out after Isidro and Gabriel but was too close to Isidro as he slipped our rifle from his shoulder. "Take it," he said, begrudgingly, misunderstanding my intentions. We had one to share between us.

"Might as well empty it of bullets," Gabriel said.

"He'll be fine."

My skin began to itch. It didn't feel like my own. I thought of my father, searched for any strength in how ashamed he'd be of me for my awkwardness with a rifle. When I had finally confessed to him that Isidro and I had enlisted, I feared he would kill me before the fascists got the chance. He reviled the new Leftist government—they were changing Spain too quickly, overrun with Communists, were church burners, to blame for the chaos in the streets and why, every third or fourth day, a politician had his obituary run in the newspaper. Didn't matter that fascists were usually the instigators. And then there were the refugees swarming in from the neighboring province. Was it his fault they'd sided with the government? Whenever someone read the news to him, he'd issue the same verdict: "Man is wolf to man. We're not good enough for a democracy. Only fools would put faith in our savage hearts." Surprisingly, when I told him of my enlistment, he merely nodded and moved chunks of bacalao around his plate, then said, "I'm glad I have a son fighting for our land." That day's newspaper had fascists proclaiming their movement required the total annihilation of the Basque Country. Someone must have read it to him. I wasn't getting the family house. What else should I do with my youth? "However," he said, "my brother is in Sevilla, your cousins, too. If you find a fascist who looks like your uncle, pretend your rifle's jammed."

Let him be ashamed, I thought, and pushed the rifle to Isidro, but the lieutenant had been feeling under the seat and produced a dusty handgun. "There are four bullets in there," he told Isidro. The way he squinted at it suggested the gun would explode if Isidro fired it. Forget denting a skull with it, you'd be lucky chipping someone's tooth. I imitated the lieutenant and checked my rifle's chamber, trying to remember the few brisk lessons we were given on the bolt-action rifle. All I could recall is how they assured us that if we kept it clean and found the right bullets for it, the fascists wouldn't stand a chance. Surprisingly, there hadn't been any speeches during our training, nothing inspirational to rouse us against those clamoring to support the failed coup.

Nearing the tavern, the moon's light glinted off the houses. The dirt in the road shimmered for it. Isidro didn't seem to notice. He was someplace else, perhaps with the two bodies and the warmth fading from them. Our lieutenant slowed. "There." He motioned with his chin toward the tavern on the corner. It was a simple tavern, stone stacked upon stone, interchangeable with any other. How could something so commonplace have within it a man whose boot was muddy with that woman's blood? My mouth went dry for the thought of it. "Lord Jesus," Gabriel said, "I am a messenger of your Grace." He crossed himself, kissed his crucifix, slipped it under his shirt. "First bullets are for the butcher's balls."

"Take the rifle," I told Isidro. "I'll use the handgun." He made no indication he heard me. We had arrived at the moment he'd long sought.

I expected the lieutenant to kick the door in, but he turned the knob slowly, and when it bumped into its end he nodded and threw it open. Six men were seated around a table, bottles of wine between them. One was a priest, red-nosed and heavy-lidded from drink, his black cassock ripped at the chest. Two were fascist soldiers in dark blue uniforms; the sewn-on patch of the red yoke and arrows looked like a flattened crab on their chests. This was the first time I'd seen the enemy. None of the men wore a butcher's apron.

The lieutenant began a declaration of their arrest, and relief warmed me. I wouldn't be asked to aim my rifle at anyone. For their part, they had two rifles leaning against the wall, a short distance from their table. They stared, confused, and the whole thing might have continued diplomatically enough had one not roared and charged at us, at me, a flash of silver in his hand. I tried to haul my rifle up, to fall back, to grab the man's arm, duck, shield myself, yell—all this at the same time. Gabriel and the lieutenant were shooting at him, their bullets missing, and just as he sliced at me, the priest's head sprayed gore, then the blade opened my arm, severing tendons and muscles while blood spurted in rapid belches, soaking my sleeve quicker than seemed possible.

There was the carving knife raised again, the light off it, but the man's face, his expression—teeth clenched, hard squint, blooming pupils—I'd never be able to match the certainty of it, the focus, a focus that put him so firmly in the moment he didn't see Isidro lift the handgun to the side of his head.

With the blast and flare from the pistol and the knife bouncing silently on the wooden floor, that furious expression would be gone, and so too an integral part of my friend who had helped me bring the sheep home through the fog, who'd shouted over their deep-bellied and nervous bleating, "So we're going to do this?" When I didn't answer, his figure emerged from the haze. He was unable to control his smile. "Let's enlist. I need to test myself against the world. And I know you, I know you need the same."

I wasn't sure I did, but I wanted to believe I carried within me a light no amount of ugliness could extinguish. Down the hill, some-where in the fog, was home—his, then mine. He'd long been plotting his escape. I never thought those plans would include me. "They'll always be there," he said, waving dismissively in the direction of our homes, "as long as somebody fights for them." He was turned away so didn't see my hand out for him to shake.

And there are moments that still find me where I pull my hand back before he notices it. They're pleasant, these brief spells when I imagine how it could have gone differently, imagine that it's possible to escape the brutality of history. But, invariably, traveling across time and returning me to the present comes the sharp clap of our hands and the rest that follows.

2

A RED-TAILED HAWK lists to the right and cuts low, its rigid shape as sharp and fixed as a knife. I lie on my back in the thick grass and stalk it through the V on my rifle stock—my finger relaxed upon the trigger, my breathing calm. It circles over us again, then catches a current and rises and grows small in the sky.

The others—Josu, Gabriel, and Isidro—sit against the base of a large pine, their rifles across their laps, save for Josu, who thumbs the bullet holes in his stock and talks excitedly.

"Four," he says. "Even if you count this as an exit hole, that still makes three. Then there are the two that tore open my shirt." He digs a finger into his uniform, where the bullets grazed him. "And three more I heard snap past my ears." He laughs and crosses himself. He's already emptied our skins of wine. Since the last gunshot in Elgeta, he's been making the sign of the cross, but only recently has he found the words to share his thoughts with us. "It's a miracle. There's no other word for it."

"The miracle," I say, "is that one never hit that French nose of yours."

"It's a miracle," he insists. "I'm here, and I shouldn't be. It's fate. It's what was supposed to happen."

"I'm confused," Gabriel says. "Is it fate or a miracle?"

I've known Gabriel all my life. We're from the same village in Gipuzkoa, a collection of farmhouses built around a church and a narrow river. Josu is from the province over, this province, Bizkaia, and by his accent my guess is that Isidro is, too. Gabriel and I ran in different circles back home, but when we recognized each other last week in Otxandio, a reunion hit us like brothers parted at birth. The truth is, I've never much cared for him—I'm certain he feels the same for me. However, when the forty kilometers that separate you from home feel like the length of a continent and those bastards from Badajoz and Sevilla and Morocco and Germany and Italy are doing all they can to dominate you, then the sight of a familiar face is as great a comfort as you're bound to find, regardless of who it belongs to. But the past several days have shown me that the war's changed Gabriel. It's fucked us all, of course. In my previous life I wasn't as tense and humorless as I've become, but Gabriel—before, Gabriel was a cabrón. A bastard within a bastard within a bastard, like those Russian nesting dolls. Not now though. He's been altered by the shootout in a tavern in Otxandio where he and Isidro killed a group of fascists, among them a priest. We only lost one of ours. Amidst the cloudburst of bullets our soldier was somehow stabbed, the blade drawing a line down his arm, rendering it useless. The fighting for that one is over, but the shootout also had an irrevocable effect on Gabriel. Now he's too finely tuned to feel the suffering created by this war. Though I didn't know Isidro before, the blood on his hands from the shootout doesn't seem to have reshaped him in any noticeable way. No lingering guilt. No mourning the loss of whatever innocence he once possessed. I get the feeling he sees killing a necessary but unfortunate consequence of war. Not me. I don't lament the act. The fascists have come here to exterminate us. Their generals have said so. They want to rid Spain of the very idea of us.

"Fate and miracles are one and the same," Josu tells him. "That all of this was written just so, that the story should unfold the way it does, that is the miracle."

It's poor form speaking like this: most of our men haven't been as lucky. To be excited for having danced around a few bullets is understandable, but after conquering San Sebastián, the fascists stood for inspection with the decapitated heads of Basque soldiers on their bayonets—or at least that's the story we've been telling. There's little reason to think that in the months since they've civilized the beast within them, that luck isn't a finite resource, a well that Josu alone may have drained before our platoon could reach it. We were split from them in Elgeta. For all we know, we're the last among us still alive.

Gabriel says, "If you want to talk about miracles, I know this guy Domingo—Ander, you know him." I nod. "He has a twin," Gabriel tells the others. "Domingo's as normal as the next guy, but his twin brother—poor thing—was born shrunken and twisted. He's half our size, eh, Ander?"

"Not even," I answer. Wind moves through the tops of the trees, rocking their boughs, into and out of my periphery. An insect crawls over my arm.

"All he can do is blink and breathe. He can't feed himself, can't clean himself, is hardly aware of what's happening around him."

Growing up, I saw Domingo's brother only a few times and then again a couple years ago at the Fiestas of San Juan. The sight of him caused heat and needles to climb the back of my neck and spread behind my ears. Some of my friends would try to entertain him. I could never bring myself to that kindness. He's a misshapen box of a human, and my throat still closes at the thought of him.

"Now *that* is as great a fortune as I've ever known," Gabriel says. "Some bullets missed you—so what," he tells Josu. "Imagine Domingo looking upon his brother day after day, knowing that inside their mother's womb it was the flip of a coin as to who would become who."

"I wonder if the brother considers it as much of a miracle," Isidro says.

"I know a girl named Milagro," I say. "At least, that's what she told me her name was. A whore at Copacabana's outside San Sebastián. Biggest tits you've ever seen. The eighth and ninth wonders of the world. Now that is a miracle."

The others breathe out a sort of chuckle, and Josu starts to object, but I let my attention wander. This talk of miracles and fate gets me thinking of my parents, who met during the fiestas in Mondragón at the end of the last century. It's been happening for me—this thinking of my mother and father—since the fighting there several weeks ago when I crouched, gripping my balls, against a stone wall as the fascists' bullets bit into it.

At the time of my parents' youth, Mondragón was a half-day's journey for my father. He would never have gone if not for the insistence of his cousin, who believed that a girl he once saw in Oñati would be there. They passed the day searching for her until my father eventually insisted they begin the long trek home. My mother then turned a corner and caught my father's eyes, and he hers. Through a fortuitous dash of confusion, she had momentarily lost her friends. She was examining the faces in the crowd when she found his.

As I watch the treetops move, I think: what about the series of coinciding tragedies and triumphs preceding that chance encounter in Mondragón, which stretch so far back in time all I see when I close my eyes is my own screaming mouth bursting out of water as dark as night? Yet here I am, far from my village, from my life there and the comfort of my ordered days, laying in the thick grass with my rifle at my shoulder, listening to my fellow gudaris who are just as fortunate as me while I track a hawk that, I suppose, fought against similar odds to be here now. It feels so improbable as to be impossible all could have happened as it did—for this, I begin to sympathize with Josu. Life is a bewildering sequence of coincidences. Josu is proof you'll make yourself crazy if you dwell on them for too long.

Isidro's thoughts must be on a similar path because he tells Josu, "Don't think yourself the beneficiary of some higher power. It will ruin you. My brother's a priest. He and the others talk like that. If we believed as they did, we wouldn't be out here giving the fascists a target they can't hit."

Josu protests, but Isidro shushes him. At once, we perk, holding our breath to make out the sound. From the corner of my eye, through the blades of grass, I see Isidro get to his feet, his rifle in both hands. He checks its action. The others do the same. I remain where I am, for the sound is clear. The tinny rattle of the plane's engine grows louder and comes from the northeast, out from the Bay of Biscay. I squint down my barrel's end and locate the grim shape in the distance. The German Dornier Do would have once been as foreign as an Arctic bird in our skies. Franco has allowed Europe's fascists—the Germans and Italians—to try bombing us from the world, to help him take from us all we were born to. I keep my rifle pointed at the plane—with my thumb, I flick off the safety.

"Stay still," Isidro tells the others. The pines don't provide much cover. I already know the pilot won't fire at us. I sense it. We don't concern him. And as the plane turns in the sky—a wide loop to return from where it came—it flies over us, lower than it should. The German in the cockpit peers down, his expression dismissive, condescending. We mean so little to him.

Though it is fruitless and might bring us harm, I can't help it. That son of a bitch and his kind have dragged us into this war. The rifle pops and the shell casing spits out, its metallic whistle briefly piercing my hearing. The Dornier Do doesn't alter its path, keeps trundling forward, while somewhere nearby the bullet I fired falls unfaithfully to earth. The plane disappears behind the high foliage of the trees and its engine drones to a chilling sort of hum.

Josu, who is sensitive to the balance of fortune that earlier saved him, charges at me, shouting. "Are you trying to kill us?" Gabriel stops him, his arms around his waist. The two fall to the ground in the struggle.

"Calm yourself," Gabriel yells, tightening his hold. I rise from the grass. Isidro shakes his head.

"He wasn't going to fire at us," I say, but then, from the northeast, comes a grumbling choir. Gabriel releases Josu and the four of us are shoulder-to-shoulder watching the sky. The black lines of the squadron—three German bombers, this time—approach. We know now that we don't interest them and watch dumbstruck as they descend in echelon formation toward Gernika.

"What do those bastards have planned?" Gabriel asks, the blare of an air raid siren echoing off the mountains. We stand like idiots and wait. Under the siren rolls the distant rumble of an explosion. I look to the others. Like me, they're squinting, trying to remember if any of our men are in Gernika or Sondika.

Josu laughs. "They're wasting their artillery chasing ghosts."

But I think of Durango, when the fascists bombed civilians, and Isidro reads my mind, saying it aloud: "Durango." There's another boom of thunder and another and another and another, and for at least a minute the explosions mark each second that passes. We run in the direction of Gernika. From behind, louder than the unending thunder coming from the town, three additional fighters split the sky overhead. They disappear beyond the pines' boughs. We enter a clearing where horses sprint in their enclosure as though ridden by demons. Filthy pillars of smoke rise to the sky, meet there and spread.

Cresting a green, low-rolling hill, we see Gernika pocketed in the valley. Dark eggs fell from the bellies of the bombers—their explosions sound like someone quickly tearing paper in half—and are tailed by fighters diving at the town, a staccato fiery orange charging from their machine guns.

"What are they shooting at?" Gabriel asks.

"Those trying to escape the fire," Isidro says.

Our rifles can do nothing against such an assault. Somewhere beyond the mountain's ridge fascist foot soldiers must be hunkering, waiting for the ashes to cool, watching with toothy smiles as more columns char the sky.

"It will soon end," Isidro says, not as a certainty but as a prayer for the village.

But it doesn't end, and from the south two more squadrons materialize in echelon formation. "No," Gabriel says. They strafe the roads and join the assault on Gernika. Another squadron bellows from the east. They bend along the perimeter of the valley, circle to swoop onto the town, break through the black towers. There's nothing for us to do, and perhaps for this reason Isidro runs downhill to the village. If the story's already written, why not stay at home and let time degrade you?

We follow him. My feet are far out in front of me. So are Gabriel's. He tumbles forward and curses, but quickly catches up to us as we climb the next hill. Summiting it is a lung crusher and there, below, is the valley and the fire's heat and the blasts punching the air but no human sound, just the deafening machinery of war. A plane angles at us, changes course by dipping in a straight dive to shoot briefly at the road obscured by a bluff, then climbs the sky. We stand to run but stop. Ahead is a family. Father, mother, two children. The bullets have dismembered the father. The other three are absolutely still, their bodies slashed open as if by a Moroccan's scimitar. Pink meat blooms from the gashes. Above, the plane arcs back.

"They need our help," Gabriel shouts. It's a thing a person should say, but he says it again, his pin eyes zigzagging. He's lost it. Whatever it is that we need to survive, that keeps us sane and holds us together, has left him. I lunge and grab one of his legs, trying to lock my arms around a knee when he shakes me off and runs to the dead family. Though we all yell at him, he doesn't stop, and the rest might as well happen before the plane even dives at him. We throw ourselves to the ground and a swarm of bullets penetrate the bluff, the plane screaming past and making a long turn in the sky. We scramble to the other side and take aim, popping rounds at the cockpit. Our bullets ricochet off the metal hull until the last bullet in my magazine punctures the cockpit's glass, and the plane veers off at once. The pilot is flustered, that's all. He ascends to take inventory.

Gabriel's back is to us, his uniform saturated with blood. Villagers are frantic over the ridge, fleeing the nightmare, and they run past Gabriel and the family without looking down, their clothes charred, faces covered in soot, eyes wide with panic. I'm on my feet and close the distance between us, sliding to Gabriel's body, rolling him onto my lap. Blood soaks through my pant legs at once. His eyes are open and empty. I shake him and yell his name and am about to put my ear to his chest then see where the bullets entered and what they've done to him. Josu and Isidro sprint past me.

I've known Gabriel all my life. I can't think beyond that, can't react, so that by the time I finally hear the bomber it's already on top of us. The whistle is like a judgment from the heavens, and in that split moment before the explosion throws me, the air pulled from my lungs and world going dark with dust and smoke, I see the bomb make contact and the light it releases. Josu tries to shield himself but receives the blast and breaks apart in pieces that don't make sense, that don't obey any understanding of the human body, and is thrown onto Isidro, who is flung back into me in a rush of earth and smoke and metal.

Later, Isidro and I squat at the bank of the river and wash alongside the others. The smell of smoke and burnt cordite clings to everyone. The bitter taste of it squeezes my throat. The world has an evil stink to it. Far behind us in the night the red glow of what was once Gernika takes slow breaths. Few people turn to look at it. Isidro splashes water onto his face, which drips black. Near us, a woman holds a dead child as though it's only sleeping. No one approaches to tell her differently. Isidro stands and says we should try to find the rest of our platoon. They will be in Bilbao by now, he is certain. I crave revenge. The smoke blocks out the stars. I wouldn't be surprised to learn they've abandoned us entirely. And so we leave the villagers behind.

Isidro never mentions it, but I thought of it as I watched him wash Josu from his face and arms, and then again as we walk through the night to Bilbao: four bullets hit Josu's rifle, three if you count the one as an exit hole, then there were the two that pulled at his uniform but didn't even cut him, and the other three that sought his head but somehow missed. This so he could later stand meters in front of Isidro and absorb the remaining violence of the bomb.

My mother had two miscarriages before she became pregnant with me. Had either of those held, I wouldn't have been conceived. If all of this is as it is meant to be, then I have more to fear than a bullet or a plane.

3

THE PLANE CORKSCREWS overhead, away from us. A ribbon of black smoke twists from a wing and marks the plane's wake. Its dual engines sound tremendous in their whirring, as though the machine, in great fear, is trying to save itself.

I am standing next to Ramón. He was my boyfriend Beñat's closest friend here. Beñat liked how he wore a bright red cord from a burlap sack cinched around his waist for a belt, brazenly inviting bullets. Air gusts past us and whips the hem of my dress against his leg. We watch the plane tumble in the sky—our reward for the last several days of grunt labor. For, I suppose, having just been shot at.

As the plane accelerates its arc toward the earth, it deposits, with surprising delicacy, a man into the sky. He hangs suspended for a moment, his arms crossed, legs bent. He is a German, a small figure against a big blue sky. The plane is a Heinkel He 111, and the earth trembles as a bulb of fire roars around it and smoke mushrooms. It was never more than what it is right now. I try to see the world in this way then start running, following the others, in the direction of the falling man.

A white fabric spills upward from the pouch on his back. The parachute balloons and suddenly stills the German's descent. He jerks forward and swings back and forth in his shouldered harness, pulling on the taut ropes to manipulate the parachute. I wonder if he knows we're behind him. Those who have been repairing the front on the eastern edge shoot at him. The knolls block them from view. I hear their rifles pop in a jumbled burst and see the German's outstretched arm as he levels his handgun. The German is precise. He doesn't flinch for the bullets fired at him as he searches the countryside below for targets. After each recoil, a wispy grey cloud quickly blows away from the muzzle.

While we run with our rifles toward this floating man, I remember how, not long ago, during the Fiestas of Bilbao, I held Beñat's hand and watched the air show in wonderment as men leapt from a small plane, somersaulted in the air, and lay flat with arms and legs outstretched. The approaching ground hadn't concerned them.

Ramón falls to a knee and looks down his barrel with one eye closed. I stand near him, brushing the hair from my face, then press my rifle butt against my shoulder, squint past the V at the base of the stock, focusing on my breathing like Beñat taught me. I let out a breath, put my index finger around the curved trigger, and fill my lungs once more. Exhaling slowly through my nostrils, I pull the trigger and a rope of blood spits from the German's head. His handgun drops in a straight line to the ground, arms hanging at his side, the wind still carrying him.

Ramón slaps my back. "Joan of Arc, hell of a shot." I keep my lips pressed tight and lift my chin. I've never been good with the rifle. If I tried a thousand times, I couldn't do it again.

THE FIRST THING I want to do is tell Beñat, but they have him tethered to a bed in the Santo Civil Hospital in Bilbao. A week into his first symptoms he asked the doctor, "Will I play pelota again?" He strained to smile. His skin was pallid and beaded with sweat. The doctor had had a long day—he frowned and said, "No, you are going to die." Beñat settled his head on the cot and studied the patchwork in the canvas tent. I held his hand. Finally, he said, "I cannot agree with your diagnosis, doctor. Heaven wouldn't be Heaven without a fronton. And the best players I ever knew must be in Hell. I'll blast that ball yet."

That was Beñat. When he had an audience, he was compelled to bring levity to the situation.

We had joined the army together, several days after we'd buried my father and brother, who were killed during an air raid on the munitions factory. My mother didn't meet the idea of us enlisting with much resistance, less than I anticipated. Beñat and I were both thirteen when we became a couple, and since then we'd done everything together. He had practically grown up in our home. My mother sat at the kitchen table dressed in the black of mourning and warmed her calloused hands on a mug. "I never once imagined," she told me, "you would wave from the doorway while Beñat went off to enlist." She sighed. "But you two are all I have left."

I had expected her to say, as she had been since burying her husband and son, "Life. We were supposed to give you life." I had half-hoped she would tell us that this was madness. Our family, she should have said, has already lost plenty. Let others go fight. Instead, she set her warm milk down and took us by the hand. She squeezed hard and, in this way, gave her blessing.

"We will make them pay," Beñat said. He had been saying this since the funeral.

"Yes," I said. I knew he wanted to hear it. "We will."

We'd thought there was little extraordinary about my joining. In Madrid an all-women battalion had secured an important bridge during a battle against the fascists, and in Barcelona women fortified the Anarchist's ranks. Here in the Basque Country, our very own Erlea inspired us all—Basque, Madrileño, Catalan, man, woman, and child—to resist the fascist's military coup. The fascists, she warned, wanted to drag us back to a time when priests told women how they must live and we all went to bed hungry. Naturally, women had to join the struggle. So when Beñat and I reported to the eastern edge of the cinturón de hierro, the Iron Belt that was our front, I expected I'd be one of many women in the trenches. We were both confident of this. Just as, I suppose, the men hadn't expected me to return after leaving Beñat at the hospital in Bilbao.

RAMÓN FINDS ME by the fire and slaps me on the back again but sees I don't want to talk about the German. A soldier announces to our group that there is a bottle of fine cognac for the man who blew off the pilot's head. A prize from General Staff. In my periphery Ramón eyes me. I don't say anything, and the soldier approaches the next group. I collect the rest of the story from those around me: the wind ultimately tangled the pilot and his parachute in a tree, which one of ours climbed to cut him down. The pilot's head was a mess. They worried all his secrets were kept there. As it turns out, his pockets had many stories to tell.

Since I feel I am entitled to a small reward, I say, "Do you remember the bar outside of Durango after we had finished burying the bodies? The time when Beñat fooled that Spanish colonel into thinking that night might be his last?" I stop. They aren't interested. Ours is a hastily stitched-together battalion of those who have retreated in recent days from Eibar and Santa Marina Zahar and those, like me, from the villages north and west of here. Most of these men know only of Beñat as a cautionary tale. I sink back.

The evening sun sets and a wash of brilliant oranges and purples cross the ridge that settles a spring chill in the air. Soon, the first stars show against the sky. The moon is trigger-shaped. We sit around a fire, passing our wineskins. I lay down and want to reach for Beñat's hand, to fool myself briefly, then hear, as though conjured by my thoughts, the tentative whimpering of an approaching dog. I know the others wish they could ignore it. They watch me from the corner of their eyes. The dog is a collie, perhaps once a herding dog, its coat white and black, its bluish-grey eyes flashing in the firelight.

"Get out of here," one of the soldiers says, swinging his arm out. The dog cowers but doesn't shrink away. It crouches lower to the ground, its tail tucked and ears folded back. "Go on," the soldier yells, and another throws a rock at it. The dog is hungry so assumes an even more submissive position.

After Beñat, we've been told to shoot them on sight. I've yet to meet a soldier who's obeyed these orders. "Go," the soldier says. Another tears off a piece of chorizo. "He won't leave us alone if you do that," the first soldier says.

"And your way was working," the one with the chorizo says.

"Don't ask for my rations."

Yesterday we began receiving meat again. For the last several weeks we've been subsisting on the state-baked black bread, but British ships have finally got through the fascists' blockade. This relaxed the grip someone held on a cache of chorizo. Aside from infrequent shipments of food, the British, like the French, have still refused to join our fight against fascism. Only the Russians sell us weapons.

The soldier waves the piece of chorizo for the dog. Its scabbed nostrils quiver. The dog steps forward but flinches when the soldier throws the chorizo into the darkness. "Find it." It turns and faces him with an imploring look in its eyes. "Jesus Christ," the soldier curses, and suddenly our lieutenant is there.

"Are you cowards trying to do the fascists' job for them?" He stands over us. He was assigned to our battalion the day before and has offered little instruction since then. His features are soft and fleshy. He takes his meals with General Staff at Hotel Gatzaga. He has a bed there, too. "If you're scared of being obliterated by a bomb, let me assure you this dog's bite will be a worse way to go."

"The dog is healthy," Ramón says. In other armies the soldier is meant to respect his superior officers, but we are Basques and before the war we were all equal and after the war we again will be. Our laws established this long before there ever was a Spain. Framed in this way, we have little patience for playing the part of the subordinate.

"I didn't know you were a doctor on such matters," the lieutenant says. "Tell me, what can I do to clear out this shit that's got me clogged up?"

"Stop talking so it can come out the end intended for it."

A few chuckle but the lieutenant squats near the dog and thumbs the button on his holster to remove his handgun. Only the officers are issued them. Some of us have yet to receive rifles, just a purse of grenades. His is a Russian Nagant. He presses it to the dog's head. I don't want to watch. "You're carrying diseases that will kill us," the lieutenant tells it. Its ears perk at the attention, but it remains uncertain.

Nobody else here knows but me so I say, "I saw the rabid dog. This one isn't sick."

The lieutenant is surprised to see me. "Qué?" He squints across the fire. I don't explain myself. I've been in the trench longer than him. "Orders are orders," he finally says and pulls the hammer so it clicks into place. The dog waits.

"Me cago en la leche," Ramón says under his breath.

The lieutenant eases the hammer down. "Here, give me that chorizo," he says. "Qué coño es eso? Not a piece, the whole thing." The lieutenant flips open his pocketknife and cuts one slice after another so they fall into the high grass in front of the dog. It waits. "Go ahead," he tells it. "Eat." The dog snouts around the grass, its tail waving. "You see," the lieutenant tells us, "he was just hungry." He stands and points to Ramón and me. "You two," he says. "You have rifles? Good. Take this dog out there," he motions outside our flames' glow. "If we don't kill it, someone else will. At least now his stomach will be full."

Neither of us look at the other. Somebody whispers, "Hijo de puta." I grab a piece of chorizo and wave it in front of the dog. When I pass the lieutenant, the corner of his lip raises as if to tell me: let's see what you're made of.

Campfires dot the landscape and each offer grey strands to the sky. The German and Italian pilots assisting the Spanish Nationalists don't fly at night, so we sit by the fires at ease.

Ramón says, "We're going to have to cross the river." I tell him I know. The chorizo casing that I can't break down I spit out and offer to the dog. Days ago I would have gladly swallowed it. The bread, black and bitter but all we regularly have to strengthen our bones, is a chore to force down. Beñat and I once happened upon Ramón and a few others standing around the body of a priest in Durango. Flies buzzed about his open mouth, but his body didn't show a single wound, despite his skin which was blackened and red. The men wondered what had killed him. Beñat tilted his head to take in the corpse then said, "The bread of Bilbao." And we kept walking. Later we learned a person should fear not only the burst shrapnel from a bomb but also the air it concusses.

The river branches from the Nervión. I chew my last slice of chorizo, the heat of the paprika finding my back teeth, and give Ramón my rifle, talking softly to the dog as I lift it and hold it to my body. It belongs to somebody, or had once. It's used to this protocol and doesn't fidget as I step in the water.

"Fleas don't like water," Ramón laughs. "But try not to think of that."

"And yet you dare to enter."

"I said fleas, not ticks."

At its deepest point the water is up to our waist. My blue worker's dress billows around me. I spit more casing into my hand and feed the dog. On the other side I set it down. "Is this far enough?"

"Do you have any chorizo left?"

"No."

"I just have this." He holds out his cupped palm. In the dark I can't see what's in it.

"Let's walk a little farther then." The dog is between us.

Some low patches of clouds pass quickly under the stars. Ahead, the blot in the ground draws our attention.

Light doesn't find the craters' bellies. The bombers, for all the fear they inspire, are far from accurate. If they ever want to hit our trenches they should start by aiming at least two hundred meters away. I recall a crater outside Durango. A speedy Heinkel 51 spotted Beñat and me in an open field and veered at us with a deafening ferocity, its dual machine guns pock-marking the earth that led to us. Beñat pulled up his pants, and we ran and jumped in the crater, scraping our arms against the blown metal bits of the bomb that had shaped it. It seemed a logical place to seek cover until I turned and saw so much of the sky overhead. "Just pretend you're dead," Beñat shouted. "The bastards up there can try all day but they'll never hit a sitting target." I doubted this, especially as the earth sprung near our heads. "Not even close," Beñat laughed, taunting the pilot.

I now stand at this crater's edge with Ramón and think of Beñat and me watching the German ultimately give up and how Beñat said to me, "Shall we continue where we left off," and how I'd rolled into his arms. Ramón holds the chorizo in his palm. The dog sniffs at it and its lips pull back when Ramón tosses his last piece into the crater. The dog looks at us, one then the other. I open my hands to show it I have nothing left. "Go ahead," Ramón says, pushing the dog's backside with his foot. It resists at first then follows the chorizo's path. I can't see anything in the crater but know the dog will find it. "Best of luck, compadre," I tell it. When we're halfway across the water, we turn and rake the dark as best we can for the dog. Back on the other side, Ramón says, "Sorry, the wine is pressing on me." I put my back to him and hear it pattering on the ground. It's no issue for them. Me, I sometimes walk a hundred meters until I'm certain I can't be seen. He ties the red cord tight around his waist and we continue but soon Ramón stops. "Christ, that bastard is still waiting for a gunshot." He puts the rifle against his shoulder. "Which star do you want me to hit?"

"That one," I say, pointing.

The rifle shot rips through the night.

AT THE SANTO Civil Hospital, many of the nurses were my age. They moved down corridors with purpose to attend to those occupying the cots lining the ward. Most of the men received their injuries in Amorebieta and Durango. Some came from as far away as Otxandio, though a few had never been in the field but suffered shrapnel wounds from air raids. There were many amputees. Beñat asked me to search the cots for Cano. He'd fought alongside us in Berriz and was in Durango when we helped with the bodies. Beñat had heard he was at the hospital—I wasn't sure how. I kept my head down as I walked past one cot after another. Sunlight angled in fully through the windows, filtering through a low-hanging cloud of cigarette smoke. The doctors and nurses were dressed in white. Some wore masks while they spoke with patients. The room stunk of sickness, the air was thick with it. With each step the floorboards creaked. The nurses smiled as I went by. I didn't meet the eyes of any soldier as I glanced past the soiled bandages from one cot to the next for Cano. Each soldier had a story I didn't want to hear. Brown liquid smeared the rim of their bedpans. Wineskins were half-tucked under mattresses. I could feel the soldiers glaring at me from their beds. How to explain my presence? My body sound and capable, I should have been with the others fighting against those who had put them here. And yet I didn't want to leave.

When I returned to Beñat's room, he was asleep. They isolated him from the others because of his condition. He slept with a furrowed brow. I took his hands, the muscles in them tight. I tried not to think of how, in a few weeks, they would turn cold, while mine might one day wrinkle, become thin and liver-spotted. I squeezed his palms to cement this memory, to never forget how he felt.

The doctors had warned me not to, but I kissed him then, watching his eyes all the while.

The sound of wooden heels on the floor echoed from down the hall. A nurse walked past the doorway, holding a silver tray of cotton balls, a rubber tourniquet, and a glass vial that rolled back and forth as it turned on the needle's point. I took the chair from the wall and sat with his hand in mine and fell asleep there, thinking I would have the nurses teach me all they could. Beñat was my responsibility.

I had moved in my sleep. When I opened my eyes I was on Beñat's chest, his restraints imprinting my cheek. He was studying the ceiling with a fierce concentration. I stretched the kink from my neck. He lifted his head, his eyes more responsive than I had seen them in days. His mouth was close to mine. His breath smelled unusual, tainted, but I didn't mind.

"Cano is dead," he said.

"I couldn't find him."

"I had a dream where we were sharing a bottle at that tavern in Durango. He told me he is on the other side now. He is waiting for me to bring him a plate of txipirones." I studied his face but couldn't tell if he was serious. "He says they have all the salted cod a man could eat in eternity but nobody's been able to find the ice chest where they stash the txipirones. He thinks it might have something to do with the sudden influx of Basques." He rested his head back on the pillow. "What a character."

I started to explain my plan to learn from the nurses, but he stopped me. "Cano told me something else, my love."

"I'm going to look for Cano in the other hospitals. If I find him—"

"There's plenty of time before you finally do. You're going to live a long life and have many grandchildren. He assured me of this. He told me I still have time, too. Weeks and weeks of it. And I don't want you by this bed between now and then. You may make a good blanket, but the cinturón needs you. We must beat back the fascists."

"I'll serve here," I told him. "If I can take care of you, that's more time the nurses have to help the others. They'll get better sooner and more will then be able to strengthen the front."

Beñat smiled. "I don't think health or math works that way. I am one man tied to a bed who gets poked with a long needle from a great distance. A lost cause. I require little observation."

"But I'm happy here."

"It's not good for our country," he said. "I'll gain some life knowing you're out there shooting holes into fascists. Your father and brother must be avenged."

I tried to think of them, but in every memory Beñat was with me. "You must do it for them," he said. "For our fatherland."

We spoke more on the topic, but the effort tired him. When he awoke next, the sun had set and the room was dark. He called my name—his voice dry, scratchy—so I took his hand. He sighed. "You're still here." His palm was moist with sweat. His voice began to drift. "Come back in two weeks. Let me know how the cinturón is doing. I'll be waiting. But if you're here tomorrow, I'll leave you for one of the nurses." He said more but the words were mumbled and nonsensical. I slept in the chair that night. I didn't answer when he called for me again. With the first grey light coming in through the window, I rose, making little sound. Beñat slept with his mouth open, his lips dry and cracked, the thick wool blanket rising and falling on his chest. I searched his hollow face for the soft, round-cheeked boy I fell in love with at thirteen. Only his dimpled chin remained. He'd lost so much weight these last few weeks. I wondered how much he had left to give. What would he look like when I returned? I stepped into the hallway.

The café across the street was already open. Slices of black bread were lined behind the glass where the glaze on pastries probably once caught the light. The bell chimed as the door closed behind me.

Several old men hunched over the morning papers at a circular table and exchanged rumors from the front. I asked if we still held the cinturón near Fika. "Claro," one said. The paper in his hands shook from tremors. "Our men are dug in deep. Not even the devil himself could move them." I sat in the far corner with my coffee and cried.

Buses no longer left the city, so I started for home on foot. Pine trees clothed the mountains save for one bare-faced peak that miners had blasted to extract iron. These deposits were why Franco's fascist allies fought us.

A lorry loaded with war supplies rumbled past me on the road home. A swelling line of dust its tail. It would be late evening by the time of my homecoming. My mother would open the door, surprised and relieved, but then have to listen as I told her about Beñat. Perhaps she already knew. His uncle had adopted him when he was six. The man was a drunk and never read the news, but this had probably legged it to him anyhow. That he'd yet to come to the hospital meant nothing. An ignorant, he no doubt feared it was contagious by proximity. Approaching home, I would see candlelight etching the windows of the first houses in the village, the shape of the orchards in the night, smell the wood smoke drifting from chimneys. I imagined my mother and me at the table, each with a cup of hot milk between our hands. Two widows far from the world where men died, where blood was spilled so that others could live, where the fate of Beñat's principles was still being determined. He was no longer able to fight for them, but I could on his behalf.

An hour later another supply truck drove past. They agreed to drop me off near a road that led past Fika. I walked the rest of the day to camp. There I quickly found Ramón. He was with Cano. "Two guesses as to the stories Beñat's telling about you," I said.

WE WATCH THE sky in confusion and anticipation, remaining at our positions, ready. The planes never fly at us. Instead, far off in the distance, the thin, dark shape of their fleets move silently, away from our front. German and Italian planes, likely—bombers and fighters. They arc over the mountains and dip into the valley of the Oka River and disappear. Then from the east a team of tranvías drift low over the hills toward the valley. Soon we hear the dull echo of explosions. An officer walks past us to the battalion on the eastern edge of the front. "What the fuck is going on there?" Ramón asks. The officer ignores us. The next who passes only shakes his head. The explosions are soft thuds. We try to calculate how far away they're falling and name the villages pocketed in the valley, asking each other if any of our soldiers are positioned there. Funnels of smoke cloud the sky and drift in our direction.

Finally, our lieutenant kneels at our trench. The men squat against the dirt walls with their rifles across their laps. I sit above-ground atop a box of ammunition. "Let me have one of those," he says, pointing at the cigarette in my mouth. I shuffle one from my crumpled pack and hand it to him. "I don't have a light," he says, pushing it back to me. I want to throw it in the dirt at his feet, but light it, pull on it, and give it to him. He takes a deep draw. "It's Gernika," he says, holding in the smoke. We look in the direction of the valley, at the dark green mountains. My first thought is of Durango: we'll have to bury the dead again. I'm not sure I have it in me. The lieutenant says this is different. "They are burning it all."

The line between Gernika and General Staff has been severed. Before it was, the operator in Gernika said the planes were cascading incendiary bombs over the whole village. The operator saw fighters cutting down civilians who ran from the burning building across from his. They lay in the street while flames engulfed the village. The bombs fell, one chasing the other, then the line went dead.

A soldier who's been sitting in the trench stands and starts walking toward the mountain ridge, in the direction of the pluming smoke. He's the son of a shepherd in Ea, a village near Gernika. "Patxi," several of our men call to him.

"Let him walk," the lieutenant says, waving in his direction, ash falling from his cigarette. "He has nowhere to go."

We ask if we have any soldiers in Gernika. "None that I know," he says. "The operator was the father of the man who laid the line." He pinches a piece of tobacco from his lower lip. "If we had airplanes of our own, or even machine guns, a little sign of God's affection. This is an unfair fight, men. What are we supposed to do here? We have no trenches between Mungia and the bay, just a few pieces of earth have been dug up at Gaztelumendi. Our front is half the length it needs to be. And where are our air-raid shelters? Where is our aviation? Where is our overhead cover? No, it is an unfair fight."

"Thanks for the encouragement," Ramón tells him.

"Of course it's encouragement," the lieutenant says. "The Basque story is one of retreating deeper to a position we can hold. No people have ever been able to dislodge us. Not the Romans, not the Moors. And now Franco and his German and Italian friends are concentrating on our country. We are shooting bullets at our own sky. That's fine. We were here before, and we will remain. It is our story." He grounds out the cigarette in the dirt and tells us to be ready. "You never know what those bastards have got planned."

For the rest of the day, though, not even bird shit falls our way. By late afternoon I strain to listen for the explosions while a messenger walks down the line, calling names and delivering mail. Our post prides itself on its efficiency. Should a letter get on a supply truck by noon, it can be in a soldier's hands hours later. It's hard not to laugh—even with the world ending, letters are delivered.

The men around me speak of distant family members in Gernika, of its fiestas, the meals enjoyed there, and of the Casa de Juntas, which houses the archives of our race and language. Next to it is the Tree of Gernika, the ancient oak of our people, in whose shade one Spanish king after the next promised to not interfere with our democratic rights. It cannot be that they've been destroyed. The village is the spiritual center of the Basque Country. It feels as if a part of us existed outside our bodies all this time and only now did we realize we should have done more to protect it.

I try to think of what Beñat might have devised to relieve us of this emptiness. Nothing comes to me.

THAT NIGHT THE valley glows red. The light cups the belly of the clouds. It veins the smoke that blankets the stars. There is a faint odor of charred earth and burning metal. We don't say much as, broken-hearted, we watch the red glow emanate and pulse. We are fortunate that the mist rolls in as we lay sleeplessly in our bags. What man destroys, the earth cleanses.

In the morning, mist darkens the tips of the pines, creating a thin break between cloud cover and grey horizon. I haven't slept enough to distance myself from yesterday. It still doesn't seem possible that Gernika is no more.

Somebody yells and we scramble out of our bags, a few point- ing at two figures who approach. I squint through the eyehole at the end of my rifle and see that they are gudaris, like us. One by one, we lower our rifles. "How goes it?" someone calls out. The two soldiers don't respond but continue limping down the face of a hill. The men's clothes have been scorched and are blotched with soot, the mist has wet their hair. Eerie messengers. I worry for what they will tell us.

"Ander?" Iker, a soldier near me, asks. He doesn't shout it, but says it softly, fearfully, uncertain as he peers toward the hill, as though he is looking across the plane that separates us from the dead. The next moment he is laughing and running to the two men. We walk after him. Iker embraces the skinnier of the two. "I thought we lost you back in Elgeta," he says.

The man, Ander, is startled and wide-eyed. The soldier next to him studies our faces and stops at me. Their clothes are patterned with blood. Finally, Ander says, "They killed Gabriel."

Iker doesn't appear much troubled to learn this. He nods and knocks Ander on the shoulder. "At least you survived, cousin."

"They've destroyed Gernika."

And from here we are told the two soldiers' story. After the retreat in Elgeta, they found themselves alone on the northern route through the pines, chased by the sound of the Italians' machine guns but concealing themselves from the planes that groaned overhead. They were four. The next day they rested in a field of high grass in the valley of the Oka River when the first plane flew over them. Soon one fleet then another followed its path and the bombs started on Gernika. The men were still far from the village but ran toward it as flames lashed the sky. They could feel its heat and the blasts that punched the air when a fighter cut down Gabriel. The next moment, a bomb sucked the air from the world, blew apart the other soldier, and threw them tumbling back with his pieces, unconscious. When they came to, all was dark. The village had been destroyed.

"You did what you could," Iker tells him.

Ander bites his lower lip and shakes his head. "We didn't kill a single one." The soldier next to him makes a reproachful sound low in his throat: dangerous benchmark for success. Ander, still wide-eyed, his tongue plugging a gap from a missing tooth, scowls at the soldier, who holds his ground. The two men share a look that unnerves me. The experience has changed them, but not in the same way.

We feed and clothe them, and Ander's cousin gives him his rifle, but though the other—we soon learn his name is Isidro—quickly makes friends, none offer him their rifles. Patxi approaches both men, asking if they know of his father, if they saw him. Mondays are Gernika's market day, and he often sold his cheese there. Neither man can help. Hours later, the first survivors walk past our trenches. Children weigh down ox carts that bump along the road, guided by adults who slowly put one foot after the other. Patxi stops those he can. Soon, other soldiers leave the trench and wait along the road. An old man points back in the direction of Gernika. He appears to be telling his story but stops, puts the tips of his fingers together, struggles to continue.

That morning, hundreds pass by on their way to Bilbao. Mainly families, though there is the occasional solitary individual or farmer directing his livestock. A young woman cradles an infant to her breast. She can't be much older than me. The baby pulls away and cries and my hands instinctually move to my stomach. I have a fleeting, surprising regret that Beñat and I had been so careful. Only a few ever look in our direction. Some who spot me tilt their heads, wondering, as I often do, what I am doing there. Later, groups carry trunks between them. One man carries the metal frame of a bed while he walks the road. In the afternoon the lorries form a scattered convoy toward Bilbao. From their open backs we see the blank faces of those inside.

The mist thickens throughout the evening, and the next day it stunts our vision. I can see no more than twenty meters in front of me. Silhouettes move about it. A deep, flat bell tolls from an ox's neck. Wheels roll over stones. From time to time, a lorry grumbles in the distance. Our lieutenant comes by and kicks at our shovels. "Moping isn't going to bring back Gernika, and it isn't going to make this trench any longer." The earth is soft under the spade as we extend the line. Word spreads that Mola's troops have entered Gernika. The Moroccan regulares are with them. It's a good thing the mist is a wall before us. To look at the mountains and know that just beyond them fascists gather would be as demoralizing as another air raid, but the men near me are excited by the news. They are ready for the fight, to avenge Gernika and all those they'd known there.

At night the mist breaks and the stars get through the clouds. First there are a few. Soon they pierce the sky with light. In the morning the German fighters will return, this time for us.

WHEN THE SUN finally crests the mountains in the east, we take our positions in the dark and damp trenches. Waiting. I feel as if I haven't slept for days. My limbs are weightless from nerves, eyes dry and scratchy, but I forget about these when my heart starts up at the sounds of the fleet—three fighters flying low enough that I soon see the sharp point of the planes' noses, their wings vibrating, the black crosses painted on their sides. A pilot glances over one shoulder then the other, blonde strands of hair whipping about his machine gunner's face. The earth far from our trench spouts from each bullet, and a soldier next to me shouts, "They're trying to knock the dirt from the ground."

We pop off rifle shots as they swoop at us, the sounds of their engines overwhelming me. I hear some of our men shout when, from a cloudbank that clung to the valley wall, five fighters—Loyalists— our fighters, join the contest. They must have been waiting for the moment they'd be behind the Germans. The fight, finally, favors our side. The Germans can't turn in time. The bullets catch one and a fiery spark jumps out its fuselage and ignites. The plane is burning in the sky before it even hits the ground.

The fighter chases after the next German plane being dogged by two of our own. When bullets hit it, whatever strings held it aloft are snipped. In its nosedive, the two Germans aboard deploy too late for their parachutes to open. They slice toward the ground. One hits it in a gruesome splatter, turning at once to pulp. The other tumbles with tremendous speed end over end. He comes to rest not far from us and we run to him. The ground has shorn off his features and reveals at his crown, through meat and blood, the bone white of skull. His skin is red and purple, limbs twisted in broken formations under his body. Grey matter flowers from his ear. Several men search through his pockets and take what papers they find. "We've got it all," one says, "leave him to gape at the show." The last German fighter is still above us, attempting to evade our five.

We dash to the safety of the trench and as we fall in, a torrent of smoke streams over the thin body of the German plane, its funeral shroud. It careens toward the mountain range in that telltale coil. We all leave the trench to pursue it. As I run, the world seesaws. Four of our fighters lift higher while one follows the plane around the bend of the mountain. The earth shakes underfoot and the growl of the explosion pulls from us all another cheer.

The mountain is large to our left, a great upheaval of earth. Circling the bend, we find a curiosity: a German, seemingly unharmed, walking to the burning wreckage. He is a young man with a strong jawline and blonde hair. From his back, the wilted silk parachute trails behind him. Branches cling to it. Some of our men yell and we quicken our pace to him, but he ignores this, steps around the ruined end of a wing, and reaches into the smoldering cockpit. The soles of his boots sizzle. Going for his gun, I think. I fall at once to offer the men cover, but he is grabbing the carbonized body of his pilot, which he tugs clear of the wreckage and starts kicking, smoke pluming off the corpse. I run after the others. They have their guns leveled at him and are yelling for him to get to his knees. All he does is kick the charred body harder, cursing in his language at it. I've never heard German before. The body is now only the idea of a body. Petrified in its final moment of horror, it's barely recognizable as human. One arm has torn on impact. The other is rigid, burned to his face when he tried to protect himself from what approached. The German's kicks lose strength. Grunting heavily, he sends his foot two final times into the burnt corpse's side. He catches his breath, hurls one more guttural word at the body, then spits on it. He turns to us and raises his scorched and blistered arms. "Me rindo," he says, his tongue thick, the Spanish almost unintelligible.

Ander, who must have been far behind us all the while, pushes past the others and points his cousin's rifle at the man. The German doesn't flinch or budge, though the muzzle is meters from him. Ander's chest rises and falls rapidly. There's the deep breathing of those around me, the air passing between my teeth, a clicking coming from within the plane. Ander mumbles something about Gernika. The German is a prisoner and so should be treated as such, but the men tell him to do it. They want Ander to pull the trigger, to see the German's head whiplash as his feet give out, to make him pay for this war they brought us. I can feel this desire coming from them, feel it take root in me, and am surprised by this.

"Egin orain," the men say. Ander jams the butt of the rifle firmer against his shoulder. Then, at once, Isidro, the soldier Ander came down the hill with, is by his side. "We can't become them," he says quietly to Ander. He should have shouted it—it's the sort of thing people increasingly do. Ander ignores him. Isidro says, "They want to dominate us through force, divide us. You and me, we're better." He puts his hand over the muzzle and shakes his head. My shoulders jerk involuntarily from the rifle shot. The sound of it rents the air and echoes off the mountain's face. Those around me buckle. Ander drops the rifle and turns away, leaving Isidro yelling and clutching his hand between his knees as blood spurts in meaty chords onto the grass. The German checks his stomach and legs, his arms bunched and tight. Several men run to Isidro and tug his hand free from his grip. I see the red, chewed stumps of his middle and ring finger, the heartbeats of blood coming from one, the splintered edge of bone breaking from the other. They work on staunching the wound while some kick the rifle away from the German and shove him with the ends of their barrels. We take the red cord from around Ramón's waist and tie the German's hands. He's saying something in his tongue but is cooperative.

Ramón and I escort him to our trenches, the German glancing at me from time to time. First, he seems confused. Soon, the slightest smile crinkles the corner of an eye. He isn't taking us seriously. I want to slam my rifle into the back of his head. Ramón holds his pants up with a hand and is happy to have his cord returned to him when we deliver the German to our lieutenant and the other officers. Our lieutenant wants to make an example of the German. The other officers remind him that, unlike Franco and his fascist allies, we don't kill people in cold blood, even if they hold a different opinion than us. The German's fate, however, is not sealed one way or the other. The officers question him about his involvement in Gernika. He says that this is his first time flying over the Basque Country. He'd traveled north the day before from Madrid to help in the large offensive that's to start tomorrow and produces his flight records to corroborate this. The corpse he kicked was his superior, a man who possessed few piloting skills but who had, through nepotism, collected the promotions that should have been his. The man had no right being up in the air. He couldn't have hit Gernika had he been told to crash into it. The German crosses his arms and says, in his poor Spanish, he's decided he's grateful for what's happened. It's kept him from killing the man on his own and ruining his family's name. The officers ask him why he is here fighting us, and the German pushes his chest out and says with conviction: to silence Communism. Color comes to his cheeks when the officers laugh at him. "Does this look like Russia, comrade?" Ramón asks him. The German frowns and looks to the others for help making sense of it. Ramón turns away in exasperation. "The hijo de puta is in the wrong skies," he says to me.

This isn't true. Anyone who has read Erlea knows that. The German and his compatriots want access to our iron ore deposits, the roads we dug into our mountains, to our ports, our factories, everything our parents and centuries of democracy have built. With those, they can wage war not solely in Spain but across all of Europe. Ramón says, "Joder, rubio, you're in the wrong skies."

The officers decide that since the German is forthcoming with information and a valuable addition to our cache of political prisoners, one that might pressure Franco to reconsider the prisoner swap we've been trying to negotiate, his life will be spared. This is communicated in Basque so the German is left to wonder at his sentence. Addressing the issue of troop morale, the officers recommend we visit the batzoki, the Basque Nationalist Party house, in Fika that night. There we can eat and drink, recover and momentarily forget.

While we wait for dusk, a messenger delivers mail through the line, and I'm surprised when he lifts an envelope and calls my name. My mother is illiterate. She'd trudge the fifteen kilometers to the front before she ever thought to put words on paper. "Here," I say, and a moment later I can't remember the steps I've taken to him. I let out a heavy breath, my chest collapsing with relief, when I see it isn't an official communiqué from the hospital in Bilbao. Beñat is still alive.

The handwriting on the envelope is familiar. I recognize it but can't recall from where. I fumble opening it and unfold the letter, reading it at a glance. Then again, slower. My aunt tells me to return home. My mother left on Sunday to visit a cousin of theirs in Gernika who lived on the perimeter of the marketplace. She's yet to return. Nobody has heard from the cousin either. She, too, is a widow, the last blood relation we have in Gernika. My aunt tells me again I must return home.

I close my eyes and feel the heat behind my lids and retreat into the pines. As the sky changes colors I sit and smoke and try to convince myself this is a mistake. My mother has hardly stepped outside our door since my father and brother's funeral. She has no reason to go to Gernika. I read the letter again and again and find more in it than is written. My aunt doesn't know the decision I made. I feel her judgment nonetheless: had I only returned home after leaving the hospital in Bilbao.

I should go now, but what could I do there but wait? Here, I am closer to the destroyed village, to the road my mother might walk. Here, I can be of better use. Beñat would tell me this. I no longer believe it. I just want to be by his bedside. No, I want to be sitting at our dining table across from him and my mother, my brother and father. I want the life we had before the others started this war.

I finish my pack while the first stars come out and don't talk to anyone as we walk to Fika, each breath filling some emptiness behind my sternum before its retreat.

WE CLIMB THE stairs of the batzoki to its second floor and sit at long tables. Women wearing dark dresses and white shoes set down a steaming pot of soup for every eight people. The wine bottles are distributed in this way, too. On the walls, murals show the passions of our life. In the bay, fishermen strain their backs hefting a net into their boat. In another corner, a crew team heaves into the waves. My brother and Beñat used to take me to the bay to watch these races. They never bet on the same team. In the painting, an ox drags a large stone across the ground. Two men play pelota at a fronton while women walk through an apple orchard. Each autumn, my mother and I collected apples to make cider for the house. A couple dances—the boy with his leg kicking high in the air, the girl billowing her dress as she twirls. The dancers are set against the waving Ikurrina, the Basque flag. This I know: people are born to be with someone specific. Beñat had been orphaned as a child, then placed in the care of his uncle, the village drunk. Until Beñat met me, the Basque Country was all he had. My eyes burn. It can't be that I've lost everyone. This is just a nightmare, I tell myself. Very soon I'll wake and things will be different.

I don't have an appetite but a sudden thirst. Something's lumped in my throat, and I try to choke it down with wine, one glass after another. I make sure to not see the table through the bottom of my glass. Ramón is several men away saying he should have put a bullet in the back of the German's head when he had the chance. He won't be able to sleep for the thought of it. War requires immediate action, and he failed. The skinny cuts of lamb are piled on platters. Curls of heat rise from them and scent the air. This is just a nightmare, I tell myself again. This cannot be all I have left.

The men talk in hushed tones, their mouths full, of the German and how Franco will be no less inclined to swap prisoners for him. The fascists didn't trade with us after the prison massacre in Bilbao two months ago. They felt no urgency then, why would they now? From there, they share stories of Gernika, of the friends and family members they are certain have died in the bombing. Nobody thinks to ask me if I've lost anyone. We've yet to avenge their deaths, the men say. I don't want to listen to them.

I stand and pass Ramón and the others and fill my glass until the wine spills over the rim then slam the bottle down. None pay this any attention. The ground is uneven, lopsided, never quite where it is supposed to be. I feel my head pulling away from my legs so clench my jaw to hold on, knocking into a few backs to the stairwell. Somebody grabs my arm and asks for more lamb. I yank free, the room teetering.

I am deliberate with each step down the narrow staircase. Then the night sky spreads above. Cigarette smoke reaches me. I squint though the darkness. The bandage on Isidro's hand is blackened from dried blood. He stands in a circle with several others. The cherry at the tip of his cigarette burns bright. I make out the uniforms of the two officers with him and the blond hair of the German. He lifts his cuffed hands to his face, bringing a cigarette to his mouth. No one appears to be talking.

"Goazen, gudari," somebody says behind me. I turn and have to close an eye to recognize our lieutenant. "Help me bring the logs."

I finish my wine, toss the glass, and follow him into the field and feel all that space beyond. Our lieutenant snaps open his holster. "I'm going to offer my revolver as a prize to the best aizkolari," he says, speaking of the wood-chopping competition. "This will help their spirits, no?" I want to tell him I can't be here any longer but that I know no other way of keeping Beñat alive. Instead, I take an end of a tree trunk. The bark is wet from the grass. "Bat, bi, hiru," he grunts as we lift it. I see him smile, his approval. Carrying the log back to the batzoki, we walk past Isidro, the two officers, and the German. "What is he doing here?"

"Who?" he says, but he perks his eyebrows. "Listen."

From inside come the sounds of the txistulari who stops the fipple flute and begins the first words of the Basque nationalist hymn while hitting the skin of the drum. Others join in. With all that has occurred, I don't know how they can be singing. I will run off, I tell myself. I'll find some way for Beñat and me other than this war. There must be one. There must. But I know there isn't. In the end, the soldiers and I are all that stand between the fascists and Bilbao, between the fascists and Beñat's hospital bed.

"Venga," our lieutenant says, "let's get the next one."

The world tilts, threatens to spin. I flex my legs to hold steady, trying to plant my feet firmly into the ground. The German smiles in my direction. "What is he doing here?" I ask again. The lieutenant doesn't answer. He's ahead of me, singing our people's hymn. This really is it, I think. "They took it all," I say. Our lieutenant turns to pat me on the shoulder, but I stumble into him and push him down in the process of pulling the revolver from his holster. In a few steps, I'm at the circle of men. One of the officers turns to look at me. So, too, does Isidro, and I know he knows. He starts to lift his hand. For the ineffective space now between his fingers or the memory of how the middle two were ripped from him, he stops halfway, resigned—this can't be stopped. He was a fool for thinking it could be. I see it in his eyes. The German's forehead creases, and he tries to say something but I have the revolver up and pull hard against the trigger. His face disappears at once under a muddy red smudge as gore jets out the side of his head and his legs fold. A sharp wail silences the world. I drop the revolver and walk away from the three men, each of them sprayed with the German and involuntarily cowering. I stop after a few steps and fall to my knees and vomit. It's all liquid and splatters over my hands. I wait and heave again and try to purge myself of what's inside me, of these last months. I usually feel better afterwards, but now I feel worse. My hearing returns with the tumult from the batzoki. The soldiers stand in the doorway, more and more coming out, trying to make sense of the scene.

Later, they argue for me. There is some comfort in their support but not much. I spend that night in the prisoner's quarters, the only person there. I imagine my mother, alone, soot-covered and in the dark, on the road that leads to our village, knowing she has me. My aunt's never been a nervous woman. Still, she could be premature in her concern, she could be wrong. I think of Beñat, a prisoner in his hospital bed. In my mind I travel the road to Bilbao. I start planning the ways I can get back to him. Twenty kilometers separate us.

The next morning, before any of the officers can decide what to do with me, the fascists begin their assault. Four of our planes are shot from the sky, and the retreat is a mess, running through the forests and the fields.

4

WALKING HOME THAT morning after the shelling, we slowed as we neared our apartment. Sandbags walled off the street. A boy in his late teens sat against them in a pink wingback chair while he read a newspaper, rifle across his lap. His hair was neatly parted, right leg crossed over the left, swinging. The chair looked more comfortable than anything I owned, probably liberated from a wealthy household. He didn't glance at us from his paper as we turned around.

When we finally rounded the corner to our block, a chalky haze sat like fog on the street and immediately dried the throat. But it was more than stucco and mortar: our neighbors were somewhere in that dust.

Their apartment building was a mountain of wreckage from which charred planks and stones and bricks—some pulverized, others intact—distended. All these hours later, men scaled it, calling down into its pockets, waiting, listening. Smoke drifted from its smoldering belly. Yet if you turned your back to it, the soot on the ground was all that hinted at the shelling that took place the night before.

Nerea kicked the frayed and perforated sole of an espadrille. Unsalvageable. She passed it to Jon who took a clumsy swipe at it. "Why do you keep thinking you're left-dominant?" she chided him. "Here," she said, "try with your other one." I wondered if they still heard, like I did, the rattling engines get louder, felt the floor tremble and the walls shudder, heard Isidro yell for us to get down, then the high-pitched whistles and the explosion that rolled toward us. I had expected the floor to collapse but the windows didn't even burst inward, just a hard drumming of pebbles against them as the planes banked east. Isidro had put his hand on my shoulder, asking if I was fine, then followed his fellow soldiers down the stairwell, hoping to rescue those buried in the rubble. The smoke looked like clouds lowering onto a setting sun. There was little the soldiers could do throughout the night but control the flames. In the morning, they returned for their bags, Isidro's cut and calloused fingertips brushing my hand. The rescue effort continued, but they had to report to their regiment to help maintain the cinturón de hierro on Mount Gaztelumendi—the city's fortification, the Basque Country's last defense.

I stepped on the sole and pointed at Teo behind the curtain of her second-floor window. "Let's see if Teo isn't busy." Her apartment was directly across the street from ours. She was the children's piano teacher, eternally seventy years old, but she had lived a life, one in which she'd been given a husband and children. She often alluded to her children in passing when reminiscing about "a simple life." I couldn't tell if they were still alive, were far away or somewhere in the city and simply chose not to visit, any of which could have explained her bitter demeanor, her hunger for my children's company, her silhouette at the window, which was an ever-present feature in our neighborhood.

I called up her stairwell. "Teo, do you mind if we start early today?" In a moment, her door cracked open. "Have fun," I told Nerea. She took Jon's filthy hand. He was four, so attracted dirt. I should have scrubbed his hands at least. We had water to spare. "I'll come in a few hours."

BACK HOME I flitted from one corner of the apartment to another, lifting an object, holding it to the light, setting it down. I chided myself for not bringing in a displaced family. Weeks ago, I'd told myself I would. Now I kept thinking: what if Isidro and the other soldiers returned? The room must remain open.

There were articles to write, but I felt purposeless, incapable of focusing on an argument. This had never happened to me before. Aside from the first weeks after my husband's death, when I was uncertain what would become of the children and me, the world had never been so rich with exigency. Writers like myself were trying to convince the French and British to lend us support, for Madrid to spare aircrafts and arms, for Roosevelt to listen to his wife, for the International Brigade to march by the hundreds down our mountains—for everyone to join the fight against fascism. But the summer sun continued its horseshoe loop, pulling in the morning shadows, and I thought only of Isidro and our kiss the night before.

His fellow soldiers had been in the kitchen, a bottle passing from one to the next. To remain with them, Nerea asked to wash the dishes, and as with everything else, Jon copied his sister. I took advantage of this opportunity to search for Isidro. My daughter had an instinct I couldn't remember possessing at her age. Incapable of articulating it, she sensed my desire for Isidro so never allowed me to be alone with him. She'd become more infantile in his presence, wrapping her arms around his legs, curling into his lap, requesting one game after another. Twice I snapped, "Stop speaking in that high register." Perhaps she was trying to assist me, a joint effort to seduce him—I would get a lover, she a father. But I was convinced she was competing against me, trying to attract a man the lone way she knew how.

I found Isidro in our sala with a copy of *The Virgin, The Nun, The Woman, The Gun.* "Sorry," he said. "I've been trying to finish it before we leave." I'd started writing to keep myself sane after my husband was killed. The pen name untethered my voice from my identity. As Erlea, I was amazed at how freely I could write on ideas long buried deep within me. I became even more grateful for the pen name when my writing gained an unexpected readership, a not insignificant number of them detractors. Some claimed to sign their death threats with a bullet's tip. I doubted this was the case. Who had such time? Nevertheless, it forced me to remain vigilant concerning my anonymity, but the week before, sensing it would impress Isidro, I had pointed to the books on my shelf. "I wrote those." We'd been sharing looks for the last week. Among the soldiers my children and I lodged, no other had been fighting since the beginning, not long after the Spanish generals had gathered in Morocco and launched their coup attempt. At that time, most of the Basques continued convincing themselves this was a Spanish conflict, a distant inconvenience that need not concern us.

"For a while," he had said, "I thought you were as big an enthusiast of her writing as me. It would explain why you were housing us. Bigger, in fact, as I haven't had the chance to read two of these. Not until Nerea hinted at it did I finally put it together."

"Oh," I said, and hearing what an idiot I sounded like, I had asked, "then you've read my work?"

"I wonder if I'd have joined the struggle otherwise."

I now looked at the copy of my book in his wounded hand. "Take it. Please."

He smiled. A film of sweat warmed my palms.

"I'll return it when I finish."

"I'd like that," I said. We should have discussed the book, I guess. I could have asked why it was that one, among the others, he pulled from the shelf. In it, I argued that being Basque meant being a minority in Spain and France and, therefore, being involved in a global struggle with other minorities: a struggle for the preservation of our identities that required not the lazy authority of ancestry but creativity, a celebration of what makes us distinct in the face of the gun and the institutional powers gripping it.

So, I suppose, I should have asked him if he agreed with my claims, asked him what being Basque meant to him, but worrying Nerea would turn from the sink and notice my absence, I hurried to cross the room. We met by the window. I hadn't been kissed in three years, hadn't wanted to in a thousand. I was self-conscious of my heartbeat. When we pulled apart at last, he was smiling. I couldn't break from his eyes but had a nagging sense that if I looked to the window, I'd spot Teo's shape behind the curtain. There were other concerns, urgent matters that would decide whether or not Spanish democracy was a short-lived experiment. In that greedy moment I couldn't recall much outside my shrinking periphery and what felt like a revelation: in war, the full breadth of emotions persist, hiding among the horror—even joy.

"How old are you?" I asked.

"I turned nineteen a few weeks ago." He was younger than I'd thought.

I kissed him again. "Happy birthday."

"And you?"

"I feel ancient, but I suppose I'm not much older." Just then the church bells began in their frantic disharmony and the low, grinding air raid siren rose in pitch. Under this, I heard the planes.

Our shoulders sagged and we both chuckled. But the planes grew louder—louder than ever before. They were tracking a direct line to us. From the window, Isidro scanned the sky. I screamed for Nerea and Jon, and in seconds the planes drowned out every sound in the living world.

WITHOUT HAVING WRITTEN anything, I returned for the children. Jon sat on Teo's lap while she guided Nerea's fingers with one hand, tapping on the sheet music with the other, coaxing her patiently. "We are hauling this piece from the past into the present," she said. I doubted she'd be so tender with them if she knew I was there. I looked for the rags she must have used to wash Jon: his skin gleamed. Her love for my children bordered on the carnivorous, but she and I benefitted mutually from our arrangement—I was given time to write, and with Nerea and Jon she could indulge her maternal impulses.

I cleared my throat. As always, she didn't acknowledge the pesetas I extended until the children were preoccupied with a jigsaw puzzle, one of the many she had. From the archipelago of pieces they'd so far joined, this was probably St. Peter's Basilica. My exchanges with

Teo were traditionally short, but I assumed she'd want to talk with an adult about the shelling. Instead, she was surprisingly cheerful. She must have figured that death, after circling and circling, had finally flown at her and missed. Still, what of our neighbors? "I'm glad to see you rid us of those soldiers," she said, slipping the coins in her pocket. Lightning bolt wrinkles creased her heavy eye shadow. "They're not what this neighborhood needs, you agree?" I wanted her to clarify, to ask if she thought we'd been shelled because of them, but Nerea passed us, and Teo followed her to the pantry, producing a treat. Her question continued to hang between us. I let it pass. It was already more than we typically shared, and, besides, I didn't know if I would see them again. A fascist's bullet, a shift in the front, a bomb racing to the earth—who could say what might happen to the men, to Isidro, to this unexpected happiness.

THE NEXT DAY, columns of foul, charcoal-colored smoke spiraled upwards from what had to have been Gaztelumendi's jagged peak and unspooled in the wind. Pin-nosed German fighters dove in the direction of the mountain before pulling up, looping and diving again. Fuel exhaust settled on the air. My children and I watched from the street as we left a talk in Plaza Nueva. The speaker for the UGT, General Union of Workers, had attempted to breathe life into the city's battered morale. "We are fighting fascism today," he told the crowd, many of them the displaced, "so our children won't have to tomorrow." My clothes itched and felt tight. Jon and Nerea kept hanging on me. Everything bothered me. I wondered which far-removed village the speaker had driven in from. Lately, people had been flinging fishing lines skewered with rancid meat from their windows, hoping to hook seagulls. The streets had been cleared of stray cats long ago. This man was too round-bellied to have been subsisting off rations like the rest of us. While I was speculating on this, Guillermo found me in the crowd. He was a former student of mine. In the classroom, he had lacked intellectual humility. These days we all profited from his unwavering convictions. We stood shoulder to shoulder, facing the speaker. "I don't have the article yet," I said. He sighed and said, "I can give you till this evening." The bombs hitting Gaztelumendi were a distant, grumbling thunder. On the walk home from the plaza, I told Nerea and Jon to forget the UGT speaker's tonterías.

We skirted a crater where soft dirt rimmed its circumference. In its guts were scorched stones and glinting metal that had clawed into the earth on the bomb's impact. When we reached the other side, Nerea asked, "What was so stupid about what he said?"

I preferred to ask the questions, keeping my opinions to myself, but I'd been emptied of patience. "That fascism can be defeated," I said. "It can't. It's like a virus. Now that it's here, it will always circulate. The best we can do is suppress it, make some progress, before its easy answers again find a poet's mouth." I scratched the small of my back, my neck, pulled at my clothes. "What's required is a commitment to the struggle. The problem with so many here," I was now practically yelling, "is they thought the headlines would always be about someone else."

"I'm hungry," Nerea said. Jon agreed with her, and his predictable confirmation is what Nerea needed to say it again, whining this time.

"Then keep walking," I shot back. "Do you see any vendors? Can you smell anything other than fuel? Show me what I'm keeping from you."

They quieted, which allowed us to clearly hear the explosions from the mountain echo off the remaining buildings. We stepped over broken sidewalk tiles that were adrift like plates of ice in freezing water. Several blocks from our apartment, we stopped short. A group of people huddled against a building's corner, pointing down the street at a soldier on the curb, slumped over, rocking like a drunk. Others pointed at a building further away, where the sniper was hiding.

Fifth Columnists. While we tried to beat back the approaching Spanish military, the Fifth Columnists, those traitors hiding among us, secretly plotted for their arrival. "We need to help him," an older man was saying. "The sniper can't still be there."

"Either you're crazy," another said, "or planning to feed us to whoever has their rifle poking from that window."

"Which window?"

"You tell us."

The old man responded, "Say it again. Are you calling me a facha? A Fifth Columnist?"

All the while no one made a move to the soldier. He drooled clumpy black-red strings that thickened in the white dust around his feet. I held Nerea and Jon to block their view, standing on my toes to confirm the soldier wasn't Isidro.

THEIR PIANO LESSONS were usually every other day, but Teo welcomed them in, smiling as though she had been expecting us, confirming her suspicion that I was an inadequate mother.

Let her think it. As long as she'll take the children for a while.

"We're hungry," Nerea told her. I was, too, and caught the smell of something sweet baking. Teo said, "Then you've come at the right time. Let's liberate the cake before it burns." I paused by the stairwell. She was parroting left-wing language, her tone pointed. "Yes, well," I said, "I suppose I'll be back in a bit." Teo had already shut the door.

As I crossed the street, a breeze churned the dust and ash and pulverized limestone and concrete blanketing the ground. They became, in the strengthening winds, a pasty cloud that soon veiled the ruins of the apartment building. With a finger, I traced the sky to our apartment, counted the second the pilot needed to wait to release the bombs. The horror wouldn't have been instantaneous for Nerea and Jon but endless as they fell through the floor and realized I couldn't protect them, that I had fooled them into ever believing in me.

I thought of their father. He had left us when I was eight months pregnant with Jon for an attempt at quick money supervising some coalmines in nearby Asturias. I resisted his decision, refusing to see him off at the train station. Nerea's birth had brought me close to death, and after it was over, I couldn't believe the wailing child they lifted into view was my daughter. It didn't seem possible she could have survived all she'd put me through. One of us had to die, such was the contest. And yet, after being confronted with the fragility of life, my husband decided to abandon us, but not before impregnating me again. I convinced myself this next pregnancy would be worse than the first, that it would end me. I screamed this to him as often as I could, which probably hurried his departure. Somehow, though, he was the one to die. This was in '34, at the start of the miners' revolt. For all I know, he could have been the first to have had his head cracked open by the Spanish Foreign Legion they brought in to quell the workers' uprising. Nerea was three by that time, Jon still nursing. They were his history merged with mine. Pulled from me, they would wither like fruit from a tree.

Again, I drew a line in the sky.

TEO SAT BETWEEN Nerea and Jon while they dipped cake into marmalade, their cheeks packed like squirrels. "Swallow what you have first," I said from the doorway. Teo's soft and dutiful expression changed at once. She stiffened her posture. I was intruding upon her time with my children.

"Did you forget something?" she asked, feigning politeness.

Her possessiveness stripped me of my ability to be cordial. "No, I just want them."

"We haven't begun the piano lessons."

I had to restrain myself from snatching what was mine from her.

"I realize that," I said, knowing the next part would tip us into new territory, "but I'll pay you regardless."

She smiled as she nodded and picked at the table. Finally, she met my eyes. "I understand you're nervous and scared, what with all the madness outside. Don't worry. The Spanish military is coming. They'll be here within days. They'll restore order. And after they get control of the factories and mines, we'll finally return to how things had been."

She waited for me to agree with her. I bit the inside of my cheek. She was an old woman, convenient to dismiss. Doing so was what allowed fascism's lies to claim her. I had denied the obvious for too long. "Teo," I said, "when you're standing at your window and looking at the world outside, I know you see a ruined city."

"I do," she said. "I see the chaos that liberalism has produced."

I'd read this in papers but never heard someone say it aloud. "What's printed on those curtains of yours? Our neighbors were bombed. It could have been you or Nerea or Jon." They had retreated from their plate—a display of their allegiance.

She noticed this, as well, and raised her voice. "And who dropped those bombs?"

I stopped. "Teo, please don't tell me you're falling for that. You don't truly believe the Basques are bombing their own people."

"Of course," she said. "For international sympathy." Before I could counter, she said, "I tried to give you a chance." She shrugged, was suddenly and oddly calm, smiled overconfidently. "I know who you are, what you've written."

I struggled to maintain a passive expression. "Nerea, Jon," I said, "thank Teo. Let's go."

THE REST OF the day, I panicked at each noise, ultimately, though, I grew weary of being in such a state. She was a solitary old lady, I kept telling myself. There was no reason to worry. That night I took Nerea and Jon with me to the street corner where I was to hand off my article to Guillermo. I titled it "The Balsam of Hope." Too often in my writing I'd grab my reader by the front of their shirt and try shaking them into action. This one felt gentler, sweeter and sadder, truer. Finishing it, I'd thought how Guillermo and some of the others would detest it. I didn't care. There were other ways to rouse people to our cause. They'd see.

We waited and waited, until it became dangerous to do so. "Come," I said. This wasn't typical of Guillermo.

During the walk home, Gaztelumendi gradually became as quiet as any other mountain. The fighting had stopped.

WE PASSED THE early morning hours as though wounded. Soon we'd have to get in line for rations, hoping the grocer would open. At the moment, I was writing at my desk, feeling the weight of Gaztelumendi's silence, glancing up often to watch Nerea read to Jon. I studied the freckles that clustered over their cheekbones in rich grapeshot, an inheritance from their father.

Nerea closed the book, and a creak sounded in the stairwell. They've come for me, I thought. With one heartbeat my body flushed and time slowed. With the next we were hugging Isidro. His uniform stunk of burnt cordite, petrol, the dank sweat of adrenaline. Something dark and human was smeared across his neck. I kissed him, nakedly. Nerea and Jon had their faces buried in his uniform so didn't see. Only when I pulled away did I note the empty door—no other soldiers were behind him. He had returned but would soon leave us again. Our fortification had been fatally penetrated.

THE CITY WAS long on the brink of starvation. In the last week conversations were converging onto a single topic: evacuation. It would occur that night. Nuns and priests knocked on doors like discreet town criers to let us know, gambling that a Fifth Columnist wouldn't shoot a person of the cloth. Isidro spoke of a diversionary attack far off in Huesca to allow the population of Bilbao to evacuate. Other families were tying overstuffed and lumpy suitcases shut with twine onto carts. I dawdled after Isidro, warming water for his bath, talking to him through the door. My children never left us alone, hovering like pesky summer gnats. He kept yawning, so I insisted he sleep. While he did, I pondered his bruises—those rings of blue and black and purple that bloomed on his arms and legs, the stories they told. I was trying to convince myself that the good fortune that brought us together would also provide us a number of days to fully appreciate what we had, time being one of them—my children and I in our home, Isidro and I together. But in the afternoon he put on his crusted and soiled uniform. He laced his boots and glanced up at me. "I'll be providing cover for you."

"We're staying," I said.

"Don't," he said.

I had expected a different response. "If Bilbao falls—"

"It will."

"If it should, we'll retreat with the army."

"Retreat to where? There's no other Basque front."

"The evacuation is for Asturias. The army has nowhere to go but Santander. Writers there have offered us their apartments."

I couldn't tell what part, if any, he believed.

"We'll be here when you return," I said and kissed him on the cheek. "Be safe."

Before dusk, the first reports of our failure in Huesca carried on the wind. Thousands of Republicans and International Brigadiers had been killed. Regardless, the evacuation was in process, its momentum stubborn, implacable. I watched my fellow Bilbaínos from the window, the determined crowd under-lit by lanterns, swell toward our valley walls. Children's cries punctuated the low, nervous hum of the collective voices. I wanted to shout at them: why had they waited so long to resist, did they think fascism would stop short of their doors? But I couldn't judge them as a whole. Among the evacuees were the displaced, nuns with children, those hospitalized soldiers able to walk. A group of them blinded by the war were tied together. Studying the crowd below, I spotted Guillermo. He held an older woman's hand, likely his mother's. He walked as if everyone was in his way. I couldn't stop nodding with indignation. Eventually, I accepted the futility of our efforts. If he had taken my article to the printer last night, it wouldn't have stalled the evacuation. All these people would still be out here.

I remained at the window until the last of the crowd blended with the gloom, until I heard the first shrill, distant buzz, that clanking of engines, the sirens echo off the mountains. I waited for the planes to enter the city. They didn't come but chased after the evacuees. In bed, I listened to the muffled thunderclaps, holding Nerea and Jon to me while they slept.

IN THE MORNING, I sensed an absence on the streets. The city hadn't been abandoned entirely, but no sound on those streets was human—a street that, weeks ago, would have been waking at that moment, should have been damp from the urine and excrement of bridled livestock on their way to market. There were gaps in the distant skyline, buildings I could never see before. Something pricked my consciousness, and when I lowered my gaze, I saw Teo's silhouette behind her curtain. I wasn't surprised she had spurned all entreaties to evacauate. She was likely the only one in the building to have done so. We watched each other. For a few seconds I thought she might be dead, petrified by rigor, a city scarecrow, until a figure on the street called our mutual attention to it. I nearly screamed from joy.

I'd never seen a man so haggard. The loose bandages on Isidro's hand were soiled and grimy with dirt and dried blood the color of rust. His steps kicked up the powder and ash. He smiled weakly at me. When I looked back to the window, Teo was no longer there.

That night, Isidro and I were on the balcony, his arms around my waist. I rested my head against his chest. All day, convoys of the Spanish military's tanks and lorries gathered around Bilbao's southern mountain range while bombers neared in widening loops, releasing with increasing impunity thermite bombs that yanked white walls of smoke from the ground. I'd packed what was most essential and what the children and I could sell when we reached Santander. Isidro said that in the morning there was to be a diversionary offensive in Basauri so those remaining could attempt another evacuation.

He was putting himself at risk by staying with us—his fellow soldiers were huddled in the barracks that had been our train station. Fifth Columnists and anti-fascist militias freely roamed the city in equal measure. The night fizzed with distant gunfire. There was a rumor that 317 had arrived in the city to help them conquer us. He was a Nationalist soldier named after the number he had killed. I would have loved to have written about him. He was representative of the fascist's lack of imagination in this war. Their identity had become our annihilation. They hadn't another idea on how to improve Spain. Their core belief was that exterminating us would get them closer to the country of their youths and safeguard the power they felt progress jeopardized.

No candles burned from within Teo's apartment, but I knew she watched us, could feel it on my skin. Clouds obscured the moon. For the moment, neither of us worried about Fifth Columnists. Hours earlier, in an effort to slow the Spanish military, soldiers had dynamited the Mesedeetako Bridge, not realizing or not caring that our electrical line ran along it. The metal girders had crashed with a terrible groan into the quick, midnight current of the Nervión River, pulling the whole city into the darkness with it. I could hardly see my fingers in front of my face, yet Teo, I was certain, followed Isidro's hands on my body. Nerea and Jon were in bed. We'd been waiting, Isidro and I, for them to fall asleep.

Tomorrow, he was saying, he and the others would sabotage our munitions factory. I tilted my head back so he would kiss me. "Will our army surrender?" I asked. The world's greatest democracies had abandoned us in this fight. Isidro's chin brushed the top of my head. He named Spanish cities south of the Basque Country that the Republic still held. "I'm not surrendering."

"And our army?"

I felt him shrug.

"My middle brother entered the priesthood in San Sebastián just before I enlisted," he said. "Xabier refuses to fight, to resist, wouldn't even when our father was dancing boot prints down our back. He won't stop believing that the worst of us possess some good he can encourage forward. We've never agreed on much, but for the last while I've wanted him to be right." I listened to him breathe. "He isn't. Last night they killed as many of those fleeing as they could. You can't redeem that kind of person. You have to silence them wherever they present themselves." That last part was mine. He was paraphrasing my most recently published article. "And if it's on the battlefield, so be it. I'm not surrendering. The Basque Country isn't the only place these ideas are being fought."

I patted for his hand, the good one. It was scabbed and split at the knuckles. A part of me hoped he'd ask me to join him. He said nothing. "So it's over?" I asked.

"I'll find you." He squeezed my hand.

"I don't even know where I'll be."

I made out a smile. "We found each other once already. We weren't even trying then."

We stepped inside, and I led him to his bedroom.

I wanted to disappear completely, into my body, Isidro's, into the rolling bursts of colors—bright and nearly transparent—that used to accompany my orgasms, but when he lifted my blouse over my head, I flinched for my smell, was repulsed by it. I'd diluted my perfume to the point where it wasn't much more than water. I kept my arms at my side while he unbuttoned his shirt with one hand, and when his chest was bare I embraced him. His skin was warm against mine. He ran his calloused fingertips down the knots of my spine. The other hand, his bandaged one, was damp, probably with blood. He held it away from me, wiped at my hip, the hard ridge of it. Of all the nightmares this war had delivered to the human body, I wanted a moment of beauty with ours, to escape, but each sensation, each thought and action, was framed by the reality outside. It made me sad for us, for everybody.

Isidro stopped kissing my neck. "Are you all right?" I bit my bottom lip. "We can stop," he offered. Then, "We should."

With the government collapsing, there would be no future for people like us. Soon, I thought, he will be killed, but in this moment I can give him, or attempt to, the pleasure I so desired. I put my breast to his face and, with my hand on the back of his head, pulled him to it while I worked to unbuckle his pants. I remember feeling grateful he was hard, that he wasn't going through this solely for my sake, and I tried throughout the night to lose myself in his hunger.

WE AWOKE BEFORE dawn. I traced nonsensical lines on his stomach, my fingers skidding over his ribs. The sun was behind the mountains, the sky through the window hinting a blanched blue. Time was against us. His stomach grumbled. Nerea and Jon would be hungry, too. "We don't have any food left."

"And for the evacuation?"

I shook my head.

"I can fetch something from General Staff."

"When you leave that will be it," I said. "I'll never see you again."

"Not for a while," he corrected me and kissed my shoulder. "Your neighbors could only carry so much. Let's see what they left behind."

On the street, there was a scarcity of oxygen. I licked my lips and tasted chalk. Isidro had his rifle slung over his shoulder as if hunting wild pigs. "I'll check this half," he said. The door hadn't been locked. I clung to the sight of him until he disappeared inside. With a foot, I shoved large stones in the street hoping to find a tin can hiding underneath. For some reason, I waited until that moment to look up at Teo's window. There she was, filling the frame, peering down the street. I sensed the effort on her part to avoid me.

I stepped off the sidewalk. The rubble was uneven underfoot as I crossed the street and saw them, the ones she was waiting for. "Fifth Columnists," I said, as though reading sandwich boards they wore.

We had troubled ourselves over Fifth Columnists for so long we allowed our communal hysteria to imagine them as something phantasmagoric, monstrous, not human. But these three were only men, boys, really. They wore checkered wool jackets, one a slouched hat, another had a cigarette like a toothpick in the corner of his mouth. Each gripped their revolvers slightly away from their bodies, a poor imitation of the sheriffs in American Westerns. "Isidro," I whispered. I could hear him scooting furniture and kicking at debris in the apartment. I considered my own across the street, the window where, just beyond, Nerea and Jon slept. The Fifth Columnists would give chase, would follow me to them. "Isidro." The one to the right pointed at me. Their pace quickened. Another cocked his gun. He had dark eyebrows, a short, wolfish forehead. I felt the sandpaper stucco of the wall behind me and thought of those grainy newspaper photos, of bullet-riddled walls, the misshapen bodies on the ground and the blackness pooling around them.

Then, two crosswinds tangled in the street, gathering ash and powder and soot, momentarily obscuring the three men. From the corner of my eye, I caught a movement at the shattered window. Isidro slid the barrel of his rifle through the gap, was crouching low and taking aim. I shielded my face for the pellets of dirt the winds flung, the winds that might with any luck blow forever. But the air was abruptly snatched from the world and the debris thinned and settled, the traitors closer than they were before.

5

XABIER   SAN SEBASTIÁN, JULY 1937

THE STAINED-GLASS WINDOWS fracture the light so the walls
are flecked in molten oranges and yellows, finding the few congre-
gants in the pews, save for Bittori Arretxea, who is tucked away
in the western nave. While the others squint, she remains cloaked
in shadows.

I stand near the confessional where we parted, unmoving as
I watch her and wait, thinking: I can remain where I am—I need not
do anything—and it will resolve itself. Silently, I recite the five Hail
Mary's and three Our Father's I assigned her for penance. She should
have finished by now, so I assume she is cycling through them again
or seeking guidance from a higher power yet.

Finally, she stands and crosses herself. I meet her near the doors,
startling her. I am only slightly less surprised. "I was hoping," I tell
her, "to continue our conversation. Can I invite you to a coffee?"
Hers is a thin, bony nose that hardens further as she considers my
request. "We need not go far," I add. "One of the cafes outside
will do."

WE SIT UNDER the shade of an elm, the leaves' shadows swaying
by our feet, silently, like an underwater plant. A grey-haired waiter
places our coffees before us. "This weather, eh, Father?" He has
to be three times my age, at least. "You'd think people had nothing else to complain about." That he speaks to me and does so in
Spanish lets me know he agrees with the measures taken by the
Nationalists today.

No steam rises from the coffee. I bring it to my lips. It's barely lukewarm. Little harm, I think. Sweat has already collected under my armpits and gathers in the hollow of my solar plexus.

Bittori fans herself with a black abanico. Its pattern is torn, so I'm sure she's had it long before her father passed. I wipe at my forehead and begin. "The confessional is a sacred space, as you know. In there I am *in persona Christi*. Here, the dynamic is simpler: two people having coffee."

"That being the case," she says, setting her cup down before taking a sip, "I blame you."

I nod for her to continue.

"Had you not told her where her husband was, none of this would have happened."

"Your sister came to me distraught—"

"She's always distraught."

"—with a very simple request. If I could alleviate her distress, why shouldn't I?"

"Because Itziar will never stop, not until she and her husband are reunited."

"Whether or not that's the case—"

"It is."

"Whether or not, I recommend you wait. Don't get involved. At this point, your evidence is thin. It's mostly conjecture."

"What conjecture? If she hasn't sold it this morning, in her dresser is a gown from Valentina's that I know she can't produce a receipt for. She's robbing everyone to buy her husband's freedom. Even from the collection plate, Lord help us. It was the only reason she attended Mass. What fools we were!" She waits for me to be as angry as she is. I maintain a neutral expression. Itziar had attended Mass because I insisted upon it, telling her I'd use the church's connections to locate her husband, on the condition she join us for that Sunday's service. Anything to see her again. I say none of this to Bittori, who continues, "I'm not sure where she's keeping her money, but it's piling up, none of it come by honestly. And now this."

"All of that is a long way from being capable of murder."

"How many," she starts, lowering her voice, "how many more will have to die? You weren't there. I'll never forget it. I'm terrified for tonight."

I have been wondering, watching the few who pass, who else was in the plaza with her. Unlike Bittori, they would have washed the bottom of their boots and shoes by now. That or tossed them into the ocean.

She says, "I doubt I'll ever be able to sleep again. Those men's deaths are on my conscience. Forever will be."

Late this morning, a band had wound through the grid of the old town's stone streets, collecting people as they played, including Bittori, until the throng arrived at Plaza de la Constitución. More than the joyful music, the presence of such a band must have enticed the people. A signal, perhaps, that with the fall of Bilbao and the war in the north finally drawing to an end, life could resume in San Sebastián. Only when the plaza filled did the Nationalists reveal themselves. They barricaded the plaza's four exits then brought forward five prisoners from Ondarreta and demanded that the crowd turn in the murderer of Commissioner Mingotsa, or else. Earlier this morning, the commissioner had been buried, his body found wedged between the large granite breakers in the mouth of the Urumea River. He'd been missing for the past three days. He was identified by his uniform, his face made unrecognizable by a bullet and the tides, his pockets emptied by his murderer.

Perhaps Bittori thought the firing squad a ruse. Perhaps she didn't think the Nationalist soldiers lining before the prisoners could actually kill their fellow man. Or perhaps her own doubts kept her from stepping forward and denouncing her sister, but the Nationalists didn't hesitate. She watched through a sudden eruption of smoke as the five prisoners smacked against the wall then crumpled. The Nationalists issued more threats. There was a speech that lasted long enough so that, when it concluded, the blood seeping from the men had spread across a swath of the plaza. The band began the music again, and those who bore witness to the execution were forced at gun point to dance in the thickening pond.

"Were Itziar not so madly in love with her husband," Bittori says, "she'd have raised the funds horizontally by now. Ever since we were young, men have fought each other to open the door for her." Some of Bittori's resentment for her sister must derive from the grand discrepancy in their looks. "But Itziar won't let another man touch her. That's probably what got the commissioner killed."

"I remind you, it's only conjecture." I wipe at my forehead again. The heat has two hands around my neck. I tell her, "There will come a time when you'll cross the plaza without thinking of it. I promise. However, I can't make that assurance if you turn in your sister. These are extreme days, but when they pass—as they surely will—you'll be left with the consequences of your actions."

"I'll have saved lives."

"The Nationalists would execute prisoners if they thought it might coax forth a few clouds. Don't let their cruelty dictate your behavior."

"They're bringing order."

I become more exhausted each time a person says this. "There are, you'll acknowledge, other means of doing so."

"Are there? Today may have been excessive, but we've seen the alternative. People like her husband. Such hideous ideas. It's a good thing he's locked up. He's determined to contaminate the world. He and my sister." She turns her attention to the cathedral. I do, too. On its front steps is where I first met Itziar, just over a week ago. Since the Nationalists' victory, most people refused to even glance at the cathedral, so I could oftentimes blatantly people-watch. Itziar was walking past and felt my attention. I tried for a warm, paternal smile. This failed me entirely when she changed direction and approached me. I might have retreated a step.

Bittori eyes the limestone as though it were made of eggshells. "The two of them, they'll tear this down if they get their way. Just like in Russia. And you and all those of the cloth will be swinging from branches."

"Let me worry about you and your family instead. I'll speak to your sister for you."

"I've heard your sermons," she says. "'God has carved a road for us. Don't wander into man's.'"

I nod. "The only remedy for the madness of these times is to remove oneself from it."

She pushes the coffee away and stands. "Then I don't know why you had to get involved."

I wait for her to cross the street then signal to the waiter. "A glass of red."

I ELBOW THROUGH the heat and hurry past the police station on the edge of Boulevard, the tree-shaded promenade that, when I first arrived in San Sebastián, the city's residents would clog at dusk, strolling slowly before the cafes and bars. Even as artillery rocked the city, they kept to their tradition. This is no longer the case, not since the Nationalists began staffing their own at the police station.

Out its open windows, at unpredictable hours, the screams of the prisoners they've brought in from Ondarreta stop us. The Nationalists could interrogate them in the prison, but few of us would hear them there. They intend to traumatize the citizenry and will continue to do so until the last person has submitted. Usually, the prison sits like a judgment on the far end of San Sebastián's coastline, exposed to the spiteful mood swings of the Cantabrian, but today I can hardly make it out across the bay. It's a grey smudge behind waves of heat—a kiln in there.

Though the station is quiet, I maintain my pace, not slowing until I've reached the port and, immediately to my left, the full breadth of the cove opening before it, the water a still plate of blue reflecting the sun, shading toward emerald along the curve of the shoreline.

In the port, docked boats float motionless. Their flags hang limp. At this hour groups of women tend to sit along the embankment, mending colorful fishing nets spread over their laps. Not today. The threat of what the Nationalists might do next has driven them inside. That and the heat. It surges from the pavement, bubbles underfoot.

Through the stone gate jutting from the ancient walls, I turn right, entering the old part and its maze of streets—Plaza de la Constitución blocks away—and climb the steps to Bittori and Itziar's apartment, my heart playing a nervous number, my tongue heavy. Their father had passed unexpectedly without identifying who would inherit the apartment. Since then, each sister has been determined to drive the other out. I knock on the door.

I should but don't pray. Before the Nationalists occupied San Sebastián, when divorce was still permitted, I'd have the occasional husband or wife confess they were no longer in love with their spouse. They felt nothing for the other person. Not resentment nor nostalgic longing. Nothing. That's what speaking to the heavens has become for me since meeting Itziar—a one-sided conversation with the stars and empty space. I struggle to see the point in continuing it.

"It's Xabier," I say, wiping my palms down my cassock. Underneath, my clothes cling to me. The other time I was here, I told Itziar I'd located her husband. The Nationalists are holding him in San Pedro de Cardeña, a former monastery outside Burgos they now use as a prison. The colonel overseeing it agreed to allow her to purchase her husband's freedom. I had hesitated to tell her the amount. A seamstress like Itziar would have to save for five years to hold that much money at one time. "Father Elejalde, that is." Only then do I hear approaching footfalls. I brace myself, try to keep my face placid, but when she opens the door, I can't help it—a smile stretches, as foolish and transparent as a schoolboy's. She's somehow more beautiful than I recall.

At the sight of me, her full lips turn down, thinning slightly. "Is there news about my husband?"

"No, no," I say. My tongue sticks to the roof of my mouth. The wine had been a bad idea. "It's your sister. She asked that I speak with you. May I come in?"

I follow her past the icons pinned to the walls: Saint George with the lance he drove into the dragon, Saint James, the patron saint of the military, and Saint Sebastián, the city's namesake, bare chested and riddled with arrows. I feel the reproachment in their eyes—those black dots of paint—as they follow me across the room to the kitchen, my own eyes traveling, for only a moment and without thought, up and down Itziar's figure. The last time I saw her I'd been walking along the river, the light from the lampposts rippling over its surface, in constant motion but going nowhere. I had turned for the rectory when I saw Itziar—her unmistakable shape—with a silhouetted man. How it goes in a city like San Sebastián: be introduced to a person and that next week you can't stop crossing paths with them. The light that filled the river glinted off the medals pinned to his chest. They stumbled in the direction of the ocean, his arm around the pronounced curve of her waistline, holding her tightly, her head tipped back with laughter.

From down the hall come her daughter's soft cries.

"I just put her down for a nap. Sit." She unfolds her abanico. It's red and lacy, ornate like the lingerie you used to see in shop displays. The air is thick though the windows are open. No wind off the ocean today. I find it difficult to get a full breath. "You go for a swim?"

"What?" I reach up, my hair is damp to the touch with sweat. Using my fingers, I comb it and wait for her to offer something to drink, but she asks, "So why is my sister giving me free reign this afternoon?"

"She was one of the many unfortunate enough to be in the plaza."

A smile dimples her cheeks. "If she's surprised by their brutality, she hasn't been paying attention. They shoot the band, too? Takes balls to be playing festive numbers."

"The band was theirs. A pied piper to attract the crowd."

She shakes her head. "And you priests think everyone has a soul worthy of saving?"

"We're lost if that's not the case."

"Please tell me they didn't actually make the crowd dance through the blood afterwards." When I don't answer, she laughs. "Shit, these fascists are determined to outdo the Inquisition. Amazing what cruelty your god allows on his watch."

I quote Saint Loiola. "'The Divinity hides itself.' We dedicate ourselves to that mystery."

She rolls her eyes. "Take that to the market and see what you can buy with it."

It's refreshing to be spoken to so informally. As if a breeze has lifted the curtains. She's allowing me to break from my own role. Despite myself, I don't. "Do you know why the men were executed?"

Her daughter's cries grow more agitated. "Hold on." She rises. My vision darts, for not even a second, to the open neckline of her blouse, the tops of her loose breasts revealed and pressed together, a film of sweat across them. "She'll start hyperventilating soon. Then nothing will calm her."

I fold my hands on my lap and watch without shame as she turns for the hallway. Glancing about, I see a photograph of her husband Raúl on the mantle. I tilt it away from the light. He's not eyeing the camera but something on the ground to his left. There's a violent intensity to his gaze made all the more menacing by the wide scar snaking from under his mustache. Those who know him must have been unsurprised to learn he'd been imprisoned. With a face like that, it was a foregone conclusion. Nevertheless, I tell him, "Had you not gotten caught." Plenty else—trivial and mundane, possibly even profound—directly contributed to Itziar and me meeting, but were it not for his incarceration, the rest wouldn't have mattered. Before she had approached me on the cathedral's steps, I had considered myself immune from temptation, hadn't even known to fear it. The Nationalists have been dumping the dead into wells—in our lifetime who will pull from those again? Temptation has similarly poisoned my convictions.

I hear her approaching down the hall so place the photograph back, thinking to it while I do: And yet…and yet I'm grateful to you. I'm here now and you're not.

Itziar's cradling her infant daughter, who, for better or worse, doesn't resemble her. "Here." She hands me the girl without warning. "I need to find a rag." The girl's little body is a furnace, flesh pink from the heat. Sweat clumps her fine hair at the nape of her neck. From the other room, Itziar says, "Don't you dare baptize her."

"The water would sizzle on her brow," I say, then hear how that could be interpreted and rush to add: "Because of the heat."

Itziar is smiling in the doorway. "You've a gift for diagnosing souls." She sits and drapes the off-grey rag over her shoulder. The girl squirms in my arms. "A worse sleeper never existed."

Itziar takes her from me and bounces her, putting her mouth by an ear, cooing in a singsong voice, "Were you not so adorable." Then she remembers, "You asked me a question earlier?"

"Whether you knew why the men were executed."

"The fascists need an excuse?"

"It was retribution for the murder of the commissioner."

Not a blink, not a twitch. Her face reveals nothing. "Shush, my love." She lifts her blouse and for a moment I see the white cotton of her bra and the shadow of an areola through it. When she slides her hand in to scoop out her breast, I shift my attention to the wall over her head. A glimpse and I'll be lost for good. I don't lower my eyes until I hear the child feeding. Itziar must sense my discomfort, the energy it takes for even a priest to maintain eye contact with her. The left corner of her lip pulls. I note the slightest disappoint-ment—how predictable men are.

"Your sister," I say, recovering, "believes you are responsible for the commissioner's murder."

75

"Before this war I'd have said nobody can be as cruel as one sister to another. My imagination doesn't match these fascists though. I suppose Bittori is attempting it in her own way."

"What's convinced her are your recent thefts." She doesn't deny it, doesn't appear the least ashamed. "You're not meant for this sort of life, Itziar. If your sister saw you take from the collection plate and if I did, imagine who else might have." I had watched, flabbergasted, while Itziar nonchalantly tipped the coins into her purse. This was days before Commissioner Mingotsa was reported missing. "Or will the next time."

"I won't be marched into the plaza over it."

"No, but they'll arrest you."

She shrugs.

"Imagine what a triumph it would be for your sister were you caught. She'd have the apartment to herself and raise your daughter as her own."

"Only to spite me. She detests the little creature."

"Your daughter's first words would be Bible verses."

"You wouldn't approve?"

"A child should be with its mother."

"The church disagrees." She presses on her breast to check on her daughter's progress. "I'm surprised you don't, too. I admit, you confound me. I'd thought all the good priests left long ago to fight for the people."

"There are other ways to offer support."

"Not anymore. The fascists have made sure of it. A shame you can't see that."

"My brother's actually a soldier," I say. "We don't see eye to eye on what will heal this country, but I—" I stop to change my approach. I never feel more inadequate than when I think of Isidro. Especially these days. "I worry about him, nevertheless. Just like your sister worries about you."

"How our army is disintegrating, you should be worried. Do you love him?"

"Isidro? Of course." She seems disbelieving, so I add, "We're two very different people. In many ways it's kept us apart. But there's much that I admire and envy in him. Brick wall or bed of roses, it doesn't matter, he'll charge right into it. Ever since we were young. I never had that in me."

"If you did, what would you do?"

Her eyes are probing. It feels like an invitation, like she's asking: what would you do right now? With my thumb, I massage the heel of the other palm. All her life men have bothered her, insisting she hear how she makes them feel. Why should I think I have anything new to tell her? "Don't give your sister this victory," I say instead. "Forgive me, but you—" You attract the eye. You're too beautiful to be inconspicuous. "You don't have the skills to be a thief."

A smile: *if you only knew.* She runs the tip of her middle finger over her daughter's temple, hooking wisps of drying hair behind her ear. "Just like those at Ondarreta, Raúl is living on borrowed time. I need to get him out. Now."

"There's no saving him, but you're still free."

"Xabier," she says, and my pulse accelerates with this bit of over-familiarity, "I've been thinking about that sermon you gave, how we should retreat from these times and commit ourselves to God's." She removes her daughter from her breast, and, again, my vision darts up the wall, returning after her shirt is down and her daughter's face is against the rag over her shoulder, the whole of her jostling for the hard pats Itziar delivers, until the girl produces a belch. She is milk-drunk, eyes rolled back, her little mouth open, every need satiated. "You have to realize—" Without warning her daughter silently spits up then settles once more. Itziar manages to catch most of it with the rag, wipes under the girl's chin and dabs at her plump cheeks which are mottled with a slight rash. "You have to realize," she continues, "for those of us who truly love someone in this world, there's no retreating from it."

I PASS UNDER the double stone arches that open to Plaza de la Constitución. Franco's supporters have renamed it the 18th of July Plaza, after the date of the coup, but even Falangists will slip and refer to it by its historic name. It is rectangle-shaped, enclosed on all sides by three levels of apartments, their uniform glass-framed doors running the length of floor to ceiling. Each was probably vacant during the execution, those inside sheltering in a room far from the balcony, the few caged birds outside forced to bear witness. The start of a dehydration headache squirms like poison across my left temple and behind the ear, pinches my jaw.

I had assumed the blood would have been washed away by now, but patches remain in the opposite corner of the plaza, their outer edges coagulated black as though scorched, the middle maintaining a ruby sheen beneath the sun pounding the plaza. Two Nationalist soldiers keep guard over the area. I tuck behind a column where nobody can see me and slap myself as hard as I can. It doesn't hurt, not as much as I hoped, so I do it again and again, but all that happens is my eyes tear up. I feel no less disappointed in myself.

Despite the horror that's occurred here, the plaza still smells of summer: the potted flowers and green vines along the balconies, heat escaping from stone. Wafting briefly from a restaurant are scents of garlic and freshly-chopped parsley, fish frying in oil.

I flinch at the hot mineral stench as I step around the mess of faint red footprints—ghostly heels, arches, toes—to approach the two soldiers standing in a strip of shade. One appears relieved to see me, as if I'd been sent to provide a balm to his spirit, or give him news about the war, that it's over, he can return home to his mother. Whatever age you need to be to fight these days, he's weeks past that birthday. I ask the two, "Where have the corpses been taken?" The church and military are aligned—in some regiments, priests have as much authority as commanding officers—but there's a challenging tone in my voice that surprises them. They squint at my cassock. "I'm going to pray for them."

The other soldier is a redhead, likely from Galicia. For centuries, the people there have been sending ships to and from Ireland. "God's already made up his mind about our enemies, Father." Yes, by his accent, Galician.

I become aware of the presence of those at the windows, their eyes and judgment. Of course, they're thinking, a priest in conversation with our occupiers. He's probably commending them on a job well done. The blazing sun throws hexagons of light across my vision.

"Were you two a part of the firing squad?" I make it sound like an indictment.

The redhead says, "So what if we were?"

But I see they weren't. Inadequacy boils in their veins. Soldiers given the responsibility to shoot unarmed men before a crowd of civilians aren't later forced to follow slivers of shade around a plaza while guarding a pool of blood. These two would never take it upon themselves to harm a priest.

"My brother's a Basque soldier," I tell the redhead, still hoping to goad them. "My younger brother." I wait, but they do nothing and nothing will come of my efforts here, so I tell them. "I've always lacked his decisiveness."

"It saved your life."

"I'm not so sure."

"We've got the last of them pinned against the ocean in Santander." He motions to the blood. "Only a matter of time before your brother's making his contribution."

"Isidro? No, I don't think so. He's always been one of the lucky ones."

"You know, when we can't find the rojo, we arrest the family members they leave behind."

An empty threat, though I wish it wasn't. I ignore the bluster. "Were the corpses taken to the cemetery?"

"It's where the dead tend to end up, isn't it?" He turns to the other. "No wonder we've been sent here to civilize these people."

"How long will the plaza be kept like this?"

"For as long as it takes."

AT THE CEMETERY, I walk down the wide avenue of family vaults, then the towering tombstones arranged on tiers that curve like a shell, like the city's coastline. We're a sociable people, and the spacing between the tombstones reflects this. They're clustered tightly together, shoulders pressed against each other at the bar.

Heat comes at me from all sides, warps the middle distance. If I can reach those waves of heat, I'd be able to disappear entirely, emerge someone different, someone capable of telling Itziar how I feel. That or turn her in. I don't need to think long on what Isidro would have done in her apartment. He'd have spoken frankly to her. He's the sort, not me, she could fall for.

I trip over the raised root of a pine tree, my limbs heavy in these searing temperatures. The Nationalists likely buried the bodies in the back, the space reserved for dissidents and non-Catholics. I climb the tiled pathway. No newly disturbed earth among the simple grave markers. There is an open pit, but nothing inside. The earth is dark down there. Cool, I imagine. I try to swallow but my throat is clogged from dehydration.

Since I am here, I search for Commissioner Mingotsa. Unlike most of the uniformed fascists in the city, he was a local, the leader of the province's Falange chapter since the party's founding in 1933. In the weeks after I was transferred to San Sebastián, those few weeks before the war, I'd see him in our pews with his wife and grown children. Had he ever been careless enough to attend Mass during the fighting, someone would have been behind him, removing a pistol from their coat. Only after Bilbao's fall did he return.

There are several mounds of earth where the newly dead have been buried, but none of the wooden markers—a placeholder for the tombstone until the ground settles—bear his name. Being a Falangist, he likely was born into money, so I return to the avenue of family vaults, where I find three Mingotsas. I settle on the vault with the least dust and stand in the heat pulsing from it as though before an open stove. I clasp my hands at my waist, lower my head. Again, I don't pray. I don't even ask the commissioner for forgiveness. Instead, I'm back in Itziar's apartment, watching along with the pinned icons as I follow her to the kitchen, then listen to our conversation, thinking *there, there, there,* and *there.* Even if I remained incapable of confessing my feelings to her, there were plenty of moments I could have warned her precisely, even wed our fates, by telling her my story of the other night.

Having spotted her and Commissioner Mingotsa along the river, I had remained in the shadows, matching their pace and watching how, between the Maria Cristina and Santa Catalina bridges and in the darkness between two lampposts, Commissioner Mingotsa buried his mouth into her neck and was moving to her breasts, which he pawed and squeezed, while her hands were at his waist, unbuckling his pants. My cheeks burned with rage and sadness and erotic anticipation. Otherwise, I felt bodiless watching Itziar suddenly step back—surprised, it seemed, to be holding his pistol. He laughed and said something I couldn't make out, palming his crotch. She turned the pistol side to side as though she'd never seen one before then swung it around, aiming at a lamppost across the river, the river itself, a passing cloud. He reached for it, but she stepped back, still playful and flirtatious. It was only when he demanded she return it, his hand rigidly outstretched, that her head listed and her posture was at once that of a person as sober as the noon hour. She raised the pistol at him, telling him something I couldn't hear but that had to have been about her husband. He lunged at her, and the pistol barked, stopping his momentum, his body collapsing, a black mist of blood and matter catching light. Immediately, she fell on him and dug into his pockets while the echo of the shot spread further. She appeared disappointed with what little she found. Still on her knees and working quickly, she rolled the body over, tumbling it into the river, and pitched the pistol in after him. I didn't move, not until I was certain she'd escaped.

What was it like, I now ask Commissioner Mingotsa. Not death, nor the confusion and surprise that preceded it, but having your hands on her, the exhilaration of believing you would soon lose yourself entirely inside her. I imagine it was worth being destroyed for.

I leave without crossing myself, and when I'm at the front gate, a military lorry swings around the corner, chugging up the hill. They've come for me, I think. They must know. I take the first step to run—tomorrow, tomorrow I'll become the person I want to be—but stop and brace myself as they start braking. I deserve what's coming my way.

Three Nationalist soldiers sit in the front seat, the windows down, their shirt uniforms unbuttoned entirely. Each holds a bottle of wine, either in hand or between their legs. Sweat mats their chest hair. "Absolutely perfect timing," the one in the passenger seat tells me, laughing. "A priest!" From the bed of the lorry, I smell blood and viscera, how they interact with burning metal, soak into fabrics and hair, and something more—there's the dank sweat of terror the sun's yet to dry. So here the prisoners are. I have to silence the cry escaping from my chest.

"You can settle this for us. We're about to come to blows over it."

"What's he doing here?" the driver interjects, but the one in the passenger seat admonishes him. "Let's focus." To me, he asks, "So tell us. What's the name of the star that brings about the end of the world?"

"This idiot here," the one stuck in the middle says, "claims it's Betelgeuse."

"Don't give him any options," the passenger warns the other two.

"A star?" I ask, brushing at a fly that's drifted from the lorry bed.

"In Revelation—the end times—a star crashes to earth."

"Into the ocean," the one in the middle clarifies. "Poisons the water and all that. It's not Betelgeuse, right?"

"No," I say. "Wormwood."

"I told you." The one in the middle punches the driver. "And you," he tells the passenger, "so confident with your fucking Betelgeuse."

"Better than this guy with the Big Dipper."

"Even he didn't believe that."

"Where in the sky is it?" the driver asks me.

All of us are breathing through our mouths. It does nothing to dull the smell.

"It's not real," I say.

"What isn't?"

"Wormwood. It's not a heavenly body."

"Then how does the world end?"

The one in the middle laughs for the question. "I'll tell you how." He hooks his thumb to the lorry bed. "By these bastards getting the better of us."

"What brings you out in this heat?" the driver asks me. There's nothing pointed in his tone. He's simply making conversation.

I glance to the back. "I came for them."

I expect the soldiers to become incensed like those in the plaza, but the passenger says, "I suppose reds are entitled to a proper send-off, too."

"So was it worth it?" I ask. Even this doesn't rile the three. They wait for me to continue. "Are you any closer to catching the commissioner's assassin?" I be sure to use the male form of the word.

"Just a matter of time, Father. Someone will talk."

I note how little of a hurry they're in to escape this heat. After the bodies are buried, they will be further yet from their crime. Soon enough, night will find them alone, then the torment will truly begin. In this moment, though, among the other's company and still so close to the bodies and this welcome distraction I provide, they need not reflect. But I do. A raven thought finds me: by not denouncing Itizar the night of the murder, I am responsible for the condition of every man in this truck, the murdered and the murderers. Not only could I have saved them but also myself—with Itizar arrested, I'd be liberated from her, free to return to the life I had before she walked past the church. I'm not sure I want it.

"My brother's a soldier," I tell them, "for the other side." I wait. They don't get out of the lorry, don't threaten me, seem more concerned than angry. "When we were younger," I say, "he would draw every boy in the village to whatever his most recent cause was. From the start, people were attracted to him. It's what I wanted for myself, but I never had it in me. I was too tentative, too cautious. Our father's fault."

"You're not looking too good, Father," the driver says.

"*Our* father, what religion he had he'd beat us with, kept our world small. My younger brother resisted in a way I couldn't. Me, I thought I could somehow redeem him by," I pat my cassock, "by this. My brother resents me for it, enlisted probably to spite me. Maybe he's right. Maybe there can be no appeasement."

The three are sharing looks. The one in the middle chuckles. "Nothing but parables from you priests until the collection plate goes around. Then you speak plainly."

The one in the passenger seat points to my cassock. "You've got to be burning up in that thing." I glance down. It's soaked through and briny from sweat. Salt deposits rim its drying hems. "Here," he says, extending the bottle, careful to keep his arm above the window frame. It sings with heat. "Take a sip." I wave it off but he insists. "Your eyes are coming loose in your head."

"It's just a headache," I say.

"A trago will set you right."

I take a pull, longer than I intend to, washing down the harsh pinch of each sip with the next. The wine is warm, months from becoming vinegar. I pass it back. "You hold onto that, Father. I've got a case at my feet."

"Thank you." I wipe my mouth. "Only," I say, "can you do me a favor."

The one in the passenger seat lifts his chin.

"Pray for me?"

They laugh. "Sure, Father. Sure. Leave it to the three astronomers here. You can count on us."

6

JUANA   SALAS DE PEDRO, JULY 1937

THE NIGHT BEFORE they left, abandoning me to serve in the war—my mother as a nurse, my father a soldier—my mother sat with me on my bed, wiping the tears from my cheeks with her thumbs, and said, "Never let our family learn of this."

We had come from Valladolid when I was nine so my father could work in the quarry. Aside from their brutal natures and loud voices, I had few memories of our family. Once far from them, my mother became a different person—joyful, perpetually awed, unconcerned what others might think of her untethered gratitude for the day. Even at that young age, I recognized she was an oddity in the village.

"They'll get you if they find out," she said now, drying her thumbs on my bedsheets. "They'll do what they did to me. They'll beat you. They'll try to make your world small." This was her sole advice. "There, there," she added. "I promise to write." Our family was illiterate, so my mother seized every opportunity to prove she could express herself on the page.

In the morning, she and my father were gone, and the house had never seemed so big.

A WEEK AFTER their departure, I began pestering the postman. I'd plan my day around his arrival, which was either on one side or the other of his lunch: a glass of wine he'd take on a well-gouged stool outside our only tavern, drinking it slowly over the course of a cigar. I'd never known a cigar could last so long. Eventually, I tired of waiting for letters that never came.

I had enough to distract myself. We all did. The threat of war was constant, straining conversations, present behind every pair of eyes. Today, the villagers would say, today we will finally be pulled into it. I believed them, as I did in the evenings when I'd overhear, "Our last night of peace. Tomorrow it begins."

Months passed like this. Yet, despite all their premonitions, the war, when it ultimately found us, didn't occur as I'd imagined. The fighting remained on the other side of the river, deep in the forest. Ceaseless gunfire, explosions that sounded like massive hammers against a giant tin sheet, dozens of bowed pillars of smoke. They produced an intolerable tension and exhausted our patience and compassion. Arguments besieged the air—none of them political. Those who cared enough had already gone off to fight. The ones who remained were on the side of survival, of life. Before, we had waited in terror for the first soldier to enter our village, now some prayed for it. Anything for this uncertainty to end.

And when it finally did end in late February, again we were surprised.

There was no rising crescendo of explosions, no tapering patter of gunfire. There was fighting and then, as though a conductor had swung his hands down, there wasn't. I looked to the others to help make sense of it, but nobody seemed to understand. Once more, we waited. Once more, the waiting needled our bones and teeth. That evening, Carlos Prieto hobbled to the plaza, breathless, saying he saw a convoy of lorries and tanks climbing the far northern ridge, toward our neighbors the Basques and the war there. He wasn't certain which side the convoy belonged to. Nationalists, he guessed. Still, nobody dared believe it could be true. The next morning, Gustavo Clemente sent his hunting dog into the forest. When it returned a half hour later, a trio of older ladies went in. They hurried back to us in the early afternoon. "They're gone," they exclaimed. They described the detritus of the camps, the burnt-out vehicles, the decimated trees, the corpses and slaughtered animals, and though they were describing a nightmare and we had no idea what had been accomplished by it, we could finally breathe.

A week later, a man in a suit representing the Nationalist forces parked in our village and explained to the mayor that we were now under their control. He provided a flag and told him to fly it above the church.

Aside from this, the mayor asked, what should we do? The representative laughed. "You think too much of yourselves. If there's ever a shortage of stones in this war, we'll be sure to let you know. Otherwise—I don't know. Pray for our continued success, I guess."

For the first months after my parents left, my thoughts were almost exclusively about them, how life had been before, where on Spain's map they might be, what our days would be like when they returned. It ultimately became too painful to live this way, so after the caravan went over the mountains, I followed the lead of our neighbors. The war was over for us. Those who had searched for it should not be mentioned. What mattered was what was before us, those who were before us—life. You'd never actually hear anyone put this to words. Instead, we spoke of flowers.

I CAN'T RECALL how it began. Gradually, there was more color in the village. Here and there a pot or two on a balcony, the morning sun striking a few green stems and closed buds against a house's northern wall. When it truly pulled me in, though, was when I approached one of our wells and saw that someone had, overnight, encircled it with blooming daffodils. From a distance it was a golden aura. Up close, something flipped in me. Others had their own moments. Within each of us we seemed to declare: enough with death and the fear of it, let's celebrate life.

Flowers began cluttering balconies. Thin gardens, at first sparse, lined houses. Promptly, they deepened. One side of a stone fence would be clothed in them. Then, the other. At first, any flower would do, but soon we prized some over others. The more vivid the colors, the more unrestrained nature's generosity with its design, the richer and more intoxicating the fragrance, the more we coveted it. Dahlias with their unpredictable geometric patterns were the most sought after. During the start of our madness, animals were bartered away for a handful of tubers.

I'd think how much my mother deserved to belong here amidst this peculiar rapture, this enthusiasm for beauty and life. Nobody would have appreciated it more, which would've brought a gentle, carefree smile to my father's face that revealed all his missing back teeth. At the same time, my mother would have criticized us for the way we'd slapped blinders around our periphery, blocking out the rest of the world and the suffering being inflicted on it, and my father would have nodded along.

I WAS PLANTING rows of bluebell bulbs in the front garden when the postman cleared his throat behind me. He was inside the gate, a letter in hand. Oddly, he didn't say a word. Afterwards, I wondered if it was because he'd recognized my mother's handwriting. I wiped my hands on my dress and took the letter from him. He turned, continuing his route. The envelope was soiled and discolored, wrinkled, fibrous, as though on its journey to me it had been soaked, then dried, then soaked and dried again. Holding it, I could picture the various pockets and pouches it had traveled in. I opened it then and there, my hands trembling. It was proof of life.

The letter was dated nine months ago, not long after they left to fight, and was a single page.

My dearest daughter Juana,

Sometimes, in the past, I have felt the entirety of the solar system roiling within me. Twisting clouds, fiery stars, primordial light, molten gases, where even the black spaces between the planets are alive. Every moment here feels this way. Your father and I are present for the birth of a new world. If you could see the spirit of these people. We come from various corners of the Spanish map, from various backgrounds, our lives up to this moment have not resembled the others'. Despite this, we're united in our belief that each individual should be free to pursue a future of their own choosing. I couldn't imagine spending a moment of my too-brief time insisting somebody go about their day based upon my own half-blind assumptions. Yet this country is full of such people. Who knew we shared it with so many barbarians? It amazes me. The fascists are certain there is one way to encounter life, to be Spaniard. If you're unwilling to accept it, you must be vanquished. Remember Erlea, that Basque bee, the pamphlets of hers I'd read to you? She's right: Since the fascists lost at the ballot box, they're trying to win on the battlefield. We can't allow them a single victory. As simple as that. It's a shame there's no God. Otherwise, he'd surely be on our side.

Your father gives his love. He says to bring some of our beans to Carmelo. Do this every Saturday, if you must. So he'll help you in November with the pig.

I flipped the page over—that was the entirety of the letter—then foolishly searched in the envelope. I shouldn't have been surprised that after all this time they had no more to say. Still, I was disappointed and saddened. I looked through the open door at the links of chorizo hanging from pegs. In the end, I hadn't needed to spare any beans. I doubt anybody would have accepted them had I offered. Instead, six men knocked on our door to slaughter the pig and break it down. I had tried to help in the kitchen. Several of their wives ran me out. I was relegated to setting the table and refilling the wine glasses. The men had even brought over their own jugs. The more they drank, the more often their voices dropped and the conversation circled back to my parents—most especially to my mother, the idea of whom perplexed them. They scratched their jaws—who would abandon their home, their daughter, their domestic obligations? They sounded like the family we'd left.

One of the men who had come over was Rafa's father. Rafa and his family lived several houses down from mine. He was sixteen years old. I'd turned fifteen by then, back when the fighting across the river so occupied us. It's a common enough phenomenon, but the light of spring that awakens the flowers can also strike a person you've known for years, whose rugged face is not much different than the others in the village, yet causes you to think that life is a thing you can give shape to with the help of someone by your side.

TWO DAYS AFTER the first letter arrived, the postman handed me another, again not saying anything. The pages were yellowed and warped, but I could read my mother's handwriting.

> *Juana,*
>
> *Your father and I had an hour to ourselves today. We sat at a café in the plaza, next to a church with ornate doors, angels adorning the pinched arc of the church's stone portal, and I wondered about the person who spent years directing his chisel and hammer to those stones. The church is now a home for the displaced, finally fulfilling its purpose. Your father had a croissant and a coffee. I picked some of the flakes from his plate. Because of our uniforms, we weren't charged for it. And leave a tip? Impossible! The waiter would have been less insulted had we disparaged his mother.*
>
> *But those angels and the man who sculpted them—the years he furrowed his brow and scraped stone as the angels took shape. Can you imagine the dreams he must have had, the wild visions? Even if it is all a fiction, what would it matter! Perhaps only pain is as convincing as a dream: both can blind you to reason when you're in them. Regardless, you see in his work that if you focus on just one thing, fix your mind to it, you can carve it from this world. For those of us trying to improve Spain, this seems a nice way of going about it.*

I read the letter multiple times. I had, in some respects, become accustomed to my mother's absence. My father's, too. It had been so long since I'd been reminded of how he could sit at a table and eat and drink next to her, practically a mute, while her mind led her to fantastical places. Reading the letter, I felt as if I was at the café with them, as if we were together again. I wanted to show it to Rafa but hesitated for the line about the church. His mother was devout, practically as much of a presence in the church as the statues. He knew my parents had abandoned me here to fight for a progress that would, among other things, strip the church of any significant power remaining to it. Everybody knew this. Still, I worried the letter might result in complications between us. Possibly between me and the rest of the village.

We were ignoring the war, even as the fighting intensified throughout the rest of Spain. Details were sparse. "It's getting worse," a villager would say to another, and that'd be all that was said on the matter.

One caught glimpses, nevertheless. In Barcelona, the anarchists and communists, tired of fighting fascists, began shooting at each other. Up north, apocalypse had been visited upon Guernica— we couldn't wholly ignore this—but what I heard made no sense. How could an entire town be wiped from the earth? Some said the Basques did it to themselves, but this seemed more incomprehensible than the town's annihilation. Besides, we didn't allow ourselves time to provide any supporting details for whatever claim we made.

"I'd heard the Basques bombed themselves," someone might say.

"How? They have no planes."

The first person would hold up their hands, indicating they wouldn't continue. We knew all too well what the collision of realities created then destroyed.

THE MAINTENANCE OF a home easily occupies the day. It kept me busy while I waited for the postman. One day passed, then another, and another. I recalled the unbearable sounds of the fighting across the river, how it seemed even the earth itself wouldn't be able to tolerate it much longer, and I worried for my parents. They had gone off in pursuit of that very thing. My father was not a violent man. He'd never once lifted his hand to me. I couldn't imagine him amidst a battle, participating in it, helping to further escalate it. What I saw instead were the wounded bodies under a hospital tent while my mother, with her renewable spirit, moved unhurriedly from one to the next, giving each soldier her care and attention. Until, that is, a shell landed and a ferocious light spread in an instant, swallowing all in the infirmary. Other times it was a group of Nationalist soldiers and their marauding sounds outside the tent, the fright of the nurses and the wounded as they waited. I convinced myself of each scene.

With such threats, why wouldn't my parents return home, to me?

Finally, thankfully, another letter arrived. I tore it open as though it could tell me where my mother and father were in that moment. The letter was dated seven months earlier.

I did a stupid thing today, and I was rightfully reprimanded for it. A wounded man was brought in. Shrapnel had slashed his stomach, spilling out his viscera. It was caked with dirt and mud. He was hunched over on his side, trying to gather it into his hands. It was too slippery, too unwieldy, he was losing too much blood. The doctor took one look at him, grimaced, then attended to a patient he might save. I rushed to the man and cupped his intestines to help him lift them back into his wound. Together, we tried, but it wasn't possible, and the man lay back, accepting the futility of it. "Just five more minutes," he said to the ceiling. His breathing was frantic. "Please, just five minutes more." When those five minutes passed, he said, "Three minutes. Still. Please." I held his hand, ours were slick and warm with his blood. I watched him breathe his last, then finally allowed myself to cry. This was my stupid thing. The doctor yelled at me in front of the others, minutes of it, he'd start to walk off, then return, his voice louder, face redder, while the blood on my hands and arms became tacky. You see, it was fine to be there with that man though we could not save him. Nobody would begrudge me that. Each of us wants a compassionate face over us as we cross into the unknown. It'd be dispiriting to the others if they saw they would be abandoned the moment their condition became irreversible.

But once the man had died there was nothing else to be done for him. Others needed me and it was wrong to indulge myself. I felt ashamed, my cheeks burned. Gently, I laid the man's hand down, over his chest, gathered myself, then attended to the next patient, determined not to make the same mistake again.

The letter occupied two sides of a single sheet of paper. I turned it over and read it again, hoping to find some hope within, some mention of my father, that he was not among the wounded, but after another reading I was even more hollowed out. I studied my skinny hands where soil caked the tread of my fingerprints and packed under my fingernails. Why would my mother return to me when there were so many dying men desperately reaching out for her, when the next man to do so might be my father? What could I offer her?

RAFA WAS SURPRISED when I grabbed his hand the next day, intertwined my fingers with his, and squeezed tightly. We were in the front garden. His mother forbade him to enter my house. There were eyes everywhere in the village. Even the stones, it seemed, would report back to her. How else to explain that she'd learned of our first kiss before Rafa returned home after having received it, she eager to slap from his lips whatever tenderness I'd placed there. She was protective of all her boys, especially her oldest. So, when I held his hand, I made sure we were shielded by the flowers. Rafa sensed I was distracted.

"Is it because of the letters?" he asked, returning the pressure of my grip. He tended to avoid the topic of my mother, even before my parents left. Just the idea of them caused issues with his family. I was always on the verge of apologizing for her. What kept me from doing so was my father, how disappointed he'd be if he learned I'd said anything of the sort. He knew the odd impression my mother made on his fellow quarrymen but would never think to apologize for her eccentricities.

"Your mom tell you about them?"

"The postman's like a wasp, carrying rumors like pollen."

"But it's not a rumor. My mother is writing to me. Or was. The letters are from the start of this whole thing."

"What's she saying?"

I readjusted my grip, the soil squishing between our fingers. Rafa also worked in the quarry, spent his days amidst its pale and fallow dust, its perpetual chalky haze. In the evenings, we'd sometimes kneel together in my garden, attempting to nurture some life and beauty from it. "Promise me," I said, "you'll never go off to fight, that if they come for you, you'll hide, you'll take to the forest, disappear for a week, there are even closets here where—"

"Hey," he said, rubbing my fingers with his thumb, "I'm never leaving you."

THE FOLLOWING DAY the postman did the best impression of a quarry stone, his face expressionless as he handed me two envelopes, both marked by my mother's handwriting. I bit my bottom lip and took them with me into the house. I closed my eyes and thought of that dying soldier my mom had attended to and how she held his hand while they had counted down from five minutes, then three, then waited. The envelopes had been opened already. Somebody had attempted to re-seal them with what smelled like pine sap. The letters were dated a week apart. I started with the earliest.

An explosion's force, the real ferocity of it, shoots upward. I'll be with some of my friends—fellow nurses—and we'll turn a corner where a shell has cratered a street, but it's not around the crater, they say, you should look if you're interested in the destruction it caused—because people will have collected the pieces by then—but instead up at the buildings that surround it. There you'll find the splotches where limbs struck and then you'll know for certain a person had been here.

This is how war changes how you look at the world.

The shelling is constant. The unpredictability of the shrapnel terrifying. It's the reason why most of my days are dedicated to amputations. These unfortunate young men. They're between your age and mine. They don't want to part with any of their body. They are like a mother who has just given birth, insisting on keeping their amputated limb within sight. They make me promise that should they die I'll bury the limb with them.

A leg severed from the body is heavier than I'd have ever imagined—an awkward weight. I'll cradle it like a newborn, the patient watching me. "It's right here," I assure them. "Everything is fine." When the patient realizes, though, they'll survive the operation, that what has occurred is irrevocable, a life as an amputee awaits, they turn their head from me. "Take it away," they'll say. "Bury it. Burn it. I don't care." They must move forward.

I was attending to one today. We had amputated his left arm below the shoulder. He was looking at the tent's ceiling. The way these soldiers will lock their vision on the ceiling, as though a message is written on the sky for them. Others do so, warily, as if the sky might open at any moment and a hand reach down for them. This soldier felt my presence by his side but didn't turn to me. "I lost my soul," he said. "There, there," I said, "it was only an arm." "No, the arm is there. I can feel it. My wrist itches." "Want me to scratch it for you?" I asked. "No," he said, "it wouldn't matter. None of it does. I don't have a soul anymore. It's no longer in me. You don't know what it feels like until it's gone." "It's probably at home," I said, "waiting for you." He kept his eyes on the ceiling. I assured him, "We all go back to where we belong. Your soul just got there first." Finally, he closed his eyes.

I wrote to your father. I want you to come here. He won't disagree. We need you. Yours is an indomitable spirit. The best parts of the world are in you. Our patients desperately need to be reminded of them. You'll be fifteen shortly. Not too long ago that was old enough for a boy to fight. Who knows. It might be again soon. Give the animals and house keys to Palacio—he is on our side. With the money in our room get to Oviedo. I will be waiting for you.

I hesitated opening the next one, dreading she would ask why I had not yet arrived and insist I hurry to her. She didn't miss me, didn't need her daughter by her side, but wanted to show how exceptional she was, how she could distinguish herself from the others. Besides, I wasn't certain her cause was mine, though we both were desperately concerned for my father's safety.

I ran my finger under the envelope's lip.

That this letter catches you at the door. Don't come. The fascists took Clara from us. She was in a lorry with three wounded soldiers. They shot the soldiers and the driver and left them on the side of the road but took Clara and the lorry. She was a skinny girl, tall, incredibly long legs, gorgeous posture. She walked as though on ice skates. Your father and the others fought tirelessly to bring her back. So much so that we forced the fascists to retreat. Our first victory. It was quickly soured. The fascists had abandoned their infirmary. We heard one of their soldiers groaning through the tarp. I was with the other nurses while the captain spoke to us, reminding us as though we needed it that the wounds in there were necessary, it was how we would win this war, but these men were Spaniards like us so deserved to be treated as humanely as we'd treat our own.

I was anxious to get in. A part of me, I suppose, expected to find Clara attending to the patients. However, the moment the captain lifted the tarp and the air wafted out, I hoped she was as far from there as possible. The flies had found their way in. Only one soldier, the one groaning, still lived. They'd shot him in the chest, but he'd survived. They were certain we'd have tortured them as they'd have done to us so executed those they'd had to leave behind. The anger in that soldier's eyes as we cared for him. The captain pulled us aside and told us, "Do all you can for him. I want him on the front and fighting for us. The last thing the fascists see will be their own man peering down a barrel at them."

The next day one of their planes flew over us. High enough so neither their bullets nor ours would be any use. It did a few loops, then a door opened and oddly shaped objects began to fall. The first thought was, of course, a new kind of bomb—they've found another method to destroy. The pieces rained down, bounced on the ground, some splattered. It was Clara. They'd tied a note around each piece. "Even heaven doesn't want red nurses." Some of our men didn't care about the captain's intentions with the fascist soldier. They dragged him from the infirmary, doused him with petrol, and set him aflame.

Tomorrow you may get another letter insisting you come and do your part for the cause of democracy, for our Republic. Ignore it. The mania will claim me once more, I'm certain, but in this moment I see things clearly, and I don't want you here. Do what you can there instead.

WHEN I SAW Rafa again I asked him who held Oviedo.

"The Nationalists."

"For how long?"

We were approaching the plaza. Rafa walked with his hands behind his back, like the old men in the village.

"September, maybe? October."

My mother's letter had been dated the twelfth of October. "Not September," I said. Her enthusiasm had never been tempered before. That she'd been sobered by the reality there made me scared for her and my father.

"Why do you ask? Did your mother write again?"

We entered the wide plaza where the wind whipped dust this way and that, covering the flowers with a film of it. Rafa and I walked to the far corner where we'd planted our seeds—mine from my garden, his from his mother's. Petunias. They'd mixed together, so we didn't know which flower belonged to whom. Our mutual affection kept them alive. We weren't the only couple in the village to do this.

"Two letters this time, dated a week apart."

"How is she doing? And your father? Do they get to see each other often?"

"She left me to be by his side, but she hardly even mentions him."

I remember, as a child, the plaza being colorless, like a photograph you'd find in a newspaper, dark blots of ink and shadows. These days it was alive with nearly every color in the natural world, especially around the church. The public garden was our priest's idea. He was aware of the competition developing between some of the houses—Rafa's mother perhaps the worst of them all—so he encouraged everyone to contribute to a communal garden instead. In this way, nobody would have prettier flowers than the church. Give what you can, the priest recommended. Though many in the village were devout, nobody donated a dahlia plant. Rafa's mom, who should have been paying rent there, offered only a hydrangea plant. "It's a red's idea," she complained to the mayor, the butcher, the men in the tavern, the baker, the donkeys in the field, anyone admiring her garden. "Each according to their means. We should be promoting individual excellence. That sort of striving lifts the whole village." Some might have been tempted to gauge the priest's loyalties were he not dutifully including every Nationalist general in his Sunday sermon.

"I'm sure they're both fine," Rafa said as we knelt by our petunias. Somebody had recently wiped the dust from their pink-tinted petals, so we rearranged the soil, nestled those that needed it, watered them. "If they weren't, you would have been notified. *That* letter, at least, would find a direct path to you."

I'm not sure why—I'd often thought the same thing myself—but this loosened something within me. I tried to stand before the tears humiliated me but couldn't do so in time.

"No, I'm sorry," he said, already reproaching himself. "That was stupid to say. Sit, please."

I shook my head, at this point my hands were over my face. "Wait," he said, "don't go." But I was running away, the colors of the plaza streaking stupidly with tears. I wasn't able to help it. I hated myself for it, for repeatedly wondering, as an increasing number of others from the village were, why my parents and others like them still fought, resisted, put themselves in danger, remained resolute in the face of the truth—life under Nationalist rule was not the nightmare they had tried convincing the country it would be. With winter the flowers would die, but at least there would be peace.

THE NEXT MORNING, on his way to the quarry, Rafa knocked on my door. I could hear him whispering loudly for me. I stayed in bed. Finally, he said, "I'm leaving something for you," then I heard the crunch of gravel under his boots as he walked away. I rolled over and tried to return to sleep. My curiosity wouldn't allow it. On the doorstep, swaddled in a towel, was a dahlia plant with four blooming orangish-pink flowers and three buds where the first petals crowned. It caught my breath. A dahlia plant, and it was mine. The morning sky was a pale blue-hued steel. As beautiful as the flowers were, the tubers were hideous, like deformed fingers or warped brown carrots. Soil clung to them. From these shot spindly roots. Villagers were already talking about hoarding their tubers and saving them for next season, but I figured there were enough warm months in the summer for me to split some of these and plant them. I examined which of the tubers might be viable. This single plant could produce three, possibly four more, by summer's end. Next year, if I properly stored the tubers, I'd have a garden of dahlias.

Though I shouldn't have, I prepared a place in the center of my garden. Rafa's mother counted her flowers as obsessively and mistrustfully as a hen her eggs. She would notice this one was missing. There would be complications, tremendous complications. I didn't care. Rafa had given it to me as a gift—I couldn't imagine a scenario where his mother would have allowed him to. Nevertheless, it was mine now, and I wanted others to see how well I could care for it.

Hours later, the postman found me still there, on my hands and knees in my garden. He narrowed his eyes at the dahlia as he handed me a letter. I wiped the soil from my hands and took it from him. As usual, he turned from me the moment I did. Once again, the letter had been opened and resealed with dollops of sap.

Your father is dead, Juana. I know of no other way to say it, to have it make sense. Your father is dead. Huberto. The love of my life. At first, I didn't believe them. I asked to see him, but they wouldn't permit it. I howled. I lost my head. Finally, they relented. The body they showed me, it could no longer hold life. Somebody put their arm around me and led me away, and I have no memory of the hours that followed, but when I came to, I was attending to a patient. I could hardly make out his pupils through the blood clouding them. Each breath stopped short, hit a wall in him. He was hemorrhaging. "Sara," he said. He reached for my face, or the shape of it. "I'm not Sara," I told him. For a moment, I wanted him dead. I wanted Sara to feel as I did. But his hand found my face. He rubbed my cheek with his calloused thumb as your father used to. I let the weight of it fall into his hand, let him cradle it. He spoke in short breaths. "Do you remember. Last summer. By the well." I told him to be quiet, to preserve his strength, but then thought for what purpose. I put my fingers through his hair, caressed his cheeks. He pulled me—as much as he could—to his lips. They tasted of iron, of blood. "Tell me," I told him, when we parted, "tell me our love story."

Your father loved these men. He and I used to think that nothing mattered more than life, but we were wrong. There are ideas. These men are still fighting for them, they are still dying for them, and through this fight for democracy and freedom your father still lives.

I stood behind the closed door, my arms at my sides. I lifted my head to the house my father would never again return to. My next thought, ridiculously, was that I could still bring him back. It wasn't too late. But how? What to do with this hollowed out body of mine? How to put it to use for the sake of my father? I remembered the dahlia half-planted, the tubers drying out in the sun. They were so ridiculous now. Pointless, obscene distractions.

I stood like that, unmoving by the door, for minutes or hours, until a knocking startled me to attention. I opened it to the priest. A slight, empty smile wrinkled the skin around his eyes. His hands were folded together at the waist. We called him El Greco, not because he hailed from Toledo, which he did, but because he resembled the long-faced figures in the master's paintings—cavernous eye sockets, cheekbones like elbows.

"May I?" he asked. His breath smelled of cheap tobacco.

I moved aside for him. So he knew about my father. I thought again of the dahlia. Rafa knew. His mother knew. The whole village knew. And this was their act of pity. For Rafa perhaps. A barbed gesture from his mother. She would want to taint the dahlia for me. Every time I looked at it, smelled its fragrance, I should be reminded of the loss now crushing me.

The priest inhaled deeply. "These flowers have long concerned me."

"The flowers?"

"Rather than focus our gaze upwards, they pull our attention down. They are unnecessary for survival, yet look how they distract us, lead us to temptation." His fingers were long and skinny, malnourished.

"I'm not sure I understand."

He inhaled through his thin nostrils once more. "Let me try another approach. Who educates a child, teaches them right from wrong, keeps them on the correct path? There is the church, of course, and the community, but perhaps most importantly the child's parents. What starts in the home engages with society. It can gird it, even improve it, or, as is the case, poison it."

If my mother were here, her gaze would have been severe and prodding, compelling him to turn away.

"Can you speak plainly? What do you want?"

"You took something that doesn't belong to you."

"What?"

"Come now, my child, it's outside for all to see."

"I didn't take anything. It was given to me."

"If that is the case, explain why I've been sent here?"

"Because she's perverse and only ever thinks of herself. Take the plant. I don't even want it."

"I appreciate your admission, but for it to count you must return it yourself. You will need to ask for forgiveness, but not from me." He chuckled to himself, self-satisfyingly. "I won't pester our Heavenly Father over this. No, this is more of a societal sin." My bottom lip quivered, my hands shook. I was biting on my teeth. The priest turned to the door, saying, "You have nudged our community out of balance, just slightly but enough, so now you must nudge us back."

I waited until I heard the front gate shut behind him then squatted and folded over and screamed into my knees. In the afternoon I returned to the garden and finished planting the dahlia and the tubers, tenderly and deliberately. I'm uncertain if Rafa's mother had been waiting until the moment I finally stood from my garden, my work there complete, but this is when she appeared at the gate. She glanced at the dahlia, snickered, then motioned to my house, as though inviting me in. "We need to talk," she said sternly.

I opened the front door for her, as one should for their elders. Let the village at least see that courtesy. I'd kept the house clean, and a part of me was proud to show it off. Quarry dust had a short existence in our house. Her eyes passed over the bare walls and mantle, the jars of preserves neatly lined along the kitchen shelf, the pressed cloth lining the basket of eggs, the lacquered sheen to the wood beams, the curtains without wrinkles, the orderly stack of my mother's letters on a stool next to the fireplace. I wanted somebody to recognize that I was all right, to acknowledge it.

"No religious icons," she asked as an observation.

"We both know I didn't steal from you."

"Do we?"

"You need only ask Rafa, if you haven't already."

"A boy my son's age is impressionable, determined to see the best in everyone, incapable of identifying ulterior motives, even what's best for him."

She spoke authoritatively, as if from the pulpit, as if she would take greater offense to me contradicting her than the theft itself. I couldn't help myself. "I didn't tell him to do it."

She raised her voice. "You didn't need to. You—"

"Then I don't understand the point of you being here."

"Let me finish," she snapped. "Such a repugnant habit of talking when you should be listening. I won't humor the consequences of your misguided upbringing."

I crossed my arms, a mannerism of my mother's. Though the beauty of the world could dazzle her, she had no patience to suffer the likes of Rafa's mother. I looked again to the stack of letters. I hated my mother for abandoning me here, exposing me to this. A part of me wanted to invite Rafa's mother to eat from our pantry and sleep in my parent's bed, but my father didn't die so she could talk to his daughter this way. I uncrossed my arms and walked to the door.

"Where do you think you're going?" she demanded.

"Me?" I opened the door. "Nowhere."

Passing me, she said, "You're never seeing my son again."

"It's a small village. I'm sure our paths will cross."

That night, I felt painfully alone. Bouts of crying were brief distractions of sorts. They'd leave me feeling even more emptied out. The Carmelos were three houses down. They had a pregnant border collie named Pecosa, for the hundreds of white dots that freckled her otherwise pitch-black face. Tomorrow I'd ask if I could get one of her puppies. Perhaps I'd even trade the dahlia for it. Keeping it would aggravate Rafa's mother, but immediately trading it away might enrage her more.

Despite my desperate need for company, when the postman delivered another letter the following day, I didn't open it. I wanted my mother back, and nothing else would suffice. If the war was over for her husband and her daughter then it should have been for her, as well. I made a resolution. I wouldn't read another word of hers.

When she ultimately returned to me, she would see that those experiences she'd had out there had not been for me. And if her death notice should arrive, the letter would sit unopened atop all the others and continue to wait for her.

This resolution didn't allow me to encounter the day with any less apprehension. Each minute crushed me, and all those that awaited were an impossible prospect. I'd startle myself by blurting, "Papa," and the tears would be out of me before I blinked. Already, over the course of his absence, I'd forgotten the sound of his voice. So what would become of my memories of his laughter? His smile? The feel of his hands? How much longer could I carry these with me before they, too, blurred into a single emotion: regret. He would never be resurrected. He would never be avenged. He was gone, and for what?

I didn't leave the house that day but swept and polished and washed all I could, and as the village turned away from the sun and the sky changed colors, I sat in the darkness and went to bed early.

At noon the next day I waited by the window for the postman. I had a premonition of worse news yet: my mother's death notice. I tried to affirm my resolution—should it arrive, I wouldn't open it—but this ache, this hollowness, this weight that sat atop me so as to burrow into my bones, I wanted a relief from it. While positioned by the window, I heard a soft rapping at my back door. Through it, Rafa's voice. "It's me," he said.

He hugged me and held my head against his chest, which stank of rotten eggs. I'd never know how he and the other men accustomed themselves to the foul smell their picks released from the stones. Yet, it reminded me of my father, the stench that had often clung to him—my eyes became heavy, my cheeks hot. "I'm sorry I couldn't come until now." It was his lunch break and he'd likely taken every back road so his mother wouldn't be tipped off. "I'm miserable. I'm suffering as I never have before. I won't continue like this. I refuse it. My mom can't stop me from seeing you." Though she was a nightmare to deal with, I found myself feeling jealous that Rafa should get to have his mother in his life. What had I done to deserve being separated from mine? "I'm sixteen," he continued. "I have a job with men who are forty, fifty, sixty years old. They control their lives, why can't I?"

"My father is dead."

"What?"

I pushed away from him and attempted to pinch the smell from my nostrils. "After all this time, it's the only real news my mother has had to report."

"When did this happen?"

"Four months ago."

"And your mother?"

"She's decided to stay, to continue as a nurse."

He groaned. "And what does she expect of you?"

"She cares more for ideas now. She wants an audience, not a daughter."

There was a knock at the front door, startling Rafa. His hands were out, as if his mother followed the stink of rotten eggs to my house. "Stay here," I said.

The postman held out the letter, an exhausted huff of air issuing from him. Both he and I had tired of this duty that continued to bind us. When I closed the door, Rafa was behind me.

"From your mother?" he asked.

I nodded. This one felt thicker than the others. Multiple pages. Rafa waited for me to open it. Instead, I took it to the fireplace. Yesterday, I'd scrubbed the soot from its belly. Not all but for most of the stones, you'd think they'd just been pulled from the quarry. I lit a match and put it to the envelope's edge.

"What are you doing?"

"Ending the conversation." If I stopped reading them, they would stop coming.

As the flames rose up the letter, curling the pages, and nearing my hand, I tossed it in the fireplace. I gathered the others and fed them one at a time to the growing fire. Rafa rubbed my back as I did so. "Good," he said, "I want you to be happy again."

When I finally finished, I told him, "Let's get out of here."

"Where do you want to go?"

"No," I said, clarifying, "let's leave this village. My parents did the same when I was little." This, I decided, is how I would honor my father's memory. "Let's start a new life, together."

"Just the two of us?"

I nodded. "There's nothing left for us here."

"My job is here," he said. "And war is beyond the village."

"War or no war, there's bound to be something better than this life."

"I'm lucky to have work. I wouldn't if my father wasn't foreman." He was considering it, though—attempting to imagine himself elsewhere.

"Even if you're determined to swing a hammer and stink of rotten eggs, what about your mother? Don't you want to be free of her?"

"She's a pain, but she means well."

"Today, she's explicitly forbidding you. Tomorrow, she'll find other ways to manipulate you. The years won't change this, only proximity can."

"Would I be able to come back from time to time? Visit my brothers?"

"We'll be in control of our own lives. We could do whatever we wanted. We just need to get out of this town."

He nodded and said *vale* multiple times, but I could see he wasn't convinced. "I should get back before they notice I'm gone. We'll need money after all." Though this was a wonderful opportunity for a kiss, he maintained his distance, as though there was something dangerous about me, as though he'd finally identified my mother in me.

"When will I see you again?" I asked. "We need to make plans."

"I'll try and come tomorrow," he said. I didn't believe a word.

He shut the door, and I watched him through the windows squat and cower and press himself against a wall, peek around it, then dart to the next one. It seemed so ridiculous with the sun high above him. In the fireplace, the flames had gone out and fingers of grey smoke rose from the crisp and blackened corners of the pages. Some portions of the letters remained. I could still see my mother's handwriting. I wanted it all gone. I opened the cupboard under the stove for the can of lard—it would act as an accelerant—but stopped halfway to the fireplace. I scooped some, cupped it in my palm, then threw it at the curtains. The next handful against the wall. From the doorway of my parents' bedroom, I threw it onto their sheets then wiped my hands on the clothes they'd left behind. I lifted their mattress off its frame and cleared the books from their shelves. The chickens in the back were getting agitated by the noise. I spiked every egg of theirs I had collected. I kept at this until I stood in the middle of the *sala*, my shoulders heaving for the breaths I took, every object in there smeared, filthy, or on its side. Now, I had something to clean, a distraction.

By evening, though, I needed to get out of the house. There was but one more lungful of air left in it. The walls were teetering and would soon fall atop me.

Outside, stars riddled the sky. Pecosa, the Carmelo's pregnant border collie, was leashed to the front gate, curled like a kidney bean. She stretched when I approached and turned herself over so I'd pet her chest. "Hey, Pecosita, it's any day for you now." Her hair was thick with dust. Gently, I rubbed the curve of her belly. I couldn't feel any of the puppies squirming. "I think they've already gone to sleep." I sat against the fence with Pecosa's head in my lap. "Who's got more freckles tonight," I asked her, "you or the sky?" The waning crescent moon couldn't compete against all those stars. They were waiting for me to make a decision. I hoped one might tell me what it would be. Pecosa's eyelids were slowly coming together but we startled for the noise behind us. From inside the Carmelo's house a group of agitated men entered through the back door. Their voices were angry—some whispered, others talked loudly—as they scooted chairs or stomped about.

"We can't have that here," someone shouted. "We can't. Not for one minute more." The others shushed him. I couldn't identify his voice. He continued in a lower volume, but his tone remained furious. "We need to prove our loyalty. It's the only thing that will save us."

"So what's the plan?"

They were talking about me. I was certain. The daughter of a red still engaged in the struggle had no place in a village under Nationalist control.

"Do we take him alive?" This was Rafa. He was whispering loudly, just as he had done through my door.

"And how will we do that? He has a rifle. Sapo saw it clearly."

"Sapo did?" another person asked.

The man who had been shouting said, "Even if he runs, we kill him. If, at this moment, he's fleeing the barn, we hunt him down. This village can't harbor reds. That bastard will pull us back into war."

"How will we know which way he's gone?"

"Sapo's watching the barn."

"Sapo can't see five feet in front of him. In the sunlight."

Rafa's father asked, "Has anyone else spotted the red but Sapo? We might be getting ourselves worked up over nothing."

"I'll kill the red," someone offered. It sounded like Rafa, or at least the cadence of his speech was similar. This was possibly his younger brother, Ángel, who was my age. Ángel possessed none of his father's softness. Instead, like his mother, he moved through the world as though it had wronged him once already and he wouldn't let it occur again.

"We'll all get our chance."

"So how will we flush him out?"

I stood quietly, softly placing Pecosa's head on the ground. I kept it there, applied some force as I pet her head. "Stay," I said and backed away slowly. She didn't rise up, didn't shake her chain, but kept a passive eye on me. When I turned the corner, I ran.

Sapo's farm was on the edge of the village. I slowed as I neared it, remaining draped in shadows. Sapo had a frog's bulbous chin, and, like a frog, his eyes bulged. With them he saw this life as though through a keyhole. More than likely his imagination had taken advantage of him and he mistook a change in the wind for a soldier.

He was outside his house up the hill, his arms crossed as he stooped slightly forward, squinting at his barn. There were too many stars in the sky, not enough shadows. Slicks of starlight pooled across the land. I should have given the barn a wider berth, but I expected at any moment for the men to appear behind me, all of them having worked or lived alongside my father. Had the fascists not killed him, had he managed to make it back to me, what sort of mercy would these men, Rafa among them, have extended him?

There was no door on the side of the barn that I approached. The only way in and out faced Sapo's house. It was hard to imagine Sapo's eyes being able to close the distance to the barn, but maybe there was something about the night that allowed him to see better. I felt along the barn as I had Pecosa's belly, trying to sense life beyond it. Crinkling paint chipped off as I knocked softly. I didn't hear any rustling inside. I knocked again. Louder this time. "Is anyone there?" I asked. No reply came. "My mother is Elena Zapico Morales. She's a nurse. She was at Oviedo, then Avilés. My father is Emilio Estrella Lugo. He died there four months ago. Maybe you fought with him. Maybe my mother has cared for you or your friends." I waited. The sounds of the heavy shifting of a horse were all I heard. "There are men coming for you," I said. "They'll be here shortly." I was surprised that the next part was difficult to say. I still couldn't believe it was something one person would choose to do to another. "They're planning to kill you."

Now, on the other side of the wall, I heard the boards shift as somebody pressed against them. "How many are there?" a man asked.

"I don't know. At least six. Probably more."

"Do they have guns?"

"Possibly. That and chisels. They're quarrymen. Did you know my father?"

"I've never been to those towns."

"Probably for the best." I heard him moving through the barn. "Wait," I called. "There's an old man up the ridge. He's watching the door. This is his barn."

Only after saying this did I understand I might have damned Sapo. I asked, "You're not going to shoot him, are you?" I had assumed it was the most difficult thing to do to another person, but the men had spoken as if it was no harder than any other demand of the day.

"It hadn't occurred to me," he said.

"Then why did it for the men who are coming here?"

"Fear," he said. It sounded as if he was ducking under something. He added. "A fear that's turned hideous." It was the sort of thing my mother would say.

"I want this war to end," I said, "but I want to preserve life. Are both things possible?"

He didn't respond.

I asked, "Is there no room for reconciliation?"

"In a country devised by these bastards? Just submission."

"Wouldn't it be worth it for peace?"

"If they're doing all this to get power, imagine how they'll wield it."

"But there must be another way than this fighting?"

"I'll let you know if I survive. I'm going to go now. Get some distance from here before I do. Protect yourself." I listened to him move, but he stopped. "Wait. Are you still there?"

"Yes."

I hoped for more of an answer, but he said, "Thank you."

I walked away, toward the night that spread from the town. There was still no relief from this ache and emptiness in my chest and bones. I was wondering if I had done the right thing when I heard Sapo yell. I turned and there was the soldier. Sure enough, he had a rifle. He paused slightly when he saw me, lifting his hand to say goodbye or perhaps to show me his wound. There was a gap where his middle fingers should have been. Then he ran. I took a step to follow him—little remained for me here—but Sapo was yelling, calling for the quarrymen, and I knew I didn't have long. I sprinted into the darkness, into the night, toward nothing. I ran until my lungs burned. If there was shouting, I couldn't hear it.

The stars were lemon-colored. They were tenuously lodged. I hoped they'd fall, a few at first then the rest all at once. I waited for it. I wanted things to end, but they didn't, and it wouldn't, and I knew I had to find some way to carry forward with that understanding.

7

MATEO   **CANTABRIAN SEA, AUGUST 1937**

THE SKY WAS as black as the sea, which the ship left, momentarily, granting us a brief weightlessness, until we hit the water again and buckled our knees. Nerea and I gripped the corner of the wall we peeked around. The hard ocean spray was pebbles thrown against our faces.

Near the bulwark of the quarterdeck Father Urza made the sign of the cross over Mudo's forehead. Two nuns stood nearby. They'd wrapped Mudo in a white sheet, possibly the one from his bunk. Blood darkened the back of it. My parents had been similarly shrouded for their simple and rushed burial. Against the sheet I'd been able to make out the perfect curve of my mother's forehead and my father's stout nose I'd inherited.

No features of Mudo's protruded. It could have been anyone there, I tried convincing myself. It need not be any of us. Then, again, it could have been any of us. "And where's Jon?" I whispered to Nerea, asking of her younger brother.

"Down in the cabin," she said. "He doesn't need to see this." She had a habit, I'd noticed, of quoting the adults like their ideas were her irrefutable own. It was the nuns who had told the priest we shouldn't be forced to watch Mudo's burial. He initially insisted on it. It would fortify our resolve, he'd said, if we bore witness to the consequences of despair. The nuns reminded him we were the last of the children—what horrors had we yet to see? There was a limit. Hence Mudo having forfeited his ghost. Did they really want to risk another child capitulating to hopelessness? They argued this before a group of us, as if we weren't there. I wanted to interject, letting them know my parents weren't gone because they'd lost hope. They had looked forward to the future and hardly ever spoke of the thing that would kill them.

Eventually, the priest relented, and so now, the two nuns lifted Mudo by his feet while the priest scooped him from under his back, nearly tipping him out of the nuns' hold. They stuttered to brace against the slam of a wave. Strange watching nuns perform a physically demanding activity. Finally, though, they got his legs on the bulwark. They had him laying across it, each of them waiting, the two nuns for the priest, who hoped the lift and fall of the ship would relieve him of the duty, but when we hit the water, the body didn't budge. So, again, he made the sign of the cross over Mudo's forehead and then, looking away, used one hand to push the body, the legs bending and going last. I cringed, expecting, I suppose, a scream as he fell, but he was silent even in death.

"Come," Nerea said, tugging on my arm, "before they see us." She was probably six or seven—three or four years younger than me—but she carried herself like she was an adult among children. Her mother was a writer, she had said, as though it explained how she was so advanced. I opened the door and we hurried down the stairs to the cabin. "Poor Mudo," she said. "To die of a broken heart."

This, too, one of the adults had said. A school mistress. There were two of them on board with us. Two nuns, as well, and the lone priest. Our chaperones on this journey away from Spain and its fascists to Great Britain, one of the world's last and sturdiest democracies. Not enough adults, if you asked me, for the three hundred of us on board.

Boarding the ship back in Santander, younger children had been wailing, parents were at war with their quaking bottom lips, arms reached for reaching arms. I'd seen it all once already. One of the nuns patted my shoulder as I neared the plank, commending me on my stoicism, saying I was setting the example for the others to follow. It felt a silly thing to be congratulated for. If any of those parents had opened their arms, I'd have run into them and away from the ship and the drearily infinite waters and its darkening sky. We squinted against the wet wind of the gathering storm out there, where, the adults had somehow concluded, some hope existed for us. Out there, German planes couldn't materialize at any moment. They were trying to hurry us aboard. 336 had been sighted in Santander. That was the rumor. The enemy soldier had earned his name by those he'd killed. Every time anyone spoke of him, the number seemed to grow, as if you couldn't evoke him in conversation without tacking a few more deaths to the total. I supposed it was some sort of accomplishment, to amass that sum while standing eye level with your victims, but some German pilots were probably in the thousands by now, especially if they were among those who had destroyed Gernika. Should one have broken through the clouds at that moment we were all clustered on the pier, they'd have been able to boast of another hundred, easily. Both 336 and the German bombers were a very real possibility, which was why they were rushing us onto the ship.

The nun and I had passed Nerea and Jon, who were just then letting go of their mother. As they did, another family caught their mother's eye. "What are those fascists doing here?" The angry tone in that mournful scene snagged our attention. I turned, along with several others, to see who she was pointing at: a mustachioed father, a broomstick-for-a-spine mother, and their awkwardly skinny son, who was likely my age and dressed dapperly as though for his portrait, as though his parents were determined to present to the older boys an object to harass and ridicule. So those were fascists, I thought. It always amazed me how one could tell. Perhaps they were too well-dressed, the mother too stiff-lipped and prim, the father too groomed. "This is the world you wanted," she yelled at them, hooking windblown hair out of her face. "Take your own child back to it." They couldn't hear her over the crying children and the agitated surf between the plank and the ship's side. The nun I was with put a hand on the woman's shoulder. "No," Nerea's mother said, shirking it off. "Those fachas—their own blood—don't get to seek refuge in another democracy now that they've turned ours to shit."

"And the child should suffer for the sins of the parent?" the nun asked.

"Why not? The rest of us are." She was going to continue, but she cringed, a hand at her stomach. We waited a long while before she finally swallowed hard and focused on her breathing, her eyes closed. My mother was in the same condition before she'd been killed. After one such spell of cramps she had taken my hand and put it on her warm belly, "Tell your sister to give her mother some peace." Whatever fight Nerea and Jon's mom had left her. She drew a haltering breath through clenched teeth and shook her head. "Go," she said, kissing them brusquely. "We'll reunite when our side is victorious." The nun took Jon's hand and the three of us boarded the ship, passing Mudo as we did.

DOWN IN THE ship's cabin, Asto, as was his natural ability, found me quickly. Heavy chains swayed overhead. He was with the other older boys. Theirs was a straight and aggressive line to me. Others warily stepped out of their way. Somehow, this didn't draw the nearby nun's attention. "Zubialdea," Asto said, calling me by the name of my house. I doubted he knew my actual name.

His was a round-cheeked smile of menace more than mischief. Whenever he flashed it, you could be certain some shade of wickedness would be delivered upon a younger boy or an animal. We were both from the same village. He was four years older than me, and, somehow, since the very beginning, he sniffed out my terror of him. I'm sure, I'm certain, his eyes opened each morning wondering: how can I dominate little Zubialdea today? Especially those mornings when he'd arrive to school with a swollen cheek. His father, anybody in the village could tell you, was a drinker.

Boarding the *Sinai* for America I had thought to myself, sure I'm leaving the only home I ever knew, but at least an ocean will separate me from Asto. When America denied us entry and sent us back to our shattered country, I half-expected to find him waiting at the port with that sneering smile of his and a mind full of evil intent. At the orphanage, while fascist planes tore apart the sky, there was the consolation that only the suicidal would venture our way.

It was too good to last, I knew. I'd learned that much from life. So I wasn't surprised when, helping Jon finish tucking in the sheets to his bed, Asto came up behind me and squeezed the back of my neck, his thick fingers working between muscle. What minor warmth I'd been feeling being helpful to someone was overcome by a pressure on my trachea. "Together again, eh, Zubialdea?" If I were his parents and had the opportunity to be rid of him, I, too, would have shoved him onto this ship for Great Britain.

In the short amount of time we'd been on it, he'd managed to attract other like-minded boys, and together they preyed on our vulnerability so as to ignore their own.

They now encircled me, Asto stepping on my toes. "You're going to help us," he said.

"With what?" I asked. The ship smashing against a wave shifted his feet off my toes.

Rather than answer, Asto turned to the others. "You should have seen Zubialdea when our school was bombed. You think all that crying at the port was bad? Enough tears from this one to put the fire out." They chuckled idiotically. Somewhere, the splatter of vomit. A few of the boys turned excitedly to try to find who'd been caught by misery.

I hadn't actually cried, but I wasn't going to correct him. Our other classmates had, even a few of the teachers. I felt nothing as we huddled under the trees while the school burned. My parents had been killed in a shelling the week before, so I was waiting on

transportation to take me to the orphanage when the harsh and galloping sounds of the approaching German planes had us sprinting
out of school. Indifferently, I watched it burn. It was to be my last
day there regardless.

"What I want to know," Asto now said, "is if you're ready to stop
crying." He dragged a chubby knuckle under his bottom lip. "What
I want to know is if you've had enough of the fascists."

Their hair was wet, I noticed. Their shoelaces were mealy, the
cuffs of their pants soaked through. They must have been out on the
deck for Mudo's funeral, as well.

"So," Asto asked, "you ready to fight back?"

Somehow, I sensed it already, but still I asked, "What do you need
me to do?"

THE THING WAS, Mudo could speak. Or at the very least he had
been able to. Why it was his mother brought him to this ship, we'll
never know. The two would have been safer under our treacherous
skies. The bombs that tumbled from the belly of German planes,
the bombs that rocked as they fell but quickly found their path and
carved it ferociously on their descent—Mudo and his mother would
at least have had a chance of dodging those. But, no, Mudo clung to
his mother and screamed in terror when the priest pried him from
her and tugged him across the gangplank. So he *had* been able to
talk. Once on board, though, he went mute. Nerea tried to charm
some words from him. Jon, too. They were gentle and patient, but
I wanted to ask him what the big deal was: why the obscene display
of emotions earlier, who were those serving, and why the dramatic
silence now?

This was my second ship, and I didn't cry once, not when I boarded
that first one, not when America turned us away, not when they told
us that the orphanage would likely be taken over by fascists before
the week was out, and not when, after we got used to the idea, they
hurried us to the port to cram us onto this, the final ship of Basque

children that Great Britain, and the rest of the world for that matter, would accept. At least you have a mother, I wanted to tell him. At least somebody back home is crying for you. What about me? Not even the ground beneath my feet will claim me.

It would have been better had he remained crying. Whatever grief he trapped inside himself was visibly damaging him. We were in the main hold, where fifteen, possibly twenty, long tables filled the space. Children sat on benches, many of them with their heads between their knees, trying not to lose the soup we'd been fed. The sour and pungent stink of sick hung in the air in surprising and unpredictable pockets. Mudo's illness, though, was altogether different—charged with rage, chilling to witness. At first, he had turned pale, then a tremor that started in his hands spread through him. "If you just speak," Nerea told him, "you'll feel better." He refused, and his dark eyes withdrew further, sinking into his skull. He'd determined to give up, even as he continued breathing. He hated us but wouldn't or couldn't tell us why. I saw it in the angry tightness of his coal-like eyes that, suddenly, rolled back into his head. He flopped on the ground like a fish out of water, and as with those fish, a blow to the head is what stilled him. Mudo delivered it himself, slamming his head into the hard edge of a radiator. A sharp, irredeemable crack like a stone splitting in two. Nerea screamed for help. I expected blood to pool around him, but what first seeped out was white and thick and haunting. He continued shaking, with greater ferocity, toward his exit.

The priest decided they'd mark the death in the book but couldn't arrive at Great Britain with the body of a child for the country to bury. "It's going to be hard enough finding places for the others," he said.

Nerea, meanwhile, had taken on the sneering characteristics of her mother—indignant, spiteful, authoritative. She swung her gaze around the cabin until she found the skinny son of the fascists. He was sitting in the opposite corner near the other radiator. With all those bodies in there, it wasn't a coveted spot. His vision was locked between his feet. He occupied as little space as possible, though he was mostly arms and legs. "You did this," she yelled at him, tears gathering under her eyelids. Had he been seasick it might have elicited some sympathy. "You think you get to destroy our country and hunt us and then, after it's turned to shit, seek refuge with us." Parts of it were her mother's words from earlier. The other parts were probably also hers. Nerea spoke from her chest, as if from a lectern. This is someone, I thought, who's seen more speeches than football matches.

The boy never met her eyes while she continued admonishing him but hunched his shoulders higher and pulled his head into his body. "My mother's friend is a soldier. He's killed other fachas like you. Right outside our home. I watched him do it. I know how to kill your kind now, too." She kicked his shin. He didn't acknowledge this. If he could tuck himself in tighter he would have, yet he seemed, at the same time, to be offering his leg for her to kick again as penance. Many others were watching by this point. "Facha," she yelled and spat at him. I looked about for help, for an adult to bring some order, but couldn't spot any, so I grabbed her by the shoulders and pulled her away, telling her that was enough. Asto had been elsewhere in that moment—I knew because he would have joined in, even if it was a private argument—but word had reached him regardless: aboard our ship is a son of our enemies whose life a young girl has threatened. She's opened a door for you.

I APPROACHED THE boy now, but he didn't lift his head to me. "Hey there," I said. His eyes stayed locked on that space between his feet, probably directing wishes to it. "I'm sorry about my friend earlier." I added, "I only just met her."

His suitcase was tucked behind his back: "So what did you end up bringing with you?" I asked. "Any toys?"

At this, he finally raised his eyes. He studied me as I tried for a smile.

"Well, go on then," I said. "Let's see what you have."

He leaned to look around me, taking quick reads of the faces nearby but nobody was paying us any attention. He slid his suitcase onto his lap and popped its clasps. The first toy he brought out flushed my cheeks with heat. It was a tin red and gold windup racer. I already knew every detail. The two flat profiles of the driver and the passenger, the gold fat 3 by both doors, the PH insignia on them, the sharp nose of its grill. I rolled a finger over its pale green tires and wanted to ask if he'd taken it from me, if he'd somehow rescued this from my things. But mine had a dented front grill and his was as if new, in the same condition mine had been when my father came into my room and brought it out from behind his back.

I put my nose to it—I didn't care if the boy thought me weird— and was returned to our kitchen, driving the car over its warped floorboards, around my mother's feet, up her ankles.

I felt my mother's presence for the first time since the orphanage put me aboard the *Sinai*. Leaving the land of my home had severed something in me. The life I'd lived before was gone, as was everyone in it. Returning after being denied by America felt like arriving to a new country. It would be a new life. It had to be. I had no choice.

I turned the car over, expecting, for some reason, it would be different than mine. But, no, there were the sharply-ridged cogs, the wire that looped from one rod to another as you wound it.

"Can I play with it?" I asked.

The boy had been watching me all the while, confused, perhaps, but whatever emotions had been passing across my face relaxed his shoulders, that neck of his fully exposed. He seemed even more vulnerable because of it. I'd become convinced I wouldn't be able to do what was required next but surprised myself by saying, "There's not enough room here. Let's take it to the deck where it can really take off."

Less than a minute ago, he wouldn't have trusted me, but I'd unwittingly bared some part of myself, so he shut his suitcase and slid it around the radiator. Though my age, he was at least a head taller. His legs and neck were too long for the rest of him. The ship mounted a wave and was smacked by another. He bent his knees to absorb the shock. I scuttled sideways, nearly toppling over. Our eyes met and we both smiled. Had he ever left that corner, he would have known how impossible and dangerous the deck was.

"Venga," I said, motioning with the racer, thinking it really didn't matter. The older boys were going to get him regardless, and if they didn't, what shot at surviving would the son of our enemies have in a democracy like Great Britain, an island likely bursting with Astos. It's why they were able to sleep in their own beds at night. Maybe Asto was right. We'd been given a chance to continue our parents' fight. We could still win. In order to do that, though, there must be fewer of them than us. Besides, why shouldn't his parents experience my grief?

The stairs led first to a mezzanine you had to cross for the next set. Hiding around the stairwell's corners, Asto and the other older boys crouched. "What store did you get this?" I asked the boy as we approached it. "My father bought me the same one. Maybe you saw him there." In my nervousness anything may have flown out my mouth. The boy couldn't decipher the tightness in my throat, the bizarre nature of the question, the quickly burgeoning panic that produced it. Had I done more than glance his way, had I turned fully so he could have looked in my eyes, perhaps he would have understood and run to an adult, but I caught only a patient and pitying smile from him before climbing the last step. I was unaware of my legs underneath me as I crossed the mezzanine. I felt only the bodies of the older boys behind the various walls.

It was now pointless and too late. Still, I turned and offered him the car. "Here," I said. "I'm sorry." Before he could take it, the boys jumped out to tackle him. It was like trying to tackle a thrashing and squawking crane. He was all limbs, and they had difficulty containing him. The only thing Asto managed was muzzling him with a fat hand over his mouth. They punched at his head to further silence him, but he was moving too much, and their fists grazed off his skull. I didn't want to watch anymore. Instead, I focused on the racer, tracing a finger over the profile of its driver, turning its crank so the wheels spun and hummed through the air. The boy had kept it in perfect condition. You could put it back on the shelf and no one would suspect it had been owned. Nevertheless, I imagined the warped floorboards this racer had once bounced over. I imagined the ankles of his mother, the love in her smile as she looked down at him, the love in my own mother's smile, her expression in the moment before her death, whether she would be any less terror-stricken if she could see her son now.

Before being fully aware of doing it, I swung the sharp nose of the grill at Asto, yelling, "Get off him." The car's nose spiked into Asto's shoulder, and he howled in pain, but it was a fleeting victory. With his free hand he struck me across the face, twisting me to the floor. I'm not sure why I ever thought it would be worse than the times my father hit me. I'd feared Asto's fists as much as I had the fascists. But on the floor, dabbing at my open lip, I thought, This is it? That's all? I've been afraid of *that* this entire time?

They tugged the boy to the stairwell, one of his legs pinned up by their arms, the other leg hopping as he tried digging into the tiles. There was another crash of a wave, but everyone remained upright. I could just make out his muffled cries. The panic in his eyes was deafening. The older boys had abandoned themselves to some collective fury, yet, somehow, each was smiling. Theirs were the angriest smiles I'd ever seen. They compelled me to action.

I ran ahead to the stairwell and up its steps. I pressed my back against the door and gripped tight the banisters on both sides and yelled. Outside, through the door, came the wild roar of the ocean, the wind. Still, I yelled. I screamed. I yelled for the adults, for the teachers and the priest and the nuns, I yelled for someone to save us from ourselves.

8

BERNABÉ   **VALDAZO, AUGUST 1937**

THE SOLDIER SEARCHES the candle-lit walls and floor, flits his eyes into the hallways' shadowed pockets for—anything. A religious icon or newspaper would tell him all he needs to know about me. There was a time you could never guess at another's political affiliation, would never have cause to wonder about it.

He's sweating still. Many would in the olive-green uniform he's wearing. That he hasn't had a chance to burn it means he's either just escaped a prison or some remnant of the slaughter up north. His eyes casting about return once more to the charred ceiling, the shriveled planks and the gaps between them where the night gets through, then the scarred skin across my neck, the blisters there, my fire-mangled ear.

"I apologize for startling you," he says. "I couldn't take any chances."

"Of course," I say.

"I didn't expect to happen upon anybody."

A nightmare had woken me an hour earlier. I never remain in bed afterwards but have learned to take myself outside. I'm safest from myself there while I wait for the land to separate from the night. Tonight's dream was another impossible scenario: Rosario and I had lost Cristobal. He was a child in the dream, Rosario and I both young. Night was filling spaces. The cold stropped its blade. Cristobal wouldn't survive if we didn't find him soon. That the dream could not have happened was no consolation. Cristobal never knew his mother, only her absence.

Afterwards, I sat against the wall outside, next to Rosario's favorite spot. All her life she had been a stargazer. She'd turn to me and marvel, *Isn't it amazing, we don't need to part with a single centavo to take in the show.* The summer air, even at night, was a heavy blanket atop me. The heat allowed me some distance from the dream.

So I was thinking of my two when a figure stirred the dark. He was twenty, twenty-five meters away. From that distance, he was Cristobal, or at least his double. They even walked the same. I stood at once, waving my arms. The figure raised his rifle in response.

He asks now, "What's the space between the checkpoints?" The chicken bone on his plate has been picked clean. With a finger he wipes the inside of the cup to get at the last drops of water. Hunger and desperation have excavated his features.

"Kilometers sometimes. Sometimes less than half." My jaw is tight from resentment. "The patrols string them together." I had given him the plate to rest on his lap, so that he might set aside his rifle, but he took the food to the table, to Rosario's spot. For twenty-three years no one has sat there. As a child, Cristobal would, on occasion, look at the empty chair and plate, then the door, as though his mother might at last walk through it. By the age of five or six this stopped. I never told him to give up on hope. He learned that on his own.

"But as I said," I tell him. "I'll take you. I'll show you the way."

"Let's go then." He starts to rise.

"Not yet." I still need to know certain things. Even with the rifle pointed at me, before he was close enough that I could make out his uniform, his shape fooled me. To have Cristobal returned, if only for a moment—my breath shook in gratitude. It forestalls any final decision.

He says, "It will be dawn soon."

"We have time."

The soldier weighs whether to believe me, rolling his fingers on the rifle across his lap. I had given Cristobal ours. I've yet to replace it, knowing I still can't trust myself with one. There is an odd rhythm to the soldier's tapping, on account, I realize, of missing fingers. I nod at the wound, a question.

He examines his hand as if he hasn't considered it for a long while. "I was trying to stop someone from making a mistake."

"Were you successful?"

"No."

"Does it hurt?"

"Less every day. What about you?"

I dab at the smeared honeycomb of scars down my neck, the blisters that rise from it. "It's not the pain that bothers me."

He points at the blackened ceiling. "What happened?"

How to explain that this house, this life, they've become obscenities without anyone to give them to. There's no way to wrench your heart from the spear. The best you can do is take hold of it and drive it all the way through. "An accident," I say.

The smoke kills you before the flames have the opportunity. But I fought to hold on. I wanted to know what my son felt. My neighbor—Oscar Martinez Garcia, a bull of a man who can give the world three sons but not fight for it—wrestled to pull me free of the house. I can only guess at how he extinguished the fire. I stopped believing everything happens for a reason. Now, though, with the soldier before me, that old faith whispers. It is a stray breeze entering through an open window and rousing the room to life once more.

Outside, one leashed dog barks insults at a wolf's scent. Under the stars and across the fields, another joins in. "Where are you hoping to get to?" I ask him.

"Wherever the fight is."

"To Montorio?"

"Is it being contested?"

"No, I suppose not. Not anymore."

The soldier stands, slings his rifle over a shoulder, and explores the room. He stops at the notches in the wall where I'd charted Cristobal's growth. There are few more joyful methods to mark the passage of time, few sadder. He considers these incisions and looks my way. I came to marriage late, later still to fatherhood. He wouldn't suspect that the notches belonged to a child born two or three years before him.

I ask, "What do your parents think of you being out here?"

He considers the question and me. "My mother has passed away."

"Childbirth?" Candlelight had pulsed across the walls that night as it does now, witness to the horror. I waited for the midwife to return with the doctor. Despite my tears, the pleading and prayers born on rapid breaths, the full measure of me breaking apart, I couldn't stop Rosario's bleeding. In my mind's eye, the blood is everywhere, thin as water but black as tar.

"No," he says, "an illness. Were my father a different man she could have received the help she'd needed in time."

"You don't get along with your father?"

"That's a way to put it."

My breath is light, light and cool, but the next I draw is thorned. There's the question again: can I really go through with it?

"Still, he must worry for you. Have you ever been so far from home?" He is a Basque, it is easy to tell. Isolated as they have been since the dawn of time, there are but a few faces they give to their children. He looks nothing like my Cristobal, just his build is all. "And in such treacherous country. Did he compel you to enlist?"

He laughs at this. I try to keep my thoughts from my eyes. "He's too selfish to care about the world. Too selfish and too cowardly."

I think of my neighbor Oscar, of him and the others—Ramón Carlos and Rivas, Gilberto and Lucio, men who live for themselves and those under their roofs.

"What about you?" he asks. "Where are your children?"

"You're right," I say, "it is late enough." I lean over to push myself out of the chair with a grunt. "There should be no issue crossing."

Outside, lit by the stars and moon, he is a silhouette, that shape. I had tried to prepare myself but my breath catches. *The child*, Rosario had said. *The child. Whatever happens, you must save the child.* It was one of the last things she said that had made any sense.

"What is it? See someone?"

"Nothing. A tender ankle. The walk will loosen it."

It hasn't cooled one degree. No candle flame touches my neighbors' windows. The houses have folded themselves into the night like children curled in bed. Regardless, I can see each of them spread across these low-rolling hills as though they were visible. I doubt the soldier makes them out. The squat stone and mortar houses, skewered with wooden beams, are rooted and unyielding. Not even the end of the world has budged them, not even the fire could destroy mine. As we near Rivas' his dog barks. But their sheep have been brought in. The dog could be barking at anything. The family is so lost to sleep that nobody shouts down to silence it. Above us, stars elbow into each other. We walk in silence. Despite his anxiety, the soldier keeps my slow pace. What fills our ears are my heavy breaths, the crunch of gravel under our feet, and the summer insects that stop chirping as we near them. It is a long walk, made longer by thoughts that take me in every direction, yet my feet don't veer from the path.

"I am thinking," I tell him, "of your father, how he didn't want you to enlist."

"I'm not anybody's son."

"Your father, I'm sure, feels differently. It is a father's sacred obligation to protect his child. This is why he didn't want you to enlist."

"No." He accounts for the outline of a distant tree before responding. "He didn't want me shooting at fascists, men twisted by fear like him."

"Is that so?"

He makes a noncommittal sound. "He doesn't have any politics. Not really. He couldn't tell you a thing Mola or Franco has said. But he's as scared as every other fascist."

"Of what?"

"Change. Power leaving the few and going to the people."

"And how many have you shot at, killed, these fascists?"

"It doesn't happen easily."

"I wouldn't expect so."

"There's no worse way to bring a country back from the brink. But it's the lone one before us now."

"Was it always with that rifle?" He adjusts his grip on it, is about to say something, but I ask, "Or have you ever locked your enemy into a house and set it on fire?" From my pocket I take a cigarette and box of matches.

"What are you doing?" he asks.

I strike the match and bring it to the cigarette.

"They'll see you."

"They're behind us now." I exhale smoke, then wave the match to extinguish the flame.

He turns and scours the night. "Then I'll get going." He steps forward and extends his good hand. He wishes to thank me.

I look at the hand. I imagine it caked in blood and mud, letting go of its heat. "Not yet," I tell him. "There's a ravine ahead you'll never find your way around at night. Cigarette?"

He shakes his head. I keep walking, pull deeply on mine, bring the smoke into my lungs, force the tip of it to glow. I tell him, "We had a doctor here once. He'd attend to this village and the three nearby. A learned man is how he'd describe himself. Forward thinking, like yourself. He'd fallen full into Marx. My wife Rosario and I had recently gotten together. I'd never been so happy, yet the doctor was determined to persuade everyone, though we lived off the land, of our miserable position in the class struggle, as if he'd sprinted down the mountain with the news. It angered me in ways I later came to regret. Had we any other doctors, the caciques would have run him out. I'd often challenge him to fights. I was older, sure, but love had me aflame with youth. In the end, the doctor and I would rather spit at each other than share any words. If only I knew what it would cost me."

The soldier is walking away from me, his weight balanced differently.

"That night my son was born, the midwife rushed to fetch the doctor. He took his time getting to us. The bastard made sure of it. So much for a revolutionary devotion to his fellow man. After I lost my wife, that was it, the others at last turned against him. I went to his house with rifle in hand, but he'd already fled, off to Madrid with his vile ideas, to finally be around others of his kind."

"Where are you leading me?" His elbow is jutted, the rifle stock gripped, his finger likely on the trigger.

"Dr. Paulo Valdez Santos. You must know him, no? He claimed his seat in the Cortes after the fraudulent elections last year. The newspaper had that red in Paracuellos del Jarama. Five thousand people, 'liquidated,' as they say, most of them women. Their crime was attending Mass. My wife was just the start. The doctor was just beginning. Five thousand people. It is impossible to imagine—no?— all those they left behind?"

He sweeps his rifle, jerking it this way and that. "You confused son of a bitch."

"Am I? Then how do I know what you'll do next?"

He starts to run, exactly where I thought he would, and the torches hit him. Again, that shape. The lights come from everywhere. Though I was expecting them, they stun me. People struck by lightning must feel the same—so much light in so little time. Behind the flashlights, the shouting is like rifle fire. The soldier understands that if he wants a few minutes more of this life he must surrender. He drops his weapon and raises his arms and they're on him. I'm grabbed, too, until someone shouts, "He's one of ours. That's Cristobal's father."

I move closer so the men are wrestling by my feet. I watch the punches thrown, the mess of limbs. It could be anyone down there. I watch and wait, by some miracle, for Cristobal to stand. It's the soldier instead, his hands bound behind him. He doesn't spit at me. His eyes show betrayal, as if I have missed some crucial point all along. It is difficult for me to maintain eye contact. I tell him, "You are nobody's son," the words hollow out my mouth. They're shoving him forward, striking his back with their rifle butts. He is, once again, just a silhouette.

I consider all these men, these boys. Why are they out here? Whose fight are they fighting and for how long have they been at it? Cristobal enlisted at the very start, when the Army of Africa crossed the Strait of Gibraltar aboard the Convoy of Victory. I'm too old, I told him. I'd be a liability. But you, you will be the one who saves Spain from the communists. For weeks after, doubts arose, often in Rosario's voice. Had I abandoned the oath I'd sworn? How could I be so reckless with the one life I was meant to protect? Then, having returned from a week of patrols, Cristobal brought me the newspaper. The massacre at Paracuellos del Jarama. Is this the same doctor? he asked. My doubts vanished then, but I would never again be so certain.

The soldier who had shouted for me to be unhanded steps forward. I recognize him from his patrols with Cristobal. His arms are open with a question. He's laughing. "How the hell did this happen?"

"Will you be among those in the firing squad?" I ask. "He is Basque. I doubt he was in Montorio."

"We have a lorry full of reds we're shipping to a prison outside Burgos. But you never know. The lorry's getting full. If we can't squeeze him in, maybe they'll allow us some target practice."

"What about Cristobal?"

"What about him?"

"Have they identified the remains?"

He waits a moment before answering. "The fire made each man indistinguishable from the other."

They could have easily brought me another's limbs to bury. I suppose I appreciate that they didn't.

"You really won't execute him now?" I keep anticipating the rifle shot, a cluster of them.

"Maybe I can get him alone," he offers. "Would you feel better if I did?"

"I don't know." The realization opens a seam in my chest. I feel it emptying me.

Before I'm aware of it, I'm hugging him. He is the first person I've held since Cristobal. He is rigid in my arms. He keeps his warmth from me. Slower than a dying man's heartbeat, he pats my back. "Yeah. Well." Even before I ultimately gave in and set my house on fire, I felt myself a scorched landscape, but if I blink, tears will slip loose. "Get on home," he says, "and try for some sleep."

Instead, I walk in the direction they forced the soldier. Doubt is a poison. The moment it enters you, you are finished. When becomes the question. Still, before it's too late, I must look someone in the eye and tell them I'm sorry. I never had my chance with Cristobal. Ahead, figures swarm the night. I can't make out his shape or that of any lorry. A hand falls on my shoulder. "You've done your duty. We'll take care of the rest." He turns me back in the direction from which I came. I allow this. I know of little else to do.

"Take care of yourself," I tell him. "So long as you live, someone is here to remember our Cristobal. He'll remain, in a way."

"Sure." I feel his questions at my back as I return through the dark for home. Alone now, it is such a longer walk. There are the scattered bell-shaped silhouettes of pine trees. Behind these, the forest is the shards of a jawbone. The low hills rise and fall. Somewhere in the far distance, not yet within sight, is my house. I imagine a rolling ball of fire in its place. I imagine coiling flames, their furious whooshing. I imagine stepping into them. It is, after all, only a matter of time.

Shades of murky blue tint the sky, cradle the blinking stars. Fewer than before. I return again and again to the soldier, how in his desperate state he had trusted me. My breath is both weak and a thing capable of crushing me. Were Rosario to return, or Cristobal, would they recognize who I've become? Or would they walk right past me, continuing to search these fields, calling my name?

The darkness dulls. The world emerges from the night. It is there before me, hinting at its expanse. I can't take a step anywhere in it without being wounded by a memory. I think again, as I have since Cristobal's death, *I hope they burn it all*. This time, though, I possess no rancor. I lack all conviction. How did such a desire ever support me? Sheep crest a hill near the horizon. Someone is out early, perhaps troubled by dreams as well. In the east, a distant light approaches. It will be here shortly. Soon, I'll have survived another night.

9

AFTER THE EXECUTIONS, we four left the cemetery from the front entrance, Rigoberto stretching his trigger finger and cursing when it slipped from his hold and curled, at once, rigidly to a hook. "My father has arthritis," he said. "His hands are claws."

"Is he able to hold a wineglass?" I asked.

"He'd shoot himself if he couldn't."

"There you go. It's not a death sentence."

"We just have to get you to the Copacabana," Heinrich said. "The ladies will straighten you out." He rose his index finger to attention. His real name was Enrique Torres. He was Huescan, likely hailed from people the color of burnt soil and varnished wood, but he was lantern-jawed with hair blonder than any German you'd find in Spain. It was translucently blonde. It could disappear in certain lights.

Marcos, meanwhile, was moving his tongue around his mouth, searching it for moisture. This sometimes happened to me, on account of the adrenaline. "First, wine." His words were slurred, dribbling down his chin.

"I remember passing a tavern," Heinrich said, opening the lorry's driver-side door while Rigoberto and I climbed into the back. There had been six prisoners here with Rigoberto and me. They could have easily overpowered us. I waited the entire ride for their first move, trying my best to appear relaxed and in control. The same nervous thrill that would eventually dry Marcos' mouth was twitching and flexing my every muscle. My eyes bounced from one prisoner to the next. I still didn't think we were going to go through with it, expected for somebody to stop our lorry or for the prisoners to overtake us, but they continued obediently playing the role of prisoners, even as we pulled up to the cemetery's front gates. Even then, with every shadow beckoning and the night opening its arms to receive them, none tried to run. I had seen it several times and couldn't make sense of it. As if dutiful compliance would somehow save them. As if a previous lack of it was what we were so upset about.

"Me cago en la leche," Rigoberto said now, lying flat along the plank, bending his finger back. "Like trying to straighten a pig's tail."

The road sloped down to the rest of San Sebastián. I detected the ocean on the air. The saline hint of it stirred me. I was from Campaspero. Before yesterday I'd never seen the ocean. As a child you'll unquestioningly welcome anything into your reality but give it a few years and you can stand up to your ankles in the sand, straining your eyes to see beyond the horizon's blue line, feel an awesome terror overtake you, and tell yourself: don't you dare let these bastards see you cry. Standing there, God or death or the ocean, something was trying to deliver me a message. I was on the cusp of hearing it, but I couldn't stop thinking: others have had this all the while, yet I've been denied.

I'd asked the six prisoners if they lived in San Sebastián, where their apartments were, but they were mountain people. No matter. The prison was packed. Plenty were bound to have a place in the city. I'd run out whoever in their family remained, then send for my mom so she could hold it for me until the war ended. That was my developing plan. I expected complications, still undetectable but they would soon present themselves, their spirits were lacing their boots.

We hugged a tight turn with too much speed and Heinrich braked suddenly, the lorry juddering to a stop, momentarily tipping, and sliding Rigoberto off the plank.

"After these drinks," he said, pushing himself up, his arms tangled in coils of rope, "one of us has to take the keys from him."

The tavern was a long stone house. Outside, a few benches and low tables were set around an oak tree that sprouted through the rain-beaten wooden slats of the ceiling. The knotted trunk was bare, but above the slats the tree flowered.

"Go ahead," Heinrich elbowed Marcos, "tell them what you just told me."

He narrowed his eyes at Heinrich. "Go fuck yourself," he said, or tried to. His tongue, it seemed, had cramped.

"Not a drop of spit in him," Heinrich laughed.

I clapped him on the shoulder. "We'll drain their barrels." The creaking groan from scooting the benches called forth the barmaid. She was a young girl—our age—and she stopped among the beads of the curtain at the sight of our uniforms.

"Well, well, well," Heinrich said. "What do we have here?"

He was teasing her. Heinrich had a type, and she didn't fit it. Even from that distance you saw the unfortunate trace of a mustache.

Heinrich said, "You're not a nun, and we're not reds. No need to be afraid. Venga, preciosa."

She walked with a limp, dragging her right leg to us. She was young, like I said, but I had the sense she was already a mother. There was a woman from my village this had happened to. The fetus had sat on a nerve, forever paralyzing his mother's leg. As the girl approached, a deepening flush mottled her fleshy neck and spread up her cheeks. I had no patience for whatever Heinrich was planning. "Fetch us a bottle of red," I told her. Her shoulders dropped from her ears.

Heinrich turned his hands up to question me, but I ignored him. By the doorway insects crawled over a lightbulb while others riotously knocked against it. Our comandante's body was now a cooling piece of meat. His superiors had had him executed earlier today, despite all he'd done for them. Before his body cooled completely, before the night was through, we'd avenge him, wholly. We wanted his superiors and this ungrateful regime to suffer. I wanted the whole city to mourn. Shooting those six prisoners was like the military coup,

135

this war, the comandante finding me. Everything was now possible. So why were we wasting our time on such a small life like this barmaid's? In Campaspero, I'd been surrounded by similarly small lives. There, the sun fell on us, too, but you'd never think it shined for you.

"When she comes back," Rigoberto said, "I'm going to have her massage my finger." He was stretching it against the table's edge. "Archers used to have that done for them, during Medieval times."

In the next breath, he said, "Goddammit."

The girl's father was bringing us the bottle.

A moment later, the man was kneeling by Rigoberto's side and massaging his trigger finger. Rigoberto grimaced as though the guy was kneading muscle. The man had a crown of unkempt hair. Like the daughter he was saving, he had heavy jowls. He made no eye contact with us.

The wine, it turned out, was undrinkable. Its astringent bite pinched my face and reminded me of the fighting two months ago near Arnedo where the vinegary and dust-covered grapes of that valley were all we had to eat. By evening, the fighting had ultimately quieted—the reds had retreated—and we were relaxing when Federico's head popped, splattering me with hot blood and soft tissue and hard bone. It was the last shot fired. He had taken my seat only a minute before, forcing me to stand, and I had been cursing him for this—doing it even more so after his face disappeared under a smear of reds and greys. We searched the rest of the evening for the gunman. Like the others, I was after revenge, but of a different sort. The gunman had exposed my own stupid fragility. I couldn't stop trembling and we couldn't find him, so with a restless moon above us, we buried Federico where he'd fallen.

The wine returned me to that place. Marcos was having his own difficulty with it. He smacked his lips. His tongue was an adhesive stuck to the roof of his mouth. I dumped my wine on the ground and told the tavern keeper to bring us beer. He rose unsteadily off crackling knees. "I know you don't think we're going to pay," I said. "You found the worst bottle in your cellar, didn't you? Doesn't matter. We're going to pay." He still refused to meet my eyes.

"And fetch your daughter, too," Heinrich said, but the man ignored him, not even flinching at Heinrich's words as the beaded curtains spread around him.

"She's already escaped out the back," Marcos said, his s's lisping like an Andalucían's.

The man carried the mugs to us. They went down easily. We had two more rounds while I waited for someone to approach from the street, to find a purpose for our being there, for the rest of our revenge. The city's heart wouldn't shatter for a dead tavern keeper. No other soul disturbed the salt-tinged air of that street. We were meant to be elsewhere.

"Come," I said, "let's get to the water."

Despite Rigoberto's earlier declaration, he didn't wrestle the keys from Heinrich. Instead, he climbed into the lorry and once more laid out on a bench, using the coils of rope as a pillow. "Wake me when we get there."

So many towns and cities are built on bones. You recognize it immediately. Not San Sebastián. It's split in two by a river, and deep green mountains nestle both halves, bringing them to the ocean. The city belonged here, was loved by all that surrounded it.

The people were Basque. Aside from the fact that they despised our presence and I'd often catch a homicidal glint in their eyes, they were a fine sort. Serious and hardworking and silent. You'd have as much luck coaxing a sentence from a mule.

I'd never given a thought beyond tomorrow, but I coveted this city and was determined to turn grey and fat here. At the same time, there was a heat behind my ears, a frustration, an understanding. Whoever runs the show would never let me call San Sebastián home. The war had liberated me momentarily from my history—rather, the comandante had. We were supposedly fighting for God and country, but neither of those had ever checked in on me in Campaspero. All my life I was convinced I'd been born to suffer from every imaginable form of poverty in a neglected and charmless strip of Spain, but along came the comandante who insisted that I, too, was worthy of glorying in the treasures of creation. And then God and country killed him.

The lorry hopped a corner and Heinrich stomped on the brake pedal. I tensed for a crash. Instead, he and Marcos opened and slammed their doors. I poked my head out. "The plaza," I complained. We'd been here earlier in the evening. "I told you the water."

"I don't remember any taverns there."

"I thought you liked this plaza," Marcos said.

"We've got the lorry. We can wander till we find one." I wanted to drink with the ocean before me. I wanted to feel the terror of that infinite darkness, a handful of meters away. I couldn't swim. I wouldn't bob for half a minute before the waves pulled me down. From out of such a darkness, anything could arrive. In Campaspero, you'd find us marveling at a puddle that lasted three days.

"What do you think they're going to say when they see the lorry's gone?" Marcos asked.

"The six missing prisoners will definitely get them worked up," I said.

"The shovels," Heinrich exclaimed.

"What about them?"

"We forgot them at the cemetery."

"We're starting to seem like amateurs," Marcos said.

Rigoberto was out the lorry bed by then. "Why are we standing around?"

We took seats under the stone arches that faced the plaza—it, too, had me flexing my jaw from resentment. Back home, the plazas were arid and colorless. There, quarry dust swirled like giddy children after a taste of sugar. Meanwhile, an island garden was in the middle of this son of a bitch. The damned thing was woozy with colors—flowers, bushes, a medley of trees, palm trees even, even a little footbridge near a pond where swans floated. Swans! Even their swans had it better than those of us fate had discarded in Campaspero. "I'll be right back," I said.

At night, that pond was like a grotto, but when I stepped up to it I realized I'd left my rifle in the lorry. I studied the swans' long, thin necks as they ignored me. I wasn't sure where I'd have to grab hold to wring them and decided, in the end, it would be too much trouble.

"You make a wish?" Heinrich asked when I returned to the table. There was a beer waiting for me.

"That we'd never heard that song."

I shouldn't have said it. We were doing miserably enough without anyone putting it to words.

"Yes, well."

Rigoberto lifted his glass off the table. "I'll never fight for a better man."

I lit a cigarette and rose my glass. The others did so with theirs.

"He had to know it was a possibility," Marcos said.

I asked, "And all the other sins under the sun?"

Marcos shrugged.

The comandante had often got me wondering: what sort of life could I have gloried in had my father exhibited this much patience and understanding...if he was so invested in my development... were there a man like this to explain the world to me...

That night we'd buried Federico, I couldn't control myself. The tears came on all of a sudden, and it was the comandante who held me in his arms. I didn't need to tell him why. Bullets had avoided me until then. It was the others they felled. I'd somehow convinced myself during those months of fighting this would always remain so. The obvious and terrifying truth, however, was that I, too, would become dust, and I'd never return from that state. That, itself, is no great revelation, but the bullet to Federico's head moved this from the abstract to something distressingly specific. The comandante was rubbing my back. "The courageous are those who carry on regardless," he said. He pulled me away but held me with his gaze. "That's you. I know it." I wanted to become the person he thought I was. Had my father caught me crying, he would have slapped me till I was on my knees.

The following day, somewhere between Castilruiz and Valdeprado we heard a shepherd boy singing. We followed his mountain song to him. His voice was pure and light. With certain notes he'd leap off a cliff's edge and soar. In a different century they would have castrated him. We left his sheep there. We might not have been able to find Federico's murderer, but now we had our own caged bird.

A few nights later, from the comandante's tent, there came his grunts over the boy's trilling gasps. Only one from our company—Ibérico, who earned the nickname on account of his piggish cheeks, flat nose, and knuckle-wide nostrils—tried to pull down the tent and rescue the boy, but we tackled him. We all owed our lives to the comandante. If this is what he wanted, however it might trouble us, why should we interfere? Quickly, though, we became accustomed to the arrangement. Even the boy. The devoted gaze he'd level at the comandante, it felt good that one among us could do it so nakedly.

For several days we joined forces with another company outside Matasejún. After the fighting, where we didn't lose a single man, their comandante stopped outside our comandante's tent. He tilted his head for the rising and desperate and vulnerable sounds within, chuckled to himself, and kept walking. So long as we were winning, all things were permissible.

Then they ordered us up here to crush the rising guerilla insurgency. I'd just returned from the sea and had gathered around with the others to listen to the boy. A colonel passed us and asked about him, what was he doing with our unit, who did he belong to, where were his parents. He was the comandante's lover, we said. His pet. He belonged to us. It seemed the most natural thing. We hadn't lost yet. The general laughed. "And here I thought I'd heard it all." But he registered our sincere expressions. They arrested our comandante that hour. We rushed the prison, not expecting for there to be that many Nationalist soldiers in a conquered city. I was at the front of our group, ripping open my shirt, demanding they shoot me—life without the comandante seemed an impossible prospect in that moment—but Marcos pulled me away. They wouldn't even let us see him a final time. The boy, like us, didn't think to lie. They brought in a doctor to examine him and confirm the particularities, then executed our comandante this morning and ordered that our unit be dissolved. They couldn't trust us together. We would be scattered across the Spanish map, like a poison that had to be diluted. Until then, we were a pen of jackals let out their cages for this, our last night together.

I finished my beer and threw some pesetas on the table. "Let's get to the water."

Rigoberto pushed off the table, scooting his chair back so it scraped the shin of a man turning the corner just then. He swore at us in French. He wore round-rimmed glasses like Trotsky and a mariner's cap. He had scraggly hair along his jawline, a hand rolled cigarette in the corner of his lips. If you'd asked me to draw you a Marxist, I'd have come up with some likeness of him.

Rigoberto bumped his chest as if he understood French. "Go on," he said, "tell that to my face again, rojo."

The Frenchman was disconcertingly untroubled. Despite being unshaven, he wore a nice suit and the polish of his boots welcomed the little light there was. More than likely he worked in intelligence. Our lorry was parked dangling off the curb for all to see. If this man didn't report to work tomorrow morning, we'd be against the wall by evening. I was getting used to the idea of remaining alive. We had to be smart, or at least not suicidal, with our vengeance. Marcos reached for the pistol that was jammed into his waistband, but then thought better of it, seeing it all play out, too. "Venga," I pulled on Rigoberto's sleeve.

The man was demanding our names and regiment number. We were halfway down the block when I turned to see if he was still there. He wasn't. "Hold on," I said and went to the lorry.

Heinrich laughed. "What are you doing with that?"

"Let's go," I said, yanking on my rifle's bolt.

Marcos grabbed my arm. "It'd be our heads," he warned.

"He's going to the Maria Cristina," I said. "Anyone with a metal pinned to their uniform is staying there."

"Ah," Heinrich sang. I was watching myself do it, my mouth, for a moment, going dry. Until only recently, I had no idea this city existed. Had I known about it over a year ago, before the war, I would have been incapable of imagining myself walking with a rifle to one of its most beautiful hotels, fearing no one.

Each hotel window reflected the night and distant streetlamps. The officers had bedded their women, drunk themselves unconscious. This side of the hotel had been shot up from the street fighting last August when we conquered the city, hundreds of divots for the night to burrow into.

I flicked off the safety. The others waited behind me, their presence encouraging me. Even before tonight, God nor country would have allowed me to live here, so why not destroy it all? I filled my chest, filled my lungs, then screamed, "You killed a good man," and let loose. Don't ask me how—I'm usually a decent shot—but I missed every window. I examined the rifle after emptying it. "How in the hell?"

Lights were turning on and Rigoberto tugged me away as silhouettes filled the window frames. There was a pistol shot. A bullet skipped off the sidewalk and thwacked into the building by my waist. Marcos and Heinrich had already turned the block. Rigoberto and I dove into the lorry's bed, Heinrich simultaneously starting the engine and pulling away, the tires spinning frantically, laying down tread behind us. We were leaving a trail of clues.

A few sharp turns later Heinrich slowed and then, from out the lorry's back, there was the ocean at night. "Yes," I said.

It was without texture, though, an impenetrable wall of darkness. As we bounced forward, I didn't feel anything for it. If it was trying to tell me something, the engine spoke over it. We followed a street to the right. The ocean was framed by buildings and the night and shrunk to a rectangle, then a meaningless patch.

Word had gone out in the city. Every tavern had closed so as not to serve us. There wasn't a light burning behind a single window. Not even a flickering streetlamp. Then I thought: it's the ocean, black water. That's how it works at night. It floods the city. We sink into it.

Heinrich jerked us forward with a sudden stop. "I'll be right back," he called, leaving the engine running.

Rigoberto was looking at me, his brow wrinkled.

"I meant to miss," I told him. "I only wanted to startle them."

"I guess," he said, "we have had a bit to drink."

There came the breaking of a window and its thousands of pieces raining to the ground. I peered outside, around the lorry's tarp. Heinrich stepped back out, ducking under the jagged triangles of glass still held by the frame, bottles of wine under his arms. He was in no rush. The sight of it squeezed my heart. Behind the wheel was another thing, but on his feet Heinrich would even amble to the trench for cover. Nothing could prod him to a faster speed. "Here," he said, handing Rigoberto a bottle. He read the labels to find the right one for me. And this was to be my last night with him? There were still things for even Heinrich to teach me. What I wanted to learn was how I could be someone other than me, how I might rescue myself from the life I'd been born to.

He climbed into the cab, and we were off again, the lorry swinging from side to side, just enough so I kept nearly stabbing myself with my knife as I tried pushing the cork down. Rigoberto and I clinked bottles. Half of it ended up down our chins. Heinrich must have been driving with his knees. We climbed a hill, the turns taken inexpertly, the tires skidding off the curb. In the next second we'd be on our backs. I waited for the world to tumble to its side, rather, for it to keep tumbling, but we slowed to a graceful stop.

"About time," Rigoberto said.

I hopped out. "What are we doing back here?"

"We've got to get the shovels."

"Besides," Marcos said, "I need to piss, and I know exactly where I'm going to do it."

It felt like a lifetime had passed since we were last here, but it was probably only a couple hours.

The cemetery was tiered. The tombstones, each taller than any man, all faced the same way: at us. The ascending levels curved inward like a coliseum and the tombstones filled the seats. They were a judgmental audience of ghosts watching us step onto the stage.

If the guerillas hadn't come down from the mountains, we wouldn't have been ordered here and the comandante would still be alive. The war was elsewhere. We should have been at it. Instead, these idiotic gamblers thought they could repel us though their own army had been unable to. We had forced them to dig their graves then stand at the lip of it. One still held the soiled white flag he'd used to surrender with.

We walked now among the large vaults toward the freshly dug earth but slowed for the two shadows ahead of us. One stood near the mound, his head lowered. The other leaned against a tall tombstone. They produced eerie silhouettes. Both were long tendrils.

Phantoms, I thought.

"Graverobbers," Marcos said.

Most knew better—get caught and we'll bury you with them. I'd heard a story recently of a graverobber who unearthed a man still alive, choking on soil, so he had to finish him with the shovel to get his watch. I doubted this. We diligently stripped them of anything valuable. Besides, who would admit to such a thing?

These two weren't graverobbers though. The shovels were exactly where we'd left them.

The man leaning on the tombstone noticed us first. He uncrossed his arms and stiffened to attention. The other lifted his head slowly, meditatively turning to us. Then it made sense. They were priests.

They were praying for the souls of those we'd killed. The shapes were on account of their robes. Ninety-eight times out of a hundred the priests were on our side, no matter the crimes we committed, but here we were crossing paths with the two who weren't.

"You did this," the priest away from the grave hollered.

With that, an electric note thrummed through the four of us and cinched tight. We knew without saying anything, without even catching the others' eyes: this would be our revenge. The city would miss these two. The priests, somehow, understood this, each in their own way. The younger of the two, the one at the grave, lowered his head and sighed. It sounded like a prayer—like, *they know not what they do*—but his eyes sought shadows to disappear into as Rigoberto hurried to the lorry for the ropes.

I got the sense that the priests had had their own complications this evening. They, too, had been pulled along by invisible forces—the younger priest willingly, the older priest barking the whole way. He was coming at us now, pointing a finger. "What are your names? Colonel Modesto will learn of this."

With the butt of his rifle, Marcos swatted the priest, who spun to his knees, clutching his mouth as though to keep his teeth from falling out. Rigoberto was sprinting back, cradling the two ropes, the ends skipping behind him. He tossed one to Heinrich. A watermelon would have slipped through the noose Heinrich tied.

"He's going to fall right out," Marcos said.

"It'll hold," he said, then asked the priest, "Don't you think?" The priest looked up, furious and puzzled, and Heinrich threw the noose around his neck, dragging him to the nearest tree. The priest was able to keep his fingers between the rope and his jugular, trying to free himself, swearing like a madman who knew only a dozen words, the rope tearing into his fingers instead of his neck, while Marcos ran after him to push the fingers down. Marcos had been right, we were amateurs.

145

I should have fired into the air to stop them. That's what the comandante would have done. He would have insisted on a sort of mercy, allowing, if nothing else, the priests to tell their story so they could die having been seen and understood.

But this, this was a chaotic and ugly scene that the young priest tried to flee. Good, I thought. Get away. I was thinking it even as I caught up to him, the air leaving him loudly when we both hit the ground. The priest never once punched me trying to wrestle free. "Shh," I kept saying. "Shh." Finally, he stopped thrashing, and in a bearhug I brought him back, both of us breathing hard, his ribcage just that, a cage that contained something wild within him.

Rigoberto was attempting knots that disappeared when he pulled on them, and the older priest's legs kicked frenziedly with each tug from Marcos and Heinrich that lifted him further off the ground. Nobody was there to intervene. They'd killed the single man who could have stopped us. Rigoberto threw the rope down. "It's these goddamn hands. Like crabs' pincers."

"You've got this," I said to encourage him, emulating our comandante's tone.

The priest sagged slightly in my arms. "I wasted my life," he said to himself or perhaps God, "but I don't deserve this."

"It doesn't matter how you lived. I was coming for you regardless."

"You know," he told me, "this won't save you."

Until that moment, I hadn't questioned whether it would. He was shivering. He shivered as if I'd pulled him from freezing waters, this though his body burned through his robe. He was shivering from that terrifying truth that reveals how suddenly this life and all it holds can be taken from you. It felt good showing it to someone. "You're wrong, Father," I said. "This is the only thing that will."

10

ÁLVARO   CASTRILLO DEL VAL, JANUARY 1938

WHEN I CAME upon the fascist, he was sitting on a log and seemed at peace. Surprisingly, I didn't hate him for this. In fact, since deciding to go through with it, I'd been buoyed by a euphoria I hoped would remain beyond this day, which I intended to be my last.

The fascist was smoking a cigarette or thumbing some pebbles or reciting poetry to the shrubs. I couldn't tell, as his back was to me, and I had time to decide where to place my crosshairs, choosing to shoot the log directly beneath him. If I missed, the bullet would rip into his ass, but I didn't miss, and he jumped, his arms flailing as he fell forward to run. My thinking had been that after passing on this blissful lightness to him, thereby guaranteeing its preservation, I'd stick my rifle butt on the ground and lean over it, pressing the muzzle to the spot between my throat and bottom of my chin. Lately, the headaches had become even more unbearable, same with the incessant high-pitched frequency in my ears I couldn't escape, and the burden and tension of survival. The headaches had begun after the shelling at Sigüenza that had claimed so many of our men. I had thought: what luck, to be so close to death yet to have survived. That night, I was on my hands and knees for the pain. It felt my head would burst from the pressure inside. I started seeing our dead, doing mundane tasks—relacing their boots, picking something from their teeth—but always I'd receive a sidelong glance from them. It was a confident, knowing look. I'd suffer in ways I couldn't yet conceive. Even before the war, I'd come to a ledge and a dark voice within me would whisper *jump*. Not long after the shelling, that voice interrupted most every thought. We are each issued a role in this life. I became convinced there was only one relief from mine. But I couldn't do it with that fascist falling every ten meters, making negligible distance between us.

Unfortunately, the others—my brothers in arms—roused by my rifle shot, rushed to me and took aim. Watching the fascist's desperate and frantic efforts, I understood it was not solely this euphoria he strove to carry forward, but that I had given him his life back and he was now attempting the same for me. If I get away, his pitiable try at flight told me, you can't put the muzzle under your chin. "Come on," I was surprised to hear myself saying. And: "Faster." Our bullets started for him but, as I said, he couldn't go a few meters without tripping, which was likely what kept saving him. Several times he'd tumble in tandem with a rifle shot, and I'd think, with neither sadness nor relief, so that's it, the two of us are done for, at which point he'd crawl forward, each limb out of concert with the other, stumble to get himself upright, and soon skid onto his face once more. Maybe a piece of the log had penetrated his leg. Nothing else explained his difficulty in staying on his feet.

I suppose it would have been easier for one of us to run after him and dig a knife into his back, but who was to guess he'd continue falling as often as he did? I began thinking the others were missing on purpose so as to prolong this comedy, all the way to the horizon if possible. If that was the case, he and I had more in common than I could have imagined—somebody, something, found humor in delaying our end.

Robles bumped me as he went to a knee. He pressed the rifle butt snug to his shoulder, and I saw that this one was it, the line was direct, a tight thread knotted straight from his rifle to the fascist. I held my breath. I waited. But Robles paused and cocked his head slightly to study me in his periphery. He was working the whole thing out—that was my life, too, in the round eyesight of his stock's end.

He still had time to ease his finger against the trigger, nothing had happened to that line, but he lowered his rifle and looked at me directly and nodded, his lips screwing to the left side of his face, an expression that said: vale, let's see, sure maybe he was a murderer of children, but who knows, he might be the one to save us all, let's see. I nodded, too, then I laughed, realizing how foolish I'd been, how I'd been looking at the world through a pinhole these past weeks.

The sky was a muddy sort of steel, the color of water off our hands whenever we found the rare fountain. A few more shots went after the fascist. The bullets wouldn't have been able to do much from that distance. It was like scaring off a wolf. So he got away. And what can I say? I could have drunk the sky. Robles was still nodding, his lips turned down, his thoughts finding my ears: let's see, he kept saying. Let's see.

And I wish it had lasted—this *let's see*, the not knowing how the war would go, the chance it might—finally!—turn in our favor. Hours later, the fascists surprised us, starting their offensive. They were a black twisting cloud of starlings while they shelled us. The only faces I can recall within that deafening intensity were those the shrapnel tore apart, the resigned look in their eyes the moment before it happened. A look that told me they'd always known this would be their end, that none of this came as a surprise, regardless of how they tensed when shrapnel met flesh.

It explained why I was among the few taken prisoner. A ridiculous confidence possessed me—I was not allowed to die. "Don't worry," I whispered to my four fellow prisoners, "we won't be executed but instead put to work, chained to each other, toiling on some project meant to bring forward the fascist's still-born vision."

I was playing my role, and this made the next few days of sleeplessness and starvation a bearable experience. I knew how the rest would go and there was some comfort in that. A diminishing supply, as it so happened.

Soon, the headaches returned, and the world was once more reduced to that ceaseless jaw-clenching high frequency, a ringing that needled the back of my teeth and that refused to take a breath. I wanted out. Thankfully, orders arrived for our captors to move camp. A two-day journey to Valladolid. We prisoners wouldn't be joining them. Unlike the four others, this came as a relief to me. "I was wrong," I told them, perhaps too giddily. "There is no prearranged story. We are in nobody's hands."

But, no, we were dropped off at a prison, which was, in fact, an old monastery in a cleared square of a grove outside Burgos. If not for all the lorries and the bored soldiers smoking dispassionately, you wouldn't have guessed it was a prison. From the outside, that is. There wasn't any fooling yourself after being shoved in. The smell was, at its most basic, festering human filth not even a breeze would touch. Underpinning it was despair, despair at being incapable of forestalling the world's end. Life had stopped for those locked inside. So miserable was it in there the ghosts stayed away.

I felt no solidarity with the prisoners, no sense of community, of having found my people. Instead, I'd press a finger into each ear and open my mouth wide to try to diminish that needlepoint frequency while watching the others move at half-speed, their eyes vacant, and I'd think, more urgently than I ever had before, I've got to get out of here. Each day was worse than the one before it.

But it wasn't as if I could bludgeon myself with the mop we'd occasionally be given. Same went for the paper-thin and dented pail of filthy water. It had unreadable stains on it. Who knows if some had attempted it before, though I doubted it could even split skin.

The opportunity finally presented itself one painfully bright and freezing January day. I was walking unaccompanied down a narrow hallway on the fourth floor and turned into a room where I couldn't smell or see another prisoner. I quickly concluded this was the first time I'd truly been alone since arriving. Meeting the moment, on the opposite wall, was a window, my exit. I remember how the breath I exhaled relaxed my shoulders. Here we were.

I stepped further into the room, to the window, and even the cold air that gusted in when I opened it couldn't tense my muscles. I was at peace. Below, blinding sunlight flared off the hard packed snow. I'd have to dive headfirst to ensure I didn't emerge from the effort a cripple. As if to prod me, the ringing in my ears intensified. Yet, past it, I heard the shifting of floorboards. A prisoner had been sitting in the corner all this while. He was perhaps a year or two younger than me. Judging by the length of his filthy beard, he'd been in here at least three months more than I had. I wondered if he wasn't trying to gather the courage to go through with it himself, but he told me, "You can't give that to them." His voice was flat.

"To who? The guards? Have they installed you here?"

He appeared to consider this then shook his head, the slightest of motions. "I happened in on my own. Like you."

"It was God then."

His was a pitying smile. "I don't think so."

"Whoever it was, I'm not giving them anything but taking it, taking my life back, my control of it."

"By throwing it out the window. You went to the same school as the fascists, did you? They're saving Spain by massacring us all." His words plumed in the cold.

"You don't understand."

He brought a hand up to scratch his chin. He was missing two of his middle fingers. The nubs moved fruitlessly over his skin. "This place," he said of the prison. "Wild thoughts find me here, too." I focused on his maimed hand, the two uneven nubs. I wondered what else he'd lost. I felt as though I'd happened upon a hermit in the woods, social isolation having pulped his mind. "Thoughts about my ancestors," he continued. "People I never met, yet I know they existed because I'm here."

In a kinder world he'd have his room and I'd have mine and neither of us would get in the other's way. "If you don't mind," I said, "I'd like to be alone now."

He ignored me. "And I keep returning to this: I have a duty to them, a duty to persist, to resist. You've heard the fascists, their chants. 'Viva la muerte!' So long as the choice remains ours, we have to choose life."

I tapped the windowsill and glanced out it, squinting for the light I was convinced would silence the ringing and end the headaches. "And if I don't want to?"

"There's a guard in here who's feeding me news from the outside. We've taken Teruel. Teruel!" Not once had I thought of the city, was only vaguely aware of its placement on the map, but for the prisoner's excitement someone could be forgiven for thinking we'd been fighting the year and a half for Teruel. "We're driving them back. Finally. The world can't ignore us now. They'll come rushing to our defense."

"This is a story I no longer care about."

"Interesting you believe we have a choice."

"I," I said, placing all the emphasis on the word I could, "do."

"If you feel that way." He looked past me at the window.

It was like being asked to make love in front of a crowd. I motioned to the door.

He nodded and stood, grimacing as he stretched. "There's a fight ahead of us yet," he said when he straightened.

I turned my hands up. "For what?" Meaning: it's all pointless in the end.

"You know, I feel for them, my ancestors. All their struggles, yet I'm the one who gets to be here to fight against these bastards for the future of the world. And you do, too." I had to give it to him. The conditions of the prison were such that they rid you of every noble and high-minded thought. Difficult to think augustly while your guts seized and the various stenches were like the foulest pair of fingers being shoved down your throat.

"I'm tired of fighting."

"Who couldn't go for a little rest? But that's not the world we find ourselves in."

We now stood face to face. There was an alertness and sharpness in his eyes that got me wondering if I wasn't actually the mad one. "You don't understand what this is like," I tried again, not even convincing myself this time.

"Of course I do." He might as well have pinched my cheek affectionately and patted it. "But I'm not letting it keep me from showing those fachas." He turned for the door, saying, "You and me and our friends, blood is pumping through us still. Just you watch how we'll put it to use." He was now down the hallway. I was certain that if I jumped he'd be standing in the snow with arms cradled to receive me, then I'd really be in trouble. This floor had once been an attic, so you had to crouch to keep your head from scraping against the low ceiling. That and the tight passage of the hallway brought his voice to me. "You'll want to stay alive to see that. I plan to."

11

JOCABED   SANTANDER, APRIL 1938

I HAVE A new name: Sister Jocabed. Mother Superior issued it to me yesterday when I took the veil, her papery eyes hardening from an almost undetectable smile, searching my own for disappointment. I admit I have not yet shed the last of my vanity. Mother Superior knows this, must have seen through the walls to my room, how I'd stand before them as though before a mirror, practicing introductions as another might model a necklace or pair of earrings. "My name is Sister Raquel." "I am the Lord's servant Sister Lucinda." "You can call me Sister Innocente."

Sister Jocabed. Even the mouth must make unpleasant contortions to pronounce it.

My parents attended the ceremony. Before it began, a boy rushed through the sparse crowd outside, reporting that the Nationalists had definitively captured Vinaroz, cutting Catalonia off from the rest of the Republic. My parents didn't seem to react to this news they'd long desired to hear—now the assault on Catalonia could begin, the beginning of the war's end. Out a window in the sacristy, I watched them brush past the boy, his palm open for a tip, and go inside.

During the ceremony, my back was to them as I faced the altar and God, awaiting an absolving light to drown me, but I was aware at all times of my father in the pew, his arms crossed while he flexed his jaw, and my mother, distressed, her eyes downcast, focusing on the rosary beads passing between her fingers. Sister Jocabed, they must have thought, good. Let her suffer more. A lifetime of penance won't suffice.

So what remains? What do I still share with the girl I had been? Only this body that she defiled, that pregnancy scarred, that yearns unexpectedly on occasion for the life it brought into creation—a sudden and tight pulling at the breasts I've yet to learn how to ignore.

"Greetings, dear woman," I attempt, turning my room's inner doorknob to meet the day. "I am here to assist you in the hour of your need. Me? Well, you can call me Sister Jocabed."

I ENTER WITH Mother Superior, as quiet as her shadow, trying not to display any hesitancy. Thankfully, this room bears no relation to the one I delivered in. None of the smells here—lye and chlorine—return me to that bed, to my fear, to the otherworldly pains I struggled to welcome and endure. The walls, like those of my bedroom, are unadorned, save for the simple, wooden crucifix above the door.

The woman on the bed breathes hard through a contraction. Her thick black hair pillows a pale face, on which unmoving droplets of cold sweat bead. None of this appears to surprise her. This is not her first—she's biting down against the contraction knowing exactly where the wave of pain will take her. I had been but a child, terrified of the moment I was in and those that would follow.

The doctor, too, bears no resemblance to the one who assisted me. My doctor was young, as skinny as an ascetic. Any lines in his face had been drawn from compassion. He was the lone person I had encountered in months who seemed to have forgiven me.

This doctor is unshaven, likely for the boils under his chin. Smaller pustules cluster tightly along his collar. He has a drinker's red-veined nose. He drapes the sheet over the woman's legs and reports to Mother Superior, "Hours to go yet."

If Mother Superior acknowledges this in any way, I miss it. Instead, she's eyeing the woman as a combatant might. The woman glares at the ceiling, breathing easier, released momentarily from the pain. I am drawn to her. I want to ask if she needs anything, how I might accept some of her burden, but I know to keep away.

The doctor nods as he passes us. We turn to leave, as well, when the woman says, her voice weak, "Wait." Her eyes are locked to mine. "Can you stay?" She lifts her hand to me as though I were by her side and could take it. "Pray with me."

Mother Superior's face is often unreadable, but from around her habit I detect the slightest smile crinkling the corner of her lips. She nods, permitting me, and closes the door behind her.

The woman's hand is back on the bed. I hold it in mine. "Shall we pray to Saint Anne?" I ask. This is who I had prayed to, the patron saint of unwed mothers and women in labor. I had been grateful such a saint existed.

I flinch at the strength in her hand as she squeezes mine. I expect it's another contraction and start to assure her all is fine. Instead, she pins me with her gaze. "You're a novitiate, right?" She lifts her chin at my white veil. "Have you taken your vows yet?"

"No," I say, as an apology, "that's still two years away. I received my veil only yesterday."

The woman's shoulders relax, so does her grip. "Good." Whatever weight had been upon her chest has lifted. "Now listen. You have to get me out of here."

"Of course. It won't be too long."

"No. This hospital. I can't be here. I should be at Mandecillo. Do you know the writer Simón Arrosarena?"

I shake my head.

"No matter. Go to Café Central. Tell the first bartender you see they have me here. They'll get word to Simón."

"There's not enough time. Besides, why would you leave this hospital for another? The baby is coming any hour."

"It was that goddamn taxi driver," she says, more to herself or the ceiling than to me. "That facha."

I cough. I haven't heard anyone use that word in almost a year. "Yes, well, I'm sure he was terrified you would give birth in his backseat."

"One hand clutched the wheel and the other was ready to grab me if I attempted to jump out."

I try assuring her. "Our doctors are just as qualified as those at Mandecillo."

"You have to get me out of here."

I look about the room for a method. "It's beyond me. I wouldn't know how. I'm sorry."

She rests her head on the pillow, her eyes shut tight, now from frustration rather than pain. "I'm supposed to be at Mandecillo," she pleads.

"Don't worry. I promise I'll be here with you."

I FIND MOTHER Superior in the infirmary. During my period of aspirancy I was here often, changing the dressing from men's wounds, spooning soup into the mouths of amputees, reading correspondence to the blinded and illiterate, penning the responses they'd dictate. Every age has its own particular sins, so receives its own particular punishments. Some of these soldiers admitted to their errors, their role in contributing to this national nightmare, and together we prayed for their forgiveness. I would then fetch the priest so that they might be absolved. Others were not yet ready to acknowledge their complicity. They prayed, instead, for time to turn itself back. Not so they could tear the uniforms from their bodies, throw down their arms, and accept the National Movement, but to stand several meters to the left or the right when the bomb struck.

One spiteful soldier laughed every time I approached. An explosion had deformed the left half of his body. His foot was now a digit-less club, his hand not much better, his left eye the white of milk and surrounded by raw pink flesh. "My brothers will be coming for me soon. Don't worry, Sister. I won't forget your kindness. For the others, especially that old bitch," his good eye narrowed in the direction of Mother Superior, "I'll have my revenge." His laugh got him choking, so I sponged water into his mouth. His tongue moved around it as though he could already taste what he coveted for the others.

Mother Superior had me report on each exchange with the wounded. I was convinced I was confirming for her what she already knew. Nevertheless, I omitted the spiteful soldier's profanity toward her. "And he didn't say anything else?" she asked.

I hesitated. "He called you a name."

"Which?"

"I dare not repeat it."

"Go ahead, my child. Doing so allows you to serve the Lord's program for Spain."

By that afternoon, the soldier was gone.

Now, she straightens from the bedside of an amputee.

He's young, about my age, and, like me, for the rest of his mortal days he'll be reminded of the gravest mistake of his life. He watches Mother Superior warily and timidly. Even the younger ones, I've noticed, quickly recognize that they should fear her.

Her back is to me as she continues down the aisles of beds. From her posture I understand I am to approach her. Before I'm at her side, she asks, "Did you pray with her, Sister Jocabed?"

There arrives a glorious string of seconds where I believe she has mistaken me for someone else, then recall, my shoulders suddenly heavy, that, no, I am Sister Jocabed.

"I did not."

Her habit bobs slightly. She knew this already. "And what did she ask of you?"

There's no point in obfuscating. "She wanted me to get her to Mandecillo."

From around the habit, a tight smile. "Is she ill, Mother Superior?"

"Her soul, yes. An infection that will spread to her child if we let it."

"Is there any saving them?"

"The only redemption is in death."

I STAND IN the expectant mother's doorway. From there, I can't detect the malady Mother Superior spoke of. The contractions seize her with greater frequency. With each, she issues an animal groan followed by quick intakes of air, her fingers clawing into the bed. After a contraction releases her, she turns and notices me.

"Did you deliver the message?"

"I walk from the convent to the hospital. This is now the entirety of my world. Perhaps I can try to get word to your family," I offer. "Do you have any here in Santander?"

She shakes her head. "I'm from Bilbao."

"And the father?"

"A soldier. The last hope we have." I know better than to ask which side he's on. I approach her bed. I want to tell her about my own experience giving birth so as to reassure her. Deliverance, or at least the path to it, came when I imagined my condition from the saints' perspective. For me, the contractions were towering and blinding, but for our martyrs I was a speck in need of compassion, a speck alongside millions of other specks crying out for them just then. How easy it is to convince ourselves that we are situated at the center of the world, and, from this position, how easy it is to be led astray. What had I accomplished that made me worthy of the saints' attention? Absolutely and undeniably nothing. With more pain and torment, though, more sacrifice—not solely in that moment but in the days left to me—I might become worthy.

"It wasn't too long ago I was in your place," I tell her.

She tilts her head back, lets out an exasperated breath. "Of course."

"I, too, was terrified. The wild things I was envisioning. But, I discovered, it all has to do with perspective. If I imagined—"

She cuts me off. "What happened to your baby?" The words scramble out as one, another contraction gripping her.

"I had sinned. Gravely. Mortally. The child is where she belongs, with a mother and a father who have not fallen."

"Goddammit," she says. If anything, it should be directed at the pain, but the tone is one of irritation for what I'm telling her. Either way, I continue.

"And I have been allowed to offer my penance, for both her eternal soul and mine."

I am uncertain how much she heard through the contraction. Eventually, she closes her eyes and her shoulders relax. I feel her cool breath of relief. She asks, "You've heard of Have You Seen?" Even in my semi-cloistered life I have. She is the mother of a slain red and is searching the Spanish map, haunting it, for her lost son. Anyone she approaches she asks *Have you seen my son?* "That will be us if we let the fascists win: driven mad by our quest to find our stolen children."

"But I know where my daughter is, exactly where she should be, with a virtuous set of parents." I try continuing my earlier point. "The kingdom of God is everlasting. We find ourselves here in the fleeting cities of men, where the ground can and will vanish underneath us. God, eternal judgment, this is all we can rely on. Take for example the young man who I had—"

"Listen," she says, "Sister..."

I bite my bottom lip, sigh. "Jocabed. Sister Jocabed."

She closes her eyes and massages her forehead, speaks into her wrist, "No me jodas. Jocabed, you put your daughter in the river to drown."

"Don't say that. Saint Jocabed, Moses' mother, made the ultimate sacrifice. The same with our Lord God. Without them, it is impossible to imagine the course of human history."

She's not impressed. "I did, too. My son and daughter. After Bilbao fell." It takes real effort for her to get ahold of her pain. Not a contraction but one building inside her. At last, she continues. "I placed them on a ship. For England. Anything to escape the fascists. Every day I regret it. Every day is one more they've taken from my children and me."

"What are their names?"

She doesn't answer for a while but finally, likely determining it can't bring any harm to them, says, "Nerea and Jon."

I pat her hand. "This will all be over shortly. Then you'll see Nerea and Jon again."

"We're losing the world that would have allowed for that." She removes her hand, locks me in place again with her eyes. "A world where you and your daughter could be reunited."

Because I know Mother Superior will ask me about this exchange, because I am certain she already knows of it, that this, too, is likely a test, I gather what strength I have to break from the woman's glare and stand. "That is a sinful world. I'll let the doctor know your contractions are less than two minutes apart."

She grips the bed and groans. The chords of her neck show. Through clenched teeth and heavy breaths, she manages: "It's your fault then." She grunts, sings a high-pitched warbly note.

"What?"

"Your goddamned head in the sand. You're complicit in—" Then the pain claims her. I wait for it to subside. When it does, she covers her face with her hands, breathes into them. She massages her scalp and seems to have forgotten I'm there. At last, she turns to me. "You had one responsibility as a mother, to your child. One responsibility to the future. To the rest of us. And you gave it all to the fascists. This is what you'll be judged for."

I brush my hands on my habit and try keeping any emotion from my voice. "I'll inform the doctor about your contractions."

THE COURTYARD SMELLS of lye and castile. Sister Sofia stands before a large, metal tub, pushing and twisting the dolly while Sister Emma feeds the first item of clothing through the wringer. She's huffing as she spins the crank. I take my position to receive it on the other end then pin it—a beige shirt with shadowy stains at the armpits—on the line. While I was with the woman, the hospital received six new patients. They're guerrillas who sought to disturb the peace Franco's National Movement has brought to Santander.

I expect Sister Emma to admonish me for being late. She detests me because, in another life, I knew carnal sin. Both she and Sister Sofia are in their forties, but Sister Emma appears much older. Her hair is a uniform grey, her face scarred by hundreds of colorless divots that she must have scratched at as a tormented child. During my discernment, I tried, daily, to please her but could never turn her to my favor. I convinced myself I'd be denied into their order on account of her dissenting vote. Even well into my postulancy I felt it was only a matter of time before she knocked on my door to cheerily inform me I'd been dismissed. I'm surprised to find myself wishing she had. That woman. Her certainty. It unnerves me. I blink hard and shake my head.

Instead of reprimanding me, Sister Emma asks, "So how is the writer?"

"She's a writer?" Writers have existed, just as the saints have, but it is difficult for me to imagine they might currently be among us. Every book I've read in the past two years has been a religious text. Before then, had I read this woman's work? "What's her name?"

"Erlea."

The name means nothing to me. "A nom de plume, surely."

"She hid behind it well in Bilbao. Since being flushed out, it can no longer serve her." The comment feels pointed, as if she is talking about me somehow, as if there's a secret of mine she remains determined to discover.

"Is she a communist?" I ask. "Socialist? An anarchist?"

Sister Emma's shrug simultaneously indicates *who knows* and *what does it matter.*

I hang the next shirt. "She's in a very agitated state."

"Most expectant mothers are," Sister Emma says. "Were you not?"

I let it pass. "She's concerned about being here."

Sisters Sofia and Emma share a look. Sister Sofia says, "That's because we finally have her, their great propogandist."

A political writer? And she judged me? What about her responsibility to her own children? Was she not being careless with their safety?

162

Sister Emma huffs as she puts her weight into the next twist of the dolly. I'm about to ask if she would like to switch positions but am stopped when she says, "Here, such mothers give birth to dead babies."

"That isn't so." I've walked past our cramped nursery several times when it was loud with life.

Sister Emma bends to pull another piece of clothing from the wash. "Still so much to learn."

I turn to Sister Sofia for clarification.

"It's an ailment of our epoch," she says, as though it is a matter far beyond our control, a physical law of nature. Sister Sofia has always been sweet to me. She once told me I reminded her of a doll she had as a child. However, she's increasingly becoming possessed by Sister Emma's cynicism, the cynicism of this hospital, these times. I refuse to let them change me as they have her.

"Is there nothing we can do for her? For the child?"

"Of course," Sister Emma says, the hint of a derisive laugh in her voice, though she is unsmiling. "That is our very purpose. We are here to rescue the children."

NOTHING—NOT THE room, the doctor, the smells, the light through the window, the sounds the woman makes—none of it resembles my childbirth, yet I am returned there. I gave birth in the middle of the night. There was but one light in the room, a harsh naked bulb, a sort of flare that the doctor kept shifting away from to not cast a shadow between my legs. At times it would halo him. More often he eclipsed it entirely, then shifted, momentarily blinding me. Regardless, I'd seen no other kind eyes in months, since I'd first started showing and it had become impossible to hide my sin.

There is no such compassion among the others in this room for the writer. I offer her my hand, which she takes and immediately and unconsciously attempts to break. Good, I think, let me receive your pain.

It is nightmarish, how long delivery lasts, how there is no exit, how the only way to get to the end is to go through it. I pray the Hail Mary, quote Isaiah 40:29-31 and Psalm 40:1. I pray to Saint Anne, Saint Raymond Nonnatus, and, reluctantly, Saint Jocabed. The woman loses control of her bowels—the same had happened for me—and the room fills with the heat of excrement. It is one more smell among many—mineral-rich blood, a tangy earthiness, the salt in her sweat, the curdled breath that lifts her screams, and the chlorine across the floor.

When her grip slackens, I shake my numbed hand then offer it again. She is becoming too weak. The doctor gently feels about her stomach, as though divining a message with his fingertips. This delicacy stops when he identifies what he was looking for. He digs his fingers into her stomach, and she folds forward in pain, coughing and hacking, sick dribbling down her chin with each retch. Finally, she collapses backwards. This is it, I think, she will die from exhaustion and blood loss, but he glances between her legs and becomes excited, yells at her to push, to cough and vomit again, angrily demands it. He tries to jam fingers in her mouth to gag her but she knocks them away, and her screaming suddenly sharpens and rises, so if the baby is crying after its first sip of oxygen, I can't hear it. The next movements are rushed. The doctor clamps and cuts the umbilical cord and Sister Emma comes forward with a freshly starched towel, swaddling the newborn. I see a limp and wrinkled leg coated in vernix and clumpy blood, then Sister Emma turns to the door. "No," the woman says as the door closes behind Sister Emma. I listen for a wail, but the woman screams again, delivering the placenta.

I'M SEARCHING THE empty nursery when Mother Superior enters. Her arms are at her sides. They might as well be crossed over her chest as my father's had been when I took the veil.

With Mother Superior, there is no hiding my intentions. "What was it?" I ask. She doesn't answer. "Boy? A girl?"

"It is a sin, and like all sins, Sister Jocabed, it is now on us to redeem it."

"But how?" I don't ask this as a challenge. I desperately want to know what powers we possess, what miracles can we perform through the Lord's love. "Where is the baby?"

"You already know."

She watches me, waiting for me to put it together. Her face is expressionless. Somehow, amidst the dry creases of her eyes, I believe I see the answer. It comes as a memory, a vision of the couple who adopted my child: a handsome, correct couple who God and nature had nevertheless challenged.

"Why not tell her the truth?" I ask. "Think of what it would spare her. Nobody needed to lie to me."

"Because you recognized your sin. She is lost. She refuses to be brought back. Without the least indecision she would damn her child as she has damned herself. This we cannot allow."

It isn't fair, but I dare not say it. And I need not. Thinking it is enough. Mother Superior's head tilts slightly, having read my eyes. "Very well," she says, "you will be the one to tell her."

"Tell her what?"

"The truth. Her child, to her, is dead."

THE WOMAN IS sleeping when I peek into her room. Her face is drawn, skin pale. This is the last sense of peace she'll experience for a very long time. I dare not disturb it. Slowly, I back down the hallway, watching her all the while.

I imagine myself sitting next to that bed and am certain I won't be capable of lying to her, though I'll have to. I must prove not only through conviction but deed that I am worthy of the redemption Mother Superior and the order are offering. Then, I hear Mother Superior's voice in my head. *You recognized your sin.* For the first time, I am not convinced my daughter was a sin. At least not one as unpardonable as this hospital.

Before I turn the corner, I stop backpedaling. Mother Superior already knows I won't manage to convince this woman her child is dead. She expects me to fail. She wants me to. I should present the woman with the conceit, one she will immediately see through. Assuming she isn't arrested, she'll leave here denying it and continue to do so. It will rot her. This is what Mother Superior wants. Ultimately, should the woman ever again wish for a calm in her soul, she will have to submit to this lie and the regime that girds it.

If I continue watching the writer, she'll wake. My look is not a comforting one. With the thoughts roiling behind my eyes, it can't be. Nevertheless, before I turn the corner for the infirmary, I pledge to myself I will not allow Mother Superior this victory. More difficult yet will be keeping this resolve from her. I try convincing myself I can do it. Doubt worms inside me.

THE INFIRMARY IS down the hall and through another set of doors. There, I find our newest patients. Sister Sofia stands over one writhing in his bed. Ruby red blood soaks the otherwise copper-colored gauze around the man's neck—how have they not managed to stop his bleeding?—yet the more intense pain, I intuit, is in his side. A bullet is lodged there, or perhaps he fell and cracked several ribs. Whatever it is, he stomps in the bed, attempting a position that will allow him to brace himself against the pain. Impatiently, Sister Sofia waits for him to still so she can change his dressing. She need only take the man's hand for this to occur but remains dispassionately above him.

In the west corner of the room is another of our new patients. He lies in bed, studying the ceiling, hands folded together at his waist. His right leg is bound and elevated. Freckles of blood pepper the wrapping. I've found myself envious of these sorts of patients, envious of the intensity in their eyes. I'm certain they can see past the ceiling. Having been grazed by death provides them with a new perspective. What is before us is thin material, and having survived the bullet or the bomb or another man's fury, they have been shown the seam, what anticipates us on the other side.

The stool squeaks as I take the seat by his bed. He is a young man, maybe a year or two older than me. He wears a checkered shirt. Matted and weather-beaten wool the color of straw lines his collar. His is a campesino's hard and leathered face, skin that the sun has already seared and blistered and now there is nothing else that can be done to it. He doesn't shift his eyes to me.

Nobody has washed him. Dirt and grime pack every fingernail. Dried blood cracks along the underside of his right palm, where he must have swiped at a wound. I clear my throat, yet still he watches the ceiling.

"What do you see?" I ask him.

He takes a deep breath, hoping it will fortify him, but his voice cracks. "When will they kill me?"

I try to admonish him while keeping my voice light. "Why would you say such a thing?"

"Because that is what happens here."

"You truly believe the regime would dedicate resources to your convalescence if that was their intention?"

"I won't confess, and I won't convert."

"Who is demanding that you must?"

Only now does he turn to me, judging my eyes against the conviction in my voice. He squints into my right, then my left. I gather all my energy to hold my smile and remain entirely in this moment, to not let him see what I've seen.

"There," I say. "Didn't I tell you?" I pat his shoulder. "I'll be right back."

I fetch a bucket and fill it with lukewarm and soapy water. None of the rags are clean. When I return, he is looking at the ceiling, just the ceiling, nothing beyond it. I soak the rag and wring it over the bucket. The sound soothes him. "'Because that is what happens here,'" I chuckle, as though it was the end of a joke. He allows me to take his hand.

I try imagining what ideas the writer put to the page, if they are among those that provided this young man with the courage to leave home, to sacrifice his earthly existence. I search for such fortitude within me but instead catch a cry in my throat. It is my daughter's name, the one I had given her. Almudena, after my grandmother. I try swallowing it. Her new parents had it changed. I was never told what it was.

Tonight, I will walk from the hospital past the convent. I will walk the thin dusty road to town, past the shuttered market, lowering my head as I cross the plaza and into the narrowing, snaking streets and keep it down so nobody can see under my habit until I reach Café Central, where I will approach the first bartender I see.

In the hospital room, I am gentle as I wash the top of the young man's hand, get between his fingers, clean away the blood and grime. His breaths deepen. Moisture returns to his eyes. I feel his body relaxing. "There," I say, "you see. All you needed was a little faith."

12

THE PRISONERS MET with the priest one by one in the cell's far corner. Chipped, colorless paint covered the stone wall behind them. They remained patient, kneeling with him when their time came and bowing their heads to his as they offered their final confessions. I was supposed to keep them from speaking in Basque but pretended not to hear those that did. Antonio dug something from under a fingernail. He held it to his nose then flicked it to the ground. The priest was making the sign of the cross on the second to last prisoner's brow and the man thanked him and returned to the bench along the wall, rotating his hands as though he had just begun to understand something important about them.

The priest waited on his knees. The final prisoner continued gripping the bars. "This floor is hard, Father." He spoke in Spanish to the expectant silence. "You might as well be comfortable with the little time we have left."

"I will stay here regardless," the priest said. "You can come to me if you wish."

The prisoner glanced over his shoulder in the priest's direction then turned back and took me in with his eyes, beginning at my worn boots, the brown pants with off-color patches at the knees from the fighting in Soria, up to the other patch at my side where a bullet along the Duero barely missed flesh. He stopped at the embroidered design of the Falangist's red yoke and arrows on my left shirt pocket. My uniform hadn't received a tear since I started here. The war continued, in Madrid and Catalonia, yet here I was. He glared at the design. "No, Father," the prisoner said, "I don't have a thing to confess, but if you want to kneel there then so be it. Unlike these fachas, I've never told anybody how they should live, so if it's souls you're out to save then maybe these two fascist shits will give you their confessions while you can still take them."

Antonio smirked at this.

"When their time finds them," the priest said, "they, too, will have to account for their actions. This moment is yours."

The prisoner faced the priest. Black hairs curled over his soiled collar. His neck was red, the skin agitated. "I don't need forgiveness, Father. Not from you, not from God, and," he said, eyeing us again, "not from these fascists who'll soon have the blood of at least two innocent men on their hands." He grasped the prison bars and spat at me but missed. "I see you don't believe me. Don't. Sleep better that way. But you know this priest is innocent. His blood won't wash off so easily."

The priest had surprised me. Others were moved by his gesture, but, like them, I suspected it was only that. While I didn't know the numbers, I assumed we had executed dozens if not hundreds of men who had families. Surely, the priest was aware of this. Yet when he learned last night that the one-eyed Navarran who received his death sentence—the same who had failed in his escape the night before—was married with five children, he asked to be shot in his place. Isidro, the prisoner attempting the escape with the one-eyed Navarran, had kept running. What prompted the escape was Isidro learning from a new transfer that Nationalists had hung his brother in San Sebastián's cemetery. This planted a dark, vengeful look in him. Before, I imagined a day when we'd get a drink together and swap stories from this war. But following the news of his brother's execution, I never turned my back on him.

He used to always be at my side, asking if I'd managed to find anything new from Erlea. Nothing, I'd tell him. Not a word since Santander fell. I'd also provide him with updates on the war—your side has us under siege in Teruel, a blizzard has frozen all guns and men, it's the coldest winter in a generation, the main task in Teruel has become amputating frostbitten limbs, your side has taken the city, we might be fighting this war for years to come, and what do you know but we wrenched Teruel back. "What did your side's resistance get them," I had asked him, "other than a hundred thousand men prematurely buried?" He shrugged. "Wanting our votes to mean something counts as resistance, does it?" He considered the walls of this former monastery and told me, "You know, Manuel, what I hate almost as much as your ideology is how you're taking these days from us." We're provided a certain number at birth. I liked how much Isidro thought about his. I corrected him, "I don't have an ideology." I pointed to the guards. "At least not theirs." He clapped my shoulder, a sympathetic gesture. "I'm not sure if I should pity you or be terrified of you." When he finally ran, I was in the women's wing. I can't be certain I would have aimed for him. The others might as well not have. All their bullets somehow missed. Here, the priest was offering the one-eyed Navarran a chance at a similar miracle.

Colonel Luna oversaw the executions at San Pedro de Cardeña, the monastery that the Carlists had converted into this prison before unifying with our National Movement. I felt as he did on the matter: the priest didn't interfere when the Navarran tried to escape, so he had no right to now. Antonio had been by my side as the priest made his request, and he winked at me. "This place is accomplishing its goal," he whispered. "The prisoners are beginning to envy the dead." And though twice I'd stood guard while they scrubbed clean the mess one of their own had caused by jumping from a high window, I knew that the priest wasn't looking for a way out. Despite the executions, he continued to perform Mass in the square and, I wasn't sure how, managed to find a way to shave. Even this morning he accomplished it. The others had muted brown and graying facial hair that covered sores and scaly skin.

Our placement in the room at the time of the priest's request— Colonel Luna at his desk, the priest before it, Antonio and me near the door—returned me to the days when the nuns would cart me to

Father Muñoz's study. Sitting at his desk, Muñoz would read a Bible passage, something unmemorable that washed over me. From a drawer in his desk he'd then pull a well-worn pine paddle, and I'd have to put my hands on the desk as he walked behind me and planted his feet. Always at that moment, I would close my eyes tight and wish for the sound of the door opening and my father's voice—though all I could remember of it by then was its low register—calling out, halting Muñoz and carrying me away, but then the air moved quickly around the paddle again and again with each feverish grunt.

One morning, when I was fourteen, Father Muñoz awoke with half his face paralyzed, hanging loose from bone. That put an end to the beatings. A heart attack finished the job a year later. We had to sing at his service. The words meant nothing to me. I didn't even bother mouthing them.

By then I no longer expected my father to come for me, or my mother—for her to appear as suddenly as she had vanished from our lives. Others waited for their parents, but I'd understood how foolish this was, that adults could feel no obligation to their responsibilities, to their word.

So, earlier this morning, I wasn't surprised when Colonel Luna reversed his decision and accepted the priest's request to stand in for the execution. I watched the priest now. He didn't relieve himself of the irritation the boils on his neck no doubt caused him but knelt perfectly still in the corner of the cell, waiting.

"Do you hear me?" the prisoner at the bars told Antonio and me. "You will be stained by this."

"Cállate," I shouted.

"Yeah," Antonio said. He folded his arms, pressing his rifle to his chest, and rested his head against the wall behind him. He closed his eyes. "You're starting to give me a headache."

My outburst didn't startle the prisoner. Instead, he tried shaking the bars. They wouldn't even rattle. "I won't keep quiet," he said, preparing to continue but stopped. His eyes shifted. The skin at the corners crinkled in a way I often saw here among those who clung desperately to some misguided hope. "I won't say another word," he told me. "I promise. Just please do me this favor: call for Javier Molina. He will—" I turned away. Molina was a Major General. I couldn't have secured an appointment to speak with his horse. "*Facha*," the prisoner shouted, and this time his spit hit the mark. Antonio watched me. I breathed out slowly and wiped the saliva from my neck and onto my pant leg then resumed my position, rifle crooked in my arm. Antonio leaned once more on the wall. "Call for him," the prisoner yelled. I buried my sigh. Blood drained from his fingers as he squeezed the rusting bars. This cell had been built less than a year ago but already the iron showed signs of corrosion. There was another like it on the eastern end of the monastery—otherwise, the prisoners were kept in what had been tool closets or wine cellars or pantries or any other space that could be locked. Often, there were dozens to a room. Less than half could lie down at any given time. Walking past them it was impossible to avoid the hot reek of human filth. We used to hold Mass every Sunday in the chapel. Two months ago, we partitioned it and pushed in schoolteachers, former mayors, leftists, card-carrying union members, those who had been denounced by their neighbors, anybody who waved a flag other than ours. And if they had run off, their parents or grown children were arrested in their place.

"He will vouch for me," the prisoner yelled, trying again. The saliva was thick and white around his lips, the lines in his forehead inked by grime. He raised his voice. It was reedy and weak, cracking from dehydration. "I'll keep shouting until somebody listens to me."

Only a few of the prisoners paid him any attention. Most sat in their own worlds a great distance from this one. They stared into their laps or at the opposite wall and scratched themselves. The priest, meanwhile, remained on his knees.

"Call on him!"

"*Chaval*," an older man on the bench told him. The threads of his sweater were torn and heavily frayed to show bare skin. "You went too high. Why not ask for El Generalísimo himself?" Several of the prisoners smiled. "Or Mola's ghost?"

Antonio opened his eyes to add: "You should've gone with someone who's gotten shit on their boots recently. Then one of us might have believed you."

The prisoner checked to see if he had at least convinced me. I didn't want him at those bars. I switched my rifle to my other arm. "You'd have bought yourself a few days."

He curled his upper lip. "Dejaste tus cojones dentro de tu madre."

"I'm forgetful like that."

Normally, of the duties here, I preferred this one. Elsewhere in the prison, I watched while my fellow guards made sport of the spiritless and pitiful. I'd feel time passing for us and think: this isn't why I fought. I had volunteered, yes, to escape the orphanage walls. Another two months would pass before the church, who'd aligned itself squarely with the coup, used who it had to help fortify the military's ranks. By then I was fighting not for God or Spain but for my fellow soldiers, the man to the right of me, to my left, for those who, unlike all I'd known before, offered their lives so the rest of us could live. They were my brothers, and despite how they disparaged the enemy, I was certain that in the neighboring village where tomorrow the fight would resume there were soldiers—be they Republicans, Marxists, socialists, or anarchists—who knew that they, too, had to be worthy of those they'd lost.

And, here, before the prisoners were marched to the wall, we returned to that same contract of the battlefield. Faced with their final moments, the prisoners, no matter the severity of their crimes, became exemplary Spaniards. They didn't bargain but sat resigned with what remained, just as I would have, and this helped us forget for the time those bars that separated us. Occasionally, I'd share my cigarettes with them and promise to deliver any final letters they may have written, and they would thank me for this. However, the prisoner at the bars soured my compassion.

Down where the hallway intersected with another, three women on their hands and knees scrubbed the tiles with soapy rags while two guards I didn't recognize stood near them. One of the women had large breasts that moved from side to side under her shirt as she scrubbed. Stooped over, her shirt was open at the neck, and I squinted to see if the Falangist brand of the yoke and arrows had been seared onto her chest, above her heart, knowing what it would mean had it been there. One of the guards tapped her backside with his foot and instructed her to get more soap on her rag. She swung at him, yelling—her accent was Basque—while he and the other guard chuckled. Behind me, several prisoners *tsk*ed. "That's Raúl Guruzeta's wife," one said to another. Two large wet circles on her shirt spread from her nipples. The fabric clung to her. She looked in my direction, not at me but past me, and I wondered if the infant that had been taken from her—surely with the nuns now—would keep her from sitting on a window's ledge or ultimately push her off it. I saw the hard corner of Father Muñoz's desk. I wished I could tell her the child would be fine, sensed she needed this assurance from someone, but I couldn't provide it.

A door closed and from the shadows emerged the large frame of another guard I didn't recognize. Against his bulk, his rifle seemed a toy replica. Father del Valle, the prison's chaplain, shuffled a few steps behind, never taking his feet completely off the ground. His arms were folded atop his balloon of a belly. Approaching the women, the guard eyed their backsides and gave the others a knowing smile. Father del Valle didn't acknowledge the scene as he walked through the soapy water they tried to work into the tiles.

"Good day, soldados," Father del Valle said to Antonio and me. We both nodded. "How many of these men," he asked us, as he did before each execution, "seek absolution and wish for the Lord's forgiveness?"

"They've already confessed, Father," I said.

"To whom?"

I motioned with my chin to the priest kneeling in the cell's far corner, certain Father del Valle knew of the priest's arrangement with Colonel Luna. If he did, it didn't impress him.

"Soldado, a rojo priest is first and foremost a rojo," Father del Valle said. "A stain on the Spanish cloth." He spoke slowly, chewing on each word as though it was tucked into his cheeks. "Did these condemned admit to their sins, their allegiance to Marxism, to fighting against those defenders of religion, property, and the family? Have they finally acknowledged that it was we and not they who fought for all that is good?"

"Forgive me, Father," I said. "From where I stood I couldn't hear them."

"I can assure you," he said, his voice rising, "that if you did you would not have heard a word of this sort of talk. Augustine speaks of the opposed forces of good and evil. And through the Lord's mercy, we can say with unwavering certainty which force we have preserved." He addressed the prisoners. "But you men are not Spaniards. You are hardly even men, and so that we can purify and redeem Spain's soul it has been decreed you must be put to death." He cleared his throat. "However, though you may die today, you still have an opportunity to live forever by His side if, that is, you confess to your crimes against His Spanish state, if you plead for absolution."

None of the prisoners lifted their eyes. A few went for the lice troubling their scalps. Only the priest and the soldier at the bars gave any indication they'd been listening.

"This is your last chance," he said. "Seek the Lord's forgiveness and unburden yourselves of the sins you committed so that tonight you may sit at His side." He waited. A prisoner coughed. "Do not make me put your names in my book. I will visit the family of each man whose name ends up there." This line used to work but somehow word must have spread that it was just talk. "Very well," he said, "your names have been written."

The prisoner at the bars glanced back at the others then stepped in front of Father del Valle.

"Are you prepared to repent?"

"I will, Father, for anything you wish me to, but you must help get me out. Please. I don't belong here."

"How can you receive the Lord's forgiveness if you don't admit to your guilt?" Father del Valle laughed and opened his arms. "I've never heard such a thing. How could I forgive you?"

"Father, I am innocent. I never fought against the Falangists. I have been wrongfully—"

Father del Valle brushed away the rest of the prisoner's speech. "I'm not concerned why you're in here. I don't know why, specifically, anyone is in here, nor am I interested in learning why. What I know is you are behind these bars because you are guilty. If you were not, the courts that are guided by the grace of the word would not have sentenced you to death. I ask though: if you did not take up arms against the National Movement, did you do so against the liberals who resisted us? I am sure you did not. Your lack of participation aided those determined to demolish the moral order. Yet you tell me you are innocent?" He snorted and joined his hands together. "As far as you and the others are concerned," he breathed heavily, "I represent the Lord's grace. You may seek it from me if you wish."

At this, something broke within the prisoner. He lowered his head. His shoulders quaked and he began to hiccup, then openly sobbed. "I just want to go home," he said.

This disgusted me, as it did Father del Valle. If you level your rifle at another then you must accept with the same resolve the bullet that comes for you.

"Pull yourself together, chico," Father del Valle told the prisoner. "The pig goes to the knife wailing. We're supposed to be better than that. At the very least, you were born in Spain. Prove that now by showing some cojones."

Despite the prisoner's dehydration, his nose began to run. Finally, he wiped at it with the back of his hand. "Please. I have a family." He didn't wear a wedding band, but this could have been taken from him.

"You should have thought of them before this moment." Father del Valle glanced around the cell.

"But I didn't do anything wrong."

"Venga, you coward," he yelled, ending the conversation, "you and I both know that is not true." Finished with the prisoner, he studied the priest on his knees. At first he only watched him, then his eyes narrowed. I had expected he would address him with an obligatory respect. Instead, he seemed contemptuous. "You put on airs, but I know," he said. "I know."

Antonio winked at me. Though he'd been timid on the battlefield, he was often smug like this, now that we were winning. It required little motivation back then to stand across from someone with a rifle to defend your land. The real struggle those days, the test of who you were, was risking your life to take away what belonged to someone else. Antonio often failed.

"I know," Father del Valle continued, "because your actions have exposed you. The fact you have survived this long is evidence of the liberalism that infects you. You'd sacrifice yourself for a rojo and yet you did nothing to stop those in nearby Palencia who dragged the priest into the street and nailed him to an electricity pole."

This was an exaggeration. I was in Palencia six months ago when we passed the town hall and stopped at the odd shadow on the ground. Above the door someone had fastened, upside down, a disfigured statue of the crucified Christ, no doubt taken from the town's pillaged church—the priest who'd once held court there had run off before the people had their way with it. The inverted statue produced a disturbing effect, as though, with his open arms, Christ was reaching out to grab me to take me away from the war. I wasn't alone in being bothered by it. At camp, others found ways to bring it up throughout the night. The next day, the details had changed. The statue had been pegged to an electricity pole at the town's entrance, a warning to all who might enter. Not long afterwards, the statue became an unidentified priest, and this was how the papers explained our day in Palencia.

"What's happened to the churches and our clergy is an unfortunate excess, I admit," the priest said. The prisoners watched him. "Worse yet is that the people feel they are finishing what you and the others began."

"No wonder you're in there with them," Father del Valle scoffed. Then, to the others: "God help you if you're following this one." Father del Valle feigned little interest in continuing with the priest. He twisted slightly to speak to the large guard. "A rojo if you ever lay eyes upon one. Get a good look while he's still around. He manages to qualify the violence our clergy suffered and refuses to recognize our struggle as the loftiest of crusades. A crusade in which divine intervention on our side is evident."

"And yet," the priest said, waving his arm before him to account for this prison, the motion meant, as well, to attract Father del Valle's attention, "you must do all this. To prove you are right, you must kill."

"Kill?" Father del Valle asked as though he had not heard him. "Kill? Yes, but not men, rojo. No, not men. We are killing a social system, and national regeneration can only come about by offing those who," he said, bouncing his eyebrows in the direction of the prisoner at the bars, "make a pact with evil."

"Were your vows so different from mine?" the priest asked. "Can you be so certain? I fear you've gotten lost somewhere between the mystery and the doubt."

Father del Valle chuckled. "When you're charged with orders from God, there can be no doubt." He took in the prisoners. "Your families will be disappointed with all of you. Though you do not repent, may the Lord in his immeasurable compassion and grace find something within you of value." He met my eyes and shook his head.

"Padre," I said. Antonio did the same. The guard led the way, and I moved to peer over his wide shoulders, but the women were no longer there.

The priests' exchange energized the prisoner at the bars. I tightened my grip on my rifle. He shouted behind me, his voice high. "A guilty man gets pardoned so a priest can be shot in his place, and me, an innocent, someone who has never harmed another, must die. Is this justice?" Father del Valle kept walking. The prisoner wiped his nose again, breathing in quickly. It was a repulsive sound. "Why is the guilty man free and I'm in here?" The guard and Father del Valle turned a corner and were gone. "Answer me you maricón piece of shit."

I made a quick motion with the butt of my rifle and felt the crunch of bone as he grunted and fell back. His hands were at his face and blood rushed between his fingers. I pulled my rifle through the bars. "That's not for the priest's sake," I said. "I'm just tired of listening to you." Antonio stepped closer. I immediately regretted my action. He wouldn't leave him alone now.

He squatted so he was near eye-level with the prisoner. "Look at me, you coward." With the tip of his rifle he tapped the prisoner's foot. The priest hung his head and sighed. I'd ruined his work. He had such little time left, and I'd fucked it up. "Hombre," Antonio said, "look at me." Over his hands the prisoner met Antonio's eyes. "When the moment comes—and it will, let me assure you of that—I will be the one across from you, and it will be this rifle, this one that should have broken your nose long ago, that will put a bullet into you. Get used to the idea. There's no one here that's going to save you. Once you understand that, the rest will be easier to swallow."

The priest put one foot on the ground then rose and went to the fallen prisoner and laid his hands on his shoulders but the prisoner jerked from under the priest's touch. Still holding his nose, he got to his feet and walked to the corner, standing like a sulking child. I opened the cell door and the others tensed. I held my pack of cigarettes to the priest. He kept his head down. My chest felt hollow. "I know the men will appreciate it," he said. His lips were dry and cracked. I avoided the prisoner in the corner. The others each pulled a cigarette from the pack, and as I lit a match for the last man, Colonel Luna and three guards entered the hallway. The soles of their boots smacked against the wet tiles. "The moment has arrived," Colonel Luna called. He walked with a slight limp and was as scarred and dimpled as the moon whose name he shared.

The match burned to my fingers before I could wave it out. The prisoner tucked the cigarette behind his scabbed ear, as if to save for later, but I lit another match. "Venga," I said. He pulled on the cigarette until the tip caught fire. With his eyes he thanked me. I nodded then stepped outside.

"Single file, caballeros," Colonel Luna said. "Yours isn't the only business I have to attend to today."

The prisoners smoked deeply and began to form a line, some looking ahead, others down at their feet. The priest held his hands at his front as though he were about to receive communion. I was struck by his repose, the certainty in his eyes. The man in back of him seemed to receive some strength from this, for he ground out his cigarette and stood with his hands at his front, his chest expanding with air, and the next did the same. I feared that the prisoner in the corner would resist, that he would remain there defiantly, bringing some censure upon Antonio and myself. Just when I thought we would have to force him out, he wiped his hands on his pants, breathed in deeply, and turned and walked to the line's end, not acknowledging any of us. Colonel Luna grinned, noting the blood. He studied the men but stopped at the priest. "This is your last chance, Father. You have acted commendably and you have earned our respect, but there are many days beyond this one for you, and there are many prisoners that will die who are more deserving than a one-eyed rojo. Say the word, and I'll call for him."

"If I cannot give my life for those I am meant to lead," the priest said, "then I cannot give them anything. I am at complete peace, Major. I thank you for obliging me."

"Very well," Colonel Luna said. "Like Pontius I wash my hands of this affair." He said to the ceiling, "I tried," then began down the hallway. One soldier followed him, and the others fell into step. The prisoner with the bleeding nose snarled at us, "I should have killed more of you when I had the chance."

"Yes," Antonio said, "you should have."

We brought up the rear, and Antonio pantomimed sticking the bleeding soldier in the ass with his rifle's tip. I did nothing to encourage him but continued admiring the priest, his composure. Even in battle I'm not sure I saw such resolve. Entering the intersection of hallways, the tiles were bone white.

"Did you know they were supposed to be that color?" I asked Antonio.

"What?" He rested the rifle on his shoulder.

"Forget it." Our boots smeared prints onto them. We banked left toward the doors that opened to the courtyard. The gray light of day filtered through the windows. A man too old to be wearing the uniform of a private held the door for us while he offered the fascist salute with his free hand. Above him, cobwebs netted the bust of Saint Sphinx, so named because the statue's nose had been chipped off and none of us knew who he was.

Outside, hundreds of male prisoners were in rows that reached to the southern wall. Gray clouds rolled over us, just above the spires. Some of the prisoners stood on their toes to see if they recognized any of the sentenced men. Most avoided looking at the eight trudging to the pockmarked northern end. Beige bricks framed the windows around the courtyard. I scanned the women's wing though I'd yet to ever spot a silhouette present when we conducted this business. The prisoner who bled from his nose set his feet and glared at those before him. We used to tie their hands together, and I wondered if we should have done so for this one. Off to the side, Father del Valle ignored the condemned, making a comment to the large guard who nodded out of obligation.

"These prisoners," Colonel Luna shouted, "are standing here for their crimes against the Spanish state, for rebelling and resisting our noble vision, for supporting the Bolshevik cause, the Jewish-Masonic cause, for being puppets to those who wish to return us to the Dark Ages of our national history. This is why they will now die. And this is why many of you will be standing here soon. However, there is one among them whose sole crime—serving as your chaplain—does not merit such a severe punishment, so I ask one of you to show the courage you've been lacking these last several years by taking his place." The men lowered their heads—some squinted at the dull bellies of the clouds. They were not getting in the way of what the priest desired. "I assure you," Colonel Luna said, "many of you will soon find yourselves against this wall. Take control of fate so this priest can live. Make your death worth something." He waited. Nobody came forward. "Cowards," he chuckled. "I knew it would go this way. None of you have surprised me. I hope you're all fed to our firing squad so you don't have to face anybody outside these walls." He scanned what faces he could. "Very well, let us end this." The large guard left Father del Valle. Antonio and I organized ourselves with the others. "I want the one with the bloody nose," Antonio said to Terejo, a Madrileño with a sharp aim for Adam's apples. The prisoner didn't acknowledge this exchange. In the day's bleak light, the blood was black around his mouth. Only he and the priest had one of us before them.

"Manuelito," Colonel Luna said to me, "come here."

"Yes, señor," I said, clicking my heels. He eyed the rifle in my hand.

"How does that shoot?"

"Straight, sir. It's never failed me."

"I don't like the look of it."

"I'm sorry, sir."

"Don't be, soldado. We're the ones at fault for issuing it to you." The soldier at his side, a skinny boy who couldn't have been any older than fifteen and was likely a relation of the Major's, handed him a rifle as though he anticipated the exchange. "Use this from here on out," Colonel Luna said. "I don't want anything to go wrong. Take García's place before the priest. Have him join Chucho in front of the one that resembles a rat."

I tried not to show any emotion but knew I failed. "Yes, sir."

"Courage, Manuelito." He clapped me on the shoulder. The mutilated skin that was his left ear moved as his lips pulled back. Returning to the line, I cursed him under my breath. The courtyard tiles were sticky with the grime of human matter. "He wants you to take the rat with Chucho," I told García, nodding at the soldier with the odd mustache. Something passed over García, the muscles in his face relaxed. I focused on my boots, on the soot that covered them. I tried not to, but I was drawn to meet the priest's eyes. He smiled softly and nodded and I knew what he expected of me, that I must do this, that he forgave me, yet I had to blink furiously to keep myself composed.

"Ready!" Colonel Luna shouted. I peered down my barrel's end. The priest's hands remained folded over the other at the front of his waist. "Aim!" His chest rose and fell. I was breathing in time with him. I aimed for the crucifix that I imagined under his shirt. "Fire!" I pulled my trigger with the others but thunder roared as if I had fired in a custodian's closet. Smoke erupted from the chamber and at once clouded my vision. The shock made me cower. I knew I held onto the rifle but was certain something irrevocable had happened to my hands. Under a high-pitched whistle, there was a distant commotion. The smoke was stinging my eyes and I pressed a forearm to them. I lifted my head, my sight was blurred, and saw the priest standing before me looking at first at his body, patting his torso, then at the men on the ground. To his right, one writhed and clutched his stomach and screamed while his guts seeped out. Another at the far edge was hunched over on his hands and knees, hacking, choking on something deep within him when suddenly bile and blood gushed from his mouth. He fell flat and went still. A chalky ribbon continued to stream from my rifle, and I understood that it had only been packed with gunpowder. The skinny boy must have done it and loaded too much. I was lucky it hadn't exploded in my hands. Colonel Luna began to snicker. Soon, he couldn't control his laughter. The boy joined him. Father del Valle smiled in a satisfied way, a wrong having been righted. Antonio was as confused as I had been. The prisoner before him lay crumpled on the ground, his left arm twisted awkwardly underneath him.

Colonel Luna bent forward with laughter. We waited for him. "What did—" he started but had to gather himself, wiping at his eyes. "What did you take us for, Father? Did you really think we'd kill a priest so a rojo Navarran, some half of a man, could live out the rest of his days?" His voice sounded tinny and far away. The laughter reduced him to a fit of coughs. When it finally ended, he cleared his throat and tugged on the bottom of his jacket. He signaled and from a door several guards led the one-eyed Navarran who limped from the bullet in his leg and was pale and dazed in the grey light.

Colonel Luna turned to the prisoners. "Let this be a lesson to you," he shouted. "There is no hope here. Nothing can save you from the judgment that awaits." He thumbed open the holster on his belt and passed his Mauser pistol to the skinny boy. Those in the front stepped back but the boy walked to the one tearing at the ground with his feet, his intestines in his hands. He was crying in anguish and didn't see the boy approach. Antonio was trying to assure me. "That priest would be there, too, had they given you a bullet." The words rippled with echoes.

I pretended not to hear him and looked up again at the windows along the women's wing, then the low sky over us all. The sound of the Mauser seized Antonio's shoulders but was a faint thud for me.

"Antonio, Manuel," Luna said, flicking two fingers in the priest's direction. "He has served his sentence. Escort the good priest to the gate." At the far left, a group of our men guarded the heavy steel door while two pushed it open. There was a square of gray light. Should the prisoners have rushed it we would not have been able to stop them all. Yet no one made a motion. Their side was losing. After a year and a half of war, the northern map was now entirely ours. A blackened wasteland, but ours. Outside was no different than the prison. I imagined that Isidro, the soldier who had escaped, was as fucked as the rest of us in here. Where could he have run to where we wouldn't be? Was there such a place? Not in Spain, I was convinced. Not for what we'd done to it and keep doing to one another.

Antonio had a hand on the priest's arm. He chuckled. "What luck, no, padre?" The blood was bright red and watery as we stepped through it. "A minute ago you wouldn't have thought you'd still be here, but, mire, usted, here we are." The priest didn't seem to understand the bodies on the ground or the Navarran who was pushed now against the wall. I couldn't bring myself to put a hand on him while we guided him out.

The week before, Antonio and I led a man to the wall in this manner. He was a socialist. Despite these beliefs, he had owned a tungsten mine. He inherited the mine and the Socialist Party card from his father. His politics and his business ran side-by-side like the wheels of a hearse and never touched. We knew he hadn't visited harm on anybody. It was just bad luck. He seemed, in a way, not to be bothered by it, as if it was a business transaction that didn't favor him but there would be more to come. Upon seeing the wall, he bent his knees and tried to dig his heels into the encrusted tiles and only then did I have to grab him to pull him forward. It reminded me of my father, him squeezing my arm, tugging me as I resisted, his jaw clenched, vision set far ahead while the orphanage walls grew large before us. After the socialist, I felt like hell. The next morning I approached Luna's door to put in a request for transfer but, standing before it, sensed this would place me on the other side of the prison bars, so I turned away before knocking.

As with the socialist, the weight of the others' eyes was on me while we crossed the courtyard. I worried my composure would break. There was a single shot. The Navarran. Antonio kept chuckling. "Coño, qué suerte." In my periphery I saw him shaking his head. "No, padre?" The priest didn't respond. What was there to say? They would just be words.

My boots peeled from the ground with each step. I raised my head as we approached the open door. In the distance and through the mist, a grove.

"What was that?" Antonio asked, but neither the priest nor I had said anything.

13

ÁLVARO   LOS RÁBANOS, MAY 1938

THE BOY SHOULD be in a robe ringing altar bells or chasing a tattered and dust-covered ball through an equally ragged plaza or searching in a mirror for his first whisker, but somebody's given him a uniform and a rifle and the idea he belongs here with us, this disparate orphaned platoon of Republicans, trade unionists, and those without a party membership card but who despise fascists just as intensely as the rest of us. We're little better than a maquis and are on the road to Catalonia, determined to beat our enemy there, to keep them out, force them back. The white poplars creak and sigh—a haunting language—while the campfire's flames dance in the boy's agitated eyes. He pinches the nub of a cigarette. A few of his teeth have already rotted, they're black and splintered. Through the poplars is the moon. It casts a silver light upon their thin and groaning tops, and, as if somebody elbowed him to explain his presence among us, the boy begins:

"My father didn't run. The fascists surrounded the village. He changed from his suit so we could bury him in it, kissed my mother, told me and my two younger brothers we were now the men of the house, then stood by the door, smoking, waiting for their lorry. It startled the fascists, how, with his shoulders back, he stepped out to meet them. Several must have hoped for a fight. One grabbed me by the arm. I stiffened my spine, too. Another said, 'Leave him, he's only a child.' When they pulled away that's when my mother collapsed, like she'd been struck behind the knees. She was crying, screaming something, but I was already out the door for the gravel pit. That's where they'd taken the other group a few days earlier. A soldier was posted as a sentry on the road. I didn't have time to go around him, so I nodded and wished him a pleasant evening. He was too confused to respond. Their smartest don't guard the roads. The second I was in the shadows I was sprinting again. They'd parked by the pit's edge. The fascists stood before the headlights, passing around bottles. My father was seated closest to the tailgate, tied like the others, wrists to his ankles, his ears at his knees. When he saw me, he shook his head and chuckled, an expression like *so this was the best my seed could produce.* The fascists, they glanced back occasionally, but the headlights were in their eyes. I unbound my father and helped him free the others. 'Now go,' he told me. I tried to say it was no use, that a guard had seen me. 'I'm joining the fight,' I started. He smacked me, a quick soundless pop on the lips. 'Go,' he shouted as a whisper. To the men he said, 'We give him a minute, then we run.' From a distance, I watched my father and the others escape. I followed them through the night. They were going to reunite with Manolo's brigade along the Arroyo de San Juan. The birds could have told you the platoon had recently regrouped along the bent elbow of that river. Each stone between Carrascal del Río and Valle de Tabladillo knew it. Clouds took the shape of an arrow every few hours and pointed to their camp. So, through the trees, I counted the lorries of fascists as they barreled past. Countries have sent fewer to conquer foreign lands. By the time I reached the river, it was almost over. Only my father and another remained. That soldier hadn't counted his bullets properly. He was rolling fallen comrades off their weapons, pushing the muzzles to his head, but they'd all been emptied. He was determined to rob the fascists of the pleasure. Finally, he palmed a large stone. As for my father, the fascists encircled him, tightening notch by notch like a garrote, until he was out of bullets. They took their time with him. Time I had to get closer, from one tree to the next. I saw each of them clearly." The boy examines the last of his cigarette, tries to pull smoke from it but draws nothing so flicks it into the fire. "Should they get scarred, grow a beard, lose half their face to a bomb, I'd still recognize them."

There will be no end to this thing. That's the bitter brew. The boy's going to live long enough to sire a few sons who will watch helplessly as fascists drag him toward a lorry, and on and on it will go.

Isidro—the second newest in our section—passes the boy a crumpled pack of cigarettes. We captured five bone-thin Nationalists the other day. Isidro pressed his barrel under each of their chins, demanding they give him information about San Sebastián—which regiments serve there, who authorizes the executions, do they know anyone who participated in them, had they, who hung the priests in the cemetery, who killed his brother, and where's Erlea, what's become of her? Like so many of us, Isidro's discomposed by the mania that haunts him. But what to do about it? If I knew, I'd be a rich man. None of us stopped him as he went from prisoner to prisoner, his spittle striking their bloodless faces. By the time he got to the fifth, I wasn't certain he wouldn't shoot him out of frustration. Nor was the Nationalist. The man had gone days without a sip of water, yet he pissed himself.

The war had, at some point, torn two fingers from Isidro's left hand. But eight remain. You only need a thumb and finger to squeeze a trigger. Many yet for him still to lose. And, afterwards, you might think it would fall to our disembodied limbs to go at the others', carrying on our noble fight, but, no—I saw early this morning, the stars still out, how it ends.

In the dream, a bullet caught me, clean through the neck. My last thought was, *so long I've been waiting for you, I thought you'd never show*. Then I was above my body, watching it curl like a fetus and sink into the earth. My skin melted away, then my organs. I was bones joining with the bones of our ancestors, and together we coiled and became a ladder that twisted amidst a starless space, and from the infinite depths of the darkness beyond I didn't feel God necessarily but judgment. We were fucked. We were terribly, irrevocably fucked. I awoke with a start, grabbed hold of my fleeing breath, my careering heart, then searched for a comfortable position to fall back asleep. What else was there to do? The lions long ago locked and loaded their rifles while the lambs have nothing stockpiled. Arm in arm, we go marching to the end.

14

AÑON DE MONCAYO, JUNE 1938

DAVID AND MARCO, my two youngest, walk into the forest and return with wounded animals, branches that resemble people, leaves in the perfect shape of a star, colorful rocks for which they invent fantastical stories. If we're lucky, Pedro, who turns fifteen next week, will consider them childish and simply ridicule them. More often, he'll snap the branches, crumple the leaves in his fist, throw the rocks as far as he can, and should the animal die, I worry that David and Marco question if their older brother isn't partly responsible, if there isn't a lesson they're meant to learn.

Today, though, David and Marco enter the forest and return with a soldier.

OR—I THINK he's a soldier. He wears no uniform but flame-bathed clothes soiled by dark, indefinable stains. Textures that make me swallow hard. He's likely out of rations and starving. Whatever fight he survived, it must have been several days from here. After two years, the war has finally discovered this pocket of the Spanish map.

The soldier's rifle is strapped across his chest. It troubles him not to grip it in his hands, one of which is badly wounded.

Our house sits alone in the woods. My husband built it: my wedding gift. He doesn't trust me, so I had supposed this—more than a desire to live amid nature—was why he moved us so far from others: nobody would have an opportunity to steal me away. Later,

I assumed it was because he didn't trust himself. Far from the village, he'd be far from drink. Now, though, I'm convinced he knew all along he would beat me and didn't want the villagers to lay eyes upon my bruises.

The soldier frowns at my black eye, my split lip, the fingerprint marks along my neck. I set my needles down to receive him. He had approached the clearing seeking help, but seeing my bruises his posture stiffens. So that's the order of things—a battle-torched soldier sunken-eyed from hunger should pity me. He slides the rifle so he can quickly sling it off his shoulder, glances at David and Marco. They wail when my husband is atop me as though they're the ones receiving his fists. But afterwards, with their father gone, you've never seen two happier boys. They live for the respite. The soldier considers the lightness in their step, their unburdened shoulders, how this picture might come together.

"No need to be afraid," I tell him, perhaps foolishly. My voice is raspy. Will be for several days yet. It was only yesterday my husband returned from the village reeking from drink. Increasingly, a more common occurrence, ever since the fascists severed Catalonia from the rest of Spain two months ago. When Vinaroz fell and all of Aragon with it, not once did we hear a muted thud of an explosion. No rifle reports. No puffs of smoke. Nothing. Even this patch of sky above didn't interest the fascists. The moon seemed closer than Vinaroz. You wouldn't have guessed it from my husband. He behaved like a hunted man, as though he was the main prize the fascists sought, as though the world now expected him to keep them from Catalonia, as though the world had ever expected anything of him. "Come in. We have a soup over the fire. Some clean clothes, too." Where there's one soldier, there are bound to be others. Something is set to begin.

MY BOYS SIT near him as he hunches over his bowl. Even Pedro.

What is it like, they want to know. The war. How exciting? How dangerous? What pulled him into it? Where is he from? Did the fascists destroy his home?

"Nothing's ever happened in my village. You could drop a thousand shells onto it and not one would detonate." Despite what he's telling them, he says it playfully, even a touch tenderly. The hard, apprehensive edges of his countenance are rounding the more time he spends with us.

Have you killed anyone? What happened to your clothes? To your hand?

I shush and scold them, but he smiles away my concern and answers, "I've been given the opportunity to stand up for what I believe in." His eyes are bright mossy green. The way the skin crinkles at their corners when he smiles, it's like a beckoning finger. He's probably ten years younger than me. Probably closer in age to Pedro.

"Our father is a soldier," Pedro says, staking some ground. His shoulders aren't pulled back. For his tone, they might as well be.

The soldier returns to his soup, face relaxed, but I see the question he's asking himself: if her husband is away, who has done this to her? "Which regiment is he with?" he asks Pedro. "Maybe we've crossed paths."

"He's a Freemason."

"And the regiment?"

"He fights with the Freemasons," Pedro says, angrily this time.

The soldier understands: the child will perceive each question as a challenge.

"Brave that he should give himself for such a noble cause."

David and Marco smile at this. Pedro only nods, setting his jaw as his father does—lips pursed, chin out ahead of the rest of his face, each tooth below battling those up top. When his father was younger, someone must have convinced him such an expression radiated seriousness, even danger. To me, it always made him look powerless—the squeaky bark of a small dog—and, at the start, I loved him for it. But that was a long time ago.

"Will you be staying the night?" Marco asks. Most questions he shouts, and this one's no different.

David joins in. "Will you?" He grabs the soldier's knee when he asks it. He is a tactile boy, always with a hand on one of us, as though being the middle child requires him to bridge Pedro and Marco.

The soldier laughs through his nostrils. A gentle smile, no menace behind it. "The fight's still out there," he says to my two youngest. "I just have to find it."

"It will be there tomorrow," I say. I'm doing this for my boys, I tell myself. They need to see—even Pedro, especially Pedro—that there are other ways for a man to be. "You won't last but an afternoon off that soup. Stay the night. We'll send you off with a full stomach."

PEDRO IGNORES HIM. Through his impotent fury, he wants us all to do the same. David and Marco notice this, but they're too excited by the presence of a guest to bend to Pedro. I watch how freely they move about the soldier when they realize they need not predict his next mood and movement. It breaks my heart that half a day passed before they truly relaxed.

David takes his hand. Marco doesn't hesitate holding the wounded one. Together, they weave around and enter the thickening trees with him. Their father often yells at Marco to collect the viscera of the animal he's skinning, *with a fist, not your fingertips!* He's still a gentle boy and doesn't understand why he can't remain so. Yet, as they disappear into the forest, the nubs of the soldier's hands over Marco's, I see no hesitation in my youngest.

Later, the boys sit near the house and direct the soldier as he attempts to whittle a dog from a chunk of wood. It's Culito they're trying to recreate. The mixed breed we once had, so named because of its disproportionately large backside. My husband had brought him home as a puppy two years ago. *I need to know you're safe when I'm not here.* But then he threw open the door drunk one night and the dog wouldn't stop barking for what he was doing to us.

David and Marco bounce the figurine about the dirt, tilt it so it urinates an imaginary stream on one tree after another. Culito had a system. He would awake determined to empty his bladder onto every tree that encircled the house. He was a patient and diligent gardener—little here, little there, what's the rush.

"Thank you," the soldier tells me. We're standing side by side. I feel the heat off his body, a body that's trying to learn again how to relax. "I hadn't realized how much I needed this."

"David and Marco, too."

"It feels so familiar. Like it's out of a dream or a memory." He says it tentatively. "The next time I blink, you'll disappear."

"If only."

He faces me. "Will your husband return soon?"

There's a flurry above us, a rush of feathers, a dance between two birds right before they come together. We both lower our heads.

"Wherever he goes after his drunken nights, he's gone for days." When he does repentantly return home, it isn't until my bruises have turned a ghostly blue. You could fool yourself they were never there, or at least never that bad.

"Is he really a Freemason?"

"He carries the card because there's no other way to get paid for a job around here, and he needs money to drink."

"Haven't you tried running off?" The birds are not being quick about their business. Pine needles drift down between us.

"It's my husband's greatest obsession that I'll pack what I can and take the boys."

"Why don't you?"

"I'd be sentencing us to death."

THAT NIGHT, WE make a fire outside. It's David and Marco's idea. Together, they and the soldier gather large stones to border the pit. In the shape of Culito's rear, David insists. Pedro remains near the house, sulking, while his brothers laugh for what they create.

Around the fire we eat soup and chew on strips of meat their father dried. Pedro is sure to tell the soldier so. He says it as though the man has taken food off his father's plate. "He must be a great hunter," the soldier says.

"He is." To all our ears, it sounds like a threat.

"The seasoning is impressive, too."

"I don't like you wearing his clothes."

"Pedro," I say, admonishing him.

"When he returns," the soldier says, "please express my gratitude."

"I'll let him know you were here."

The fire leaps about Pedro's eyes, then he shifts and they go black.

"Perhaps," I say to the soldier, "you can share a story with us. My father used to require it of his guests. Your grandfather," I tell the boys, "had a bad leg and an even worse pair of lungs. But also a desire to see the world. Everyone in the village knew, if a stranger was passing through, point them to Justicio Vallarte's door. He'd travel through their stories."

"Is that how you met Papa?" Marco asks.

"No. Your father was always just there. So," I say to the soldier now, "what's happening beyond the trees?"

"A story from out there?" He's scratching his chin with his wounded hand, searching the treetops. "I'd have to change every ending."

"About your home then."

"That I can do." He repositions himself on the log, sets down his bowl. Before he starts, he palms his mouth to catch a sneeze. I'm touched by this courtesy. My husband cackles like the schoolyard's menace for how we jump and tense when he sneezes. "Like Marco, I'm the youngest of three boys. The difference in age is the same, as well. Once, at this exact time in our lives, when I was nine and Xabier was ten and Aitor fourteen, the three of us stole a boat.

197

Somebody had seen a whale, and I convinced my brothers this was our moment. We each had a knife no bigger than—David, hold out your pointer finger. Well, slightly bigger than that. The plan was: hunt the whale, get rich off its meat. A good plan, I'd say. Turns out sailing isn't as easy as the old fishermen make it look."

David asks, "So what happened?"

"Something my village talks about to this day. We managed—"

He stops, turns to peer into the impenetrable night. I'm about to ask what he's heard, when over the crackling of the fire I suddenly hear it, too. Voices and the snapping of branches. At least a dozen men not trying to hide their approach. The soldier says to me, "Nobody knows I'm alive."

I keep my voice calm for my boys' sake. "In their bedroom you'll find a half-made chair. Behind it is a loose panel in the wall. My husband hides his bottles there. It'll be tight." He drags his foot about where he sat and takes his bowl with him. I whisper to my boys, though it is specifically for Pedro's sake, "Those are the fascists out there. Just be respectful. If they enter the house and find your father's papers, they'll hunt him. But they won't go in there, will they? Because we're not going to give them any reason to."

The men must see or smell the fire. One by one their voices drop and others shout lowly for them to quiet. There's the quick slide of rifle bolts, bullets shucking into chambers. "If we remain calm," I say, "they will, too."

From out of the forest's darkness comes a gruff voice, a command. "Who's out there?"

"Me and my sons," I call.

Movement in the night, then the fire's faint glow slips over the fascists' shapes. They've fanned out, more than twenty of them. Each bends their knees as a predator on the hunt, their rifles against their shoulders. A few lower their weapons when they see that my sons are only children. The officer in the middle, the one with the gruff voice, asks, "Who's in the house?" To his men he orders, "Aim at the windows."

"Feel free to search it."

"And we won't find your husband cowering under a bed."

"He's in someone's bed, but not mine."

Now they see my bruises. I'd forgotten about them this past hour.

"Your husband do that to you?"

"Does it bother you he did?"

The officer's lips curl into a derisive smile—another woman who's yet to learn her place. "How does it work here? The man needs a little break so makes sure nobody's tempted to run off with you while he's gone?"

"Ask him when you get to town. Look for the one who's filled himself to the brim."

It feels good speaking this openly about my husband before his sons, but Pedro's chin is out in front of his face again.

The officer pays this no attention. He studies the house, squints at the windows. "It's tilted."

"And that he built sober."

He levels a grocer's eye on my boys. To Pedro he says, "We'll be back in a few years for you." He then signals to the others—a sideways jerk of his head—and they blend into the forest once more. The four of us maintain a steady watch on the night as though the fascists might yet leap from it. When I'm certain they've gone, I reach over and squeeze Pedro's knee but he slaps my hand away. "You did so well," I tell them. Marco is smiling at the praise, shakily. His lips are determined to turn down. "It's over," I assure them. Their father's been yelling at the walls about fascists for over two years, since before the war began. "After all this worrying, and for what?"

DAVID AND MARCO want the soldier to sleep between them. He assures them he will, but the excitement of the day has exhausted them, even Pedro, so they're asleep while the soldier and I sit at the lopsided dining table passing back and forth a dust-covered bottle of neglected grain alcohol. We haven't touched flame to candle should the fascists return.

"I knew I was putting you at risk."

"No more than is typical for us."

He rubs down a splintered divot of the table's edge. It's probably the drink, but I'm focusing on his hands as though they provide an answer. But to what? Long dormant parts of my body tingle their response. He says, "I can remain here until your husband returns."

"Don't."

"I'll leave my rifle then. Hidden away should things ever get too bad."

"You're going to need it."

"Our side has more rifles than men now."

"My husband knows every corner of this forest. He gives a second glance when a leaf's out of place. Besides, I've had every opportunity to poison him. I'm incapable of it."

"How can you be so resigned?"

"Maybe before—while my father lived and Pedro was a kinder child—I could have run off. Too late now. He'd kill us if I tried."

He's shaking his head. In disbelief, perhaps disappointment.

"You'll see," I say. "Live long enough and life empties you out so you're only a vessel for others."

"And not for hope?"

"I have hope. I hope my boys don't become my husband. That they don't make the mistakes I did."

The soldier passes me the bottle. I put my hand over his. With my thumb I stroke the uneven nubs of his missing fingers. The slightest tensing in his muscles carry into his hand. "It's been so long since I've been touched with any tenderness," I tell him. "I've forgotten how that feels."

"I can't give that to you. I'm sorry."

"A wound?" There are, I think, other things we can do. Still with my hand on his, I scoot closer until my leg presses against his. That slight change in warmth moves through me. But when I find his eyes in the dark, I see pity in them.

"I've promised myself to another," he says. For my sake, he adds, "Otherwise…"

I stop him. "There's no need." I let go of his hand but remain where I am. Out the window, the fire's embers are a pure red against the black. With each breath they fade. "What's she like?"

"Mariana?"

I nod.

"She's a fighter." He probably means nothing by it. I feel the thorn, nevertheless.

"A soldier?"

"No, a writer." I wait for more, so he adds, "She is Erlea."

He expects a reaction.

"You've never heard of her?"

I open my arms to show him my world.

"She's a political writer," he says. "She helped me put words to my ideas."

"Which are?"

"Not my brother's." He considers a high corner of the room, then waves at the window. "They killed him, my brother who believed there existed something salvageable in everybody, even the worst of us. They hung him in a cemetery."

"I'm sorry."

"I can't stop imagining his murder. It's different every time. Yet I always see him forgiving his killers before he thinks to forgive himself. Me, I can't."

I don't say anything. I know enough to know there exist no saints among us. Even my father would be hounded from time to time by his personal set of demons.

"Mariana was right," he says. "She was always right. This ends only one way. We must rid the world of them entirely. There can be no peace until we do."

Wouldn't it be nice to be so confident. "I envy her."

"She'd laugh if she heard someone say that. She and her children are refugees in their own country."

Though she has children, I imagine she's his age, that she still possesses her youth. Mine passed me by—the world, too—while I was trying to keep my husband from getting upset. "I never had any luck with this life. What I look forward to is the next one, of getting to start again."

"But this is the one you were born to."

"And the one I brought my sons into." I stand. "You'll still stay the night? I haven't driven you away, have I?"

The faint light outside etches kind lines around his eyes. "I told David and Marco I'd wedge between them."

"Terrible to be jealous of your children." I take the bottle and finish the rest of it. Like swallowing one of the embers.

THE MORNING SKY is a creamy blue, the color of a starling's eggs, and just as delicate. It could crack from our breaths spilling upon it. Pedro awoke sullen and left before breakfast, saying he was going to check the traps. I manage to convince the soldier to stay for lunch. It will be fish, David promises. So he and Marco lead the soldier to the river with their poles. He takes his rifle with him. At no point can I remember him not having it within reach. I keep thinking of his offer. The rifle has kept him alive this long, yet he believes I need it more than him.

The trees sliver their shapes as the three recede. Then I'm alone. It often occurs so abruptly. One minute my sons are clinging to me, my husband jealously observes my every step, I feel like my head is being held under water, and then everyone is gone and I have more air than I need.

This morning I remain outside, sitting where I did last night. The ashes from the fire have drifted over the stones that remain in the outline of Culito's rear. His coat was silver-black. The ashes thinly dusting the grey rocks evoke it. I'll have to point it out to David and

Marco. To this day my husband has blamed us for the dog's death. Often, when the boys make a mistake, he'll yell at them. *And you think you deserve another dog?* But even at their most playful or lonesome they've never asked for another.

Looking still at the rocks, my focus shifts. Boot prints in the ashes. They could be Pedro's, though I don't remember him walking in this direction when he left. Would the soldier have been so careless? And then I recognize the shape of the boot.

My vision swings left to right, behind me, back in front—the trees blur, the world spins. He's here, somewhere. I hold in a breath to calm myself, search the gaps in the trees. "Arturo?" I call. Best my husband comes now, with the soldier and his rifle far away. "Arturo, show yourself." The thing is, I never know exactly how it will go, what he will be capable of, so my heart clogs my throat when I see a figure through the trees. Then there's another figure and another and more yet, all of them in the fascists' dark blue uniforms. And at the front, leading them to the house, is Pedro.

"No," I cry. Something in me breaks. It stops my breath. I clutch my stomach. A surprise: there are other ways yet to be hurt.

The officer from last night walks alongside him. "O sea que…" He's smiling, draws the words out, practically sings them. "So someone *was* in there after all." He flicks a finger at the house. Several of his soldiers look anxiously at one another. "Go," he commands. One charges in, obligating others to follow. Were David and Marco inside, they'd have been shot on sight. If Pedro understands this, it doesn't register on his face. He wears a hardened expression, as if all this is my fault. "I suppose," the officer says, "you did tell me to search it." I'm not worried they'll notice my husband's papers. They'll pass right over them hunting for the soldier.

"You won't find him," I say. "He left hours ago."

"She's lying," Pedro says. His voice cracks with a truculent note.

I want nothing more than to grab Pedro and hold him to me. Perhaps I haven't lost him for good—not yet—but he's at the officer's side like a devoted adjutant, and I discover I'm pegged to the log.

"Where are your other two?" the officer asks.

"Foraging for mushrooms." Yesterday, before the soldier's appearance, we had spoken of doing so. The officer judges the possibility of this from Pedro's tight lips that curl inwards.

Inside the house there's a brief shout and the crash of glass. This perks the officer's posture, but a moment later the soldiers file out, shaking their heads, while one holds the broken pieces of the frame that held my father's one photograph, contrite, on the verge of offering an apology. With another flick of his fingers the officer orders him to toss it to the side. He then draws a tight circle with his finger. "Search the perimeter. He could be hiding nearby."

"I already said, he left this morning." The photograph of my father has been gashed by broken glass. It sits in the grass, nearly severed in two, about to be trampled by the soldiers. I try for a quick inventory: does anything of my life before my husband remain?

"If we find him, you'll be wishing it was your husband's fists you were contending with."

Pedro shifts at this. The officer doesn't seek to assure him. He must figure there's little more he can get from my son. I turn back to the firepit, my husband's boot print in the ashes—deal first with the soldier, then it'd be my turn. "You won't."

After completing their sweep, the fascists gather around the officer. I hear him sigh. He stands directly in front of me, trampling the print. "Normally, I'd make an example of you. But who would tell the story? The trees? I'll entrust your husband with the honor." To Pedro, he says, "You'll let him know." Pedro gives an uncertain nod. Much of the fight has left him. "If the soldier returns, you know where to find us. I promise we'll spare your mother." With his toe, he taps mine. "So, which way did the red go?"

I motion behind me.

"We came from that direction."

"He's a soldier. He's searching for the war."

The officer considers this, doesn't appear convinced. He smiles while studying my bruises. His vision drifts to Pedro, the pieces of the picture frame, then the teetering house. "What else could I threaten to do to you?" I don't acknowledge this or his final derisive chuckle. To his men he says, "He's somewhere in the forest."

They move away with all the discretion of a marching band, every footfall snapping branches. Pedro's head is down. When I approach him, he steps back. Angry tears streak his face.

"My boy." I open my arms to him. "You need to know: I've never been more hurt. But not for anything you've done to me." Again, he steps back. "Please," I say. "I need to know you'll be able to forgive yourself."

"I heard you," he yells. "Last night. With the soldier. What you wanted to do with him. You're lucky I didn't tell the fascists."

"I'm sorry you heard that."

"I heard it all." His arms are down and he's crying openly. Finally, I can bring him to me, but the moment I touch him, he pushes me away and runs off. I watch him go and wait, wait for the sounds of him to disappear, wait to see if the silence might deliver my husband. When it doesn't, I start running, too.

IN A FEW months, the snowmelt will turn the creek into a wide, uncrossable river, further penning me in. These early summer days, the frigid and swiftly moving water is at my knees. It rushes between large stones and hurtles against the creek's sharp bends. I listen for shouting while I run along its bank, until, finally, further ahead I see David holding Marco. The two are pressed against a tree, their expressions terror stricken, eyes fixed on something near the creek, a carve in the earth I still can't see. I run towards that, not my children, fearing the gruesome scene I'll find.

But the soldier is still alive. His face is scratched and he's bleeding from his mouth. As I come up the bank, I see he's kneeling on my husband's back, hogtying him. My husband's complexion is ashen from drink and mottled bright red with fury. He twists as he yells at

David and Marco to untie him. Neither child moves. They only press harder against the tree. All goes still—my husband's attempts to thrash himself free, even, it seems, the noisy water—when my husband spots me. It's a jackal's smile. "There she is," he yells. "There's the slut."

I ignore him and crouch next to David and Marco. "I need you two to go home. Don't run. Walk as casually as you can while collecting mushrooms. There are soldiers nearby. The same from last night. If they find you, say you're foraging. Whatever you do, don't run. And when they ask, the soldier left this morning headed for town. Our lives depend on this story. Now go, but slowly."

They start. David turns around first, then Marco. They look at me, their father. He shouts, "Tell Pedro where I am."

I smile warmly at them. "A casual pace. Collect every mushroom you see. I'll be back soon."

I don't turn until long after they've vanished from sight. My husband is laughing at me. Snarling laughter. "Even when you try to give yourself to a man," he says, "he won't take you." I walk down to the bank, wondering where he got that bit from. Not Pedro. And had my husband watched us through a window last night, he would have broken down the door. No, he's just guessing at this fact. He's always been able to sense my vulnerabilities. "How you tried to convince me otherwise. All those wasted years worrying." Drink has deadened his tongue. Bloodshot squiggles his eyes. He'd probably been driven out of town by the fascists' presence and thought, when he saw the soldier leave the house this morning with our two youngest, that he could best him.

The soldier extends the rifle. I think of the woman he promised himself to. She'd probably take it. I wave it off. A shadow passes over the soldier's face, a coldness. Like the season changing to winter, I feel the warmth bleed out of him. It will be on him to kill my husband. My eyes go to the trigger. What force does that curve of metal exert on him? It is there for one distinct purpose. I signal for him not to do it. All this my husband misses. He's still laughing. "No wonder we're losing," he says. "Our side's so amariconado they get the women to do the killing for them." To me, he orders, "Now release me."

"Shush." I kneel and search through his back pockets worried I won't find it but, no, there it is. He tries glancing over his shoulder. "What are you doing?" I pull his Masonic party card from his pocket.

"Roll him onto his side," I say. "Get him against this rock." The soldier does, and I put the party card in my husband's front shirt pocket so it pokes out. "Bitch," he barks and spits at me. It mostly dribbles across his chin. He thrashes wildly now. Blood seeps from his wrists, further sinking the rope binding him. "Fucking whore!"

He tries to bite the card, then reach it with that chin.

I stand. "Leave him for the fascists to find."

"You're going to kill me," my husband shouts.

"No," I say. "Not me."

He shouts for help, screams Pedro's name. "Call the fascists to you," I tell him.

"I'm sorry," he says. "I'm sorry." He's apologizing not to me but to the soldier. "We're on the same side. We have the same enemies. The fight needs every one of us."

The soldier doesn't acknowledge this but slings the rifle over his shoulder. He says, "Was it Pedro?"

"He heard me last night."

My husband is yelling over this that he'll change, he'll never lay a hand on me again. All he wants is to love and protect me.

"I knew you'd kill me one day," I tell him, "that it was only a matter of time, so I stopped caring about myself. Our boys, though. I had no other way to keep them safe." If I caressed his mud-streaked cheek, a final goodbye, he'd try to bite me, so I turn up my hands and grimace.

He's screaming at us while we walk away. "I'll kill you. I'll slit your throats." The soldier turns back from time to time, as if trying to puzzle out a riddle—we can leave these brutes to destroy themselves. Then, my husband must accept there's no saving himself, but he still has a chance to be buried with company. He shouts, "A red! Come quick, a red!" He's shredding his vocal cords for the effort.

I point to the west. "They'll be arriving from this direction."

The soldier looks off to the east. I try imagining what awaits him there. He must, too. His body's stiffened. Those kind lines around his eyes and mouth are gone. His time with David and Marco was but brief relief. He is, once more, the leery and troubled young man they brought to our house. I want to tell him to let go of that person and remain with us. But in what world would that be possible? Fascists prowl this forest. Mariana is out there. So are his brother's killers. Turning back to me, he asks, "Will you be all right?"

"For the first time in a long time, I don't know. It's an improvement." I lean toward him and kiss his cheek, one side then the other, holding my lips there. "Thank you."

I watch him cross the creek. Only when the trees on the other side begin to conceal him do I turn, heading for the north, re-entering the forest's cool and fragrant shadows. A bird sings nearby. Above, the branches whoosh and rustle. I can still hear my husband's shouts when I bend for my first mushroom, grabbing it by the base and wiggling it from the earth's soft clutch.

15

WE HAD SUFFERED a numbing series of losses before we came upon Isidro alone on that sun-blanched road beyond Huesca. The comandante, the captain, then Felipe—previously the highest ranking among us—had been killed, in that order. We'd buried Felipe in the morning. Several hours later, Isidro's blurry shape limped toward us. Since then, we hadn't lost anybody, so I tended to stay close to him, but I hesitated as he stepped into the church and lifted his collar to cover his nose.

It was the warm fetor of turned meat. Nothing can so catch the throat, issue a warning. I blinked hard to bring color to what was around me. The pews had been ripped from the floor and heaved one atop the other. We craned our necks to the vandalized statues we passed. At their bases rose the acrid reek of piss.

"Let's get back to the others," I said. The comandante, the captain, then Felipe. A mine, a German shell, a bullet in each lung. There were other ways to die, and this reprieve couldn't last forever.

Isidro let out a scratchy breath, pointing to the Virgin, her eye sockets scraped hollow.

I had especially liked Felipe. He was a gangly man, his proportions wrong for war. Once, outside Segura de los Baños, he took cover behind a tree where, from my vantage, I saw a quarter of his body poking out. I yelled for him to pull in tighter, but he didn't hear me over the rifle fire and he smiled cheerily, his eyebrows steep crescents as if to say: life is a remarkable thing and what are the odds I'd be here to participate in it, and, sure, sometimes you'll have fascists hurling bullets at you but, look, I found this tree and isn't it a fine example of the interconnectedness of creation.

I suppose I agreed, so, months later, watching him drown in his own blood, though a world of air surrounded him, I kept repeating: I'm still here, I'm still here. I'll honor you by surviving, by continuing this fight. I swear I will. But leaving his buried body behind, knowing soon, surely, I'd be the one suffering so, I wondered if I wasn't getting the worst of the agreement. "The others are probably wondering where we are," I told Isidro.

Behind the altar someone had painted *Why would God allow us to destroy his temples.* The paint ran to where Jesus and his cross lay in several pieces. It wasn't a fear of belief since to do this you had to believe in something. Isidro continued toward the far corner of the church, toward the smell's source. The stench rushed blood and heat to my ears.

The statue was of Salome with her platter. They'd removed John the Baptist's decapitated head. She held the platter like she was presenting us with a dish brought from the kitchen. The flies' incessant buzzing sounded electric. They crawled lazily around the priest's open mouth and across his thin lips before flying off and landing along the rim of his clerical collar which was on his head at a tilt like a crown. His face was a deep purple, the skin sagging unnaturally, his eyes open and vacant and sunken. Whoever did this made an uneven job of it. I had to look elsewhere.

Isidro lit a cigarette and waved it under his nose. He asked, "It wasn't our side, was it?"

He was getting worked up. I shrugged. It most likely was our side, but who knew. It depended on this priest's politics: for what purpose he used the church, whether he supported the people or the power. Or maybe it was simpler than that. Maybe a parishioner coveted his horse or never felt properly absolved, a restlessness that gnawed at him, that he figured had to be somebody's fault. It often amassed at my temples, this wish for absolution, and I'd think I would do anything to get back to who I'd once been.

"They didn't reach the ceiling," I said to say something. The mural of clouds and winged cherubs remained untouched. On closer inspection, I saw the bullet holes. With that, fingers moved up the back of my neck, but I knew I wouldn't find anyone behind me. Isidro breathed heavily as he walked to the crucifix, sidestepping some shit, and righted the top half of Christ. I wasn't sure if Jesus was a sucker or not, a fool to let others have their way with him all these years or if by making an offering of himself he'd been freed from this panic that crushed me. Whatever it was, he hadn't done it for my sake. He'd gone up there, and I was still fucked.

Isidro held another piece of the crucifix, uncertain what to do with it, and let out a long breath that caved his cheeks. "My brother," he said, "was a priest." Aside from his Basque accent, I knew nothing of where Isidro had come from, and I preferred it that way. The more nebulous his character, the less defined his story, the easier to consider him a totem sent to ward off not only danger but any sort of excitement. Since meeting him I hadn't fired my rifle. "Fascists hung him in a cemetery," he said.

I didn't need to look at the head on the platter to know what he was getting at. Instead, I peered again at the gouges in the ceiling's plaster, the faded yellow hair of the cherubs, the wispy clouds surrounding them. Half a century ago, ropes harnessed a painter and that hair was as close to gold as he could mix his paints.

Taking it in, I stepped back, and the rest happened in parts and all at once. My elbow caught an empty pedestal. I didn't grab for it as it fell. What would have been the use? It smashed on the ground in the sharp, explosive sound of rifle fire, and I was still turning to the shattered pedestal when the figures sprang from the vestry, those two boys who had probably followed us in and must have been sweating back there with fear and anticipation and who knows what ideas of

211

heroism or retribution when they thought we'd begun firing at them. I cowered as their bullets splintered upturned pews and cut the air with deafening pops. In my periphery Isidro stood by the altar, his rifle against his shoulder, as steady as the statues. It was quick. Four shots, maybe five. The boys weren't any older than fifteen, and the bullets threw one down, splayed out. The other was on his hands and knees, crawling, not toward his dropped weapon but away from us. In the weak light of the church, the blood pumping from his neck was black on his skin and collar. Isidro stepped closer. I raised my hand, opened my mouth, but couldn't make a sound. My throat might as well have been slashed by a bullet. Isidro's eyes bounced almost imperceptibly, then a rifle report. The muscles in the boy's left arm seized, went still. Only then did my voice return as it does when you wake yourself from mute dreams with your howling.

"Were you hit?" Isidro asked, his rifle pointed now at the other boy. Each breath was a wet, raspy chore that shuddered the boy's body. His arms were open to embrace the bullet-riddled vision on the ceiling.

"No." But I didn't check. I could have been. I'd known guys who denied they'd been shot even after showing them the blood soaking their uniform.

The boy startled when we came into his line of sight. Eyes white and lidless, they jerked between Isidro and me. His legs thrashed but his heels weren't able to catch the floor, and a crackling moan, animal-like, mewed from him. I wanted to quiet the panic in his eyes, to ask: what more can we do to you, what is left to fear? You've been set free. His terror, pure and unguarded, persisted. It overwhelmed me as he lost color, and suddenly I thought: I can save him, it's not too late. Nothing mattered more.

Long ago, in a different life, at the war's inception, I had been a part of the social revolution in Zaragoza, assisting the displaced, working in education centers, that sort of thing—trying to unite my fellow Spaniards against those bent on dividing us. I spoke in slogans. Our fates are intertwined, I'd say. A grand design exists. Without you, there is no me. This, I promised, is what will save Spain. Ultimately, I became frustrated with our inability to halt the momentum of the right. Whatever we built, the fascists destroyed.

However, two years of war later, time came together for me in that church. I still wanted to believe, to stand at that shit-smeared pulpit and say: of course it's obvious but don't you see, this fighting has accomplished what the other side was after, it's divorced us from one another. To hell with survival, with sacrifice, with martyrdom. I have a brother, too, Isidro, and he wasn't much younger than this boy when the war took me from him. I doubt he'd recognize the person I've become. So let's help this child, perhaps then we might save ourselves.

I started to bend to him—"Shh," I said—but Isidro already had his rifle at his shoulder. I heard him draw in a whistling breath through his nostrils, knew he'd closed his eyes, that he wouldn't open them until he pulled the trigger. He was thinking of a tree in a cemetery, of a rope digging into a sturdy branch, into a neck. The boy meant something else to him. I wasn't able to stop him, couldn't turn away in time, and saw what the bullet did, how the boy's face pinned to the ground and bloomed as the sounds of the world converged at once into a high-pitched wail.

All that evening I worked my jaw for my hearing to return. Isidro sat alone against a tree. Everyone avoided him. I did, too, or he did of me. He wasn't slump-shouldered. His chin didn't press on his chest. Instead, he sat rigid, examining the inky distance ahead, probably thinking as I often did: sure, I'm still here but have I survived? Despite myself, I pet the earth like it was an obedient dog.

When I awoke that night it was gradually, to Isidro's voice. He sat nearby and stopped talking to glance at me before continuing the conversation. My eyes finally adjusted. We were the only ones in the area. I wondered if I'd been answering him in my sleep.

"Two more," he said.

"Two what?" I asked, the boy's face returning to me, how it disappeared under a bullet. "Oh," I said, "that." I pushed the heel of a palm into my eyes and searched for the others. It was common enough to be woken by someone talking themselves down. The best thing to do was find a quieter corner under the stars. Too late for me though. "It had to be done."

"Did it?" A challenge, not a question.

"Of course. We can't let the fascists win." I figured I still needed the talk as much as he did. "Look, it was them or us. That's the contest—their vision for tomorrow or ours. This—death, how you're feeling right now—it will get worse if we don't keep them from crossing the Ebro. And what then? What will all this have been for?" I was emptier for having said it. I thought of the things I'd likely been telling him in my sleep, what I'd felt in that church, and I sat up, my weight on my elbow, to let him know how we agreed, but instead I said, "I'm tired, too, but we can't stop now. If we do, somebody else will have to fight this. They'll start at the beginning, making all the mistakes we have to arrive at this point."

"You don't understand. I thought I was better."

"Better?"

"Better than—" He waved his injured hand, a vague gesture. "Than them."

This cleared my head. He was wrong, and he needed to hear it. I thought of more slogans. We have to fight the fascists, and we have to fight them with their weapons, not only for Spain but for the world. We can't begin to comprehend the cruelty they'll revel in if we aren't victorious. Instead, I said, "We're on the right side. We're the good ones."

"Tell that to the two boys in there."

I laughed. "The ones who humiliated that priest? The ones who were going to kill us?"

"They weren't. Not in the end."

No point saying I'd wanted to stop him but had failed. "There's no other way," I said. "If we were at war with some other group for some other reason, sure. Maybe we could shake hands and work together to bury the past. But these bastards won't allow it. It's them or us."

"It's collective suicide." He wasn't wrong. Someone visited every abattoir across Spain, inquired about their sloppiest craftsman, then issued them command of a regiment.

"You know the old song: we just need to hold out long enough for the rest of the world to recognize this fight for what it is." I arched my back, twisted from side to side. "The night's having its way with you. That's all this is. You'll see. In the morning you won't feel so rotten."

Even in the darkness I made out his disappointment. He stood and walked off, and a bird leapt from a tree and circled above him in a broad arc. Who knows if it meant anything. I remember waiting for someone to shoot it from the sky. It was wide in the middle and would have fed several of us.

The next afternoon we reached the Ebro, where our section was immediately disassembled and absorbed into various companies. Lose the Ebro and we'd lose Catalonia. Lose Catalonia and we'd lose access to the French border. Lose the border and we'd lose this war that trudged on regardless of revelations.

16

IMANOL   EBRO VALLEY, NOVEMBER 1938

WE WALK AT a slant, one foot crossing over the other, each landed step sliding in the soft dirt of the mountain's slope. We're stooped, lest our heads break the mountain's crest and provide a target for the fascists who might be tucked behind the scorched trees. During last night's ambush, a small group of ours—about nine or ten, mostly Andalusians—fled behind the line. Because Isidro was the newest among us, the lieutenant offered him the opportunity to venture out among the fascists' battalions to see if we might be able to locate them. Recognizing this as my chance, I volunteered to accompany him. We were given strict orders: if we could bring them back without risking our lives, great. Otherwise, return with their whereabouts, and maybe we'd be able to cajole the 226th to assist us with rescue efforts.

In another life, in another time, Isidro and I occasionally ran into each other. His village neighbored mine and was pocketed in a valley where a single road unraveled from it, winding and opening to the sea. Mine belonged to the mountains of Gernika, near a dramatic gulley—like the one now alongside us. The houses there dotted the ridge of the cleft. In Isidro's village there were shepherds, but more looked to the ocean for how they might survive the day. The ocean for us, on the other hand, existed as the stars did, a distant navigational reference point.

Who knows if either village remains: his or mine. That Isidro has yet to recall them is, perhaps, why I still haven't shot him, the only person in this war-battered valley who knows, or might know, that I killed my brother.

"Bertsolari," Isidro whispers behind me. He's leaning forward, squinting. In the distance, the heatless light of the November sun glints off something. I peer through binoculars. "A lorry," I say.

"One of ours?"

"I can't make out any markings." I pass the binoculars, and while he studies it, I think how right now, with him by my side and us a thousand miles from the rest of the world, I can lift my rifle to his head and pull the trigger. First, though, I need to hear him say it. I've been waiting for the slightest slip, for that sliver of a moment when his thoughts are unguarded and in his eyes I can see for certain that he knows what I did to my twin.

Isidro lowers the binoculars. "It's not ours," he says. "It wouldn't be. Not this far out. Etorri, Bertsolari." And he takes the lead, walking before me, the back of his skull a widening target.

BERTSOLARI. THAT'S WHAT he said with a lift of his chin when he joined our battalion three days ago and spotted me among the ranks. He didn't say it joyfully or startled but instead as a flavorless acknowledgment. Of course, he seemed to be saying, why wouldn't our meandering routes through this nightmare of time and Spain reunite us here? Meanwhile, my palms had moistened and my mouth had gone dry. I'd somehow convinced myself I'd never again see anyone from home. I patted about for my rifle and attempted a smile that would reach my eyes. However, he casually turned from me, and our lieutenant continued the tour.

Later that night, when he passed us again, reliable Castor, who couldn't let a single order pass without poking it with a dozen unnecessary questions, asked, "Bertsolari? Why'd you call Imanol that?" Here it comes, I thought. I shifted to my knees to quickly stand, but

Isidro never mentioned my brother. Instead, he spoke distractedly about Basque fiestas and their bertsolaris, the improvisational poets who competed against each other as though in a duel. I'd been one of them. My brother, too.

Those minutes at the fiestas were my most cherished. Despite my desire to be as effortlessly carefree as my brother, I vigilantly maintained a sense of myself. Regardless of the scenario, I'd watch myself doing it, like a bad actor certain he wasn't fooling anyone. That's how I experienced most moments. However, on stage I'd manage to silence that self-doubt, exist in the present, trust in my intuition, and finally release control. I never found that elsewhere. By the time I came into a greater sense of my improvisational abilities, the bertsolaris were beginning to be distinguished between two groups—the illiterates and those who brought to the competitions not solely their own experiences but all the Basque texts they'd studied. My brother and I belonged to the former. Increasingly, our kind were getting trounced. Only my brother could make it to the final round and even win, on occasion, the txapela. It hadn't been all bad for me though, or so I'd thought. During one of my mismatched defeats, a girl with a tender heart stood in the crowd. She was so moved by my humiliation that she followed me from the stage, and, months later, we married. My parents and brother immediately took to her. She made me a more serious person, a more dedicated shepherd, even a better bertsolari, while my brother continued searching the night for good times. I'd long felt the unwelcome member of the family, but after bringing my wife into our home, the mood among the others shifted to *ah, so that's why we kept him around.*

My brother was in no rush to marry. The women liked him too much. So long as his knees held up, he planned on climbing into strangers' beds. Concerning the house, then, the decision became a fairly easy one for my parents: my wife and I would inherit it. The lone person this surprised was my brother.

"No me jodas," Castor said, slapping me on the knee. "We've had a goddamn poet with us this entire time and you never even spit one verse our way."

My cheeks burned. I settled against the tree, continuing to study Isidro. He was under the other tree, which was basically charcoal. How a bomb can annihilate one while leaves still cling to its neighbor is a mystery this war has yet to unlock.

The others nudged and punched me and called for a song. "No," I told them. "A ram only shows off its horns when there's another to slam against." I noted the tremble in my voice. I had long ago lost the melody, the words, access to the place within myself where I was able to trust what I'd say or do next. "Besides, the verses are in Basque. You wouldn't understand them."

Isidro stopped them before they thought to ask, saying he couldn't improvise, then continued on—to the next campfire, I assumed, to the next person from home who he hadn't seen in years and wouldn't be surprised to find in the Ebro. I suppose it wasn't an impossibility, even if it was one I hadn't previously considered. Over the past two years, the fascists had been scattered about Spain in their corners while they relentlessly ground into ours. Now we were all claustrophobically pushed into the Ebro. Anyone still determined to raise a rifle for a cause had received an invitation here, where the war, the oddsmakers were saying, would be decided. Nevertheless, I watched the night close around him. He hadn't mentioned my brother. That's how I knew he knew. And, yet, he hadn't mentioned my brother— perhaps he hadn't heard. I couldn't find him that night among all the sleeping bodies.

"I DON'T LIKE being this high up," he says now.

Traveling along the ridge allows us to cover ground quicker and provides us a more expansive view of the burnt and scarred earth of the Ebro Valley. "Sure," I say. "They'll see us but at least we'll see them. No surprises like last night."

"But look behind you."

I do so haltingly, distrustful of Isidro, of turning my attention from him. There is nothing behind us—bomb-scraped mountains, blackened folds in the earth, a tiered mountain range silhouetted by pale grey smoke.

"They see us," he says, "and where do we run? They'll cut us off before we can get back."

I consider this. When we first arrived at the Ebro, you couldn't find a square meter of soil undisturbed by trees. The sky was often concealed entirely by a canopy of branches. It reminded me too much of home, so there was some comfort when tens of thousands of the fascist's shells tore hundreds of thousands of trees from the earth. They now lay broken in their own ruins like charred and splintered bones. The valley resembles our decimated cities—there are massive breaches in the skyline. "Still," I say, "it's better than being surprised. At least up here we have a chance."

"It's not an either-or. Last night could have been avoided."

"So it was the lieutenant's fault then?" I'm trawling for gossip to take back to the others. Most of us like the lieutenant.

"What's done is done."

Their ambush had cleaved us. Those nine or ten mostly Andalusians in one direction, the majority of us in the other, and the dead left behind. I emptied my rifle but never hit a fascist, always the way it went. I've tried everything. Aiming to the left, the right, closing my eyes. Nothing works. My bullets just sing through the air, never piercing the enemy.

Last night, among the charred faces and the acrid reek of singed hair and fabric and the copper stink of new wounds, I couldn't find Isidro. Good, I thought. The fascists have done the job for me. It's taken care of itself. But, no, after being chased through the night, there he was bringing up the rear, dragging wounded Castor with him.

"What do you think of him, the lieutenant?"

He allows some time to pass. Finally, he says, "This is a war of idiocy so it's appropriate he should be among those leading it."

"Why do you stick with it then?" It's something I've often asked myself.

"There's no other way of beating the fascists. I forgot that for a while."

Before I can ask how so, we hunch against a charging wind, loud as a train barreling past. In the moment, we wouldn't be able to hear a convoy of tanks a hundred meters off. There aren't any, at least none I can see. Instead, dark clouds gather along the east, the wind its emissary. Moisture is in the air. You can rub it between your fingers. A storm, a proper one, would be nice, provide a temporary relief from the shelling. This one will, like the others, sit on us long enough to soak all we own, puddle up the roads, then clear out before night, the sky full of stars and the moon, billions of little lights giving away our position.

The tattered ends of the wind stream past us. "How many more Basques do you imagine are here?" I ask. "You think many of us remain in the fight?"

He doesn't answer but slowly lifts a hand, quieting me. We've come to the mountain's slope. I try to peer around his shoulder. "Shit," he says. He steps aside so I can take his place. A circle of black shirts huddle in another dried-out vein of the land. Last month, Prime Minister Negrín had ordered the withdrawal of our International Brigades, believing this would put pressure on the fascists to send their Germans and Italians home. At long last, the war would be Spaniards against Spaniards. That was the thinking. So back to England and America and Ireland and Belgium and anywhere else free people can think free thoughts went the only help we ever received in this war. But the thing about fascists is they're impervious to international pressure. They'd look at you open-mouthed and squinty-eyed if you tried to explain why they shouldn't slaughter civilians. Whatever these Italians are standing around, they've got their attention fixed to it as if money is on the line.

Isidro points down and I nod. Descending sideways to the gulley's belly, we lean back, keep our weight from toppling over our legs.

There's a further cut in the earth down here—a ravine hardly wide enough for a person—but we remain on the shelf above it. The fascists would certainly hear the gun shot now: it would peal through the gulley, be cupped by the mountains, lead them back to me. He has no idea, I think as I once more study the back of his head, that a group of fascists are keeping him alive.

We Basques have a bump others are born without. It's a small, rounded bone between the skull and the neck. I'll aim above it, I decide, when we get enough distance, when another freight train of wind howls past, when Isidro finally admits to knowing the truth. Were the others in my company to learn of my crime, they'd tie me up for the fascists to happen upon before I could explain myself, not that I'd be able to convince them that what I did was necessary. I can't even convince myself.

"Aside from me," I try, "when was the last time you came across one of our breed?"

A slight, disinterested shrug.

"And what about from home? For me, it's been over a year and a half. Not since early '37, just after Gernika."

"Burgos," he says. "They have a prison there. A converted monastery."

In prison, what's there to do but talk? It's like sharing with your section any food you may have found. Every story is passed around.

"When was this?"

Again, a shrug.

"After Gernika?"

"Tough to remember much before Gernika." He's surveying the tops of the gulley, like a rodent will the skies for a shadowless hawk.

"Anyone we knew in there?"

"Were you a part of Balenziaga's or Saizarbitoria's?"

"No."

"Then probably not."

I try to recall which battalions were decimated in the weeks following Gernika, but Isidro isn't asking. The thing is: while others were fleeing southwest from Gernika to Bilbao, I rushed directly southward, out of the Basque Country and into Spain, not once wearing the uniform of the Basque Army. Had I considered the ocean, had I been composed enough to think *fishing boats, France, escape,* I'd have a vineyard before me right now, the crackle of a phonograph lazy on the air. Instead, I hurried south to get far from the house I had inherited, the field where those I'd left behind would soon find my brother's body.

Ever since I inherited it, my brother would drunkenly stumble into walls, no matter the hour. He'd often pass out in the field, once directly in front of the door so my father tripped over him in the darkness of early morning. My wife was the only one among us who felt sorry for him. I resented her for this, which, in turn, brought a sneer to her face every time I entered her line of sight, and on and on it went.

"You don't understand what it's like," I tried to get her to see. "What growing up with someone like that does to a person, to a twin." My brother had always been more talented, more gregarious and charismatic, better liked, confident he'd meant to be born. "His triumphs have always weighted me—now, too, this defeat?" The first defeat, I pointed out, he experienced from me.

"Of course you'd be thinking of yourself," she said. "Have you ever considered his fall?" But how could I with the way he'd begun eyeing me. I'd never felt so despised.

Months passed like this. Months with a rift between my brother and me, with a rift between my wife and me where, often, I couldn't find her, and when I did she'd put forward the ludicrous proposition that I should renounce my inheritance so the two of us could strike out for the Americas. She had an uncle on her father's side in Uruguay and another on her mother's in New York. Once we got there and the moment my back was turned, I was certain she'd board a ship to rejoin my brother.

I hardly slept during this time, and after a while I noted how people were commenting on the lushness of her hair, the glow of her skin. Had that radiance always been there? Were they just now noticing? This was in April, and toward the end of that month the sky began to shake. German planes flew overhead in packs of three. The bombs they dropped onto nearby Gernika seized the ground with tremors. Our sheep huddled and bolted, huddled and bolted. Behind them, over the ridge, smoke rose under angry rips of thunder. All of it was surely coming our way.

I searched for my wife—this great threat might finally reconcile us—and found her around the corner of the house, a thin puddle of vomit at her feet. She was wiping her mouth when our eyes met. She could have been sick from terror and panic, but in her eyes I saw where she went all those times I couldn't find her. My mind was more unsettled than the scattering sheep. I was capable of any dark thought.

Another squadron of Heinkels assaulted the sky, then another, but over their deafening sounds my brother called my name. He was waving for me to join him out in the field. A lamb is breached, he said, but his eyes told a different story: I don't lose, they said, and we always knew how this would end. Again, he waved for me to join him. I nodded, yelled I'd be right there. He started back for the sheep, and my wife doubled over again. She didn't see me step into the house for the rifle.

HIS VISION SWEEPING the two ridgelines, Isidro stumbles momentarily over a large rock. "Fish in a barrel," he says.

"And the family?" I ask. "How are your brothers?" I don't ask about his father. I detest the man. When I was eleven, he slapped me at the fiestas of San Juan for crying, too loudly or too long I suppose, when my Basajaun figurine shattered at my feet. To this day I've never been struck so hard. "How are Aitor and Xabier?" I ask.

He stops, and when he turns, I probe his eyes.

"Xabier is dead," he says. He says it as though I should have known, as if I'd asked him if we were in the Ebro just now, eternally at war, eternally on the verge of defeat.

"I hadn't heard. He was a priest, no?" With the rifle's tip I scratch my head. "It wasn't our side, was it?"

A silent, derisive chuckle, mostly just air through his nostrils, which says the lieutenant isn't the only idiot in this division. "Fascists. They hung him in San Sebastián's cemetery." He points to the vertical slope at our right. A wall of hard earth, actually. "We'll probably be fine up there. Fighting chance if nothing else." I hop over the ravine, then tilt my head back fully to gaze up the slope that claws at the sky.

"Up there?"

"Our sole chance."

Soon, the burn in my lungs spreads to my thighs and calves and wrists and shoulders. Invisible hands crush my ribs. The wind muffles our heavy breaths but does little to cool me as I blink hard against the sweat dripping into my eyes. The mountain, at times, feels like it's about to tip over. There are but a few degrees of pitch to it. Isidro is also hacking, climbing without pause, pushing himself further and further, to pain, to distraction, to a greater distance from me, this unexpected vestige from a home that he, too, it turns out, has been trying to forget.

Somehow, we reach the top. Isidro first, gulping air, hunched over and, I can see, smiling. He's choking with a sort of unreadable laugh, his hands on his knees.

"What is it?" I ask between breaths, getting to my feet.

He lifts his head quickly, a nod to what's before us, and I don't even need the binoculars. In a narrow pocket of the valley, still far off but visible between a cleft of the earth, are our nine men, the mostly Andalusians. They're huddled tightly together, as though hatching a plan. Isidro bounces his eyebrows and smiles—it's going to work out after all.

He stands and straightens. "Shall we?" Not once in all the time since the lieutenant brought him to our fire the other night, reintroducing him to my life, have I seen him smile, but there's now a contented lightness about him. It takes me back to years ago, before this war, to a fiesta in his village—my brother in front of the audience, me off to the side watching them smile warmly, their concerns momentarily forgotten, while my brother led them to his story's denouement—the priest in it was gradually being seduced by a forest nymph—when they became, Isidro among them and along-side him his brother Xabier, a laughing choir. Even the bertsolari my brother was competing against laughed, acknowledging what we all knew: he'd been beat.

"I miss my brother, too," I tell him.

"Which one?" We're walking side by side. For the first time he appears interested in what I'll say.

"I only had the one."

Proceeding downhill—it was practically a flat-faced mountain as we scaled it but on this side it slopes at a gentle, accommodating decline—we lose sight of the mostly Andalusians. I quicken my pace to keep up.

"You think there's any going back?" I ask. "Back home, that is." What I suppose I want to know is how I'd be able to.

He doesn't hesitate. "No." Then adds, "At least not for me." I think of his father. What did Isidro endure at home with that man who probably had children because he'd tired of beating the mule? "Not that one."

I'm picturing my home, the forest at its edge. I imagine a pair of scales among the trees that a grey- and wild-bearded ascetic with pristine wings squats next to. Behind him, there's the presence of a lake, a soupy fog shifting over it, and on its other bank: whatever awaits us next. Were I to approach that wild-bearded man today, he'd condescendingly turn his lips down at the sight of me. Probably even laugh. Wouldn't bother with the scales.

"You think rescuing these guys will help clear some of what we've done these past years?" I motion to the hill, our nine men some-where on the other side.

He says, "I met someone. In Bilbao." By his tone I understand it to be a woman. "A writer. Our writer: Erlea."

I recognize the name but admit to never having read her. He appears surprised, suspicious—why am I here then?

"'The war will make us unrecognizable to our former selves,' she wrote once. Scar us, mutilate us. The whole gambit. Shred our hearts, those parts, at least, not hardened to stone. She went on for a while, practically the whole page. 'But,' she said, 'we must fight regardless.'"

"A fair description of our options," I say.

"For a while, I tired of that idea of hers. I despised what this war turned me into."

"The price of survival." My legs remain cotton as we approach the bottom.

"I was ready to quit. But then a letter from her found me."

"What did she say?"

His lips draw tight. "We have to win," he says. "If we don't, we lose more than our country."

Ascending the next hill, every limb and organ complains.

"Should *you* make it back home," he says, "you think you'll participate in the bertsolari competitions again? You had talent."

I'm about to thank him for that kindness, then realize he's mistaken me all this while for my brother. Though not identical twins, we looked similar enough—nature trying variations with my features that never quite worked together.

"No." There's no point correcting him. "I don't think so. You have to trust yourself to be up there. It's the only way you can be surprised by the story you tell, with the verses spilling out of you."

"That's gone?"

I remember my brother's alarm and confusion when he turned to see the rifle I was raising. Behind him, black clouds of smoke from Gernika were towering and curling toward us, like a wave. I should have given him an opportunity to speak. It haunts me that I didn't. For years I had watched him on stage, incapable of guessing what he'd say next—were I able to do so, perhaps I may have once won a txapela—so that even now I've no idea what he was about to tell me. But it was too late. The motion that lifted the rifle also had me pulling the trigger. "Yeah," I say, "it is."

Nearing the hilltop, we're breathing hard again. The wind rides over it and pushes on us, and, once more, Isidro approaches the top first. At this angle, all I see is his shape suddenly stiffen against the vast darkening sky. I hurry to him as he draws a line from the north to a point, then the south to a point. "What?" I say, the wind carrying the word away.

Our nine men, the mostly Andalusians, haven't moved. The wind must be swirling in their ears so they don't hear the two small caravans of fascists closing in on them—one from the north, the other the south. On this hilltop, we can see the roads that they're unable to. There isn't any urgency on the part of the caravans. They have no idea our men are there, are unaware even that another team of fellow bastards approaches. Each, for the moment, believes themselves alone.

The group from the north are closer to our men, but once those from the south arrive, ours will lose any cover they may have had in a firefight. I'm watching the whole thing as though it's already started. Isidro shakes me to get my attention.

"Did you hear me? Go for the others. This is it. I'll be bringing them to you. The fascists won't be able to help themselves. We can pin them in the gulley, but we'll need everybody."

There's time, sure, to reach our nine men, to get close enough so they might hear him over the wind, but a minute or two later the first caravan will round the bend, spotting their retreat. They'll never make it to the gulley.

"We have orders," I tell him.

"It's their only chance. Take the ridgeline. Even if you're an open target, it's the quickest way. Go!"

He yells to our men. It thuds off the wind.

I take my first step—not back to our battalion but to the nine, to possibly save them, perhaps to my death, but also, no matter what occurs, to my salvation. There's no second step, because Isidro grabs me by the back collar and throws me down before I've completely realized what's happened. He stands over me, the flash of a smile. "Go," he says, "a few more seconds and all this will be for nothing." He starts for our nine, and I scramble to my feet and run, too, never turning around, not once, the wind at my back pushing me forward, to our battalion, to more of this life where maybe, in this moment or the next, I'll finally come out on top.

17

GABLE   EBRO VALLEY, NOVEMBER 1938

I'M BLEEDING FROM my side and clinging to the higher branches
of a bare roadside tree. Having lost my rifle in retreat, I'm stripped
among the clothed, at war without a shield. I panicked, and this
charred tree was the first to call to me. Now, I'm too exposed by the
road but too terrified to climb down.

The last month of counterattacks have butchered our men in
hordes. I haven't slept properly in weeks so encounter the world
with an insomniac's detached but unrelenting terror. Memories have
disconnected from time and lost their sequential order. I can't be
certain of much, just that, near home, there's a field: pines huddle
in one of its corners, in another corner is a gurgling creek, in yet
another a gentle rise of hills, and there between them all my wife
and I laid while our infant daughter climbed over us, babbling like
the creek. I don't actually have a daughter, nor a wife, but the field
exists, and all I want is to complete the picture. My bones and soul
ache for it. Whenever I've imagined it, it takes place in the month
of May—spring's peak, life conquering death, summer's promises
before me wider than the ocean. A better version of life than I've
known. It seems a thing worth fighting for, a reason to keep going.

I reach for a higher branch—the moon past it is full and battered—but pain shoots through my side, doubling me over. Fires dot
this rolling horizon of the Ebro that had been forested when we first
arrived, dressed in evergreens. It's now cratered, the soil churned by
hundreds of thousands of shells into a muddy pulp in which the

corpses of men and horses settle. Burnt cordite and petrol are the air we breathe. Nothing will grow here again. If we beat them back, is this what our side wins? A stupid question. We're on the cusp of defeat.

A German plane roars overhead. Moonlight and firelight glint off its metal hull, etching its shape through the branches, when a shell cuts the air and the low night goes wild with color. There's a chance it missed our men. Then my stomach twists for a distant but approaching rumble and a faint light on the trees. I hug the branch tightly, try to become it, as the lorry's headlights creep up the road. Soon, its lambent outer rim is on the tree, then on me. I feel its warmth but can't jump down to run, not from that height.

The lorry continues bouncing over the uneven road, mud spitting from under its tires, and the headlights constrict to two sniper scopes then spread across the trees and the deep puddles ahead. I don't breathe. All it would take is for someone to glance up. But they pass right below. Fascists sit on wooden slats in the lorry's back, their rifles between their legs, encircling ten of our men they've taken prisoner and are likely driving to one of their pits. I should yell, cause a distraction—several might escape. These men have their own dreams, their own fields, perhaps actual memories. But I do nothing, and know it will find a thousand different ways to haunt me.

The world dims and the lorry keeps bucking, and I see Isidro among the imprisoned, his posture straight, straight as it was that evening he leaned against the tree on the outskirts of that dusty village, after he and Héctor killed those two boys in the church, locked in argument with himself and all the world. The rest of us peered into empty sheep pens, parted picked-over stems, followed sickly chickens to wherever they may have laid their eggs, or merely collapsed in a patch of shade—anything to avoid Isidro.

The next day, continuing to the Ebro, I must have been too inside my head because I found myself walking alongside him. When a soldier on the fascist's side was in this condition, an unfortunate chaplain was probably ordered to be audience to his self-loathing and doubt.

You wouldn't want to risk sending in a soldier. Doubt for a soldier, especially one belonging to a platoon like ours constantly in retreat, was a disease worse than malaria or syphilis. Those infected attracted fascist's bullets, so we'd learned to give them a wide berth. I was slowing my pace when Isidro said, "Two more." I didn't acknowledge him, still slowed. "Two more, Gable." It had been my name ever since joining with Mantilla's battalion last year. I didn't look much like Clark Gable, but you could swap his pencil mustache for mine and nobody would notice the difference. Pathologically, I kept it well-groomed. My thinking was: if I could control this one thing...

"Once the bullets fly, that's the arrangement," I said, my tone light. "Besides, Héctor owes me three wineskins. I'm glad fortune finally favored our side."

"Nothing's changed except the world is worse off. There's not a number of their dead that will make it any better."

"Keep it to yourself," I said. "Nobody wants to kill or die for a lost cause."

But he wouldn't let it go. "I'm not the person I thought I was."

"Who is?"

"I've become the very thing I left home to fight."

"Worse yet will happen to you if we lose."

"Every fire burns itself out."

"Meaning?"

"The fascists will ultimately destroy themselves. Think of all we've lost because we've engaged them on their terms."

I couldn't help but laugh. "Brother, you've got it bad. What I'm thinking is: this is what the fire has done to Spain. If we can't contain it here, imagine how it will spread to the rest of the world."

"We all know this is pointless."

"Sure," I said, drawing the word out, my eyes loping right and left. I cursed and danced on one foot. "Stone," I said. "A jagged bastard." I bent down to untie my boot. "You go ahead, I'll catch up."

He's a dead man, I thought, watching him as he approached the next of us to disturb. That night we made camp on the outskirts of the Ebro, attaching ourselves to another platoon, a group of anarcho-syndicalist laborers, exactly half of whom were prematurely bald. When I wasn't trying to make sense of that, I'd scour the forest's sawtooth treeline. In there was death, possibly mine, likely all of ours. Alcaraz, our commanding officer, had been talking to theirs when he returned with a letter. Letters were passed from one platoon to the next until they found their recipient. More often, the person would have long ago been buried behind us, so into the night's fire it would be tossed. But that was for the mail that found us. There had to have been thousands of letters traveling throughout Spain. I imagined them like comets. Round and around they would determinedly go—solitary, adrift—until the end of creation.

"Isidro," Alcaraz called out. Just great, I thought. This sentiment was reflected on others' faces. Alcaraz should have pocketed it for a few days. Rarely did they contain good news. I hoped he would ask for Isidro's rifle before giving him the letter but even that didn't occur to him. We kept Isidro in the corner of our vision. He sat away from us, within the light of the fire's reach. For a long while—one minute, five, then ten—he held the letter in his lap. I'd seen him read leaflets so knew he wasn't illiterate. By the time he opened the envelope, the others' attention had drifted elsewhere. I couldn't find Héctor. He owed his life to Isidro—whatever happened next should be his mess to tend to.

Isidro began reading. He frowned but immediately, wonderfully, I saw a fish-hooked smile. Maybe this would bring him back to us. But he frowned once more. Now, others were watching as he recoiled slightly then flipped the letter over. There was no text on that side. He looked in the envelope, found nothing there, dropped it with the letter, and stood, his hand over the bottom of his face and across his jaw while his eyes flitted about the ground as if for an answer. Taking his rifle with him, he entered the forest.

"Where's Héctor?" I asked. Nobody knew. "Alcaraz was the one foolish enough to give it to him. Have him read it." When he couldn't be found, the others returned to whatever they'd been doing earlier. "Fine," I said. "Fine." I bent and tilted it to catch the light.

My dearest Isidro, it is I, Mariana. I write to you in haste. I'm a prisoner in a hospital bed in Santander's San Marcos Hospital. A nun has provided me this pen and paper and has pledged to put it in hands that will find their way to yours. Her name is Jocabed. In Bilbao you promised to find me after this war, but, first, I want you to find her. I've had a daughter, Isidro. You and I have had a daughter. Sister Jocabed assisted with the delivery. The doctor claims it died in birth. The nuns, too. They're lying. Our child is now with a family sanctioned by the church. That or the orphanage. I never even got to hold her. I don't know what they have planned for me next, but whatever it is, I won't let them break me. I refuse that story. I put Nerea and Jon on a ship for England. We can only get them back, get our child back, if our side is victorious. We will be, because we must be. Afterward, imagine all we'll tell our baby. I hope to see you again soon, in a world far more just than the one descending upon us. Your dreamer, Mariana. Onwards.

I eyed the forest. "I wonder."

Quatro was by my side. "What does it say?" He couldn't start a sentence without four twitches of his upper lip. I had practically stopped noticing it, but I thought then: how many of us are dead because that tic kept you from warning us in time?

I folded the letter and returned it to the envelope. "Says here," I said, whacking his chest with it, "while you were gone, your wife has earned you a small fortune on her back."

He chuckled. Again, the lip danced. "I'm glad one of us is having fun." He turned to the others and opened his arms. "Chicos, I can finally afford land of my own."

I waited for Isidro. While I did, another platoon found us, then we shifted to merge with another, and though Alcaraz fought it, our platoon was parceled out before Isidro returned. I put the letter in my sack. It was a tolerable weight. I figured Isidro and I would never cross paths again. Nevertheless, I held onto it. And now that I see him I have no idea where my sack is or the letter therein, nor my rifle or the men we were with that night. I can't be certain any of them still live.

I squint at Isidro, try to will him to glance up. His vision is traveling around the lorry bed, from the fascists and their rifles to his fellow prisoners, searching, I can see, for an escape. Whatever doubt he possessed on that road to the Ebro is no longer a part of him. He has a child out there. All the reason a person would ever need to fight. Slowly, so as not to draw attention, his head lifts and our eyes meet. The look he gives me says *Of course, a tree, I should have considered that.* In the next moment, as each figure becomes indistinguishable, he offers the slightest nod. Not a farewell but a see you later. Is he convinced that I, too, will be caught? No. Somehow, he believes he'll survive. And if so, might I? The road curves to the left and the lorry with it. I'm alone again with the restless night, the silent fires in the distance, and the moon above, exhausted and ash-colored.

Not long after, I hear distant and successive rifle pops, then several others, their fading echoes. Inexplicably, the fascists continue shooting. I picture their anger as they pull their triggers, the bullets tearing into my fellow soldiers, into their bodies, each bullet taking them further from who their family would recognize, taking us further from the world we've fought for.

I wait for Isidro to come back and tell me to hurry down, tell me, *Hey, Gable, they might have killed everyone else, but you and I remain. There's a fight before us still.* Ahead, no shadows disturb the night. Nevertheless, I wait. I wait longer than I should. Finally, I try again for that higher branch but the pain in my side won't let me reach it. I'd have as much of a chance of flicking the moon. In minutes the lorry will return, bouncing on the rutted road for me, and I can't expect to be so lucky again. I start scooting down, all the while hoping that high branch will whisper to me, tell me to keep waiting, bend to me like a mother, but soon one foot is on the ground, then the other.

18

FAUSTINO   BARCELONA, JANUARY 1939

I KNEW 491 when he was still Juan Matas Reynoso, when, despite his fascination, he would hesitate at wringing a chicken's neck, when he couldn't hit an olive jar off a fence post from seven meters, when his mother would call him her Juanito. This was before my parents brought him in and my father loaded us all onto a ship for Cuba where, for nearly a decade—a part of my life I primarily recall in the sickly-sweet smell of rotting tobacco leaves—my father amassed a respectable fortune as foreman of a large nickel mining operation. I rarely saw him during those years, but I remember him pining, always, for our return to Spain. 491, too, searched the Eastern horizon with intensity. He fought daily with the neighborhood boys and showed little respect to our schoolmasters. My mother thought him a devil and regretted ever adopting her late sister's son, but I heard the noises he made at night while he thought I slept. I knew the truth.

For a Spaniard with connections, those American mines held a treasure, so had it not been for a series of strikes and a timely invitation from an old friend in Segovia, I think we may have never left the Caribbean. Instead, as 491 and I entered our eighteenth years, my family made the voyage across a calm Atlantic back to Spain, unaware that as we approached the Iberian Peninsula, General Franco had seized command of the Army of Africa in Morocco. Disembarking in Cádiz, the world had tipped irreversibly toward apocalypse, and my father enlisted 491 and me into the military for his side. He explained his decision to my mother. "Two less mouths now."

491 WASN'T IN need of a nickname, but the war christened him over and over so that, though we grew up as brothers, when I finally saw him again in November of '38, I no longer knew what to call him. Before the fighting in Badajoz, he was simply Matas, then Mata Rojos. Not very clever, but it fit him and his deft brutality in Utrera. But in Badajoz things changed quickly. As for me, I possessed none of his confidence and knew very little as to why we fought, only that I wanted to live. I developed the strong conviction that, so long as I didn't kill anybody, nobody had the right to put a bullet into me.

On the third day of fighting outside the Alcázar, we finally entered the ancient fortress walls. The Moroccan regulares charged in while we turned our attention to an ill-timed diversionary attack. 491 claimed to have dispatched twenty-seven rojos, and if I hadn't been by his side for most of the battle I would have doubted him, just as the others did. Outside the walls, near the Guadiana River, he would hit a target then take a pebble from the ground and put it in his pocket. He was methodical. His rifle would recoil and in the distance a fountain ruptured from a chest or neck or head through which the rojo's life bubbled out. 491 would then grab the nearest pebble, slip it in his pocket, and squint through the round eye-sight on his stock's end to locate the next target. That night, he and I sat at a campfire next to a burned-out church. Men carrying the stench of weeks on the road bragged of how many rojos they'd shot. As the conversation continued around the fire, each man upped the one before him. If one killed four then the next killed six. 491 began to smile. I felt out of place and when it was my turn to speak, I looked to him. He said that, because of him, twenty-seven rojos were wearing the Spanish earth that night. The men laughed and called us children. 491 stood and emptied his pocket of the twenty-seven pebbles. They fell onto the handkerchief where the men kept their cheese and chorizo, and somebody yelled at him, saying that was the last clean food they had left. "Each one of these is the life of a rojo," 491 told them. A man with a thick beard and a teardrop scar who'd been sitting against the trunk of a palm tree took the cheese and chorizo from the handkerchief and shook off the pebbles. 491 bit his lower lip, as he often did when he wanted to focus his anger. One of the men told him to calm down and tried to hand him a skin of wine. Another, still laughing, cut some chorizo for him, but he walked away, disappearing among the shadowy skeletons of houses. I followed the sound of shattered windows under his boots and finally found him near the bloated corpse of a cow.

In the distance was the campfire that belonged to the Moroccan regulares. The spices over their fire reached me despite the cow. They appeared at home among Badajoz's Arabic structures. It was they, not I, who belonged here. They had joined our column in Zafra, and after we took the city, our Lieutenant Colonel had pushed two peasant girls into a house where forty regulares waited. "Don't worry," he told a revolted officer, "they won't last more than four hours." But the officer flung his rifle from his shoulder and pushed past the Lieutenant Colonel to the door. The Lieutenant Colonel pressed his handgun against the small of the man's back. "Take one more step," he told him, "and we'll sew a wig to you and throw you in next." Afterwards, I kept my distance from the regulares, but they intrigued 491. There was a potential for cruelty that he was just beginning to understand. Not since we were children in Segovia did I see him so matched to his surroundings. Then, in Medina de las Torres, he watched in awe as those frenzied regulares climbed over their own dead to get at a rojo standing ground near the front doors of a cathedral, squeezing his trigger with unwavering fury though he had run out of bullets. When they finished with him, 491 approached the corpse, tilted his head to the right then left, and for reasons I couldn't understand at the time, put a bullet into what was left of the man's head.

Now, as I sat next to him, I wanted to talk of Cuba and those we'd left there, if he remembered the name of our first housekeeper and her beautiful daughter. I yearned to feel my feet under me, to return to a familiar place, but he asked how many stars I thought were above us. I hesitated before answering. The stars gathered in blue-tinted, hazy brumes. I couldn't tell one from the other. "I don't know," I said, "billions?" How about below us, he asked. Do you think there are more or less? I told him I thought there were probably about the same number. He said that couldn't be and told me how many there were above and below and why to our right there were so many more than to our left, and how it all had to do with the war we were fighting. The northern provinces were the enemy and though we had fared well in Badajoz he foresaw horrible casualties for our side in the eastern provinces of the country. He knew this because of the stars.

He never used to talk this way. Lately, he had begun speaking like a savage mystic. I thought of the twenty-seven men filling with gas along the riverbank, of the lice still biting at them, of the contract he had entered into with death. He didn't mention this or those by the fire but went on about what was above us and below us and, after some time, asked why I didn't fire my rifle that day. I felt the question had been coming. "But you're mistaken," I told him. 491 studied me for a few moments. "I hit two men," I said. "I can take you to them." He faced the stars again. I tried to discern his expression in the darkness. He started to say something but stopped at the sight of the prisoners, hundreds of them, being led toward us. Our men held torches in one hand, rifles in the other. Neither the soldiers nor prisoners acknowledged us. They marched silently on the road leading to the bullring atop the hill. The bullring's silhouette was the only remaining Spanish shape in this otherwise Arabic landscape.

491 grabbed his rifle and asked if I would accompany him. My carotid artery pounded against bone. There was something wrong with his voice. It was pinched by excitement, like an overeager child's. I told him I'd prefer to get to bed. He wished me a good night and hurried in the direction of the bullring. I waited until he passed the regulares' camp, then stood and managed to find our sleeping quarters under some palm trees. Soon, the rifle shots started from the bullring. They were sporadic but kept me awake. I thought about

the day and felt far from home, though no longer knew where it was or if I would live long enough to return to it. I resented 491 that he wasn't disturbed by similar concerns and fell asleep after several frustrating hours.

MORNING CAME QUICKLY. Two uniformed men with several stripes on their sleeves went up and down the rows of sleeping men, yelling and kicking at any trying to get a few more seconds of rest. 491 wasn't in his bag.

The city had changed during those few hours I slept. From the bullring, the rifle shots and screaming were now ceaseless. The city seemed incapable of bearing the sounds. Everything looked grey. Occasionally, an *olé* whooped from the bullring. "What's going on over there," a soldier asked one of the men with stripes. He answered by assigning him and three of us, solely due to our proximity to the man who asked the question, to report to the highest commanding officer at the cemetery on the edge of town. Walking there, I cursed the soldier under my breath but stopped at the sight of blood running downhill from the bullring in five rivulets, like fingers reaching for us, discoloring the ground. "No me jodas," one of the men chuckled. "I never thought it was actually possible." But on the far side of the bullring we saw a street where a wide stream of blood blackened the gutter and gathered into a turbid pond at the bottom. It had a sweet and coppery smell to it. One of the men couldn't stop coughing. I didn't feel well, either, on my empty stomach. "It's because of the minerals in our body," said the man who had asked the question. "That's why blood smells like that." At the entrance of the bullring two trucks were parked, and the Moroccan regulares handled the dead. Their tan uniforms and white cloaks were saturated with blood, red as their fezzes. They worked mechanically, carrying the bodies by the arms and legs and hoisting them into the bed of a truck before returning to the bullring for more. There was a pause in the gunfire. I heard a few guttural cries, the cheering from our men, a collective, anticipatory *ooh* that rose to a crescendo as if an escape had been averted, then applause. "What's happening in there?" the soldier by my side asked again.

Another truck teeming with slaughtered rojos pulled away from the bullring and passed us on the road toward the cemetery. "Joder," one of our men said. Not long after, a boy pedaled past on a bicycle, unconcerned by our presence. At the cemetery we helped the driver unload the bodies. There were already at least two hundred laid out in lines, their arms draped over each other in awkward embraces. Many must have been killed during the start of the fighting as their graying upper lips were already pulling back, giving way to death. The commanding officer was furious that we were the only ones assigned to him. "Get rid of these bodies," he said. One of the men with me said, "You can't expect us to be able to bury them all."

"I don't care how the fuck you do it," the officer said. "This is now our fucking land, and I don't want to see these fucking rojos on it." I thought it unnecessarily dramatic but knew to stay quiet. You survived by keeping your head down.

We each took a shovel, cursing the officer and the soldier whose question put us in our position, but before we dug a shallow hole wide enough for three corpses, another truck came from the bullring to the cemetery. This time, four Moroccan regulares sat on the tailgate. They shared a cigarette and joked with one another while bodies jostled heavily behind them. So we began unloading the dead. I hesitated touching their hairy forearms and muddy ankles and bare feet, their damp armpits moist from fear. They were difficult to handle. Their clothes and skin were soaked through, the blood warm and slick. For many, their bowels had released their grip in death. We worked while continuously smoking. Most of the bullets had entered their chests, though some destroyed their jaws so that their mouths swung open across a shoulder. "What should we do about this one?" a soldier asked, pointing at a still-blinking rojo. Blood clouded his eyes, and he breathed with his mouth open. Flies grazed at the corners of his lips. A bullet had sheared a hole through his trachea, which wheezed with each breath. The commanding officer glanced down then turned away. "He'll be dead by the time you dig his grave." I helped the soldier remove him from the truck, incapable of looking at the dying man for fear our eyes would meet, but jumped back at the sight of a shirtless man underneath him. "What's this," I asked. Two red and gold banderillas drenched in blood hung from the shirtless man's back. The blades' talons had popped an organ—blood hemorrhaged from him. Between his shoulder blades was a gaping wound, and when I turned him over, I saw where the sword exited. Through the cartilage of his nasal septum somebody had punctured a hole and managed a ring through it, resembling a bull. "That," the driver said, laughing, "is the work of Belmonte." Belmonte had been Spain's greatest bullfighter. One of the soldiers digging holes with me pumped his fist. "We've got Belmonte," he said, astonished.

"Don't be an idiot," the driver said. "You think Belmonte gets his hands dirty with this war? He pays somebody to wipe his ass for him."

In the next three trucks, we unloaded others killed in this manner. The whooping and cheers from the stadium grew louder. "Belmonte is perfecting his craft," the driver said pointing at a man with only a sword wound, no ring through his nose or banderillas, and this time the sword had not been run straight through him but instead the killing had been done cleanly. As in a good corrida, the sword's tip cleaved the heart, and the man had died instantly. His ears had been cut away.

I CAN NO longer remember who came up with the idea. After several hours of digging, we started piling the bodies against the cemetery wall and dousing them with petrol. We stood upwind but the smell of the burning flesh and hair overwhelmed us nonetheless. A lieutenant colonel came in his truck and yelled at us and the officer and the Moroccan regulares. The stench had reached those in the city center, and they couldn't think straight from it. So that put an end to incinerating the bodies, but it relieved us of having to dig such a large hole for all of them. 491 didn't return to our sleeping quarters that night. And the next day the soldier had gone from Belmonte to The Matador. I assumed the officers learned of 491's last name.

At least two dozen of us were at the cemetery digging pits. The ground under the charcoaled bones still smoldered. Soot had darkened the tombstones and crucifixes and flowers. The trucks arrived with the same consistency as the day before and always there were at least two men killed in the style of the corridas, missing an ear or two, but the trucks also contained the bodies of women and children, their warm bodies pocked by bullets. Some of the soldiers began to complain until an officer said that children of rojos grow up to become rojos and that the wombs of these women were rojo factories. Still, one soldier refused to handle the dead. He wouldn't take part. "There will be eternal repercussions for our actions here," he said. "What eternity," another soldier joked. "You think God is a peasant woman looking over her potato field?" Nevertheless, he stuck his shovel into the earth and crossed his arms. He was promptly court-martialed and shot in front of us. For the rest of the day, my hands shook as I dug. The rules were changing.

491 didn't sleep among us that night either, and the following day our column proceeded north. I bundled up his sleeping bag and shouldered the extra weight. By then, he was known as The Matador of 212. Those of us who had been digging were assigned to the second column. This put us closer to Madrid and closer to the fighting. Leaving Badajoz, we passed the ceremonial shooting of seven high-ranking Loyalists from the Popular Front. They appeared tired but well-fed. An officer to my right said, "We must prove to our fellow Spaniards that we don't just shoot workers and peasants." Thousands of people crowded in the square to watch. A full-sized band played a festive number that I hummed to distract myself as we marched out of the city.

I WAS BADLY wounded during the retreat in Guadalajara but was fortunate to have been shot in the upper thigh. Those who couldn't walk on their own were left behind, clawing in agony toward camp. Any reaching to grab hold of those running away were brained by a lieutenant colonel half out of his head who alternately screamed *solidaridad* and *patria* before each bullet. At camp, I lay down with the rest of the wounded. Several hours later the rojos could be seen coming over the ridge. Of those in the makeshift ward, I was one of three who managed to get to my feet and escape. The phantom bullet floated like a serrated bone in the meat of my thigh. We watched from afar while the rojos descended upon what was left of our camp.

After several days my wound became infected, and I was put on a train to Sevilla. All through that first week I went back and forth about whether or not I should apply the salves to my infection, but in the end decided the wound was too far up and that I may not survive the amputation. In the hospital I listened to the exploits of 303. Others spoke as if he were over two meters tall and as impenetrable as a tank. I tried to tell them of the boy who couldn't even hold on to the flailing body of a wrung chicken. They shushed me, and the commanding officer entered my name in his book. I learned to keep my mouth shut. There was no shortage of news regarding 491's heroics. In June, he aided General Dávila's Army of the North with the capturing of Bilbao and the surrender of the Basques. Six weeks later he played a significant role on the coast in the falling of Santander. In late August, during the house-to-house fighting in Zaragoza, he killed three-dozen men.

BY FEBRUARY I was deemed fit to hold a shovel, and I found myself in the Ebro countryside, digging trenches in anticipation of the others. 491, meanwhile, had traveled south to recapture Teruel. The fighting in the Ebro was sporadic and half-hearted through spring, but with the start of the rainy season the rest of our infantry arrived and we managed to get momentum on our side. We fought for months. A day or two before the final push, while walking with a bowl of hot water and my razor and bar of soap, I spotted 491. The evening before, one of the ten prisoners we had taken into the forest to execute had escaped. I had tried to evade the firing squad assignment, as I had in the past, but lately the rumors had begun reaching my ears. Those who I was close to warned me. So that night I'd been lined in front of a soldier with two missing fingers on his left hand. His glare was defiant but rooted in a desire I recognized. It had little to do with any similarities regarding physical characteristics but he reminded me of my old friend. He wore these years of war as if no other life beside this exhausting one ever existed. Studying his expression, I recognized a kindred refusal of this moment. He broke from my gaze and looked off to the forest at his right, inviting me to do so, as well. Rather than follow his vision, I closed my eyes and tried bending my finger over the curve of the trigger, listening to my galloping heartbeat, feeling a paralysis cement my limbs and my throat constrict when I heard the commands to aim for their hearts and to fire, then the clustered pops. The prisoners fell into the pit, one onto the other, but my prisoner was gone. Who knows how much lead the others threw at him as he wove through the forest. It was inexplicable. My friends pled on my behalf to the commanding officer. It will be the firing squad for him if you report this, they said. He blew a hole in the rojo's forehead, we can all confirm it. The bastard has a third eye. There are ten bodies lying on the ground, they said. Put his name in your book with the others. We all see him sleeping with his friends. Put his name among the others.

That next morning I made several resolutions I knew I wouldn't be able to keep. Then I saw 491. We were born months apart, but the years had aged him in a way that reduced me to a child. It seemed unfair. Adult lines etched deep into his brow. The sun had leathered his skin. His posture was flawless, boots clean, and he looked to have grown. Before, we could stand back-to-back and it'd be impossible to tell which of us was taller. I could say now without hesitation he was, by several fingers.

"Juan," I called out for him. "Juan," I said again. "Juan Matas Reynoso. Belmonte. Mata Rojas. The Matador. 468." But he kept walking, and a soldier came from out of nowhere and told me to speak with more respect to 477. I laughed at him. "You mean Juanito," I said. And once more I called to him—his back was to me. "Juanito." I said it again, "Juanito." There wasn't a wrinkle in his uniform. "Juanito, teach me how to wring the neck of a chicken. I can't do it without retreating in fear. Juanito, my mother's passed away from the flu, and I've nowhere to go. My father was a drunk who abandoned her the moment he laid his seed. Will you take me in? If not, it's the orphanage for me. What do you say, Juanito?" He ignored me. "Maybe," I said to the soldier, "the fighting has affected his hearing. Me, I'm as deaf as an old man." The soldier eyed me with suspicion.

491 turned a corner and that was the last time I ever saw him. He would die a month and a half later in Barcelona. He was standing in front of a washroom mirror when a single bullet entered his left temple and came out the other side, shattering his jaw.

The rumors were immediate. Some said it was the work of a professional hired by a wealthy Englishman, revenge for one of the lives he took. Someone dared tell me he'd died from his own hand. With the war ending, what purpose did he have to go on? Simple and ridiculous mythmaking. Anyone who knew him knew he was incapable of such a thing.

HE WAS MURDERED during the final days of January. The last of the rojos in the north were fleeing to the French border. Along with a few cities on the coast, Madrid was all alone now. It took nearly three years of war for the rojos to figure this out.

A letter arrived from my father. Good news, he said. He'd purchased a tungsten mining company on the cheap from a socialist's widow and wanted me to be the foreman of it. I'd proven myself worthy. He arranged my discharge with a colonel who'd once served under Yagüe. Come the week's end, I was free to leave. Just like that.

I had wanted nothing more for so long, but I sent word back that first I had business in Barcelona to tend to. I'd see him afterwards.

I used the colonel's name and my father's, called in favors I wasn't owed, then booked travel in what had to have been the loudest train in Spain. Despite my poor hearing, the thunderous rattling kept me from thinking on any one thing for more than a few minutes at a time. Even after disembarking in Barcelona, the roar of all that machinery continued echoing in my head.

Barcelona, like so much of Spain, was an odd contradiction that winter. Some of its neighborhoods were stripped of color, reduced to rubble that husks of buildings leaned in, buildings that a strong breeze would soon topple and clear from memory. Other blocks shimmered in Mediterranean golds and blues. You suspected a single bullet was never let loose down those streets. Where I was going was far from the water. A small path had been cleared for people to walk between the ruins. In my uniform, the few locals I passed turned away from me. I hitched my rifle further up my shoulder and tightened my coat. The remains of buildings inclined like drunks against one another. It was a haunted place. Every window on the street had been blown out. The façade of one appeared untouched but behind it was a mess of mortar and stones and rebar. There were children's discarded clothes nearly at the surface, sodden from rain. Atop another pile of stones a lone boy of about five bent and threw pebbles in the air. He watched me vacant-eyed as I passed. The gagging odors of decomposition were everywhere. I thought of all the steps I'd taken during the war that had, through blind fortune, put me where death in that moment was not. So many other men I knew—dozens, hundreds—every step they'd taken in their lives, every decision they'd made, had ultimately led them right into the bullet's path. The threat existed for me still. Is this the right course, I asked myself. Is this?

I turned several blocks then several more and saw the young soldier standing outside the door waiting for me. "The third floor?" I asked him. He nodded. I climbed the empty stairwell, expecting, for some reason, to be stopped.

On the third floor, the apartment door was cracked open. Inside, another soldier stood at attention. "They've cleared it of 491's things?" I asked. He didn't answer. His one job, so far as I could tell, was tending to the candles. The dresser drawers had not been pushed back in, the bed had been stripped of its sheets. I placed my palm against the bathroom door. The faint streak of blood remained on the tiled wall. Air whistled in through the punctured window, the glass around the hole was fractured in a spiderweb pattern. I tried swallowing but could not. If he'd only been shaving there, I thought, the bullet would have grazed him, maybe missed him entirely. The cold kept seeping in and with it came the names of the dead, of those I'd watched die and tried to not think about whenever I closed my eyes. As I stood in that doorway, one after the other assailed me, pegged me in place, like they were waiting for just this moment. Luis Barrera Tomás. Teodoro Blanco Bonilla. Roberto Pérez Delgado. José Mari Costa Pedra. Joaquín López de Vega, who caught a bullet on the side of his face. *Where am I*, he cried on the ground. *Where am I? What has happened here, what is this*—until he fell silent. Fernando Rodríguez Duero, who told me, *I kill not because I like to kill but because I love to live*, but I saw him in Guadalajara sitting on the ground away from the fighting, blood running down his face while with outstretched hands he tried to ward off an approaching darkness. Pedro Salvador Torres, whose family owned over two hundred head of sheep and whose spinal column a bullet grazed and who fell face forward, drowning in the mud of Plasencia before we could turn him over. Javier Torres Villalobos, who shielded his eyes with a hand while peering up to locate the plane when a swarm of bullets threw him to the ground, and he begged for the rosary he kept around his neck, but the bullets had made such a mess of his torso that I had to knot a shoelace and give this to him. His crying kept him from completing his first Ave Maria.

The past returned. I felt stripped, meat and bone exposed, standing in that doorway, repeating over and over, "Juan Matas Reynoso, Juan Matas Reynoso," as though it would make it all less real. But, no, 491 was gone, too, and his end had to be as final and inglorious and solitary as the others'. Of that I was now certain. I could see him, my old friend, in this washroom the moment he was suddenly thrown onto his side. I could see him trying to get to his feet, panicking, incapable of comprehending the spray of blood that slowly moved down the tiled wall. And I thought for the first time of the fear that connected him to me, that connected us all—the men we'd served with, those we'd fought against, every wretched one of us that contributed to this war—and for the first time in years, I didn't feel alone.

The soldier who had welcomed me in was behind me, asking if I was all right.

"Of course," I said, wiping at my face, "it is just happiness."

BACK AMIDST THE rubble, my eyes not yet dry, I came upon a man hefting a ten-liter steel gas can in one hand. With the other, he clutched an infant to his chest. His movements were hurried and panicked. He would have been sprinting if not for the weight of the can. He hadn't seen me. I followed him to a black and yellow Hispano-Suiza, a brand of luxury car whose name I knew because my father's former business partner used to go around in one. As a child, I'd run my fingers over its hood ornament of a stork in flight, dirtying its ridged wings with my prints until someone, sometimes the chauffeur, oftentimes my father, yelled at me to stop.

The man set the swaddled baby on the passenger seat and, in his rush to fill the tank, dropped the can, which had no cap. I approached at first because I was curious, then because I thought I could be of some help, but nearing the man, I saw that he was too unkempt to have been raised among money. He had to have stolen the car, just as he did the steel can, and more than likely the gasoline in it. He probably steered the dying car into the ruins figuring that we Nationalists had already had our way with the neighborhood, so why would we stick around.

I swallowed to clear my throat and dragged a finger under my nostrils. Before I could speak, the man spotted me, dropping the steel can once more. His knees were muddy with ash and gasoline. "You will want to set that right," I said of the can and the gasoline that was again spilling out. He did, peaking at the infant across the seat, then the narrow road ahead, and the rifle across my shoulder. He worked out the math. When he faced me, it was with a full chest, the sort brave men present to the firing squad. This man's clothes were threadbare, he hadn't shaved in more than a week, his mustache was untrimmed, his cheekbones had been cut by hunger. I'd seen enough rojos to know he was one. Even rats spawn, but I read plenty of this man's story in his jumpy eyes to understand this wasn't the case for him. "Whose baby is that?" I asked.

He hesitated, then set his jaw.

"From whom did you steal her?"

"She was already stolen."

I peered around him to look at the child. She was wrapped in a thick yellow blanket against the cold. A wool cap was pulled over her head. Despite the falling temperatures, she was likely sweating. I was worthless when it came to guessing infants' ages.

"Twice now? She doesn't look a year old."

"She isn't."

"Who does she belong to?"

He tightened his lips. Again, he filled his chest, as though he'd rather take the bullet than divulge a name. "I won't allow you to take her back to the fachas."

My first impulse was to impose my will upon him. I was the one with the rifle, I belonged to the victorious side. My friends had died for that victory.

"What day is today?"

The question confused him. "Saturday."

According to my father's letter, I was now free. I no longer belonged to the army whose uniform I wore. The war, I sensed, would never be finished with me, but I was finished with it.

"Where are you taking her?" I asked. "Back to her parents?"

The man noticed my red-rimmed eyes. This disarmed him. His bunched posture slackened. "First," he said, "out of Spain. To safety. Afterwards, I'll reunite her with her mother." Then, as if an afterthought, as though this would be the greater challenge, "Or at least try to."

"The roads to France are being bombed."

"There's no other option."

The rest of my life would consist of overseeing the excavation of one mineral mine for its treasures, then another. I'd never be leaving this country that had demanded we sacrifice our one glimpse at life to destroy each other. I went around the car. The fuel cap was where I had remembered it. I unscrewed the cap and motioned to the steel can. "Hopefully enough remains to get you across the border."

He bent for the can but kept his eyes on me, supposing it a ploy.

"Go on," I said. "Give it." As I poured the gas into the tank, I saw there was a single suitcase on the backseat. The whole thing—the kidnapping, the escape—must have come about suddenly. He was being hunted. If he wasn't bombed off the road, whoever had first kidnapped this child would track him down. They were likely on their way now. He'd be executed the moment the child was taken from his hands. "Is this really worth the risk?" I asked.

"To do the right thing?"

I didn't answer but put the empty can in the backseat by the suitcase, then left him there, climbing into the car.

I kept my hearing attuned for footfalls behind me. Anyone who would steal a child and a Hispano-Suiza would not hesitate at bashing in a Nationalist's head with rubble to possess a rifle. I turned the corner just as the car engine flooded with gasoline and growled. It was too loud. If anyone after him was in the vicinity, they'd hear it. There were so few buildings still standing to muffle the sound. When the car's engine finally faded, when I strained but could no longer hear it, I stopped and allowed my shoulders to relax. I looked up to the sky. It was blue and uniform and impenetrable. Against it, the plume of my breath thinned to nothing.

19

PALE WHITE BREATHS rose from the crowd, thin and tattered, insisting weakly that we remain. Some shared a blanket as they walked. Others crossed their arms tightly over their chests, their shoulders bunched, wearing all the clothes they'd managed to throw into suitcases when the air raid sirens had rung.

Snow dusted the pines, collected on the branches. Through them, the occasional snowflake became visible, then disappeared against the light. Ahead of us, somewhere, was France. Behind us on this muddy road: the years of war, the remains of our country, those we'd been forced to leave behind, more dead than we could count. If we were able to, the number would be meaningless, incapable of conveying what we'd witnessed and endured. Nevertheless, we tried to make sense of it, which was likely what kept us talking. I caught snatches of conversations around me.

"They've already said: if you burned a church, it's as if you killed a banker—you're going against the wall."

"During all that time a fascist never laid eyes on our daughter, thank God. Not once. I sometimes wished this war might scar her. A mother shouldn't say such things, but, don't you see, she's too beautiful."

The conversations were snagged on a loop. Similar words, the same inflection points. Were we so hungry for confirmation from each other that we continued to exist? Was there no other way to be certain unless someone saw us, nodded, said they understood, said please, keep going?

"Melons, that's all I smell. Overripe and mushy melons. Even after a bombing or among the dead—it's as though I'm standing in the middle of a field where melons wither on vines. I suppose it's a blessing."

And what would I say were I the type relieved by talking? Would I ask what had been the point? All we'd fought to bury now flourished in Spain. Or would I say, instead, I still believed the world could be saved. I had to. In Spain were those we needed to return for.

"What I can't forget are the wounded outside the Vallarca hospital. They hobbled toward us on crutches. The ones without dragged themselves down the street."

Maybe I'd tell my own defining story, the one that prods me still. I had a brother once. I had two, but the other, the oldest, was like my father. They cared about shepherding, the demands of the day, the season. Their concerns ended where the sheep stopped grazing. Winter, so far as they'd been told, didn't ignore you if you were a communist. Hunger spared no fascist. Then why bleed out for an idea? If they were determined to choose a side, they'd have found common cause with the fascists. Especially my father. He was ruthlessly self-interested, violently so, unyielding, life's path and purpose prescribed by a church you dared not question. Power flowed from it to him but stopped there. Any deviation from his wishes, any challenge to his commands, and he'd lay into us. Never enough to keep us out of the field. My face in the dirt, blood and soil every taste and smell, I'd wait for the kick that would deliver me to bed for days. It never came. He knew just when to pull back. Life had wronged him a thousand different ways before robbing him of his wife. He made sure we knew that. He made sure we felt his pain.

"The wounded of Vallarca were howling not to be left behind. Flailing. It opened their wounds, soaked their bandages. Yet how they continued waving, as though to strike at demons or repel their fast-approaching fate."

My oldest brother learned how to avoid our father's fists. Xabier and I weren't as successful. Not that we tried. Him maybe, me not so much. I'd rather keep dropping my shoulder against the orthodoxy dictating my life. What warmed me, even when our father was at his worst, was having Xabier there to endure it with me. So when Xabier joined the priesthood, that hurt more than all the beatings. A great betrayal, no matter his motives. By then I realized that the world was as perilously positioned as I was. We were both of us in need of saving. *How* came through Mariana's writing.

"We swatted at the wounded as they grabbed at the lorries we'd overloaded with mattresses and bird cages and furniture and suitcases. No matter how careful we were, the blood soaking their bandages got all over us."

But more than a year ago, fascists tossed a rope over a high branch and cinched it around Xabier's neck. This changed me, for a while.

Were anyone willing to listen to me now, I'd tell them I served in this war not only to fight against fascism but to escape my father, to finally live, to drink up all of this life I could, to fight alongside those equally impassioned, to search for that kinship I once had with my brother, to suffer grandly, make things a little easier for others, and be able to answer when it was asked of me: so why were you given this time under the sun?

When I learned of Xabier's murder, all that went into the grave with him. I was blind for revenge.

Claiming it, I sought forgiveness, became desperate for mercy and grace and an end to this war without end. However, a letter arrived—I had a child. A new family awaited me.

"While we beat the wounded back, they begged not to be abandoned. Each of their wounds was from the war. That they survived was an insult to the fascists, who don't like leaving behind unfinished business."

Our daughter was kidnapped by the church, by the regime, by fascists. I guess I forgot I was a part of all those I'd met and that they were a part of me, that together we were fighting not solely for our future but for those who will follow us.

Submission wasn't an option, never could be, so rather than make a final and suicidal stand in Barcelona, I retreated with the others toward France. There, we would regroup. Our side still held Madrid and Valencia. The fight against fascism continued, would continue, for as long, at least, as I drew breath. It was the only one way to reclaim what was mine. The soldiers surrounding me, I was certain, were similarly motivated.

"It took all we had but we managed to beat the wounded off. We left them half-naked in the cold. How they foamed with rage. They cursed us for a dozen generations. And now look at us: no lorry and just these few possessions."

So I suppose I was thinking of her already, of the woman we called Have You Seen, when someone shouted and a high-pitched buzz suddenly grew loud in the western sky. We scattered, running into the forest, high-stepping through snow. You hardly heard the screams as the German fighters dove again and again and again, spitting lead into the masses.

THE ROAD WAS behind us somewhere. For close to an hour the Germans chased us deeper into this balding forest, making a sieve of whoever they caught. They were refueling now and rearming. Miguel and I still wore our uniforms, as soiled and flayed as they were, so we attracted others. First, a mother and her daughter. The girl had managed to keep her checkered blanket, which she wore over her shoulders. Her teeth chattered for the cold and her face was drained of color, save for her nose burning pink. Then an elderly couple, and finally a family of four. The father wasn't much older than Miguel and me but deferred to us on account of our uniforms. Thousands had been on that road, yet we were unable to find any others. Until, that is, Miguel looked over my shoulder and said, "Joder, Isidro, you're never going to believe this." I turned then chuckled—there she was.

THE FIRST TIME I saw her was in Belorado. By that point she already had her name. "Has visto a mi Demario?" "Has visto a mi

257

hijo?" "Has visto a mi girasol?" Have you seen my boy? Have you seen my sunflower? I wondered if she had sense enough not to wander over to the fascists' lines or if she even approached them asking whether they'd seen her only child, the son they'd killed. She always showed you the photograph. It was from years earlier, when he was fourteen or fifteen. He had thick lips and a surprised expression, as if somebody had just warned him: in a few years, you'll be gone. His ears jutted out at ninety-degree angles. Adulthood had likely sharpened his features, but I didn't recognize him. He'd belonged to Lieutenant Colonel Díaz's regiment.

Demario wasn't that common of a name. I knew of one other, a soldier I had fought alongside in Calahorra, which is where Have You Seen found us. Unlike so many battles, this one was a set-piece. There was a lull in the positioning when someone said, "Christ, she's still alive," and Have You Seen hurried our way, her hands up at her chest, her bony fingers nervously intertwining as they often did. Demario—our Demario—anticipated the others. "I'll put a bullet in whoever points to me."

She'd pop up all over the map—Logroño, Toledo, Lleida—to give people her son's name. "Demario, my little sunflower, have you seen him?" I doubted my father and surviving brother spoke my name these days. If they did, if they pictured me in this pine forest where the thin branches provided little cover and we stood out starkly against the snow, they'd probably say to each other, "That's what he gets for joining a fight nobody invited him to." But Have You Seen showed the photo to all she crossed paths with, told his name, gave his story. "He was born small, and he stayed small. Kids in the classes below him quickly passed him in height. 'I'm going to fight for Spain, for liberty,' he told me. 'I want to see what I'm capable of.' He was so small, though. 'But Demario, do they even have a uniform that will fit you?'"

She became a mascot of sorts. You could forget all about her, live three different lives, then you'd spot her stepping cautiously over the rubble to ask if you'd seen her son. The world was constantly shifting underneath us, atrocities no longer shocked as they once did, a shared madness coursed through all, but there was, at least, this one constant.

Outside Peñalba, she found us at a bad time. Rayo had lost his best friend an hour earlier and remained standing over his broken body. He'd managed to close his eyes, but the mouth no longer fit together properly. It was a throat-tightening scene. Marrow had seeped from exposed bones and mixed with blood so that Rayo was keeping vigil in a pool of milky crimson. "He's dead," Rayo shouted at her when she approached. He was speaking of her Demario, not his best friend. "I can write to my mother anytime I want. Why do you think you haven't heard from him? I'm not sure who lied to you at the start, but they did you a disservice and fucked the rest of us. Every person in Lieutenant Colonel Díaz's regiment was killed, your Demario included." She listened, and we waited for her collapse, but when he finished, she asked the next soldier. "What about you, have you seen Demario, my little sunflower?"

Sure, there were times she could be a nuisance, but even then your heart broke for her, for yourself, for all those ideas you'd fought and everyone who'd fought alongside you. After news of my brother's hanging, I, too, felt compelled to ask strangers: Did you know my brother, can you tell me a story about him at the end, anything that might bring him back? After I got my revenge I longed to ask: And what about me? Have you seen me, who I once was?

The last time I saw Have You Seen was in Tarragona, seven or eight months ago. I'd mostly forgotten about her, until I received the letter from Mariana: we've had a child together, Isidro. A daughter the fascists have stolen from us. *Search for her. Fight for her.*

Occasionally I'd notice a skinny, nervous woman in the distance, and I'd squint to make out her features. Seeing it wasn't Have You Seen, I'd think of how much time had passed since Tarragona. I'd hope she'd found what she was looking for. Not her son, since that would be impossible, but a truth she could live with, a sort of peace.

But, no, here she was.

THE FATHER ALONGSIDE us was looking past her for the thousands of others who'd been on the road, his head on a swivel. She always approached the soldiers first. Wide-eyed, she'd study our uniforms, imagining, I guessed, her Demario in one.

Her bones couldn't have weighed much more than a sparrow's, yet the snow still crunched under her feet. The shoes she wore were made of a thin material that the snow had darkened and the cold afterwards had hardened. I wondered if she could feel her toes.

"Have you seen," she asked me, "my son, my Demario?"

As she started, Miguel whispered appreciatively, "It's nice some things don't change."

"He's twenty now. Your age maybe. Maybe a year or two less." She held the photograph to us. The boy in it seemed younger than he ever had before. "Have you seen him?"

I reached for her chin to steady her face. "Who did this to you?" She had a black eye. It was a few days old. The mark was cloudy along its perimeter, the bruised skin already beginning to sag. Likely someone short-tempered pushed her away then reached back with a fist when she persisted questioning them. You selfish bitch, they might have said. We've all lost someone. Or: we've lost everything. Or: we're all lost now.

She pulled out of my hold and asked Miguel. "Have you seen my Demario?"

"Sorry, darling, still nothing."

"Where did you come from?" I asked, but she turned to the older couple.

"This is my sunflower. Demario. He enlisted with Colonel Díaz's regiment in Asturias. Have you seen him? It's not a recent photo. He's a young man now, but you'd recognize those eyes. The sweetest child. Always so affectionate. 'Mama,' he'd say after each meal, 'you'll give me gout by twenty.' They were the simplest plates, really, but how I loved cooking for him."

"I hadn't heard that one before," Miguel said to me.

"I did once." I closed my eyes to remember. "Torrellas, maybe. He's a sweet kid, that Demario."

"Too gentle for this world."

"Well," I told Have You Seen, "I guess you're joining us." She was showing the mother and young daughter the photograph. I told the group, "Those planes will return soon, and when they do, I want us over there." I pointed to a far-off mountain whose face you couldn't see for the trees carpeting it. Everyone else, I figured, was hiking to the protection they provided. In the meantime, we were easy targets.

I KEPT GLANCING behind me to be sure Have You Seen remained with us. "I'm expecting her to wander off and show that photo to a squirrel," I told Miguel.

"If she does," he said, "let me know. I'd eat it raw." A little while later, he asked, "Do you really think it's over? The war?"

"Not for a long, long time."

"It will be hard to keep it going as a refugee in France."

"We're just regrouping. So long as we hold Valencia, its port, we can sail down the Balearic. I'm eager to see southern Spain."

"Getting a boat might be an issue. The French have fascists, too."

"Along with their neighbors. No shortage of fascists. I think that's been our problem."

"I can't remember a time without war. I'm not sure I know how to make friends if people aren't wishing me dead."

"The French will oblige."

The treetops cracked and groaned—from far away came the sound of one collapsing. The silver sky went on forever. Should there ever be a last day, this would be the light of its dawn. By midday, the end.

Miguel's forlornness gave way to a renewed determination. He said, "Even if Madrid and Valencia fall, the world won't tolerate this new arrangement on the map. England, France, maybe even America. People will fight like we have. They watched us long enough. We let them know it's possible."

"All we did was find new ways to lose."

"Only way we can be certain of what tomorrow brings is if we give up."

It was more than zealotry. We had faith in humanity. We believed in tomorrow. If we didn't, we'd have stayed home or joined the fascists in their attempt to dominate Spain. "That's right," I said. "Rest your shoulder while you can. The rifle butt will soon again be kicking into it."

There began a slope to this field of trees. Further ahead, a quiet and muddy road bisected it. Seeing it stopped us. We listened for the planes, all of us except the older man, who seemed to be mostly deaf. The trees' cover was as thin as mosquito piss. The last time we'd walked on a road, we'd been shot at, so we were hesitant to cross this one. As we started for it, the girl began crying. This agitated the two kids—a pair of boys, possibly twins—each less than five years old. Their parents had them when they were about my age. They carried them against their chests to muffle their whimpering. The older woman leaned close to the girl and said, with just enough sweetness to confound, "I once had a granddaughter like you. She couldn't keep quiet either."

The father was by our side. His son's arms were wrapped tightly around his neck, his legs out wide, face buried against his shoulder. I had no memory of ever being held like that. The body heat surely helped both. He saw me eyeing them. "Do you have any children?" he asked.

The question stopped me. Nobody had thought to ask before, so I'd never shared with anybody Mariana's letter, our last night together in Bilbao, and how, in a city emptied of people, we'd made a life together. Which allowed fascists to imprison her in a hospital bed and take from us what was ours.

We halted before the last trees before the clearing. "It feels like a thousand years ago since I was in Bilbao," I started, but he wasn't paying attention. Instead, he lifted his chin at the road and said, "They probably have rifles trained on it, no?" It was a dull, muddy strip.

I swallowed my story and told him, "If that was the case, we'd see bodies."

"Maybe we're the first trying to cross it."

"I would feel better," Miguel agreed, "if we weren't so alone."

The father said, "Thousands on the road and now no one?"

Standing there, the air became perfectly still and the trees stopped creaking. We glanced up at them. All you could hear were our vaporous breaths. It was the sort of silence rifle shots like to break.

"Nobody's on the road," I said.

"But can you be sure?" the father asked.

At this, his wife spoke up. "Of course he can't." She was admonishing her husband. We were all speaking in loud whispers. She readjusted the boy clinging to her. "We're here because you were convinced the fascists were going to burn Barcelona."

"They will. They mean to extinguish us."

This sort of talk couldn't have been good for the children. Have You Seen kept to the side, absently smiling, uninterested in our conversation and whatever threat was ahead. She looked to have one foot in placid memories.

Any moment the planes might return. "I'll go first," I said.

You never hear the one that hits you. In this cold, I doubted even the Germans could aim straight. They'd give me plenty warning.

There was no burp of gunfire as I stepped from behind the last tree. Soon, it felt like I was walking through a world stripped of air. Snowflakes materialized out of nowhere, hung and shimmered, then disappeared. For a moment I didn't know where I was going or who I'd meet there, but after a few more steps I found myself on that simple muddy road, considering its plainness through pluming breaths.

Waving to the group, I saw something glint down the road, near its bend. "What's that?" I sensed no threat.

The light was angling off a car's windshield, the car only half-visible as I approached it. It was yellow and black, probably worth more than what most people earned in a life, and was parked next to a tree whose gnarled branches faded into the whiteness of the backdrop. Then, rounding the bend with the others behind me, the sight locked me in place: a man floated under the tree.

"Turn the children away," Miguel yelled.

The older woman shushed him to lower his voice. Too late for the girl, who screamed unremittingly. I mostly heard my short and deep breaths as I stepped closer until I stood before the man. He wasn't more than a meter off the ground. His head was crooked to the side, chin down, lips slightly parted, skin not yet a bloodless blue, his expression aggrieved, like he was disappointed to learn that it hadn't been worth it, that in death he'd find no peace either.

"Who did this?" one of the women shouted.

It seemed obvious he had. Nobody else would go to the trouble. His hands were unbound. He'd stepped off the car's rear fender. Miguel was in the driver's seat, heaving with his shoulder as he cranked the key in the ignition. A heavy click sounded. "Out of gas," he said.

"No, no, no." This was Have You Seen, with a commotion of movement uncommon for her. She was rushing around the car to something on the ground, an open suitcase. "No, no, no." She lifted from it a baby swaddled in a mustard yellow blanket, a grey tasseled wool cap on its head, tufts of fine light-colored hair curling from under it.

So the infant had frozen to death, and the man slung the rope over the branch. The child was too much for me. I couldn't look at it. I turned back to the man. The rope was thin and squeaked against the branch ever so slightly, though no air rocked the body. I wiped my cheeks with the heel of my palms.

Miguel was trying to take the baby from Have You Seen, who wouldn't release it. She held the wrapped bundle as tightly to her chest as the parents were doing to their sons to keep them from witnessing this scene. Like Miguel, I could imagine her refusing to part with it long after she should.

"That's enough," I said. Lieutenant Colonel Díaz's regiment—every last man—was massacred during the fall of Santander, not long before I'd learned my brother had been murdered. Since then, the two of us have been wandering this country searching for those the war had taken from us, but watching Have You Seen cling desperately to that miniature corpse I thought: maybe this is where hope ultimately brings you. I tried banishing the thought but couldn't. I yelled, "That's enough."

She stopped, though not because I yelled at her. She said, "There's a pulse."

I would have thought she was stalling, but she had a startled expression, frightened and excited. Miguel stuck his hand in and felt around the baby's neck, while the rest of us waited in that strange and vacant light. He pulled away quickly, as though he'd been bit. "It's weak, but it's there." The others rushed forward to surround the baby, ignoring the hanging man. The possibility of being shot at had vanished. They rubbed its hands and feet, blew warm breaths upon them as they worked in a frenzy to bring it closer to life. The older woman produced a sliver of chocolate from an inner pocket and smeared it to paste between her fingers then dabbed it over the baby's motionless lips and in its mouth. "There's no warmth." Her voice trembled and cracked. Her husband held her, and the two were turning their backs on us, when the baby stretched and its mouth twisted for a silent cry. Any fascist within a kilometer would have heard the others' blooming and joyful laughter. Trembling, I reached in with my bad hand to touch the baby's fingers and toes. There was the faint heat of blood—she'd probably keep them all. "The poor man," the mother of the daughter said. "What a horrible, horrible mistake. Oh my god, what a terrible mistake." I'd convinced myself that my brother had arrived at something akin to peace during his final moments, but this man's pinched face said otherwise. He looked merely asleep, in the merciless grip of a horrific and unending dream. I need only seize his arm to wake him from his nightmare.

Miguel patted my shoulder. "We'll have to leave him here." To the others: "Let's get to that mountain. The planes will be back soon." He again patted my shoulder. I was considering the baby. Have You Seen clutched her tightly. Nevertheless, it'd be so easy to take the infant from her. "Right, Isidro? The planes? The mountain?"

Hours later we reached it and soon found a mother willing to share some of her milk. Have You Seen hovered, nearly an extension of the child. Afterwards, I watched her approach other women and explain our story, begging for milk they might spare, holding out the baby as though standing before an altar. Not once did she ask if any-one had seen her son. The last time I saw Have You Seen, a woman had just removed the infant from her breast. Have You Seen cradled her and gently patted her. I was glad to eventually lose them among the crowd as we continued to France. Fight, I reminded myself. As vile of an enterprise as this is, you must fight.

Throughout the journey, I was there and not there. I was among the masses under the dense canopy of trees, thinking I must not yield, and I was still standing in the road before that hanging father, wanting to be told what I could offer for my own penance, waiting for another miracle, for more of the lost to return.

20

THE FIRST ONES were waiting in the forest in Spain, beyond the sloping mountain line that tapered to the sea.

I was twelve. Every newspaper showed a parade. Tanks in Madrid's streets. Women sitting on soldiers' laps, smiling, offering fascist salutes, their legs crossed at their ankles. "Finally," my father kept saying, "finally that mess is over." What had been the trouble, I wondered. They looked like they were having more fun than we were. Then you saw the buildings behind them, those still standing.

It made sense why our government chose Argelès-sur-Mer. There probably wasn't a wider belt of sand in all of France, and so close to Spain. When my father learned they'd transform our beach into a concentration camp, he cursed like a madman on the street corner—"France will become the world's dung heap!"—and issued every threat, as if his anger might somehow reach the politicians in Paris and halt the refugees' advance.

The gendarmes hammered posts along the shoreline and stretched a mesh of hooks across them. Then the Spaniards began to emerge from the thick, zigzagging line of dark green that followed a fold in the mountains. At first there were a few. Soon a column of people spilled out the Spanish side of Catalunya. It didn't seem a country could have held them all, let alone a forest. It was impossible this beach would. Yet here they came.

With their batons, the gendarmes enthusiastically prodded those first arrivals, corralling them to the beach, but they were defeated creatures. I stood on the sidewalk next to my father and some of his friends. Women held children's hands while balancing suitcases bound with twine on their heads. A woman with a crutch, one pant leg knotted at the knee, even managed it. The men were loaded down like mares. They walked bow-headed toward the water. Then I saw something of a curious sight approach. A boy my age pulled along an emaciated sheep. They were the only two who met our eyes. I wondered about the journey they'd made together when a nearby man on the sidewalk stepped into the street and grabbed the rope from the boy, who resisted. There was a brief struggle until he received a hard knock from a gendarme and the sheep went with the man. I expected my father to say something. He squinted at the smoke he exhaled.

"How long will they be here?" I asked.

The boy lunged again for his sheep. This time the gendarme lifted the baton over his head. I flinched for the sound it made. *"Allez!"* he yelled, and kicked at the boy. Onward! The boy held the side of his head, checking his hand for blood, while an older man—I don't know how many tattered blankets were tied around him—helped him off the ground. The gendarme waved his baton and yelled. *"Allez! Allez!"*

EARLY ON, ONE of those first evenings, some friends and I couldn't resist this great curiosity. Gran Hotel du Catalunya, we were calling it. The wind arrowed off the water at a cruel angle, as sharp as the razor wire perimeter. Gendarmes patrolled with little interest. Mostly they huddled together, their collars up, passing a bottle between them under hastily constructed sentry boxes. Lorries were scattered at the edge of the shoreline. Those gendarmes pulling higher rank sat in them, occasionally wiping the condensation from the windows to glance at the beach. The wind rattled the chains in the truck beds and flung rain at us, blurring our vision as we crawled closer to the dunes.

"Look at those *sauvages*," my friend laughed. We got the language from our fathers. Watching them on the beach, it made sense. Their desperation was vulgar. It disgusted us. We pointed and giggled while they dug at the sand like a bitch about to give birth. Soon they'd collect enough driftwood to construct tents, but that night our giggles turned to uncontrollable laughter for their frantic burrowing.

I was up early the next morning with my father. He swore when he saw the grey bodies tumbling loose-limbed in the surf. They ultimately pulled their own from the water and buried them in the least desired spot on the beach. It didn't seem fair. To have come so far and survived so much. The image I kept returning to was of the women smiling victoriously atop tanks in that decimated city, their arms out, saluting like Germans. They'd rather destroy their country than share it with those on the beach.

A WARNING SPREAD through town: the Spanish women were loose, insatiably carnal, determined to corrupt the virtue of any young Frenchman who wandered near them. Even our priest thought the warning ill conceived. "For too long, anxious mothers and impatient maidens have failed to appreciate the male mind. No reason to expect they'd finally figure it out in our times." He added, "I foresee this rumor producing the opposite of its desired effect."

My friends and I occasionally spotted young men in two's or three's near the beach's wire perimeter, aspiring for a nonchalant posture while their eyes probed for the Spanish women they'd heard so much about, had practically been promised, these reds who would split everything with the collective, including their bodies, but none of the women accommodated them.

Once, Louis, who was a year older than me, had us crouch behind some bushes. He cupped his hands around his mouth and shouted, "If you're that desperate, rut a sheep," then dove against us. We watched them through the tangle of branches searching for us, their arms rigid, fists clenched, but seconds later they fled as casually as they could, and we were on our sides laughing.

Some of the older men possessed less shame, the years of lonely nights having leeched it from them. They'd walk along the perimeter, hands behind their backs, scrutinizing the women as they might live-stock brought to market.

What surprised us was seeing Old Leon before the fence—legs far apart, arms crossed, defiant. He was obsessively anti-Communist. Ever since his wife passed, you'd find him in church more often than our priest. A few of the townsfolk were too curious to leave him be. However, after nearing him, they reported that he was threatening those inside, saying we should have greeted them with bullets the moment their feet touched French soil. "I worked my whole life for France," I later heard him say, "and for that I earn a pension of fifty francs a month. But we're handing you filthy refugees two hundred and forty a month."

Where did the money go, I wondered. I hadn't questioned before how they were staying alive, nor that we might have a role in it. I assumed we were trying to kill them, if not through neglect than from despair or boredom. "We're too accommodating," my father told our neighbors. "That's our problem. Our government should learn from the Germans and Spanish. Make it bad enough and these reds will return home, you'll see. Regardless of what awaits them." However, the driftwood lean-tos had been replaced by proper bar-racks, the lumber having been paid for by us, I supposed, and though no fish gathered in those waters, they were being fed. My father, who never had one good thing to say about the drunks we'd come across in the street, now said, "Our own are dying of cold and hunger in the gutters, but we're keeping these lazy Spaniards' stomachs full."

Other than complain, he did nothing to change the situation. Nobody did. Mostly, they watched the horizon, waiting for one large wave to resolve this mess.

WE BEFRIENDED A few gendarmes, my friends and I. They took us in their lorries, and we drove along the border with them. On my own, I'd never have dared it. Over there was so awful that people wouldn't trade all the hunger and sorrow of the beach for it. I had begun fearing getting too close to the sloping mountain line and the forest lest it somehow pull me in. But with the sun above me and the gendarmes at my side, I felt invincible.

One of my friends spotted them—three Spanish soldiers. We were in the lorry's bed, and he shouted and banged on the truck's roof, pointing, and we smiled excitedly as the truck bounced on the road, the wind in our faces. I'd never seen a sadder lot. Our gendarmes were clean-shaven, wore crisp uniforms. At the right angle, their buttons popped with light. These soldiers were hollow-cheeked, sooty, hobbling, each an exhausted collection of bones. They didn't acknowledge us as we approached. The lorry cut them off, and a gendarme muttered a few words of what probably passed for Spanish, pointing in the direction of our town and the beach.

The soldiers' flaking white lips were thin, split at every crease, burned of any moisture. Their eyes were set deep into faces that had been blistered from the sun off the snow. They'd paused as the gendarme spoke to them. One gave us a recriminating look and said something in Spanish, hooking his thumb as if whatever he was talking about was directly behind him—it sounded like a warning you'd give a simpleton—then they resumed their pace.

A gendarme swore at him. Another hollered, "It's the beach or Franco's gallows." He called our names and we jumped from the bed and they drove around the soldiers to come behind them, the gendarme on the passenger side slapping the outside of the door, hooting, the truck's grill nearly clipping their backsides as they were forced to begin jogging. We were alongside them like collies pushing a flock of sheep, my friends yelling, *"Allez! Allez!"*

The one I was closest to, there was nothing but frustration and reproachment in those eyes. He was the oldest of the three, about my father's age. *"Allez,"* he said, shaking his head. It sounded different out of him. I wanted to reclaim it. Swallowing hard, I reminded myself I was where I was supposed to be, I needed not fear a thing—the gendarmes were behind me, the sun directly above, my friends at my sides as we hopped a lip of hard-packed dirt for the road to town, to the beach, its human reek, and everything else awaiting the soldiers there. You're all right, I tried assuring myself. You were born to this country. The forest was a smudge of green behind me. Beyond it, the ruins of Spain and those Spaniards giddy to be among them. I attempted to smile as the women had on the tank. It was wobbly, but I managed to hold it as I cleared my throat and steadied my voice, then drew in a breath to yell. What came out was splintered and strangled and got the Spaniard chuckling. Even my friends joined in. There was some satisfaction corralling him and the others to the beach and watching them processed at its gates. Some but not much. It was too cheap and easy a victory.

That night I tried it out again. "*Allez!*" Onwards! The only place I wouldn't be heard shouting was among the trees near the coast, with the ocean's roar batting down my voice. I filled my chest and cleared my lungs with each shout. "*Allez!*" The moon was full and low. It was a cloudless night, and the waves were emphatic—pulling back noisily to hurl themselves once more in a swollen tumult upon the shore. I could hardly hear myself, but what I heard wasn't impressive. A pup trying to bark. I reached deep into my belly for another roar—"*Allez!*" till I drained the breath out of me. I couldn't even convince myself despite keeping at it until my throat became raw and I felt woozy and my temples ached. Walking home, dejected, I blinked repeatedly, closing my eyes tightly. The path along the coastline had me nodding at gendarmes who wouldn't reciprocate the gesture. I wondered if the others had told them about me. Not a silhouette inside seemed drawn to my presence. Sometimes, if I was alone, they'd approach to beg for food or francs. Occasionally, with a sneer, they'd demand it. That night, I was invisible to even them. The waves and the wind had everyone's attention.

I had taken my first step for home, away from the coast, when a sound—a child's cry—stopped me. Of course there were infants in there. All of humanity was in there. But that cry pierced the noise. I felt it drive into my chest, run right through me. I returned to the fence. In the distance, the full moon's tail lay upon the sea. Close as it was to the horizon, the moon was without an aura in the cobalt night. The waves were white as fresh snow. I searched the beach and saw them nearby, three women around a little girl who held onto two of the women's hands, so she could hoist herself up. What I had mistaken for a cry was a squeal of joy. She immediately plopped back onto the sand and reached for the women's hands again. The low moon was upon everyone, so I was able to see the crescent outline of the infant's full smiling cheeks. She, like the others, was cast in purples and blues and shadows. I moved my mouth around and swallowed, dragging my hands over the bottom of my face. My parents had a baby after me. She lived for two weeks before the relentless cold of that winter and her fever and cough silenced her and carried her off. My father demanded that I help him make the casket. It was little bigger than a shoebox. I never forgave him for that. I tried to keep from thinking of those months of anticipation and the black time that attended it. This was difficult to do—I had memories of my mother laughing, but none from after that. Watching the little girl rise to her feet once more, I thought of who we could have become. The women pulled their fingers from her grip. She wobbled and shrieked before falling again. I pushed a knuckle into the corners of my eyes. If any of my friends saw me just then, there'd be no end to the taunts. This didn't stop me from remaining there. *"Allez,"* I said. I'd been rehearsing the line for so long it slipped from me without thought. For the first time that day, it sounded like something good and true and necessary. The little girl insisted the women again stretch out their hands. One did, then another. She met their eyes and smiled, hers big and untroubled, and grabbed hold of their hands and pulled herself up, shifting her weight, jerking her hips from side to side, searching for balance, to root herself. ■

ACKNOWLEDGEMENTS

My gratitude to Eric Obenauf, Eliza Wood-Obenauf, and Brett Gregory at Two Dollar Radio. Thank you for the care, attention, vision, and fun you have brought to this dream collaboration. To he of the unshakable faith, thank you to my former agent Michael Nardullo, who helped this novel find a place in the world. Thank you, Tim Wocjik, for your assistance with foreign and audio rights. For the early endorsements, thank you to master storytellers Phil Klay, Margot Livesey, Philipp Meyer, Richard Russo, and Laura van den Berg, with special thanks to Joseph Boyden and Andre Dubus III, who are among the most generous and big-hearted people I've ever met. I'm humbled by it all.

Many of these chapters were first published in different forms in literary magazines. Thank you to the tireless people staffing *American Short Fiction, Boulevard, Copper Nickel, Electric Literature, The Florida Review, Gettysburg Review, Glimmer Train, One Story, Ploughshares,* and *War, Literature, and the Arts*. With two exceptions, these chapters were elevated from the so-called slush by those magazines' first readers. Such journals are essential to American literature, as is the work performed by these readers. Who knows where this book would be without them. In shaping those chapters early on, I had the great pleasure to work with editors Rebecca Markovits and Adeena Reitberger, Dusty Freund and Jessica Rogen, Wayne Miller and Joanna Luloff, Kelly Luce, Jacob Wolff, Mark Drew, Susan Burmeister-Brown and Linda Swanson-Davis, Patrick Ryan, Ladette Randolph, and Jesse Goolsby.

To my brilliant friends and fellow scribes who read drafts of these chapters, thank you to Akshay Ahuja, Sean Conway, Blake Hammond, Alexander Lumans, Liz MacDonald, Nicholas Mainieri, Davis Mendez, David Moloney, David Parker, William Pierce, and Gabriel Urza. Thank you, as well, to the many outstanding writers who comprised the University of New Orleans' MFA program in Madrid those many summers ago, most notably Amanda Boyden.

Thank you to all past and present within the University of Massachusetts Lowell's Honors College, especially former Dean James Canning and our dauntless leader Dean Jenifer Whitten-Woodring.

As for help with historical accuracy, I am fortunate to have been able to field my questions to some of the greatest Spanish Civil War historians there are. Thank you, Xabier Irujo, Nick Lloyd, Paul Preston, and Alan Warren for your patience, scholarship, and guidance. Thank you to Ana Teresa Nuñez at the Gernika Peace Museum for helping me place my characters in the right place and time in the first chapters. Thank you, as well, to the Association for the Recovery of Historical Memory, who allowed me into their office in Ponferrada to observe the critical work they do. I am indebted to Asun Garikano and Bernardo Atxaga for their assistance with Basque history and culture, as well as for their friendship and support. Thank you to Ander Caballero, who should he not know the answer, certainly knows the person who will. The books most vital to my research on the Spanish Civil War include: *The Spanish Holocaust* by Paul Preston, *Tree of Gernika* by GL Steer, *Beyond Death & Exile* by Louis Stein, *The Spanish Civil War* by Hugh Thomas, and *Ghosts of Spain* by Giles Tremlett.

Despite these many authorities, I occasionally had to defer to the stories my narrators were telling me—should any historical inaccuracies exist, I am solely to blame.

Several chapters would not exist as they do without the inspiration of the work of others. To that, I'd like to dedicate Chapter 3 to GL Steer—a co-writing credit for that chapter is more likely in order. In Chapter 12, several of the statements made by Father del Valle and Colonel Luna were appropriated from the letters and speeches of Cardinal Isidro Gomá, General Francisco Franco, General Juan Yagüe, Monsignor Anselmo Polano, and the prosecutor of Juan Caba Guijarro, all of which I came across in *The Spanish Holocaust* by Paul Preston, to whom I dedicate the chapter. Chapter 18 is dedicated to Jay Allen for his reporting on the massacre at Badajoz and to Alice Oswald for her book *Memorial*. Chapters 6 and 19 to

Svetlana Alexievich and many in her books *Secondhand Time, Zinky Boys,* and *The Unwomanly Face of War,* whose experiences I hope I have honored in some way.

Mila esker to my family and friends in the Basque Country, Boston, and California's Central Valley, and to the many dear others I've met on the road. Thank you to my in-laws Celeste and Robert Sticca, for your generosity and support.

To my parents Amador and Mary Zabalbeascoa, thank you for giving me the tools I needed to write this novel, along with an early love for the Basque Country, be it on the Spanish or French side, this land that shaped all those who came before us and that I first explored as a child alongside my brothers and earliest fellow adventurers Mikel and Jon. Thank you to my aunts Ana, Karmele, and Mari Asun, and my cousins Beñat and Arkaitz, who have been showing me around there since the beginning.

Lastly, thank you to my wife and best friend, my first reader and editor Katie Sticca. This novel, this life, they wouldn't be what they are without you. And thank you to our beautiful and joyous son Nico, who makes it all make sense.

Photo by Katie Sticca

JULIAN ZABALBEASCOA's fiction has appeared in *American Short Fiction, Electric Literature, The Gettysburg Review, Glimmer Train, One Story,* and *Ploughshares,* among other journals. He divides his time between Boston and the Basque Country in Spain. *What We Tried to Bury Grows Here* is his first novel.